A Dance With Seduction

A Dance With Seduction

Alyssa Alexander

This book is a work of fiction. Names, characters, places, and incidents are the product of the author's imagination or are used fictitiously. Any resemblance to actual events, locales, or persons, living or dead, is coincidental.

Copyright © 2017 by Alyssa Marble. All rights reserved, including the right to reproduce, distribute, or transmit in any form or by any means. For information regarding subsidiary rights, please contact the Publisher.

Entangled Publishing, LLC
2614 South Timberline Road
Suite 109
Fort Collins, CO 80525
Visit our website at www.entangledpublishing.com.

Select Historical is an imprint of Entangled Publishing, LLC.

Edited by Alethea Spiridon
Cover design by Erin Dameron-Hill
Cover art from Period Images

Manufactured in the United States of America

First Edition July 2017

To Joe, the bedrock of my life
and
To Josh, I am proud to be your mother

Chapter One

"Get out of my study." He hunched over the bit of Russian text he was translating, though her scent told him she was near.

She always smelled clean.

Strange, given her various professions. Gunpowder or perfume would be more appropriate.

Of course, she didn't leave, which meant his work would be disturbed for the remainder of the evening. The warm fire and soothing glass of brandy he was about to enjoy would *also* be disturbed.

He'd been looking forward to that brandy.

Maximilian Westwood did not look up from the Russian missive. Perhaps if he did not meet her gaze, she would go away. The Flower could exit his study by whatever mysterious method she'd entered and leave him in peace.

Light footfalls approached him from behind, followed by the quiet, decidedly feminine sound of a throat being cleared.

She was still there, confound her.

"I am not in that line of work any longer, mademoiselle."

The nib of his quill was becoming dull. He eyed the feather carefully. Yes, most definitely dull. Opening the top drawer of his desk, he reached for a short knife. "I suggest you find someone else." Breaking the Flower's ridiculous spy codes was less important than his other tasks. Such as whittling the point of his quill.

"I have a need for you, monsieur."

He scowled at the quill and shifted in his chair. Her voice was sultry and sensual, as befit her profession—well, one of them, at any rate—but her words sounded as if she were advancing a sexual liaison.

"I am no longer in His Majesty's employ. I've retired from code breaking." Thankfully. He only wanted to study words on the page, and as he excelled at translations, his services were in high demand.

Blowing on the nib to dislodge any loose shavings, he was careful to turn away from the desk so the debris did not scatter onto wet ink. He still did not turn to look at her, though he could sense her prowling around his study. Baffling that she could enter the house without even his sharp-eared assistant discovering her.

"This matter is not related to His Majesty, monsieur."

Something stirred against his shoulder. A light touch, little more than her clothing brushing his. Her scent came again. *Soap.* Not overly sweet as some ladies used, but plain soap.

Maximilian ignored it. He wanted to work, and letters and words were easier to understand than gorgeous spies masquerading as French opera dancers and mistresses. He bent over the paper and pretended the Flower was not standing beside him.

The nib of the quill scored the paper as he tested it. Perhaps he'd oversharpened it due to the distraction of his visitor.

"This matter is only for myself." Her voice layered over

the scratching of the quill. Even when she spoke English, the words were accented, though he had never been able to determine the precise region of France she heralded from. "It is coded."

A small, gloved hand slid into his vision, blocking his view of the Russian text. Between her fingers was a scrap of paper. He brushed her hand away even as his mind recorded the note. Two inches on the vertical height, approximately four on the horizontal length. Eight square inches with two lines of text across.

The paper reappeared in front of him, still held tightly in her fingers. He supposed persistence was a necessary quality for a spy.

"I shall pay you, monsieur."

Hell and the devil. Being a second son, his inheritance was not large, and the government did not pay translators particularly well—or code breakers, for that matter. Maximilian's pockets, while not light, were not exactly heavy.

With a sigh, he finally looked up into the Flower's face.

Her beauty simply stole his breath—no doubt as it did every other man. An oval face was framed by a riot of inky curls and a defined widow's peak, with eyes the same deep shade as her hair and narrowed in watchfulness. As she usually did when she worked, the Flower wore all black. A small ebony coat, breeches, and boots. A cap was clutched in her other hand. The Flower might be dressed as a man, but there was no mistaking the flare of hips or the exquisite face.

Or the determined light in her eyes.

"Just this note?" he asked, deciding he would make her pay well for a coded message, since she had interrupted him.

"*Oui.*" Her full pink lips curved up in a satisfied grin. "Your fee is two pounds?"

He leaned back in his chair and eyed that grin. He didn't like it. Or her. Too sneaky by half and so gorgeous a man might forget all boundaries of respectability. "Five pounds."

"Five?" One black brow rose to a wicked point. "My brain, it has been lost, do you think? Two pounds, ten shillings."

"Four and ten." He would have accepted the two pounds from anyone else. The loss of the brandy and his solitude was worth more than two pounds.

"Three pounds."

"Three and ten."

"Acceptable."

He set her paper beside the two sheets already on his desk, where it lay like a bright beacon on the polished surface. Dismissing it for now, Maximilian picked up his quill again. Dipping it into the inkwell, he turned his mind back to the Russian text. "Return tomorrow night, and I shall have it for you."

"No." Leaning over, she tapped a finger on her note with gloves that matched the rest of her ensemble. She would be near to invisible in the dark with all that black clothing—which was her intention, no doubt. "I have need of it now. *S'il vous plaît.*"

"I cannot break the code now. I am translating Russian for a client who already paid me." Setting his fingers on the original Russian letter, he skimmed them over the lines of text until he found the place he had left off. "*You* have not yet paid me."

"*Mon Dieu!*" She muttered it, but a coin landed on the Russian letter. Another. Then more, until three pounds ten lay scattered on the document.

His temper spiked. There was an order to his projects. The Russian project first, tomorrow he would translate a Greek paper on the study of water fowl, *then* Vivienne La Fleur's spy code.

"I still cannot do it immediately." He shoved the coins off the Russian letter. "Your note is too complicated—the symbols, the order. It will take time."

In his peripheral vision, he saw her shoulders sag in defeat. A small movement, but she always stood so straight and tall, shoulders back and head high. A dancer's pose. Even the slightest movement of those shoulders showed.

Quite deeply at the moment, he wished the gentleman in him would stay quiet.

"Very well. I will have it by morning." Sleep would be unlikely, though staying awake all night to translate an interesting bit of text was not a new occurrence.

"Thank you. *Merci.*" Her voice sounded odd. Hoarse, perhaps, as if she were going to cry.

"Mademoiselle La Fleur." He turned his head, angled it up to look at her. "If you are going to be a watering pot, get out of my study."

Pointed chin jerking up, she cleared her throat. "I am not a watering pot. My throat is sore. I have recently recovered from an illness."

Spinning on her heel, she stalked across the room, dark curls swirling through the air like a—well, he didn't know. No one had hair like the Flower.

For once, her boots made more noise than a whisper.

Now it was his turn to grin.

...

Impossible man, that one. Maximilian Westwood was all that was ordered and controlled. Sitting there in his coat and waistcoat, though it was nearly midnight and he was alone. Ah, but he was not *so* proper. Stubble ranged over his squared jaw, which he surely would have shaved had he known it was there.

Also, a man ought not to have such an agreeable shape to his face, nor eyes that focused on every detail of a woman.

Pitiful locks on his windows, however. Vivienne slid between the sash and the pane to drop onto the grass at the rear of his town house. She shut the window, satisfied not a single squeak could be heard inside. Her town house was close enough to Monsieur Westwood's home that she chose to walk, even late at night. As a kept woman, she did not live in as respectable an area as the monsieur's, but she was not in danger.

And then, of course, there were her knives.

She slipped through her own back door and into the comfort of the kitchen a scant quarter hour later. The fire was out, and a late-night chill hung in the air. Curled in a chair beside the cold fireplace was Anne. The housekeeper's daughter.

Or so it was said.

Thirteen now, and oh, how fast her sister had grown this year. It was all Vivienne could do to keep her in gowns that didn't show her ankles.

"Anne." She shook a narrow, girlish shoulder. All angles and points as she grew, Vivienne thought Anne would be as tall as their mother. Certainly taller than herself, but that did not require much growth.

"Vivienne?" The girl's eyes fluttered open to reveal two dark pools of sleep befuddlement.

"Hush, *ma minette*. Bed now, yes? Come."

Anne was limp as a sack of potatoes, and as useless. Vivienne prodded the girl until she was walking, such as it was, with Vivienne's supporting arm around her waist. When they reached the servants' quarters, Vivienne stripped off her gown. Anne had become thin in the middle and would need proper stays soon. Nearly ready to be a woman, this daughter of her heart.

Vivienne swallowed the lump in her throat as she settled a nightgown over Anne's head. "Into bed. It was much too late for you to wait for me."

"I wanted to say good night." Anne covered a yawn with work-roughened hands. "Did you see Mr. Westwood about the note?"

"I did." With a gentle touch, she guided the girl to the bed.

"You could have managed any of the short words I taught you for your work," Anne said, slipping into the small bed. "I would have read the remainder for you, but for the code."

"I know." She could only be grateful Anne worked so hard to learn her letters. Vivienne had never learned more than what was necessary. No time when one was fighting for survival as a girl. Later, when she had become a spy, to tell her spymaster she could not read would have meant being turned away from espionage—toward prison or death instead, given her past.

Vivienne drew the coverlet up, tucking the edges around Anne's shoulders as she liked. "Monsieur Westwood will have the translation in the morning. I will soon find out what it means. What I must do."

"No one can hurt us, can they?" Big brown eyes watched Vivienne over the edge of the coverlet. Anne's fingers clutched at faded seams, her knuckles white.

Memories of their father had faded, but not enough.

"No. Of course not." A lie. Truth would only cause fear. She smoothed the hair across Anne's brow, tucked a lock behind her ears. "It is nothing to worry over now. Until Mr. Westwood translates it, we can do nothing. So we must wait and take action later. Now, sleep again."

"Good night." Anne turned over, burrowing beneath the coverlet.

Vivienne blew out the candle on the bedside table and let her eyes adjust to the dark. She waited, listening to Anne's breathing. Did everyone tell lies to children? She supposed they did, as sometimes one must pretend there were no villains in the world.

But there *were* such men, as Vivienne knew.

As Anne knew.

It was a short walk to her room a floor below. Vivienne drew the drapes but did not light a candle. Instead, she let her eyes adjust once again to the dark before moving to the wardrobe. She pushed aside the silk and lace nightclothes provided by her commander and spymaster until she found a well-worn cotton shift. She shrugged out of her coat, removed the knife hidden beneath, then stripped off the other tied around her thigh. A third was hidden in her boots, which she pulled off before slipping out of her breeches.

The first knife she slid beneath her pillow. The second was set beside it on the mattress. She laid the last one on the bedside table, hilt toward her so she could easily grasp it. The shift was soft against her skin and fell to midthigh, freeing her legs for the next part of her nightly ritual.

Plié, deep enough so her bottom met her heels. Count two, three, four. Stand again. First position, fifth position, spin, another *plié*. She continued the routine, her arms working as she lifted them over her head. The muscles and sinews of her legs would strengthen, fiber by fiber, to assist in her work. Dancer, spy, thief. All required her to stay strong.

A body was no different than a pistol or a knife. She had long ago learned to care for her weapons. In those days she had loved the familiarity of the training rooms, the routine, the comfort of knowing that space was both home and sanctuary. That town house, empty now but for the spies Angel and Jones, was still home.

Jones, too, had been a comfort and refuge. Training beside her with his quiet strength. She had given him her body in their youth, when they both understood that spies could never have love.

Those days seemed very far away.

When she was breathing hard, she strode to the washstand in the corner of the room. The pitcher stood sentinel over the matching basin, their white porcelain sides painted with a floral pattern. She despised the ornate and fussy rosebuds painted across the base of the vessels, but she had not been allowed to pick the decor of the room.

Splashing water into the basin, she dunked her hands into the cold water. The plain, homespun soap lying on the washstand barely lathered, but she used it each day, washing, rinsing, then patting herself dry with a strip of soft linen.

Once she had hung the linen over a rack to dry, she sat down on the end of the bed to let her heartbeat return to normal. Her hands lay limp in her lap, palms up. They were delicate, with fine, narrow fingers. Competent hands, skillful fingers—unmoving and quiescent, at the moment. It would not last, of course. Even in sleep she could not find respite. She must listen for intruders, for soft sounds that were not the house shifting or a carriage beyond the windows.

For Henri.

Lord Wycomb was inclined to arrive in the middle of the night with an assignment, and though he had never touched her beyond a caress or stroke, he sometimes looked at her in a most disturbing manner. He had not done so at first, when she was young. In these last years, she had found his eyes on her more often.

Each night she listened for him.

She slid into the bed, repositioned her knives just so, and mentally listed her tasks for the morning. Breakfast with Henri, as he demanded. Rehearsal—she would enjoy that. Burglary into the house belonging to a member of the House of Lords suspected of turning traitor—she would enjoy that also.

First, before breakfast, Maximilian Westwood. She would have broken the code herself, if she could. Instead, she must rely upon the most proper, reclusive, damnably attractive man she had ever met. She needed an expert, however. Mr. Westwood had been England's best code breaker during the war. More, he was no longer used by the government. He was only a translator now, with his own private business.

Which meant he was her best chance at remaining undiscovered.

Chapter Two

Maximilian propped his chin in his hand and frowned at the small symbol resembling the Egyptian hieroglyphic letter *A*. It wasn't actually an *A*. The vulture wasn't shaped correctly, and it faced the wrong direction. It wasn't a logical progression in the code, which should have been a mathematical substitution cipher. The vulture changed the rotation.

On 13 October, go to No. 14 Hanover Square. Yes, that part of the message was easy. A date and an address. *Document will be hidden in a copy of* Sense and Sensibility *by A Lady.* Truly, spies were an odd lot. Who would hide important documents in a novel where any young debutante could pick it up? *Deliver document to 22 Neva Street.*

At the end of the message was the vulture. He could not understand its purpose there. He pulled the scrap of paper closer, leaning over and squinting despite his spectacles. A signature, perhaps? Interesting, that little drawing. Quite well done, in fact, and vaguely familiar.

Maximilian yanked on the bell pull recently installed by his assistant. The bell clanged somewhere distant in the house.

Nothing happened. Not for ten long, silent minutes.

He jerked the embroidered pull again, then rubbed a thumb over the vulture mark. Damned if he could remember where he had seen it before. Daggett would likely remember. Or he would have a record of some type in the maze of notes he used as a classification system for the documents Maximilian translated.

"Sir?" Daggett staggered into the room, mouth open on a yawn.

"Why are you wearing a nightshirt?" Maximilian leaned back in his chair, eyeing the skinny legs poking out of the bottom of the nightshirt. Surprisingly scrawny considering the round belly above it.

"It is nearly four in the morning." Another jaw-cracking yawn. Daggett blinked and absently rubbed the side of his ear. "I was sleeping."

"Oh. My apologies." Maximilian looked down at his own clothing and realized he hadn't changed in nearly twenty-four hours. Well, he was still working. "Do you recall seeing this symbol?" He tapped the document with his forefinger and noticed the digit was smudged with ink.

Daggett peered at the vulture, thin lips pursed as he considered the drawing. "Yes, sir. I am uncertain as to where, however."

"Can you find out?"

"Of course, sir. It will take some time, though. There are quite a lot of documents I must reference. You have completed so many translations—" He broke off, peering closely at the Flower's message. "What are you working on? I did not enter this document in my records."

"No."

Daggett tugged on his nightshirt. "Sir, I cannot be of proper service to you if you don't allow me to accurately record your work. Or your visiting clients." His mouth turned down in offended grimace before his eyes popped wide. Two shocked circles of gray. "Oh, sir, I have failed in my service. I missed a client. I must not have heard the door. My deepest apologies. It shall not happen again. I shall be more vigilant in the future—"

"It was the Flower, Daggett. Even I didn't know she was here until she was standing next to me."

"Oh." Relief sent his assistant's shoulders sagging. "Well, in that case—but, have we decided to work on codes again? I thought we had retired from that work." He frowned and leaned over the note again.

"Just this code. She is paying rather more than the usual rate."

"I must record it, sir. One moment." Thin legs marched out of the room into the connecting office. They marched back a moment later supporting the man, a ledger, and quill. "When did she arrive, sir? Before or after midnight?"

"I don't know." Maximilian could not see that it mattered. He bent over the note again to study the vulture mark. Until he knew what it meant, he could not complete the translation. Most dissatisfying. In good conscience, he could not charge her the full amount.

"I must record the correct date." Daggett's quill hovered above the ledger, poised to begin his notes.

"Before midnight, I suppose." When he was still hoping to be left in peace with his brandy, the fire, and the Russian text.

"Very good, sir. The price?"

"Three pounds ten shillings." Finishing it would require additional effort. Flicking at the buttons of his coat, he shrugged out of it. "If I cannot break it fully, I will have to repay some of the money."

"Naturally. You are most honorable in that regard," Daggett said, his chest puffing out. The nightshirt swirled around his legs as he set the ledger under his arm. "I remember when the German consulate asked you to translate a letter into Russian, French, Persian, and Swedish, and you could not complete the Persian letter. We had to repay—"

"I'm quite aware, Daggett." An expert in eleven languages, and he could not complete the task. Persian was a language in which he was less than proficient. Germanic languages and Romance languages had similar roots, but Persian—well. He must work on mastering that one.

"The Germans were quite pleased with your level of service, however," Daggett finished cheerfully.

"Go to bed." Maximilian shifted his shoulders, wishing briefly that Gentleman Jackson's was open at four in the morning. A round of boxing might clear his mind enough to decipher the vulture.

"If you are awake and working, sir, then I shall be also." Daggett drew himself up. "We must find the vulture reference. We must not disappoint the client, even if it is the Flower."

...

Monsieur Westwood was bent over his desk when she returned just before dawn. Aside from being in his shirtsleeves, it appeared as though he had not moved. Vivienne studied him from the shadows before stepping into the room. The line of his back, strong and broad as he dipped his quill into one of the four inkwells on his desk. Marvelously thick hair stood on end, so that what should have been a smooth, burnished mahogany was spiked with cinnamon and gold and even russet.

Sighing, he leaned close to the paper, as if his spectacles were ineffective. She had not seen him in spectacles before. They made the strong planes of his face seem more scholarly. She shifted, intent on stepping close to the desk, but his head jerked up like a wolf scenting the air.

"You are back," he said, in that brusque voice he used. It did not change for anyone, so far as she had heard.

"Have you completed the code, Monsieur Westwood?"

"No."

Panic sliced through her, as cutting as her own knives. "I gave you time, as you asked." Striding to the desk, she looked down at him.

He removed the spectacles, dropping them to the desktop. Bare fingers rubbed against his closed lids, as if clearing away cobwebs. Monsieur Westwood's hands were wide and strong, with long, powerful fingers. The hands of a farmer or laborer, perhaps. Elegant they were not, though they were gentle with a quill.

"There is one figure I cannot decipher." He sounded exhausted, as if his bones required rest. Shadows were deep beneath eyes that missed nothing. A niggle of guilt crept into her heart.

She pushed it back out, as she had paid him handsomely.

"This symbol, what is it?"

Reaching out, he set one finger on the note. Paper shushed across the wooden desktop until it was in front of her. Seeing the sloped handwriting again made her stomach clutch.

"The vulture." The monsieur angled his head in the direction of the message, candlelight edging his cheekbones and jaw. The stubble shading his skin had grown since the night before, and now that the spectacles were removed, he appeared less scholarly and a little more dangerous. "It's similar to Egyptian hieroglyphics, but it's not quite right. The feet are out of proportion to the body, and the bird is facing the wrong direction. It might be a signature, or it could have some meaning that modifies the code."

She knew what the symbol meant. It would not affect the words of the message, but it did chill the skin at the base of her spine. "What does the message say?"

"I believe it states: *On 13 October* — that is tomorrow."

"I am aware, monsieur."

"Oh. Of course." He looked oddly put out that he could not instruct her on the date. "On 13 October, go to No. 14 Hanover Square. Documents will be hidden in a copy of *Sense and Sensibility* by A Lady. Deliver documents to 22 Neva Street."

"Neva Street? You are certain it states Neva Street?"

"Quite certain."

Vivienne bent over, staring at the vulture drawing. The mark — yes, she knew it well. The French spymaster signed all of his messages in this way. She understood what he wanted her to do — steal documents from an Englishman on Hanover Square and deliver them to a Frenchman on Neva Street.

The chill at the base of her spine grew, spreading over her until it settled in her belly. She would not steal the documents. Absolutely not. It would be treason. She gritted her teeth and forced her chest to fill with air, then constrict again. In and out.

Do not show fear. A spy never shows fear.

Turning her head, she looked toward Monsieur Westwood. He, too, was bent over the letter. The unknown mark must have offended him. A great frown creased his forehead. Large, dark brows slashed downward. He had a prominent nose, though it was not unhandsome. Ah, but then there were his lips. Some men with such lips, they would be very great lovers. This man used a generous mouth to snarl at paper and ink.

"Thank you, monsieur."

"Unfortunately, I cannot accept your money. I could not complete the cipher." Frustration edged his tone, and he flicked his finger at the paper. "Damn vulture."

"You did complete the message." She did not want to speak of the Vulture. "Thank you for acting quickly."

Ignoring her gratitude, he narrowed his gaze on her lips. "Your accent is difficult to place. I have been trying for years, and despite my experience, I cannot determine the origin. It is not the French spoken in Paris, certainly. The nasal tones are not right."

"No?" Amused, she grinned at him. "I shall not ruin the game by providing the answer to your riddle."

The scowl crossing his features was ferocious. "Your accent is like the vulture symbol—both trouble my memory. I've seen the symbol before but don't recall exactly where." He picked up the paper and folded it carefully, end to end, lining up the edges just so. "My assistant will find it, though."

"The vulture—I know the drawing." The cold returned, moving from her spine to ice her belly. She did not want Monsieur Westwood to remember, or the chattering assistant to find it in his records. "It is not a code, but a man. He means nothing."

"A man." His gaze searched her face. They were a curious shade, his eyes. A mix of green and brown, with starbursts of gold fighting through both. "Are you in trouble, Mademoiselle La Fleur?" he asked softly, handing her the message.

"No, Monsieur Westwood." Except she was. "Good-bye."

It was a simple matter to slip from his study. In the early-dawn light, she left by the back door of his town house. Minutes later, she walked through mews already bustling with life. Grooms, coachmen, livery boys. Each with assigned tasks. Wash this, mend that.

Loosening her walk, Vivienne pushed her cap low over her face. She was not tall, so she would be a young male, one growing into himself. She hunched her shoulders in that way lanky boys did before they understood their shoulders to be wide as a man's. Cap low, a whistle between her teeth, and boy's breeches—she was just another groom, sauntering through the mews on his way to work.

Unfortunately, her work that morning involved lying to her commander.

"Bonjour, Henri."

She received him in the boudoir attached to her bedchamber, as was her habit. Henri preferred to maintain appearances, which was also why she used the French pronunciation of his given name. Anne and the housekeeper had come with her during her training. The lame footman she had known in the old days. The others—the day maid, the groom—were hired.

Vivienne reclined on a chaise and found her pose. Breasts forward, one arm dangling carelessly along the back of the chaise. The satin negligee slipped over her legs as she curled them onto the seat. Smiling flirtatiously, she angled her head so he would not see the telltale pulse pounding in her throat.

So he would not think she might commit treason.

Henri bent and kissed her cheek. "You are a vision, my darling."

She accepted his kiss and the slight rasp his whiskers left behind. He was the same age her father would have been if he'd lived, but his eyes still perused her body, lingered here and there. Lust, she supposed, was the least of his sins.

She suppressed the repulsion beneath her skin, burying it deep so he would not see. "Thank you, Henri. You are well?"

"As ever." He was lean from his daily rounds of boxing and fencing, and handsome with his patrician features and the hair silvering at his temples. Elegant. No large laborer's hands for Henri. "And you, Vivienne? Are you well?"

Why they bothered with these niceties, she did not know. "Well enough." She shrugged, using the Gallic gesture she had worked months to perfect. "Rehearsal was difficult yesterday."

"Too taxing for you?"

"Of course not." As though such things would tax her. "The soprano, she had the vapors again."

"Ah." He did not even pretend to care. Already his focus had turned elsewhere. "Did you retrieve the documents I requested? I asked for them nearly a week ago." He sat and crossed his legs. Each elbow rested on an arm of the chair, then he pressed his fingers together to form a many-steepled roof.

"Of course." She angled her head toward the sheaf of papers folded and sealed on a nearby table. Could willpower cause another person to stand, pick up an object, and walk away? If it was possible, she would will it so.

"Good." Cold eyes flicked to the documents, back to her face. "You were unnoticed?"

"Do you doubt me, Henri?" She questioned herself, sometimes, as she could not always read the documents—but the quickness of her fingers and her stealth were dependable. These she took pride in. "Have I not been trained well?" She brushed a finger across the raised design of the brocade covering her chaise, idly, as if his answer had no import.

"Of course, darling. I trained you myself." A man could be utterly still and wholly terrifying. Lips that never smiled. Eyes that never warmed, watchful eyes to haunt one's dreams. "Has something happened, Vivienne?"

"I am tired, that is all." If she denied it easily, he would leave soon and read nothing in her face. "I had to wait hours for the lord and his mistress to retire before I could obtain the documents. The lord—he was enthusiastic." The roof had been cold and damp beneath her buttocks as she waited for the eager gentleman to finally stop playing with his long-suffering mistress. She counted herself lucky she had not succumbed to an ague.

"You have shadows beneath your eyes." Henri's voice was quiet. Sharp. "You must take care, Vivienne. I cannot allow my best weapon to fail me."

"Of course not." That would be intolerable. "I shall sleep well these next nights, with no assignments to complete." Aside from meeting a Frenchman, perhaps, if she were to commit treason. Tomorrow was 13 October.

"Sleep must wait, as I do have a task for you." His tone did not allow her an opportunity to refuse. Nor did the eyes that searched her face with such suspicion. "The Prince Regent is hosting a soiree tomorrow evening. Lord Lynley will be attending, as usual. He is charged with passing a note to Prinny from a Tory supporter." He paused and set a finger to his sleeve. An offensive white thread lay there. He captured it between thumb and forefinger and flicked it away. "The prince must not receive that note. I have arranged your invitation to Carleton House."

"*Non.*" She had not said it aloud, had she? Fingers twitching on the arm of the chaise, she struggled to refrain from leaping up.

"I beg your pardon?" He was angry. His voice became colder when he was angry.

"No, Prinny certainly must not receive the note. I shall retrieve it." But she could not be in two places at once. Stealing in Hanover Square for the Vulture and at Carleton House for Henri in the same night was impossible.

Her commander did not speak for a long moment. Perhaps he understood her heart beat as quickly as a fleeing rabbit's.

"Bring me the note at first light."

He stood, much later than she had willed him to, retrieving the sheaf of papers she had stolen. Folding them a final time, they disappeared inside his coat. "I will have more orders for you soon, Vivienne."

After a final, slow caress of his finger on her cheek, he turned away and let her breathe. The door closed behind him. Soft, but firm. She let out her breath. It was uneven, but she ignored that. He did not guess. Not yet.

She had time, then, to decide what to do.

Chapter Three

"I am glad Mr. Westwood could read the code. I was ever so surprised to find the note under my pillow when I woke. If it hadn't been wash day, I might not have seen it." Anne carefully set the edge of a kitchen knife on a peeled yellow onion.

Vivienne eyed the sturdy worktable and its stacks of bowls and partially completed dishes. Frightening. Terrifying, even. A knife was much easier to wield in combat than in the kitchen.

"Not like that, dear. The knife will take your fingers clean off." Mrs. Asher, the housekeeper, repositioned Anne's hands before looking up at Vivienne. "What did the note say?"

"Nothing of import." So many lies. "The agent, he must have confused my room with Anne's."

Both heads jerked up. Two sets of eyes narrowed on Vivienne. She was being skewered by family, though Mrs. Asher was not a blood relative. Wisdom suggested she turn away and ignore both females so they could not guess what was happening.

Wisdom did not always follow love.

"I have been given two assignments this night. One of them will make Henri very angry." Even now, with only Mrs. Asher and Anne, she used the French pronunciation. One small lapse might mean two, which might become three. "The other assignment will make someone else very angry." Worry and dread hunched her shoulders so the knife tucked inside her stays pressed against her breastbone.

"What will you do?" Anne sawed at the onion, hacking off uneven bits. With luck that particular vegetable was not needed for dinner.

"I do not know." Leaning against the table, Vivienne absently fingered the transparent, papery onion skin piled there. She felt stretched as thin as that peel. But transparent? She hoped not.

"You cannot risk your position, miss, if I may be so bold." Mrs. Asher dropped a lump of dough onto the sturdy wooden table and began to work it. Forearms dusted with flour, she kneaded, pressing and turning the bread. "We have food and a roof because of what you do. Don't risk that."

Mrs. Asher was right. Without Vivienne's position with Henri, they would have nothing—but Mrs. Asher and Anne did not know the whole of it. If she defied Henri, she might be deported or hanged. It had always been so. Even when the English declared the Flower their best spy, when the French raged because she could steal their secrets and elude them so easily, Henri still knew she was once a pickpocket and thief on the London streets.

I am all that stands between you and the gallows.

He had said those words, and she remembered each syllable as if he had spoken them yesterday. Could she still be sent to the gallows? She did not know, and there was no one to ask but Henri.

She was tied to him.

"Perhaps if you tell Lord Wycomb about the second assignment, he will let you do both," Anne suggested. She sniffled and used her plain cotton sleeve to wipe away a tear.

"No, that I cannot do." Vivienne was reminded why she did not slice onions as its pungency stung her eyes.

"I don't understand why not." Anne stopped cutting the onion and looked up with eyes amusingly red and teary, but Vivienne could not find the strength to smile.

"Henri is not—" Vivienne swallowed hard, lowered her voice. She must be careful. Walls had ears. "Henri provides for us, but it is not because he cares so much for us."

"No, miss." Mrs. Asher folded thick, work-reddened hands over her stomach, dough and all. She planted her feet squarely on the stone floor. "It is *you* who cares so much."

Vivienne shook her head. It did not signify. These women, her sister and the woman who had cared for her until Vivienne could see Anne settled—they were her responsibility.

If she did as the French Vulture asked and was discovered, she would be hanged for treason against the English.

If she did as Henri required of her that evening, she would remain alive to protect Anne from the Vulture—and she would not have the whole of the English government out for her blood.

"Henri, then," she murmured, looking about her. Gold autumn sunlight flickered into the room to illuminate the onions and bowls of pudding and flour, mocking their difficult subject. "I have made my choice."

"Good." Anne's voice seemed strong in the quiet kitchen. "Mrs. Asher, I think this onion might be rotten. It's making my eyes water."

"Lud, girl. It's not rotten, it's supposed to do that." Mrs. Asher peered over Anne's shoulder. "The more you hack at it that way, the worse it will be. Let me show you. A woman needs good knife skills in the kitchen to land a husband or a position."

Now Vivienne did find the strength to smile. Her sister, someday, might have a husband. Even children. She could see Anne as a woman, preparing a simple meal in a warm, comfortable kitchen in a sweet cottage somewhere green and open. Perhaps a child would be tugging at her skirts and a great, handsome man would kiss her cheek. Mrs. Asher might still be with them, knitting by the fire in a rocking chair or holding a new babe and helping Anne to care for it.

It was for this Vivienne fought so hard. Espionage was her life and it was good, but it was not for Anne. Mrs. Asher and Anne trusted her to protect them, sleeping each night secure in the knowledge they were safe because she was there.

She would do what was best for all of them.

The Vulture could go to hell.

Chapter Four

"Sir, you do not have time to attend a soiree, even if it is hosted by the Prince Regent." Daggett huffed, his chest swelling with indignation. "You have *work* to do. Important work."

"Yes, Daggett." Maximilian stared into the mirror. His cravat was crooked. Damnation, how was a man to get these things straight without a proper valet? He'd let his go last month due to finances and had been dressing himself since.

"You should be working on the French medical text. The completion date is quite finite. Only two days remain." Daggett lifted his pudgy frame to the balls of his feet. The ever-present ledger waved in the air, a herald of timeliness.

"Yes, Daggett." Maximilian tugged one last time before abandoning his ministrations. It was only a neckcloth. No one would care if it was crooked.

"The prime minister has asked that you translate a letter from India. Quickly." Brushing imaginary lint from Maximilian's sleeve, Daggett made an irritated sound in his throat. "You cannot ignore his lordship."

"Yes, Daggett." He usually avoided these *ton* gatherings.

A lot of bored people wore ridiculous clothes and gossiped about one another. Silly, really. Except a gentleman did not refuse the prince—at least not a man whose livelihood still depended to some degree upon the government and the monarchy, even if the missives were diplomatic letters instead of coded military messages.

"Do you suppose Mademoiselle La Fleur will have additional messages to decipher?" Daggett asked. "I should like to schedule them in advance, if so."

He'd lost the thread of the conversation. "Mademoiselle La Fleur?"

"Will she be a regular client again?" Daggett's quill hung suspended above the ledger, feather quivering with anticipation as it waited to record Maximilian's statement.

"I sincerely hope not." He didn't want the Flower as a regular client. Maximilian no longer wanted to be wrangled into spying and code breaking and Frenchwomen working for the English government. He had done what needed to be done during the war against Napoleon. Now the war was finished, and so was he.

"Hmm." Daggett scribbled something into the ledger. "I shall make a notation that she may be arriving with more frequency. Perhaps she shall even arrive during the day instead of in the dead of night."

Moreover, the Flower didn't smell like a flower. Nor was she delicate. She was like a hardy thornbush. It quite amazed him that the men of London only saw the exquisitely beautiful opera dancer and never the sharp, strong woman beneath.

Of course, in the *demi-monde*, men didn't notice what lay beyond the surface. Living in the center of that world and supported by a wealthy protector, the Flower made a very effective spy.

"Sir, you have made a mess of your cravat. It is quite wrinkled. Do have a care, next time." Daggett sounded quite angry.

"It is only a cravat." Frowning, he studied the mangled mess in the glass. "Give me another. I'm going to tie it the old way instead of one of these new methods the dandies use."

When he left the town house, the second cravat was also wrinkled and not the least bit fashionable. But it was around his neck and tied, and Daggett assured him he would not be an utter embarrassment to his assistant.

Carleton House was ablaze with light when he arrived. As usual, it was full of raucous, half-drunk guests. All Prinny's favorites, of which Maximilian was one—to his everlasting surprise. He'd helped the regent pen a coded love letter to his mistress, which she had delighted in. Now he endured the odd dinner parties and balls and excessive drinking and eating, because a favorite did not refuse the Prince Regent.

Tonight was no different. Music played, glasses clinked, elaborate gowns shimmered everywhere. A young lord fondled a widow's breasts, and after ensuring it was not his married brother doing the groping, Maximilian turned away. They might be lovely breasts, but a gentleman would perform such acts in private rather than a crowded salon—and with more respect.

Judging the tenor of the party, he decided it was already beyond salvaging and searched for his host. If he greeted Prinny and made a point of speaking with one or two of the guests not already swimming in their cups, he could return to his work quickly enough.

He found the Prince Regent ensconced on a settee, looking like his corpulent body had been planted on the seat. Beside him, with her hand on his arm and her head bent toward his, was Vivienne La Fleur.

The Flower.

Only not as he'd ever seen her.

Dark curls bounced and flirted around her face as she

laughed aloud at something Prinny said. Her mouth was wide and red and lush, her laughter throaty. Color rose on her cheeks, and her eyes were bright. Not with drink, he saw, but with pleasure.

"Monsieur Le Roi, you are a naughty man." She sparkled up at the prince, then angled her head. "I have my protector, and so I must decline."

"Mademoiselle La Fleur, your loyalty pains me sorely, though it does you credit." Prinny took her hand and raised it to his lips. He appeared to want to gobble the Flower right up, like a French pastry at the end of a long meal.

There was something about her vivacity in the midst of the *ton*, the confection of white lace and pale-blue satin she wore, the laughter lurking beneath her curving lips—all of it could lure a man. Maximilian couldn't decide if he would count himself luckier to drown in those dark eyes or turn and sail away.

The prince caught sight of Maximilian and grinned. "Max, my boy! Do meet Vivienne La Fleur, the best opera dancer to grace the King's Theatre. Mademoiselle La Fleur, may I present The Honorable Maximilian Westwood?"

"Mademoiselle La Fleur." Maximilian ignored Prinny's use of the utterly ridiculous name Max and bowed in greeting. "A pleasure to meet you," he said, meeting the spy's eyes as he bent low.

"Monsieur Westwood." Not even by an eyelash did she reveal she knew him already. Instead, she sparkled up at him as she had done to Prinny, coy and gorgeous, with her hair artfully styled to appear as though she'd been well tumbled.

He did not care for it. The riot of hair made him think of beds, a warm female body, and the Flower's hair spread across a pillow.

"This is a most delicious soiree, is it not?" she asked, smile quirking up on one side.

"Delicious," he repeated. Not a word he would have chosen, as it made him sound like a milksop.

Her smiled widened, and he knew she laughed at him. "You do not have a beverage, Monsieur Westwood. Come, we must rectify that, do you not think, Monsieur Le Roi?"

"You must see to his comfort, my dear," Prinny said, still gripping her hand. "Not before my own, however."

She laughed again and bent forward to whisper something in the prince's ear. The regent's gaze darted toward her bosom. She knew her quarry well, it seemed, as the glimpse and the whispered words served to have her host relinquishing her hand. "When you return, then."

Mademoiselle La Fleur stood, and even with heeled slippers she just met the height of Maximilian's shoulder. "If you will excuse me, then." Sinking into a deep curtsy, she fluttered her fan over her bodice.

Now it was Maximilian who was given a glimpse of cleavage. Her gown barely covered the lavish breasts presented by the plunging bodice. Little blue flowers dotted the sleeves and neckline. They moved with every breath, every shift of her breasts.

Reluctantly, he sent his gaze over her head to study the gold *chinoiserie* paper covering the walls. He was a gentleman. A pretty spy would not change him, however luscious the breasts she offered. When she rose, he politely offered his arm and wished the Flower to perdition. He wanted to leave immediately, not drink wine or brandy or another liquor bound to muddle his brain.

Or see the lovely curve of her breasts.

They were not something he usually saw when she came to his study. Nor did he see a smiling woman. This was not the solemn spy who slipped into his home with codes to be broken and weapons too numerous to count. This was a charming, playful woman—and a stranger to him. He could not reconcile the two.

Then again, perhaps he could. Neither of them was truthful.

As they started to move through the crowd, he cast his mind around for a suitable conversation topic and said the first thing that came to mind. "You do realize, mademoiselle, that the Prince Regent is not yet the king. You cannot call him Monsieur Le Roi."

An amused smile curved her pink lips. "This, I know. He delights in my words and that a pretty Frenchwoman finds him attractive. Accordingly, I call him king, and he laughs and thinks much of himself."

She was excellent at deception. Hopefully the prince never discovered it.

"If you would like an escort to another group or to find a refreshment, I would be delighted." Could one's tongue turn black and fall out if one lied often enough? Perhaps he should ask the Flower. "However, I do not desire a drink."

"This, too, I know also, Monsieur Westwood." She did not look at him as she spoke, but waved to some acquaintance or other with her fan as they passed. "You need a good woman and a good tumble to set you straight, not a drink. I told the prince the same."

He nearly choked. "I beg your pardon?"

"A tumble." She slid dark eyes toward him. "Not from me, you understand." Ah, there was the Flower he knew behind the focused gaze. She was only playing at being an coquette, then.

For a moment he was disappointed.

"Do you know your cravat is ridiculous?" she said. "Did your valet allow you to leave your town house with such a monumental disaster?"

Suddenly the damned linen felt too tight, though a moment ago it had been comfortable. Thing felt like a noose around his neck, now that she had spoken of it. "It isn't too wrinkled. I checked."

"It should not be wrinkled at all. Come."

Sliding her free hand around his arm, she linked her fingers together in the crook of his elbow and led him from the salon. Guests lingered in the hall, deep in conversation or flirtation. Gazes flicked their way, and though she smiled gaily, they did not stop until they were in a dim offshoot from the main area. He wasn't certain why he followed along. He should have shrugged her off, but her hands were insistent on his arm, and he couldn't seem to dislodge them.

"This is a pathetic attempt," she said, turning him so his back was pressed against the wall. "I cannot help the wrinkles, unfortunately."

Maximilian let the sound of her words wind through him, trying to determine the dialect again. He closed his eyes. "*Français méridional*, is that right? Meridional French, influenced by Occitan in southern France."

Small, silk-clad fingers had reached for the base of his throat. They stilled, then tangled in linen.

"That is right." Insistent hands tugged and loosened the starched white fabric. "My family came here when I was only a little girl."

"Are they here in London?" Curiosity about the Flower's past trapped him, the minutes and years swirling in his mind. "Do you see them often?"

"No." Long lashes covered her gaze, fanning out to create shadows on her cheekbones. "They have all died."

"I am sorry." He was, though he did not care for much of his own family. Pain did not enter her expression or her tone, but the lack of emotion revealed more than he'd expected.

"It was long ago." Breasts rose as she breathed deep, the valley between shadowed in the unlit hall. "You are tall, monsieur," she said softly. "It is a good height."

She began to retie the fabric, smoothing and twisting.

He should have stopped her. A dark hallway was his brother's venue, not his. Yet the cravat *was* ridiculous, and she appeared competent. "You have considerable experience with such knots."

She pursed her lips in a coy, knowing smile. "I am an opera dancer. I have a protector. Do you think I would not have learned to do this?"

"I suppose mistresses must learn these things." Her face was shadowed in the hall, and he could not see her eyes. He discovered he wanted to so he could gauge what lay behind them. The Flower lived in the same world as his brother—courtesans, glasses overflowing with brandy, and infidelity—but she did not seem to possess a similar dishonorable nature.

Through the dim light he searched her features, but there was nothing he could translate to thoughts. No code to be read. Her eyes were downcast, hiding any glimpse into her soul. "What will you do when you are old and have no more protectors?"

Her hands ceased their ministrations.

Devil take it. Had he asked that question aloud? He stepped away so she could not finish whatever concoction she was making with the cravat. "My apologies. I have no right to ask—"

"Stop." Her fingers fisted in the cloth and pulled him back to her. Strength was in those hands, in her dancer's arms. "When my role is no longer agreeable, I shall find a new role."

Her face might be unreadable, but he *could* decipher her words. She spoke of spying, not dancing or being a mistress. The brisk tone was one she used in his study, serious and sober, rather than that of an insipid tease sitting beside Prinny.

He felt a bit more on even ground with this Flower. The other one—the one that seduced a man with smiles and laughter—he did not understand.

Quick fingers looped the cravat, pulled. He hoped she knew what he was doing, as without a glass he could not repair it.

"There, it is finished. Not as fashionable as some, but the best I could do in this hallway." Stepping back, she cocked her head to study it. "The Mathematical Tie would suit you best, but the starch is insufficient in this cravat. It has been handled too much."

Setting a hand to this throat, Maximilian ran his fingers over the folds. It *felt* correct. Better than what he could do, at any rate. "Thank you, Mademoiselle La Fleur." Clasping his hands behind his back, he stared at her.

She watched him steadily, as though assessing him. Did she find him lacking? Or did he meet some unknown expectation? The flickering light from the wall sconce at the end of the hall lit her face, then shadowed it again. The shape of her lips was visible, however, even in the shadows.

"Do you never smile, Monsieur Westwood?"

"No." Letters did not require smiles. "Do you when you're not playing these games?"

A faint line formed between her brows—a thinking line, as erotic as it was intelligent. Smoothing away again, her face became that of the opera dancer who dallied with a prince.

"Life *is* a game, is it not, monsieur? Endless parties and routs and balls." Her smile was brittle at the edges, though she spoke with a bright enthusiasm that might have fooled some men. She'd returned to her frivolous role.

The change irritated him, though he couldn't say why.

She held out her arm, waiting for his escort. "Come, we must return, before the prince begins to wonder if I have taken it upon myself to tumble the unhappy gentleman and make him happy."

Chapter Five

She should not tease Monsieur Westwood so, but his respectability demanded it, as did the deep frown turning down the corners of his handsome mouth.

If she was needling him, she would not worry about her assignment.

There, now she was worrying again. Her stomach clutched, as though a hard fist had plunged into it. The Vulture would not yet know she was disobeying his command. She had one night, this night, when she would not yet need to be on guard against him.

Enjoyment could not be allowed, however, as she had not seen Lord Lynley and completed her assignment. What if he had left before she arrived and Prinny already had the note? She would have failed. Henri would be displeased, and then she would have both him and the Vulture to worry about.

"I *am* happy." Monsieur Westwood muttered it to himself as they reentered the soiree. She had heard him do this once before. That muttering had been about a Prussian code she'd brought him.

"Hmm?" Vivienne looked up at him. Brows were angled as they would be if he were hunched over a difficult code, but he was still handsome, a squared, strong jaw the culmination of a face formed of sharp cheekbones and full lips.

"It does not signify." Shaking his head, he looked away, but his frown did not ease. "Prinny is waving at you."

Indeed, he was. Most leeringly so. It was a wonder he did not fall from the settee. She smiled at the prince, a knowing little half smile. It would make him feel like the king.

Expanding her smile to the man standing beside him, she realized it was Lord Lynley. Blond and handsome in that angular way some men had about them, he did not seem dangerous. He bent his head to speak with another man—a bishop, judging by his gaiters. Lynley's hand dipped into his pocket, moved there, so many fluttering bumps beneath the fabric as he fingered something.

She had not yet failed.

Heart pumping, the rush of her blood—these were the beginning of her assignment. Whatever was in Lynley's pocket was her goal, the one set for her by Henri. Her lips curved up.

It was time to work.

"Mademoiselle, do you intend to pierce my arm with your fingers?" Monsieur Westwood's tone was dry as he looked pointedly at her gloved hand. "I did not give offense again or ask any unforgivable questions, I am quite sure."

"I beg your pardon." Vivienne let her fingers relax. They should be quick and limber, not frozen to the monsieur's arm from the thrill of the hunt. "I must return to Monsieur Le Roi."

"I should say so. Prinny looks like a windmill, beckoning you that way."

He was quite right. She laughed, a true laugh that did not come from this role she played. Monsieur Westwood looked down at her but did not smile, though she thought perhaps one corner of his mouth had twitched.

She had never seen him smile. Most strangely, she wanted to.

"You are right," she said, curbing both her laugh and her foolish desire. "Monsieur Le Roi, he would not like it said."

When they reached the settee, she let her fingers drop away. Monsieur Westwood's arm did not look injured from her fingernails, but as strong and steady as before. Perhaps playing with quills day in and day out created some strength.

"Lord Lynley." Monsieur Westwood inclined his head in greeting. His eyes crinkled at the corners, just a little, as he turned to the bishop standing watch above Prinny. Perhaps such lines were as close to a smile as she would see from the monsieur. "Bishop Carlisle," he said. "Very good to see you again, my lord." He reached out a hand, which the bishop accepted.

"And you, Maximilian." The bishop seemed an incongruous guest this evening. He appeared quite respectable with his sober, dark clothing and lined face—not at all as entertaining as the rest of company. "Do convey my well wishes to your mother."

"I shall," the monsieur said. To Vivienne and the prince, "The bishop was my father's oldest friend."

The bishop looked very carefully at Monsieur Westwood. Then, also carefully, he looked at Vivienne, gaze lingering on the plunging neckline of her gown and her unruly curls. The lines around his mouth drew down. She had received such disapproval before from other men of the cloth. It was not of import whether this gray-haired, staid bishop believed her to be immoral.

It was Lord Lynley she focused on. He was fingering the little something in his pocket again. Trills of anticipation skittered across her skin. Palms itched to lift the note, to touch fabric and smooth paper and know she had taken something.

"Carlisle isn't as prudish as some others, you know," Prinny said, gesturing toward the bishop. "Though he does try to keep me on the straight and narrow on occasion. Like today, attempting to talk politics instead of pleasure."

"As the bishop has done most of my life, as well, Your Highness," Monsieur Westwood said to the prince. The lines around the monsieur's eyes crinkled again as he slid his gaze toward the bishop.

"Not politics," Carlisle corrected with a slight nod of his head. "Advice on matters of state. Now that I have delivered my message, I will be taking my leave." The bishop folded his hands over a trim middle. "Lynley?"

Lord Lynley's eyes flicked toward Prinny. "No, I shall stay a little longer."

To deliver his note. It was clear. The intent was bright in his eyes, if one knew to look.

Not if I steal it first.

Her pulse hitched. The air seemed dense on her skin, as though it weighed more now than only a moment ago. She felt every shift in its flow. It was always so when she took something. Stealing was a skill, one that took time and practice to perfect. A craft, she supposed.

She was good at her craft.

"Bishop Carlisle, I'm too busy for matters of state." The prince gestured to a footman waiting nearby and plucked a glass of wine from his tray. "You may go."

"Quite." The bishop bowed, revealing a skull beginning to bald at the crown. "Your Highness, Lynley." He nodded. "Maximilian, I shall no doubt see you soon."

"I will join you as you take your leave, sir, if I may," Monsieur Westwood added, clearly seizing upon the excuse. Relief was barely hidden in his voice.

"If you must, Max." Prinny raised his glass in mock toast, the pale-gold wine sloshing over the edge to discolor his gloves. "You too often leave early."

"Farewell, Bishop, Monsieur Westwood." Vivienne smiled when she saw the monsieur was irritated again by the prince's words. Such fierce brows the monsieur had. "Our time together was quite *charmant*," she added.

"Indeed." He bowed to her, attention already elsewhere, though his cravat did look better. "Delightful, Mademoiselle La Fleur."

Striding through the crowd, he was a step ahead of the bishop. Monsieur Westwood was very tall, taller than the other men in the room. It must be interesting, watching everyone from such a great height.

"You were gone a long time, my dear," Prinny said from his comfortable seat on the settee. He sulked like a little boy, his lower lip curled under.

"I missed you every moment, Monsieur Le Roi. You have other company now, I see." She angled her body so that she stood beside Lord Lynley. She smiled at the prince, at the lord. A warm smile, so they would see her face and not her hands.

Lynley nodded his head to her. "Mademoiselle." He was not like Prinny, with his excess and his women and his plump body. This man had sharp eyes that missed little.

Suddenly the challenge was more enjoyable.

"Lord Lynley. I have not seen you at the opera lately. Have you tired of my performance?" She pouted, just a little, and set a hand on the arm that had been fingering the note.

Apprehension suddenly rose from deep inside her, and her mouth went dry. What if she were caught? Never, in all her years, had she been afraid to steal. Never had she believed she might fail. Except this time, it was more than thievery. She thought of Anne, of the Vulture, and of Henri.

Failure was unacceptable. She must complete the assignment.

"I could never tire of your performance." Lord Lynley

leaned down with an enticing smile. "Unfortunately, I had important matters distracting me from your charms." Still, his eyes, they lingered on her shoulders, her bodice.

So she leaned her body toward him, exposing the valley between her breasts, to say, "Then my charms must try harder," and slipped her hand into his pocket.

...

Maximilian was not unhappy. What was happiness, after all? Certainly not a tumble with an opera dancer, or the raucous world of Prinny and his ilk.

He pushed open the door to his town house. Awaiting his arrival was a single candle casting a glowing circle over a faded rug and a pair of urns his mother claimed were from Greece. They were not, since the carvings purporting to be Greek letters were quite fabricated, more's the pity.

Daggett stood halfway up the steps to the upper floors, a stack of ledgers under his arm and a cup of tea in his hand. He appeared to be retiring for the evening, given the tea he usually carried to bed. Maximilian glanced at the utilitarian wooden clock squatting on a narrow table near the door. It was too late to go to Manton's or Gentleman Jackson's. Perhaps he had enough time to work tonight.

Narrowing his eyes, he studied the yellowed clock face.

"Daggett, you moved the clock again." He did not comprehend how his instructions could be misunderstood. Mathematical angles were precise.

"It is not visible from the hallway unless it is angled this way, sir," Daggett said. "I must be able to record the time when going in and out of your study."

"It is supposed to be angled toward the front door for optimal visibility when one enters the house." Setting a finger at the base of the clock, Maximilian pushed the left side two inches backward. "From the door, one may choose to go in any direction from this entryway. If it is only readable from the hall, one must move farther into the house to check the time, then retrace one's steps to go upstairs or to the study. It is a matter of efficiency."

"Yes, sir." The man sighed.

"Good." Maximilian began to peel off his gloves, content now that the clock was angled properly. "I intend to start work on the German text tonight." When his assistant didn't answer, Maximilian glanced up and found the man staring openmouthed. "Yes?"

"Your cravat, sir."

Daggett had noticed. *Of course* he had bloody well noticed. The Flower had tied it into some confounded knot Maximilian probably couldn't undo.

"What of it?" he bit out, tugging at the offending linen. It came apart more easily than he'd expected, but it was still a mess of loops and tucks and folds.

"Sir." Daggett swallowed. "It looked *perfect*. How did you learn to tie your cravat in that manner?"

"I didn't. The Flower corrected it for me." Thankfully, it was now undone and hanging from his fingers.

"The Flower? You were with the Flower?" The ledgers slid out of Daggett's hand and tumbled to the steps, a few slips of paper fanning out on the dark wood. "She has a protector, and she is a spy. Sir, well—she is *adventurous*."

"I wasn't with her in *that* way." Unable to determine if he was insulted or not, Maximilian narrowed his eyes. Did the man think Maximilian couldn't take the Flower to bed? Or that he was *unadventurous*? He acted honorably, unlike many men in society. "She attended the soiree at Carleton House and took offense at my untidy cravat."

Maximilian shoved the linen into his pocket and marched toward the study, leaving Daggett to scramble around the steps and retrieve his ledgers.

Unfortunately, Daggett's voice trailed down the hall behind him. "Oh, meeting her at the prince's makes much more sense, sir."

Now Maximilian *was* insulted. Not that he wanted to be with Vivienne La Fleur in that manner. She was too— too— Well. Too much. In every way possible. She practically breathed sensuality, as her entire body was formed to draw a man's gaze. She was a spy, which he knew from experience meant devious and sneaky and incomprehensible. One never knew where one stood with a spy, and particularly the unreadable Flower.

She was also pledged to another man, a fact he never forgot.

As he stepped into the study, the betraying scrape of wood on wood floated in from the hallway. The clock was being shifted on the tabletop again.

"Make a notation in your ledgers for me to terminate your employment tomorrow morning," Maximilian shouted down the hall.

"Yes, sir."

Blast the man. Daggett did not sound abashed in the least.

Maximilian shut the study door quietly and firmly. He had work to do. Mademoiselle La Fleur and her cravat-tying skills should not be of interest to him. The German ambassador wanted a translation of an English book on etiquette for the ladies of his entourage. A silly frippery of a book, but it was business. The ambassador was willing to pay handsomely, so Maximilian would do the translation.

Vivienne La Fleur and her coded messages and sensual voice would fade away once he could begin to work with the words. Words, at least, made sense.

The Flower was impossible to decipher.

Chapter Six

"The Flower did not take the document from the book, my lord." The agent's voice was quiet, even fearful. "It was still there this morning."

"Did you retrieve it?" The Vulture did not look up from the thick tome splayed open on his desk, but kept his fingertips resting on the thin pages and their tiny printing to mark his place.

"Yes, my lord. I have it here."

Cold fury filled him as the agent set a small square of folded paper on the corner of the gleaming mahogany desk.

"Burn the letter." The Vulture did not need to read it to know what was inside. It was not of any import, as it was only a test to see if the Flower was as good as the reports indicated. He also wanted to determine if she would do as commanded, but the Flower had clearly ignored his directive.

No one ignored the Vulture.

She was nothing. A mere slip of a girl. A pickpocket. A common thief.

Perhaps she was not *so* common, he allowed. She

had access to places he could not go because he would be recognized, places many of his quickest agents could not access. It was why he needed her. Anyone could pick a lock, but not everyone could slip notes into the pockets of politicians during Prinny's gatherings or a dinner party with lords and their mistresses.

The fire across the room flared as his agent dropped the letter into it. The scent of burned paper could not overpower the burning wood, but the Vulture fancied he could smell it nonetheless.

"Leave me." He needed to think, and he needed silence.

"Yes, my lord." The agent bowed quickly then retreated from the room.

The Vulture leaned back and watched the dancing flames. Setting his elbows on the arms of the chair, he pressed his fingertips together. Tapped them.

The threat to the girl had not been enough to turn the Flower as he had expected. He had meticulously researched her and knew everything about her past. It had taken months of work, but he knew everything until she entered the service. There was a gap there—presumably she had been in training—and then she had emerged as the Flower. A dancer capable of slitting a man's throat and lusted after by dozens of London dandies.

What man wouldn't desire to bed such a beauty?

The Vulture wondered, vaguely, if the younger sister resembled the Flower. His tastes did not run to shy, untutored young girls, however. He preferred experienced, creative women. Those women would—and did—allow anything. Perhaps he should send round for one tonight. Or two. He had an endless supply. It was good to have the owner of a brothel in your pocket. He yanked on the bell pull, already anticipating a satisfying night.

While he waited for his men to bring a woman, he would

make plans to find the proper incentive for the Flower. He could still use the little girl to achieve his goal.

He would simply have to make good on his threat.

Chapter Seven

"Sir." Daggett swept open the study door.

Maximilian continued to scratch the quill against paper without looking up. Daggett never minded. They had an arrangement whereby Daggett would talk and Maximilian would pretend to listen while he worked.

Daggett cleared his throat, then went silent again. It must be important. Maximilian looked up to see his assistant sketch a short bow and usher in—"The Right Honorable Lord and Lady Highchester."

Ah. His brother and sister-in-law.

Maximilian sighed and considered pretending he hadn't heard their entrance, but they would enter whether he acknowledged them or not. Which, of course, they did while he was still thinking.

Lady Highchester came first, looking pale and wan and, well, gray. She often looked gray. Even when she wore something with a little more color, such as today's pale-blue gown, she still seemed drab. Daniel Westwood, Baron Highchester, followed her, handsome and windswept, with a dimple that deceived women from Kent to Cornwall to Northumberland, and every dark alley in between.

Maximilian ought to know, as he had spent the better part of his life correcting those deceptions.

"Highchester. Lady Highchester." Maximilian set his quill beside the document he had been translating. He required a break anyway; his eyes ached, as he'd forgotten his spectacles again. Maximilian stood, buttoning the jacket he'd loosened while he'd worked. "Welcome."

"Hello, Maximilian." If voice had color, Lady Highchester's would be as gray as the rest of her. "I have come to say goodbye."

He waited until she settled on the edge of an armchair before he sat again. "Where are you going?"

She pressed her lips together. A moment passed, then, as though she'd recovered from something, "To the country." Her fingers tangled in the strings of her reticule. "I thought it proper to inform you of my departure."

Highchester stepped behind her chair and set his hands on the back of it, the ruby in the family crest winking on his ring finger. "My lady is expecting again." He looked quite bored, his gaze moving slowly around the room. Was that how one usually felt regarding the birth of one's second child? Bored?

Maximilian did not know what to say. Felicitations on becoming a father, or felicitations to Lady Highchester for not having to further suffer her husband's affections?

"My felicitations to Lady Highchester," he said drily.

Her ladyship nodded her head in acceptance.

Maximilian peered at her plain face. She suddenly looked a bit green instead of gray.

"Will Highchester be retiring to the country with you?" He couldn't decide if he wanted his brother to stay in London where Maximilian could keep an eye on him, or in the country where there were fewer scandals to become embroiled in.

"My lord will be staying here to pursue his own amusements." Her ladyship's voice was cold and small, her gaze becoming as dreary and defeated as the rest of her.

Above his wife and out of her sight, Highchester raised a brow. "I have a few business matters I would like to attend to before I retire to the country." His tone was easy, but Maximilian saw the intent behind his eyes.

Something angry and hot burned in the pit of Maximilian's stomach. Women, gambling, drink—that was Highchester's *business*. It always had been. Maximilian did not need further explanation, and apparently neither did his wife.

"Excuse me. I don't feel well. I'll be in the carriage." The lady stood up quickly, skirts swishing. Her reticule fell to the floor. "I shall see you in a few months, Maximilian." She flew out of the room, leaving behind the reticule and a sense of urgency.

Highchester made a noise low in his throat that smacked of disgust. "The cow is sick all over the house. There's a chamber pot in every room. I can't bear to have her in London anymore." Moving around the chair, he kicked his wife's reticule out of his path and strode to the brandy decanter. "I've sent her and the boy off to the country so I can have some peace."

Maximilian didn't say anything. He couldn't *think* of anything to say to that. An heir and an expecting wife would be a blessing. Not that Maximilian wanted either, but if a man did, they would be a blessing. At the very least, they deserved basic consideration.

"With luck I'll have that spare and can stop doing my duty for the family line." Highchester flipped over a snifter. "My lady is like an icicle in the bedchamber." The handsome rakehell waved a hand in the air as though dismissing both her and any potential children.

"I would be, too, if all of London knew of my spouse's

affairs," Maximilian said derisively. Disgust threaded through him, and he found he could no longer sit.

"Defending my wife's honor again, brother?" Highchester raised the empty glass as if in toast. "You always do the proper thing."

"Someone must." Maximilian stalked to the window and set his back to Highchester, studying the carriage for signs his sister-in-law might need assistance.

"Let's not talk about Lady Highchester when there are more enjoyable things to discuss. Carleton House, Max?" His drawl was coated with mocking admiration. Crystal clinked against crystal. "An opera dancer as well? I am truly shocked at your recent company. What has my chivalrous brother turned into?"

"I'm not—" Maximilian spun on his heel.

"That little French morsel is one I'd like to get my hands on, but she's been kept by Wycomb for at least two years. A shame. Brandy?" He raised the decanter in Maximilian's direction, the movement itself a question mark.

"No, it is only ten o'clock in the morning."

"Ah, I'm a little late for my first glass." He grinned, a lopsided, crooked grin that often allowed him to do as he chose without repercussions. "So, dear brother," Highchester said, settling himself into the chair his wife had recently vacated. "Tell me about the delicious little dancer. Everyone noticed you returned to the ballroom with a different cravat style. Did you tup that one? If so, you've got more bollocks than I gave you credit for. Her protector is known to be vicious in guarding his property."

"Highchester." The ache behind his eyes slipped into a throbbing mess. "Mademoiselle La Fleur might be an opera dancer and Lord Wycomb's mistress, but she is still deserving of respect."

"I'm sure she does. A man can still want to bed her, can

he not?" He raised his brandy glass in a mock salute. "Did you tup her in the hallway?"

"God's elbows." Temper spiked at Highchester's disregard for her. "Of course not. Mademoiselle La Fleur retied my cravat. That is all. What of your lady wife?"

"She's likely vomiting in the carriage, and I don't intend to join her there. I've other places to go." He settled deeper into the armchair, despite his claim. Bright-blue eyes studied Maximilian with a combination of amusement and cynicism. "What fun are you getting into, baby brother? The exquisite Mademoiselle La Fleur would not be retying your cravat if you did not have some relationship with her."

He hated that superior stare, as though Highchester knew more than he. Well, perhaps Highchester did. More women, more gambling, more drink. If that was knowledge, then Maximilian preferred to be ignorant. There was right and wrong, duty and selfishness, and a difference between marriage vows and bachelorhood.

It was exactly this dissolution Maximilian tried to balance by being a proper gentleman. The Flower was as deserving of respect as any lady of the *ton*.

"Mademoiselle La Fleur is an acquaintance. A kind one who took pity on a man without a proper valet with a poorly tied cravat." It seemed he'd been reduced to lying in order to be a gentleman. Except he could not tell Highchester that she was a spy and he, himself, a former code breaker.

"You would have me believe you didn't imagine what you could do to her? Any man would want to bed that French strumpet."

"I haven't given Mademoiselle La Fleur any thought in that way." Something niggled at the base of his skull. That wasn't quite the truth. He'd pushed all of those thoughts away until he saw her sitting beside Prinny, laughing and glittering like a diamond in sunlight.

The Flower was with Wycomb. Wanting her would be a hopeless endeavor.

"Well, Max, I *have* thought about her in that way, and so have most of the men in London. The way she moves on stage…a man can't help it." Highchester tapped a finger against his brandy glass and grinned into it. "She's small, but she has a magnificent pair of breasts."

Damnation. Maximilian had no right to think about the Flower's breasts. Yes, they were magnificent, as were her sleekly muscled legs and the flare of her hips in the breeches she wore on assignment. And her lips. Any man would imagine the taste of those lips.

Highchester sent him an satisfied smile. "You're flushed, little brother. It's creeping up your neck."

Maximilian opened his mouth to say something, but not a word came out.

"Sir, sir! I have found the vulture!" Daggett skidded into the room from his adjoining office. He clutched a ledger against his chest, the binding frayed with time. As soon as his feet slid to a halt, he began to back out again, all obsequious bows. "Oh. Oh. Lord Highchester. My apologies. I forgot. So sorry, my lord. I'll just—"

"Cheese it, Daggett." Highchester laughed and tossed back the last of his brandy. "Max is grateful for the interruption so he doesn't have to answer my questions." The snifter landed on the table with a sharp *snick*. "Don't think I've forgotten, brother."

That last was delivered quietly and gave Maximilian a chill. It was then he saw the bright light of avarice in his brother's eyes. *I don't want my toy, I want yours. I'm going to take it because I can.* Oh, yes, he knew that look.

He also was no longer a young boy bullied by his older brother.

"Good day, Highchester." He jerked his chin up. "If you're

lucky, the door handle won't hit your arse on the way out."

With a flourished bow, Highchester quit the room, whistling through his teeth.

It would not be the last he saw of his brother in the near future. He'd best warn the Flower, he supposed. Highchester could make a nuisance of himself when he wanted a particular woman, and it might cause her difficulties.

Family could be the very devil, and his particularly so.

Daggett cleared his throat.

"Hell." He'd forgotten the vulture symbol already, damn Highchester's lascivious predilections and foolish greed. Maximilian spun around to face his assistant. "What did you find?"

"It was before Napoleon's hundred days and Waterloo." Daggett rushed to the desk and dropped the ledger onto it. He riffled through pages, then pointed at a series of precise lines. "There. It is exact. This is a missive intercepted on its way to Calais with the symbol of the vulture at the bottom."

"My spectacles." Maximilian patted the pockets of his worn coat, to no avail. "Where are my spectacles?"

"Here." Daggett scooped them up from the desk where they lay between a scattering of inkwells.

Maximilian looped the frame over his ears as excitement spun inside him. He leaned over the ledger and was grateful Daggett faithfully recorded every document that entered his study and every translation that went back out.

"I remember now. Orders from Paris—subversive ones, as I recall. The writer was against Napoleon." The memory was coming back to him. The paper had been four inches by six inches. Script slanted to the left, with a narrow nib. "I didn't understand what the drawing meant then, either, and assumed it was a signature."

"We found out who it was, eventually."

"We did?" He jerked his head around to look at Daggett.

"Who?"

"Marchand. A French spymaster who called himself the Vulture. He was never caught. We couldn't even determine where he was hiding."

"Damnation."

What had been written in the note to the Flower? Maximilian squinted slightly as he stared up at the carved ceiling, as though doing so would bring the words back into his mind.

On 13 October, go to No. 14 Hanover Square. Documents will be hidden in a copy of Sense and Sensibility *by A Lady. Deliver documents to 22 Neva Street.*

The implications were clear. The Flower was to deliver documents to Marchand, or at least take orders from Marchand. Ergo, either the Flower was a double agent, or she was in trouble.

Neither was something he could ignore.

Solitude and words would once again elude him due to duty and espionage. Particularly as 14 October was today. She would have been stealing the documents for the French last night, before or after Prinny's soiree. Perhaps she'd even had the documents in her possession while she'd tied his cravat.

That sort of lie, he thought sourly, was why he'd retired from code breaking.

"Find out where she lives."

• • •

The floor of Anne's room was hard. It was also cold on Vivienne's bottom. The surface was bare wood with some type of shining lacquer applied. Fingers tracing the grain, her eyes followed suit in the thin light from the candle stub.

A soft sigh came from the bed as Anne turned over in her sleep. Vivienne watched the rise and fall of her chest to see if she breathed easy. It was an old habit from their childhood, when she would put her hand on Anne's back to see if she still breathed in her sleep. Their mother had done the same, she remembered.

Twenty-four hours had passed since she'd ignored the Vulture's command. He would know by now that she did not intend to comply. He might have flown into a rage. She had not met him before, but she had heard of his temper. Even his own spies feared his wrath.

Vivienne could not predict what consequence would result from her choice. Her life might be considered forfeit—so might Anne's life.

That Vivienne would not allow.

Anne could not come to Vivienne's room for protection, or Henri might question why Vivienne stood watch over her. Nor could she change the locks or post a guard without Henri noticing. So Vivienne must go to Anne. She would sit on the floor of this tiny room for the remainder of her days, her back against the door and eyes on the window, if that were necessary.

Vivienne tensed as a sound filtered through the night. Fingers reached for the knife beside her, but she did not stand up. Not yet. Listening, she waited, assessing the sound. After a moment her muscles went lax. Wind, rattling a windowpane somewhere on this floor.

Closing her eyes against the wavering candlelight, she leaned her head against the door, but not to sleep. Rest would not come. She wanted to listen to the sounds of the night and bring them into her. If she knew them, she would know one that was out of place.

Wind. A creak of the floors as the house settled. The tick of the clock beside the bed. The footman snoring in another room down the hall. Then, loud against the backdrop of house sounds, a shush of feet on floorboard. Not in the hallway behind her, however.

Beside the bed.

Vivienne did not move. She kept her back against the door, her eyes closed, and listened to those soft footsteps growing faintly louder.

"Oh, Vivienne." Anne's voice was sad. It should not be so sad.

"Go back to bed." Still she did not open her eyes. Buttocks numb now from the floor, skin chilled from the cool night air, but she would not leave until morning. "Go."

"Not if you are sitting awake," Anne said softly. "I will not be able to sleep."

Soft fabric brushed against Vivienne's ankle. No doubt it was the hem of Anne's shift. She opened her eyes to observe a pair of bare feet peeking from beneath a hem of thin cotton swirling through the pale light of the candle stub. Yes, the dratted girl was standing right in front of her.

"Go to bed," Vivienne said again and straightened, glaring at Anne. "I am not sitting awake, like so, while you also sit awake. It is absurd."

Anne was young enough still to pout, her lip pushing out. "No. You're worried someone will come for me because you made them angry. You're protecting me like you used to with Da." Thin arms crossed over her chest, and though her tone had been petulant, she also sounded stubborn. "I shall sit with you."

Anne settled on the floor beside Vivienne and drew her legs up beneath her shift.

"Obstinate girl." Vivienne would have done the same. The fact squeezed a little fist around her heart, and that fist clouded her judgment. "At least put slippers on so your feet will not be cold."

Her sister ignored her.

The wind still rattled the windowpane. The snoring

footman did not cease his snoring. And so it was the two of them. Alone in the dark and on a cold floor.

"I love you, Anne."

"I love you, too."

A thick braid bumped against her arm as Anne laid her head on Vivienne's shoulder. Toying with the tail of the plait, she ran her fingers through soft, freshly washed hair. Vivienne, too, had washed her hair that night. It was just as soft, though bound tightly at her neck so it could not be used as a weapon against her.

A wry chuckle slipped from Vivienne's lips.

"What is funny?"

"If we meet our deaths this night, we will at least have clean hair."

Anne snickered, a little-girl sound that warmed Vivienne's heart. Another sound followed, unobtrusive, like the swish of dead leaves beneath one's feet.

There were no leaves in Anne's room.

Chapter Eight

The shift in awareness came quickly.

Vivienne's knife was in her hand before she thought to seize it. Blood beginning to pump, heart beating furiously in her chest, she closed her mouth and forced herself to breathe through her nose. She must stay calm. Vigilant. Determine whether the threat was in the hall or outside the window.

Vivienne put her mouth to Anne's ear, ignoring the tickle of hair on her nose. "They have come," she breathed.

The girl stiffened, muscles tensing, though she could not know who *they* were. Terror radiated from her so vividly, so sharply, Vivienne could almost smell it—but Anne did not move.

Good girl.

Vivienne waited for the next sound. Which direction would they come from? She could not move until she knew. Sweat slicked her palm so the hilt of the knife slid against her skin.

Now fear clutched in her own belly. She did not sweat. It was not tolerated. Sweat and terror would make her knife inaccurate.

Another sound met her ears. A scrape. Perhaps a branch on the window. Or perhaps not. There was no tree, and so no branch could scrape.

They were coming in through the window, then.

Again into Anne's ear she whispered. "When I say so, run into the hall. Hide behind the secret wall in the linen closet downstairs. Take the footman and Mrs. Asher with you." Mrs. Asher would know to go straight to the closet and to take Anne. They would be safe.

Anne shook her head, and Vivienne heard her breath tumbling in and out in a mad rush.

"You must hide." Vivienne clutched at her sister's arm, pressing her fingers into young skin to make her point. *Hide!* She wanted to scream it, but could not. "Do not come out until I let you out, or until morning, then run far and fast and do not return to England." It was the best she could do.

There was no time for a proper good-bye.

Swallowing her sorrow, Vivienne rose to a crouch, balancing on the balls of her feet. She took a second knife from her boot. One knife for each hand, hilts solid in her curled fingers. Comforting, even.

She would not be alone when she faced the intruders. She would have her knives.

Vivienne studied the window, the outline of the drapes. The fabric would move, ever so slightly, once they entered. There had not been any movement yet. She had another moment, then, to gather herself for the battle. To center and quiet the mind, to control breath and push away fear and sorrow.

She turned her head to look at Anne and saw the girl's eyes were wide and petrified. Anne tried to smile bravely, but her smile wobbled and tore at Vivienne's heart.

She would carry that valiant, trembling smile with her.

Always.

"*Go.*"

Anne's thin, taut body sprang up, as an arrow might be loosed from a bow. She wrenched the bedroom door open and slipped through, the hem of her nightgown a whisper in the night as it disappeared from view. The candle sputtered in the draft from the door, then was extinguished, leaving a thin trail of smoke.

Vivienne spun on the balls of her feet and set her back to the door, arms raised. There was no light to glint on the blades of her knives. No movement in the air. But she felt the intruders. In the dark. In the night. The drapes had moved while her back was turned, and she had not seen. They were in the room.

The shadow sprang at her.

Her breath stopped. Turning to the side, she shot a leg out, up and high. It connected with the column of a neck. Someone else's breath wheezed out. She ignored the sound and took satisfaction in the feel of flesh against her booted foot.

Vivienne arced her knife into the air. The man jumped back, but another was in his place. The whisper of a blade slid through the air, perilously close to her side. She did not hesitate. A thrust, a parried slice. Neither made contact, so she leaped forward.

Even as her blade slashed through fabric and skin, air rushed in her ears as the other man sprinted past her. Out the door. To the hall. *To Anne.* Vivienne spun, flailing outward with her knife, but it was too late.

The man was through the door and away.

With a howl of rage, Vivienne sprang toward the hall. A foot rammed into her back. She slammed into the floor and skidded through the bedroom door. Pain rode up and down her spine, but she pushed to her knees.

She was too slow, too clumsy.

Anne. She must protect Anne.

A shout rang in the hall. "Oi! Who is it?" It must be Thomas, the footman, but he was lame. He could not run well and would not be of use against these men.

On her feet now, pounding down the hall. An enemy in front, another behind who was not fast enough to stop her from finding the servants' stairs. They were narrow and steep, but she plunged down them as fast as her legs would allow, bouncing off the plastered wall.

A scream came from below. Vivienne recognized Anne's voice and needed nothing more to spur her forward. Her stomach heaved and pitched, and her breath would not become steady in her lungs.

Jumping the last few steps, she landed in the hall of the first floor. Here, light flickered from a candelabrum lying on the floor, a few scattered candles still burning. She sped down the hall at a full run. Mrs. Asher slumped on the floor, hands clutching at a forehead trickling blood.

The first intruder, tall and wide and muscular, had his arms around Anne in a great, farcical hug. The girl bucked and kicked her feet, but she was no match for him. Vivienne heard Anne's whimper, the male grunt.

Not Anne. You will not take my Anne.

No time for hesitation, but he was too close to Anne. In the dark she could not separate their shadows enough for the thin blade of a knife—but she could see which part of the shadow was the man. Vivienne kicked out, foot connecting with his kidney. He staggered, and Anne broke free.

Henri's voice was loud in her memory. *When the enemy is down, a spy pounces or risks losing the advantage. Advantage means life.* Her foot lashed out again, and she heard ribs crack.

"The closet," Vivienne called to Anne.

Again her sister did not listen. She dropped to her knees

beside Mrs. Asher, sobs bursting from her throat.

"Hide!" Vivienne shouted, leaning down to pull Anne to her feet.

Pain exploded in her head.

Suddenly the world consisted of throbbing agony, spinning stars, and tumbling hair as the neat coil at her nape came apart. The floor rose up to meet her. More pain burst into life in her knees and wrists as she fell. A sharp cry grew in her throat, and she could not keep from giving it voice.

She would not fail.

She could not see properly to throw her knife. Her vision was blurry, but she could see well enough to launch herself at the man who stepped past her toward Anne. More pain in her shoulder as they tumbled to the ground. Dimly she heard Anne's cry for help as the other man lifted her into the air and began to run toward the front of the house.

The footman's lurching footsteps came from the other end of the hall. It was too late for his help. Vivienne's knife thrust in and out of flesh. Again. She could not think of the life taken. There was only Anne and her mewling cries growing fainter as she was carried away.

Vivienne did not look at the intruder whose life was spilling onto the hallway floor, but pushed to her feet, panic roiling inside her.

"Here, Miss Vivienne." The footman huffed, thrusting a pistol at her. She fumbled with it, unwilling to take even a moment to shove it in her waistband.

Mrs. Asher was on her hands and knees now. Blood matted her hairline, but she was lucid, her breath wheezing out a whispered, "Anne."

She would heal, Vivienne thought, letting that small relief fill her as she spun away.

"Into the closet," she shouted to the footman as she raced down the hall. "Take Mrs. Asher. Do not come out until I return or until morning."

"Aye," he returned.

If she was fast, she could still reach Anne. Head hammering in tandem with her footsteps, she concentrated on the open front door and steps beyond. On the cobblestone street and the London night.

It was deserted.

They were gone.

Chapter Nine

Maximilian had quite a few words for the Flower.

Never mind that it was midnight. After midnight. Maximilian flipped open his pocket watch, turning it so the carriage lamp shone on the surface. After one in the morning, even.

Well, she was a dancer and a mistress. No doubt she was accustomed to late nights. Besides, it had taken Daggett this long to unearth her direction. Now Maximilian was riding in his brother's cast-off, second-rate carriage, intent on confronting her.

In the middle of the night, it seemed.

The *clip-clop* of horses' hooves competed with the pattering rain. He smoothed down the front of his greatcoat, then clasped his hands together in his lap while deciding what to say when he arrived.

Are you a double agent?

That might result in his death, likely by pistol or knife. She was no doubt competent with both. He had no experience with knives himself. Marksmanship was a skill he possessed, of course, having honed it during the war—though he was no longer accustomed to carrying a weapon, despite occasionally practicing at Manton's.

He would have to rectify that if he were to continue having dealings with spies. As he would in the next few minutes.

Perhaps he should begin by asking her, *Are you committing treason?*

Surely one did not open a conversation in such a way. It seemed a bit harsh. Maybe he should begin the conversation with some pleasantries.

How was your most recent performance? Did you dance well? Oh, and are you committing treason?

Perhaps that was *too* pleasant.

The carriage jerked as the footman-turned-coachman slowed the horses. Maximilian didn't wait for the steps to be set down, but jumped from the carriage on the wet cobblestones. Tilting his head back, he squinted through a light rain at the facade of Mademoiselle La Fleur's town house. Every window was dark and silent. Not even a whisper of life.

She was probably sleeping. Or gone. Or—devil take it— entertaining her protector.

He should not have come. Waiting until morning would have been prudent.

"Do not move." The Flower's voice was low and deadly. The click of the pistol cocking certainly didn't ease the menace he heard there. How the bloody hell had she sneaked up behind him?

Something poked against his back, and he assumed it was the pistol. The powder would be wet and useless in this rain. Probably. Possibly.

He really ought to have brought some type of weapon. It was a mistake he would not make again.

"Mademoiselle La Fleur."

"Monsieur Westwood?" Surprise bounced along the edge

of her sensual voice.

"What are you doing on the bloody street instead of inside the house?" he asked. They would both be soaked through in another minute.

"I'm looking for—no. It is not important." The pistol pressed firmly into his vertebrae. "Why are you here?"

He swallowed hard. "I know who the Vulture is."

The pistol jerked against his back as she gasped. If she pulled the trigger, she would sever his spine.

Time spun out to nothing but sight and sound and breath as he waited for her to make a choice. The jingle of harness, rain trapped in his lashes, light slanting over the walkway from a neighboring house. The clean scent of the Flower, made stronger by the rain. All were more intense in that moment.

"Sir?" The driver called from atop the carriage.

The word spurred the Flower into action, and the pistol eased away from his spine. "Send your driver away," she whispered. "Come inside." Then she flitted into a rain-soaked shadow, leaving him seemingly alone on the street.

He had half a mind to step back into his carriage and go home. A fire waited for him there. Work, too. Dry clothes and brandy. Any of them were better than standing on the street in the middle of the night, rain dripping from the brim of his hat.

Yet he couldn't ignore the fact that the Vulture was sending the Flower coded messages.

"Take the carriage home, John." He cursed himself even as the words came out of his mouth. "I'll hire a hackney on my return."

"Are you certain, sir?"

Yes, he was bloody well certain. He couldn't leave now. *In too deep, Maximilian*, his conscience said. "Go home, John."

He waited in front of the silent house as the carriage pulled away. It disappeared into the darkness, and he wondered if he had taken leave of all of his senses. Rain pelted his greatcoat and the back of his neck. He hoped the Flower would return soon from whatever dark place she'd disappeared to.

"Monsieur. Come in." The words barely carried over the rush and rhythm of rain. He could not see her at first, then, yes. There she was in front of the town house and wearing men's clothing again, as he could see her legs moving up the steps, one after the other.

He strode to the entrance and started up himself, but the damn things were slippery. He nearly slid off the top step and gripped the railing to keep from tumbling down.

It was a sign from fate, he thought, as he scrambled to get his legs back under him. He should run, fast and far. Becoming involved with the Flower would be complicated and likely dangerous.

Looking behind, Maximilian checked for the carriage. Perhaps it wasn't too late to turn back. But, no. That damnable duty again. He hadn't shied from duty when he'd first been recruited for code breaking, and he wouldn't do so now.

The door to the house was open, revealing nothing but midnight and silence. Mademoiselle La Fleur was a shadow against the dark interior. She made some unintelligible gesture he theorized was "come in" given the circumstances.

So he did. Stepped right into the lion's den. Or the dancer's lair.

It was more or less the same thing.

He passed by her and into the shadowed entryway. The town house smelled feminine and flowery and perfumed, and not the least bit like her. If he had given any thought to the matter, he would have expected it to smell fresh, as she did.

The door shut behind him. A quiet *snick* that spoke of restraint and—fear? Was that fear? Then he caught some strange scent in the perfumed interior.

Fresh blood.

He whirled to face her, prepared to fend off an attack. A knife ready to slit his throat or aimed for his gut so the death would be slow and painful. She only stood there, a shadow pressed against the door. Harsh breathing filled the quiet entry, the uneven rhythm loud now that the rain was shut outside.

"Excuse me. I must see to—" She broke off, shaking her head with erratic movements. "Wait a moment, please."

She pushed off the door to stride down the hall, dancer's legs moving with a quick, determined stride. He followed, deciding whatever blood had been shed in this house, it was not here in the front hall.

His eyes had adjusted to the dark, revealing the outline of the Flower, yawning doors to other rooms, and the shape of paintings on the wall and statuary on tables. All of it a jumble of shadows and forms.

She must have cat's eyes, she walked so confidently in the dark. No wonder she was able to enter and exit his house without detection. He could not hear her, though she was only a few feet in front of him. It must be the dancing. She moved with grace and fluidity, feet stepping as lightly as clouds kissing the earth in the quiet early-morning hours.

He couldn't quite accept the fact his brain had devised a phrase as ridiculous as clouds kissing the earth.

Maximilian set his fingers against his forehead and rubbed—and ran into her when she stopped. A light *oof* puffed from his lips as he registered her body against his. He could not feel her shape, but the contact still sent a jolt straight through him.

"I beg your pardon, mademoiselle," he said stiffly.

She only shook her head and turned toward an empty wall. Her hand reached through the dark, touched something, and a door creaked open. Stepping back at the sudden glare, he was certain a host of spies would spill from the narrow space to swarm the hall.

The glare was only a small stubbed candle, illuminating a heavyset woman in a shift and wrapper and a young man in a long nightshirt. They huddled on a stone floor in a room barely big enough for both of them.

"Good." Sagging shoulders accompanied the mademoiselle's uneven sigh. "You are both safe. Are you well, Mrs. Asher?"

"It's a small cut." The heavyset woman stood. Blood matted her hair, and her hands trembled as they pulled together the edges of the wrapper. "Anne?"

"Gone." The Flower's tone was bleak. "She is gone."

"Oh, my dear." The older woman flew through door and straight at Mademoiselle La Fleur, drawing her in.

"I should have helped, Miss Vivienne." The man clambered to his feet. He limped forward, clearly injured, though Maximilian saw no fresh blood. "You needed me. Anne needed—"

"No, Thomas." Mademoiselle La Fleur spoke firmly, even as the older woman looked to be squeezing the breath from her. She patted the woman's back, two perfunctory taps, before disentangling herself from determined arms and turning to the man. "You went into the closet as I asked. They would not have hesitated to kill you and Mrs. Asher."

"What in the blazes is going on?" Maximilian stepped into the circle of light from the candle. He did not care for feeling ignorant, and whatever ghastly episode had played out here, it was time he knew.

The light from the candle stub shadowed the Flower's eyes as she faced him, giving her a mysterious look. It suited the scene.

"Do not quibble now, Monsieur Westwood. We have a dead man who must be removed." She spoke woodenly, as though she were discussing the rain outside. "The facts I will explain later."

The blood. He'd smelled it, hadn't he? Death and violence and fresh blood.

"Who is it? Marchand?"

She hissed out a breath. "Do not say the Vulture's name. Not just now. I do not know what ears—" She whirled away, hair fanning out in wet coils to lure him in. "Thomas, bring the carriage. Mrs. Asher, find linens, towels. Something to wrap the man in. We're going to dump him in the Thames."

"Absolutely not." Maximilian drew himself up. Murder he was not having any part of. Disposing of dead bodies he was also not having a part of. "There are authorities who must be contacted. An inquiry into the manner of death. You cannot—"

"He was a French spy." She said it flatly, her eyes dark and hard in the weak candlelight. Resolve firmed her chin. He could not say why that tugged at his heart, but he wished it didn't.

"Then the authorities must be called." As stubborn as she, he would stand firm against her resolve. There was a proper order to things, a logical method for answering questions.

"His manner of death was a knife in between the ribs, angled up just so, in order to pierce the lungs and heart. A fast death." She continued as if he had not spoken, lips thinned and turned down, brows rigid and without expression. "His murderer is myself, with my own knife."

Dear God.

"If he is not removed and all traces of his death washed away by morning, it will be more than my life at stake. More, even, than the young girl abducted tonight. It will be the country."

Maximilian drew a very deep, very resigned breath.

"Bloody, buggering hell."

Chapter Ten

The body hit the Thames with a splash that made Maximilian's skin crawl.

"I should have stayed at home." He shuddered as the dead Frenchman bobbed along the surface of the river. Turning away, Maximilian gritted his teeth and breathed through his mouth. God's eyes, the very air by the docks was ripe with rotting…something. "I should have stepped back into the carriage when I saw your windows were dark."

"Yes, I suppose your papers and brandy are most important," Mademoiselle La Fleur said testily.

"I beg your pardon?" He sounded like a cur beginning to bristle and knew it. Turning sharply, Maximilian aimed his feet in the direction of the carriage. Not far, it sat like a specter on the street, the lame footman perched on top.

The Flower fell into step beside him. She sighed, rubbed a hand over her face, and tugged at the cap bundling up her hair. "My apologies, Monsieur Westwood. I am tired and a little sick, I think." She tapped a hand against her chest. "Here."

"Anyone would be after killing a man, even if you are a

spy." He must remember the man was a French spy and the Flower had acted to save an innocent. If he let himself forget that, his body would surely rebel.

"It is not the man, or not only him." Her voice was barely audible, but he heard sadness there.

"Then what?" He wished he could smell *her* instead of this other stench. Whatever clean scent she used was lost among the garbage and sewage and heaven knew what else in this part of London. At least no one would question someone dumping a body into the river. Happened all the time down here, he suspected, which meant they should leave the area. Quickly.

"Monsieur, I cannot do what comes next alone." The clear tones of her voice broke, and she coughed before she spoke again.

Please, no tears. Crying women were, well, frightening. There was no logic to female tears that he could see. His mother regularly had hysterics—though he couldn't imagine the Flower having anything resembling hysterics, which was a point in her favor.

"Please." Her voice was very, very soft. Embarrassment, even desperation, colored the word. "I need your assistance."

"Well, damn." Sometimes being a gentleman was the very devil. Not to mention that little matter of the Vulture, which had sent him to her doorstep in the first place.

"Monsieur?"

He sighed. "What assistance do you require?"

She, too, sighed, though it was more like letting out a breath she'd been holding for too long. "It is complicated and requires privacy. Come." She jerked her head toward the carriage.

Maximilian found himself inside the vehicle as the carriage lumbered away from the docks. Mademoiselle La Fleur sat stiffly in the seat across from him, hands gripping each other. She didn't appear as if she would to cry at the moment, but he did not intend let down his guard. If she did cry, he must be prepared to find his handkerchief quickly.

"What trouble have you gotten yourself into?"

Her brows snapped together beneath her cap. "The trouble—it was not started by me."

"But it *is* trouble." Of course. "Marchand."

Her breath was short and angry now. "You know of Marchand?"

"The vulture is his signature. I decoded one of his messages a few years ago during the war. My assistant records everything and was able to locate it."

"Ah. The inimitable Daggett." She shook her head, apparently as resigned to Daggett's ways as Maximilian was himself. "I had hoped you would not recognize it. If you know, you may die. Do you see?"

Of course he could see—in the same manner he could see through the muddy, brown water of the Thames. "It's still quite unclear," he said carefully.

"It is complicated. Most complicated." She leaned forward and rested her elbows on her knees, as any man might have done during a difficult explanation. If she'd been wearing a gown, her breasts would have popped right out of her bodice.

Closing his eyes against the thought, Maximilian forced the image from his mind. He had promised himself years before that he would not treat women as Highchester did.

"What is important now is that one of Marchand's men is dead," the Flower continued, not bothered by any possible fantasy. "The Vulture will know I killed him."

Right. The Vulture. Not that quickening in Maximilian's veins or the pulse beating in his belly. Setting his mind back to the issue at hand, he shifted his body on the cushioned seat.

"Did Marchand order your death? Is that why the Frenchman was in your town house?" Perhaps her disguise had been penetrated. He imagined the French would be brutal to a Frenchwoman working for England—which made him wonder what ideology caused her to be an English spy and not a French one. She was a fascinating mix of truth and secrets.

"Marchand is not going to kill me, as I am still of use to him, but it was not me he wanted this night." The narrow shoulders, normally so straight and square, slumped. "If he wanted me dead, I would be."

"The girl." He remembered the hurried, panicked conversation with the housekeeper. "Marchand wanted the servant girl."

"If I do not do what Marchand asks, they will kill her." Jagged words pierced the air, as if something had torn in her heart.

God help him. She *was* going to cry. What should he do? He fumbled for his handkerchief.

Unbearably grateful when Mademoiselle La Fleur did not cry, he let out a breath as her shoulders straightened again.

"Anne cannot die." Her tone was harsh, words echoing with conviction. "I will not tolerate her death. She is innocent."

Maximilian studied her face, shadowed beneath the cap she wore. Her eyes were hidden, but the small, pointed chin he could see clearly enough in the light from the carriage lamps. It was angled up, her mouth set in a determined line.

He understood a part of her, he supposed, despite the many unreadable layers of her character. Mademoiselle La Fleur was likely responsible for many deaths, directly or indirectly, but the death of a girl with no ties to espionage was a different matter than killing a spy. A life was a life, but there was a difference between innocence and war.

"What assistance do you need from me?" he asked.

"The messages from Marchand may be coded, like the one I brought to you a few days ago. If so, I will need you to decode them."

"The last message was a simple substitution code." He shook his head and shifted against the carriage seat. "If I gave you the substitution parameters, you could do it yourself."

"I do not think so." By the light of carriage lamps he saw that her face was blank, even the determination wiped away. There was no emotion or expression on her fine-boned features or in her words, nothing he could translate to an expression he could understand. "I might be wrong."

Confound her, she was right. The code might change. Or she might decode it incorrectly. He scrubbed a hand over his face. "What does Marchand want?"

"A double agent."

He had been afraid of that. Leaning forward, he propped his hands on his knees in a mirror image of her stance. He could clearly see her face beneath the cap now. "I will report you if you become a double agent," he said carefully.

Her eyes glittered when she met his gaze, two dark obsidian shards. "And the girl?" she asked softly. "If I do not do what they ask, she will die. She was taken because I did not do what they asked the first time."

"Ah. The first message I decoded."

"Yes." She straightened, then spread open her gloved hands so that they rested palm up on top of her thighs. She stared at them, as if they held the answer to some mysterious question. "It might have been stolen English documents that would be useful to the French. Or it might have been nothing but a simple message. Whatever it was, I was to take it to Marchand."

"You did not," he finished for her, suddenly understanding what had happened. She had gone to Prinny's soiree instead of acting on behalf of the French and had *not* betrayed England. "Now the girl's life is at stake."

The carriage slowed, and he noticed the stench of the

Thames had dissipated. They were back in the semifashionable area of town where the mademoiselle lived.

"What will you do?" he asked.

The carriage rolled to a stop at a soft *whoa* from the coachman above. Neither of them moved to get out. Silence stretched between the seats, thin and taut.

Finally, she whispered, "I don't know."

The carriage door opened, letting in night tinged with gray light. Dawn was closing in. The lame footman poked his head through the door. "Miss Vivienne, we're home."

"I will be out in a moment." Mademoiselle La Fleur did not look at the footman but kept her gaze steady on Maximilian, eyes dark and wary. "What do you suggest I do?" she asked when the footman's round face disappeared from view.

"Hell. I have no idea." He ran both hands through his hair, gripped it, tugged. "I cannot let you spy for France."

"I will not let her die."

"Why can't you speak with your commander? You must have a commander. A spymaster."

She was so quiet he could hear the swish of the horses' tails outside. It was not cold enough that her breath was visible, but he imagined it was nearly so. The damn carriage was frigid with the door hanging open in that manner.

"I cannot approach my commander," she finally said. "Marchand does not want the English coming after him, and my commander would do so. If he did, the Vulture would not hesitate to kill the girl and find another double agent."

Confound the woman, she was right again. Marchand would simply find another spy without the Flower's scruples—such as they were.

"What if we find her?" she asked suddenly, leaning forward again. "If we find the girl and bring her back, she will not be leverage. Everyone can be told. The Vulture can be stopped without the girl dying."

"*We* find her?" He did not like the way that sounded. "I am not a spy, mademoiselle, and I have no desire to engage in espionage."

"You are the only person I can rely on to assist me. I cannot approach an official code breaker, as he would be required to report it and Anne would die. Yet Marchand must be stopped."

Maximilian narrowed his eyes and studied her delicate features, wondering just what he was setting himself up for. Spies were tricky sorts. One minute a man was studying languages at university with dreams of scholarly accolades, and the next he's in a muddy field breaking codes for Wellington. Except the Flower was difficult to resist, even when asking him to do all manner of unsavory things. There he'd been, working on a simple Russian translation. Without warning he was decoding messages from French spies and dumping a dead man into the Thames.

Hell and damnation and all of God's teeth. If he didn't help the Flower, the girl *would* die. Maximilian had a sudden image of a pretty little girl huddled in a filthy room while Frenchmen taunted her. Or worse. No, that he could not tolerate, and the image would haunt him now that it was lodged in his brain.

"I'm not killing anyone," he said. He had to draw a line somewhere. "Not even for an abducted girl."

"I would not ask you to kill anyone." She shook her head, and he watched, fascinated, as a long curl tumbled from beneath the cap to float around her face. By all that was holy, did she plan such things to torment men? "Only decoding messages, monsieur. That is all."

"Well, we better locate her quickly, before your commander finds out or Marchand kills her. Now, can we leave this carriage so I can come inside and get warm before

I walk home?"

"Thank you, Monsieur Westwood, but you cannot come into my town house." She slipped from her seat and moved toward the opening, her body making not the slightest noise. "Henri will be arriving soon, and he cannot find you here."

"Your protector." The word made his stomach twist. What occurred between them was not his affair, but that did not stop him from wondering if the man treated her well.

The Flower's eyes met his, as difficult to read as Persian.

"The carriage will take you home." She stepped from the vehicle, turned around, and shut the door without another word.

Chapter Eleven

Her room was very cold. Or perhaps it was only Vivienne who was cold.

This feeling was not *only* cold, however.

Temperature simply raised one's flesh in little bumps. This was deeper than the skin. It was bone deep. Heart deep. She could not think of a word in French or in English that explained this cold inside in her.

She had failed Anne.

Life had left a man's body only hours before—and she had taken that life. She was trained to do so, but her work for Henri involved theft, not killing.

It felt deserved, now, that she should sit in her room wearing nothing but her shift and let the cold ravage her. There was no comfort to be found. Not in the bed she sat cross-legged on, nor in the knives she had set out on the expensive, frilly coverlet. Not in the pale light of dawn as it broke over London. Not even in the pencil drawing Anne had given her when they were young.

She smoothed the paper over her bare knee and studied

the drawing in the half-light of dawn. Two figures made of sharp angles and crooked lines. One tall, one short. Both with childish scratches around their heads that must be hair. The short figure smiled a broad smile, though she stood crookedly on legs of very different lengths. The taller figure did not smile and did not frown. Only a straight line for her mouth.

Vivienne had never smiled in those days, and Anne was adamant about correct details in her pictures. Vivienne touched a hand to the mouth of the smaller figure. At least Anne had smiled as a child. She'd had done everything she could to see that bright, happy smile.

The scratching on her door was quieter than the wings of a moth against a windowpane. Still, she heard it and tucked the drawing beneath her pillow. Not the secret place she hid things from Henri, but it would do for now.

She did not move from the bed when the door opened, though she was very conscious of how far from her hand her knives were. Six inches. Life or death could be decided by as little as six inches.

Death was not at her bedroom door, however. It was only Mrs. Asher wearing an apron over her nightgown. The blood was gone from her hair, and only a small cut remained.

"Miss." Sorrow filled the single word. "I've cleaned the hall, and Thomas removed the dirty linens. If his lordship arrives for breakfast, he won't see anything amiss." Dim light shone on Mrs. Asher's lips as she pressed them together and shook her head, messy topknot trembling with the movement. "I wish—"

"There is nothing to wish. It was done, and we must move forward." A brisk, confident tone would make Mrs. Asher feel better. The energy it cost Vivienne to create such a tone was only one more deserved punishment. "Even now, I have been thinking of a plan to rescue her."

Always lies. She had no plan. She had nothing but an

empty space in her heart and fear filling her mind.

"Good." Mrs. Asher nodded once, sharply. "I can help, too. I know some lads from the old streets still. They're not always honorable men, but they have brawn. If you don't mind my saying so, they remember you and Anne well enough. Always good for a bit of mischief, too, that lot is."

These men knew everything about her. They'd known what Big John did to his wife and daughters in those days, yet had turned a blind eye. No, she did not want to ask them, even if they had brawn and mischief in equal measure. One could not rely on such things.

"I will bear that in mind. Now, as to Henri, I do not know if he will arrive this morning. If he does not, you will go to sleep. Thomas, too. This house will be shuttered today."

"Aye, as it should be. What of you?"

"I must make plans. I do not have time to sleep." She would not be able to sleep, even if she tried, as she did not know what Anne was enduring. Rising to her knees, Vivienne was careful not to disturb the knives. "Mrs. Asher, if at any time Monsieur Westwood arrives, he must be allowed entrance. Even if Henri is here, I will find a way to receive him in secret."

Monsieur Westwood would be the key to finding the girl, though she could not rely on him any more than the lads from the old streets. A reclusive scholar who did not like to be disturbed would not be of much use against a French spymaster.

She would not even have told him anything of Anne if he had not arrived just when she needed his strength.

That did not signify.

Marchand, he would use codes. She could not decode them herself, so she would use Monsieur Westwood.

She could not do anything until the Vulture contacted her again. Until then, she must spy for Henri, laugh with the

Prince Regent, and pretend the very breath of her life had not been stolen.

"I will find Anne, Mrs. Asher. Do not fear." She fisted her hands. Perhaps if she could make Mrs. Asher believe it, she would believe it herself. "Monsieur Westwood, he will assist us."

Shamelessly, she would use Monsieur Westwood—and hope she did not lose her temper and stick her knife into his shoulder when he became irritating.

...

Maximilian set the pistol case on one of the short tables at the rear of Manton's Shooting Gallery. It wasn't a set of Manton's pistols, as Maximilian could not afford the high price, but they were a respectable enough pair. If he would be consorting with the Flower in the near future, he had best make sure his weapons were in working order.

A crack rang out as another patron shot at the wafers lined up at the other end of the gallery. The acrid smell of black powder hung permanently in the air of this building, as did the continuous hum of voices as gentlemen came and went, practicing their marksmanship and placing bets on the skill of others.

All quite satisfactory, he thought, opening the solid lid of the pistol case.

"I haven't seen you here or at Gentleman Jackson's of late, Westwood." The smooth baritone voice was familiar and pleasant, and Maximilian grinned as he turned to face the speaker.

"Angelstone." He nodded at Alastair Whitmore, Marquess of Angelstone—a spy, actually, but a decent enough one—and then broadened his grin when he saw Angelstone's companion. "Well, Langford, I haven't seen *you* at either place of late, either."

"The end of the war brought many changes, as has marriage and fatherhood." The Earl of Langford clapped Maximilian on the back, genuine enjoyment gleaming in bright-blue eyes. "We've less need for marksmanship and boxing now that we've retired—well, you and I, at any rate." His voice lowered, though he did not modify his demeanor.

"Are you still active, Angelstone?" Maximilian asked quietly, turning back to the pistol case. His pair was sitting quite comfortably among the velvet, wood gleaming and barrels catching the light. He rather liked the lack of engravings and adornment. Much more practical than some of those elaborate carvings one saw.

"It's different now that I'm married." Angelstone's voice, too, had lowered so the words would not carry. He leaned over Maximilian's pistols casually, as though nothing was being discussed beyond a pair of inferior, non-Manton pistols. "What of you? What are you doing now?"

"Mmm," was the only statement Maximilian's currently empty brain provided. Lying had never come easily to him, and he was certain the Flower would not appreciate him imparting information. "Work."

"That's rather cryptic, though not unusual for you, Westwood." Langford's words competed with a pistol shot from down the row. He stepped to the table beside Maximilian and began reloading his own pistol, pushing the ball deep into the barrel with the ramrod. "Translations, isn't it?"

"Books, letters, messages for various embassies." Maximilian shrugged, concentrating on removing one of his pistols from its velvet nest in the box. It felt as if he'd last held them in his hands yesterday, never mind the months between. "Still the occasional code."

"Ah. We never quite retire, do we?" Angelstone reached for Maximilian's second weapon, the queue at the base of his neck shifting over his shoulders as he drew it out. "There was that code for Prinny's mistress, of course. It's a difficult life you lead," he added, grinning.

"Indeed." Maximilian snorted and began loading his own pistol. "I wasted a perfectly good afternoon devising a code for love notes." He had yet to receive his fee, come to think on it.

"Well, it put you in Prinny's good graces." Langford sighted down the length of his pistol, aiming perfunctorily at the row of wafers at the far end of the room.

"Coding love notes is a far cry from Wellington's missives." Maximilian stepped beside Langford and chose his target, then settled into his stance.

"Oh, how far you have fallen, Westwood." Angelstone replaced Maximilian's second pistol in the case before leaning a hip on the table. He crossed his arms, lips curving beneath tawny eyes.

"Things are different, as you said." The butt of the pistol was warm in Maximilian's palm, so he lifted it and aimed at the first wafer. "What *isn't* different is that I can hit more wafers with my second-rate pistols than you can with your fancy ones. You always were my favorite agents, particularly because I could best you both with a pistol."

With that, Maximilian aimed his pistol and fired, hitting the wafer where he'd intended—precisely in the center.

Langford threw back his head and laughed. "You're right, Westwood. Some things never change."

...

Vivienne stared at Marchand's latest message, lying on the polished tabletop as though it were an innocent visitor in her bedchamber.

The note had been folded inside another paper and

tucked inside a chicken delivered by the butcher's boy. He had not been the regular runner, which Mrs. Asher had not thought about until she'd hacked the bird down the middle with her massive cleaver and discovered the now-split note inside.

At least the inner paper was cleaner than the one it had been tucked inside.

Vivienne set her forefingers on the two pieces of the note, moving them over the tabletop. It was not precisely in halves. One side was larger than the other. The cleaver had not sliced evenly.

Finger tracing the markings, she tried to decipher them. Some were letters, others numbers—and the vulture at the bottom, of course.

Beneath that, an added note.

I am well.
~ A

A single line only, but she knew Anne's handwriting as well as her own. The tail at the end of the second *l*, the points of the *m*. The angled cross mark of the *A*.

Relief and fear rocketed through her—Anne was not dead yet, even after these two days she had been missing. Vivienne had guessed it, because if the Vulture killed the incentive, she would not be motivated to comply. Still, Anne's hand was steady, which meant she could not be seriously injured.

Hope was a pitiless pair of butterfly wings beating inside Vivienne's chest.

She held the two ends of Marchand's message together, joining the letters, but it did not make sense. At least, she did not think so.

Small words she could read with ease. "His," "her," "at,"

"the." Even medium words. "Lord," "street," "paper," "Whig," "house." Even longer words like "London," "king," "France," "prince," "Whitehall," "Parliament." Anne had taught her those words for her work and was even teaching her words such as "ambassador."

The words of Marchand's note, now split in two, those words she did not recognize.

She hunched over the message again, the cream-colored squares of paper more important than their small size would make them seem. Mrs. Asher had assured her the letters did not make sense together. They did not all form words and sentences, she said.

Hopefully, it was coded. She must see Monsieur Westwood with this note to be sure, and it would be embarrassing if the letters *did* form sentences. He might look at her in that manner he had. One brow up, the other angled in a frown, as though he could not decide precisely how to interpret her words.

If Monsieur Westwood could decode the note, it might lead her to Anne.

Brushing the two sections of the note into her hand, she strode from the muted, feminine bedchamber Henri had decorated for her, her cumbersome skirts swishing about her ankles.

She did not have time for hope, only time to gather information.

There was no way to go but forward, which meant asking questions. She would track Anne in the traditional way. Questioning others. Espionage. Trickery, if she must. But not in her own home.

Mrs. Asher stood at the butcher block in the bright, open kitchen, hands on her aproned hips, scowling at the chicken as though it had offended her. Blond hair was knotted atop her head, additional gray strands threading through it each day.

"I'm sorry." Mrs. Asher did not look up from her contemplation of the display in front of her. "I noticed it wasn't the regular boy, Miss Vivienne, but I didn't know it mattered."

Clutching the halves of the note in her fist, Vivienne stepped to the butcher block and looked down. The chicken was still splayed open on the block, though it had been quite brutally dismembered now.

Mrs. Asher's face was red as she glared at the shredded poultry and raised her arm. The cleaver whistled through the air, then sliced into bone and flesh with a terrifying, angry *thwack*!

"You could not have known the delivery came from *him*, Mrs. Asher." She could think of nothing else to say to ease the housekeeper's heart.

"I should have."

It was a natural reaction, thinking if one had been more observant, more careful, one might have changed the course of fate. If only she had secreted Anne away that night, or sensed the spies creeping through the second-floor window a moment earlier. If only she had obeyed a Frenchman and become a traitor. *If only*.

Anger and guilt bubbled up inside her, along with a cold fear. It was not Mrs. Asher who had failed, but Vivienne. Miserably so. "Mrs. Asher, I want you to tell me everything the butcher boy said."

The woman pressed her lips together.

"I want to know what he looked like," Vivienne said. Sunlight shone on the tight sleeve of her rose-colored gown as she set her hand on the woman's shoulder, squeezed. Softly, before letting her hand drop away again, she added, "Tell me what he said, please. What he wore. Nothing is too insignificant."

"He didn't look French, Miss Vivienne, but as English as

I am." The knife blade caught the light as it came down again. Vivienne could no longer identify the parts Mrs. Asher was hacking away at.

"Of course," she soothed. "If he was good at his work, he would look and sound English." No one wanted to think they had failed to see a villain, and Vivienne hoped her words would bring comfort. "It is not so hard, if one trains for a long time."

"Aye. You would know, I suppose." Mrs. Asher sent Vivienne a sly, almost amused look. "Well, I'll tell you, he looked like an ordinary butcher's boy and spoke not a word. I didn't pay him much mind."

"Was he taller than me, or shorter?" Vivienne drew herself up to her full height, which was not much, so the answer would likely be obvious and would make Mrs. Asher feel useful.

"Taller. Definitely taller than you, miss." She looked Vivienne up and down, as though measuring.

"Good. Do you see? You remember well enough."

Mrs. Asher shook her head, a most ferocious frown on her lips. "You are getting thin again. I swear, that theater works you too hard, as does his lordship."

"I am not hungry." Food was not important just now. "The boy's hair? Brown? Blond?"

"Light brown, I think, almost blond. Not dark like yours, at all." Mrs. Asher turned and set her hands to her hips. "I'll set you up with a bite to eat." She strode into the little room that served as their larder and pantry.

"Truly, I am not hungry. Light brown, then, Mrs. Asher?" Vivienne set her elbows on the table and leaned on it. Light brown, taller than her. It was not enough to track him. "What color were his eyes?"

"Eyes?" Mrs. Asher's voice floated out from the open larder door. Crockery rattled, competing with her words, and Vivienne struggled to understand them. "Those I don't remember. His nose, now—*that* I couldn't help but notice. Beaky, it was. A big 'un. He was young, too. Older than Anne, but younger than you, Miss Vivienne."

The housekeeper emerged from the larder with a hank of bread and a ladle that had clearly been misplaced and was now recovered. Still, she had given Vivienne something. Age was approximate, but with the nose, the hair, it was information to work with. Rising up on her toes, she planted a kiss on Mrs. Asher's round red cheek.

"Thank you." She plucked the bread from the housekeeper's hands and took a bite.

"Oh, go on with you." Mrs. Asher threatened to smack her bottom with the ladle, so Vivienne went on, a little bit lighter of heart. "Miss Vivienne?"

"Hmm?" With her hand on the kitchen doorjamb, she turned to face the housekeeper, who had exchanged the ladle for her cleaver again.

"*Get him.*" The words were as violent as the cleaver splitting the chicken's breastbone into two pieces.

"I will." There was no mercy in her voice.

She had none.

Chapter Twelve

Monsieur Westwood was bent over his desk when she slipped into the study. He never seemed to be anywhere else. Did he not rest? It was always work with this one.

Vivienne could only be grateful for it.

She hesitated in the doorway, watching him scratch away with his quill. He worked without gloves, probably to be more efficient and practical. A single candle was set at his elbow, casting its light over an array of documents and multiple inkwells. Quills lay side by side on the desktop, as if marching across the polished surface. Behind him, flames crackled and spit in the hearth, illuminating the shelves lining every wall. Books towered and tumbled about, their leather covers muted in the firelight.

Had he read them all? Most likely. It made her feel stupid.

The monsieur's quill paused in its scratching.

"Hello, Mademoiselle La Fleur."

How did he always know it was she? Even with his face nearly pressed to his papers, he knew. "Hello, Monsieur Westwood."

Turning to look at her, he pulled off his spectacles and her stomach did a funny little flip. The strong jaw and broad shoulders, the muscular thighs beneath nankeen breeches made him seem so male. But the hazel eyes punctuated with bursts of gold, the full lips that ought to kiss rather than frown—it was these that drew her focus.

"Did you receive a message from Marchand, or do you have another body to dispose of?" Oh, that wry tone made her want to smile, though there was little to smile about.

"A message." Boots silent on the thick rug, she crossed to him and offered the two sections of the note.

Wide, strong fingers plucked it from her hand. Delicately, carefully, as though he did not want to touch her skin. But just as he wrote without gloves, she picked locks without gloves, so they *did* touch. A brush of finger on finger. Rough skin, warmth, and then he was bent over the message, spectacles looped once more over his ears.

"It's in two pieces." Brows raised in question, he peered at her over the top of the lenses.

"The housekeeper's cleaver discovered the note."

"Method of conveyance?" Attention shifting to his task, he looked back at the note.

"A chicken."

"That must have been a surprise."

He did not push aside the document he had been working on. It was more an orderly shifting of duties. Paper on top of paper, straightened just so, then the entire stack was moved to the side of his desk and squared against the corner before he bent over the Vulture's note. Powerful hands ran over the lines of text, then settled lightly on Anne's scribbled note. "There is a message. From the girl?"

"Yes. I recognize her handwriting."

"She lives. Good." He pushed his spectacles up the bridge of his nose with a forefinger. "Let us see what Marchand has to say."

"Is it the same code?"

"I cannot tell at first glance."

The vulture signature was the same, but the rest was a jumble of letters to her. She set her hand on his shoulder and leaned over, looking at the two scraps of paper.

Muscle shifted beneath her hand. Staring down at her fingers, at the shoulder beneath it, the note was forgotten. His body was warm and solid, and she felt strength there as well. The faint scent of sandalwood drifted on the air, and Vivienne wondered how strength and sandalwood could cause her pulse to hitch.

She heard his breath then. A little strained.

"Step back, if you would, please," he said curtly, shoulder moving again beneath her hand. He did not look up at her. "You are distracting."

"I beg your pardon?" Taking a step back, then another, she let her hand slip away from his shoulder. She could not help staring at his profile. She was *distracting*?

Something odd fluttered in her belly again. Strange, but not altogether unpleasant. She could not decide if she liked it. It left her feeling unsettled inside and aware of every inch of her skin. She very much feared this fluttering had unleashed something she had not known was inside her.

"The code is identical. They have not modified it." Quill flew over the paper while his eyes narrowed in concentration. Such concentration he had.

She could focus, too, and block that uneasy, slightly delicious feeling inside her to think only of the note. "What does it say?"

"Wait. I am not finished."

The thick rug gave way beneath her boots as she shifted impatiently. He knew the code—he should be faster. Finally, when her patience had spun out almost entirely, he spoke.

"Bond Street, noon on 21 October. I am hoping to find a gift for my mother. Perhaps she would enjoy some jewelry. The gift must be delivered unopened to the Nelson Hotel, Room 12. Marchand's vulture signature completes the message." Monsieur Westwood paused, his frown ferocious. "I must have made a mistake. That message does not make sense. Jewelry? Gifts?"

"No mistake, monsieur," she said softly. A message like this she could understand. "It is a conversation."

"What?" He removed his spectacles and rubbed a hand over his face. Leaning back in his chair, quill dangling from one hand, he looked up at her with bleary hazel eyes.

"Someone on Bond Street will say to me he is looking for a present for his mother. I will say she might like jewelry. He—or she—will give me something to deliver while we speak." Thinking, planning, she began to pace the room. "A letter, most likely, or the business would not be conducted in the open. He wants me to be a simple courier. Nothing difficult. It is a test."

"How is it a test?"

"Because it is a simple task. Accept a letter over here, and take it over there." She shrugged and stepped yet farther from him. "Any of his agents could do it."

"Explain." Frowning, he lifted his spectacles and peered at the lenses, as if looking through them again would help him understand.

"The Vulture wishes to determine if I will do as he commands, now that he has the girl." There was no choice but to do as Marchand demanded, even if Anne was well. "I will do as he asks."

"What of the letter?" He stood now, towering over the desk and her with shoulders that seemed overly broad, though not frightening. They were simply masculine—and she felt foolish for even thinking so. "You don't know what you're delivering."

"True." The war was over, but there were still secrets to be uncovered and sold. "Delivering a message without opening it is part of the test."

"You can't do that."

He set a hand on her arm. Perhaps he meant to stay her, or simply to punctuate his words, but for a moment, all of the world contracted to that single point of contact. The unleashed thing in her noticed only his hand, warm and strong through the sleeve of her coat, before his hand fell away and the world expanded again.

She took a deep breath, a very deep breath. "Monsieur, any letter will be sealed. If I open it and Marchand discovers I have done so, I will have proved myself untrustworthy to him." Once more the world contracted, this time to a single thought. A single fear. "Anne might die."

"What will we do, then? You can't deliver the letter without knowing what the consequence might be." Solemn finality edged the words when he spoke.

"There is a way to open such a letter, but it is difficult and will take time." She shook her head. "What if I *did* open it? It might be a letter about jewelry, or some other innocuous thing. If it is also coded, I would not know what it said, at any rate." Which Marchand would hope for. He would want her to deliver it, not to decipher it.

"Confound it, you're right. It is an impossible situation." He ran both hands through his hair, gripping the mix of cinnamon and russet and gold. She was becoming accustomed to this movement, and it nearly made her smile. "I'm coming with you."

Now there was no desire to smile. "Do not be absurd. You are not a spy."

"No, but I am a code breaker. You'll likely need one to decode the letter. Need *me*."

"Perhaps." Ideas formed and broke apart and formed again. "I need you," she said softly. "Yes. I need you."

His gaze dropped to her lips, stayed there a moment before flicking back up to her eyes. Others had looked at her lips in such a way, like they wanted to nibble and taste. Some tried, despite her protector. Monsieur Westwood had never looked at her just so.

He made her think of kissing.

Vivienne had never *wanted* to kiss someone before. What would it be like? Wishing to feel those lips against hers—it was too much sensation to feel inside a body. Heat. Uncertainty and need pulsing low in her belly. Shock, as this man had never looked at her in such a way before.

"Come with me, the day after tomorrow." The invitation sounded awkward to her ears. She *felt* awkward. Something had changed inside her and between them. "I only need you to be nearby when I receive the letter. To read it, and other things."

He watched her solemnly. They were close, too close, so that she could see the gold spears in the depths of his eyes.

"Other things," he said softly, gaze falling to her mouth once more.

• • •

I need you. She'd whispered it in low, soft tones, watching him cautiously with those dark eyes. Below them were her lips, pink, curved, and calling to him simply by existing.

If there was ever a woman he should leave be, it was the Flower. Not only because she was a spy, but because she had an arrangement with Wycomb. It was not quite the same as lusting after another man's wife, but close enough.

Maximilian dragged his gaze away from her mouth and forced his mind back to the problem—a meeting on Bond

Street, finding the girl, and stopping Marchand.

Maximilian would not let the Flower go alone.

"What, exactly, does 'other things' entail?" he asked.

"I do not know, for certain. I must see the letter first." She shrugged, an expressive movement full of Gallic indifference. A pink flush tinged her cheekbones and made him think of all sorts of other things.

Whatever it meant in the Flower's world, it was bound to be more unpleasant than in his world.

"Also, you must bring the tools to open the note," she continued, stepping away from him. Skimming a hand down her thigh, she smiled suddenly. "I can hide much in my clothing, but not everything."

"What do you usually conceal in your clothing?" *That, you bloody idiot, sounded both debauched and stupid at the same time.* To busy his hands, he scooped up the two halves of the note. He couldn't think what to say to excuse his momentary lapse of intelligence.

"Monsieur Westwood." She cocked her head to the side, a little half smile fluttering about her lips. Not quite the smile she had used to laugh at his cravat — that one had been colored by the role of coquette. This was soft rather than mocking. "Those are my secrets."

The Flower reached out, hand cupped to receive the paper he offered. Black wool shifted over her shoulders and torso, leaving him wondering less about the weapons lurking beneath her clothes than her figure.

Gaze dropping to trace her shape, he speculated for only one moment before his brain properly engaged. Eyes wheeled in his skull as he tried to avert them, refusing to ogle the Flower as men of his brother's ilk did.

It was too late.

Curved hips in breeches, a narrow waist nipped in by the coat — he could not see her breasts, but dear God, in that moment he wanted to. Desperately.

Gripping the back of the chair to steady himself, he tried not to breathe in her clean, simple scent. Everyone used fragrant soap—even *his* soap smelled like sandalwood. Not the Flower. Her lack of perfume was as dangerous as an opiate.

"Day after tomorrow." He tried to wipe the burgeoning image of her breasts from his brain, but the confounded organ defied him. So he did not turn to look at her again, lest he look at some other improper part of her.

"*Merci.*" The word was very quiet. Very thoughtful.

He did not hear her retreating footsteps, but he did hear the door close as she left.

Her damnable scent lingered.

Chapter Thirteen

The sun shone bright, and Vivienne was playing at being a pretty opera dancer, so she surveyed Bond Street with fake delight from her seat on the barouche. A pair of dandies passed on their horses, and she waved, beaming at them—as though she were not on any kind on mission. As though Marchand would not be in some window on this street, watching her every move. It was her test, after all.

Hopefully, Monsieur Westwood would do what he was told.

"Thomas, do set me down. The most lovely milliner's shop is just there." Breath turned to fog in the chilly autumn air as she called to the footman.

"Aye, mademoiselle." Thomas slowed the barouche, and the horses' hooves clip-clopped to a halt on the cobblestones.

"Thank you, Thomas."

Flipping a coin to the young boy who'd run up to hold the horses, Thomas limped around to put down the steps. The walkway was solid and steady beneath her booted feet as she stepped onto it, the breeze as sharp as the sun was bright. She set off at a slow meander, looking at window displays and waving at acquaintances.

Wiggling her fingers inside her fur muff, she checked for the knife she'd hidden earlier. Yes, it was still there, warm from the heat of her hands and the fur. Gripping the hilt, she took comfort in the feel of the weapon in her palm. It was best to be ready. If she were not, it could be seconds before she found the knife. She could die in those seconds and knew it well.

"I am hoping to find a gift for my mother." The stranger's voice was pleasant and not French at all. It was also not far away from her right ear.

She did not look at this stranger, this courier. One did not look unless it was necessary, because then one could be forced to give a description. Instead, Vivienne bent to look at a display window. Pretty snuffboxes were scattered beyond the glass, their ivory lids glowing in the sunlight.

"Perhaps she would enjoy some jewelry." Vivienne inclined her head toward the display, the curls peeking from beneath her bonnet sliding over her shoulder to dance in the wind. "Not from here, however. There is another shop down the street with much better workmanship."

"Ah. Well, these snuffboxes are nice." The man bent over to look through the window, just as she was doing. He, also, did not look at her.

Still, they each sized up their opponent's measure. She could see in her periphery that it was a man with a top hat and dark coat. A cane hung from his forearm, dangling inches above the walkway. It likely held a sword. She assumed he was studying her pale-blue skirts and the muff she carried, thinking similar thoughts about what weapon she might be hiding beneath the white rabbit fur.

The letter was nothing more than a bump against her thigh. Using the fabric of skirt and pelisse to hide the transaction, she accepted it and tucked the letter into her muff beside her knife.

It was over—at least this portion. The man with the cane walked away as though she did not exist. To anyone on the street, he might not even have noticed her, he was so focused on his next destination, which meant Marchand would be focused on her, wherever he was hiding. If he was not watching her himself, someone he trusted would be.

She would have to be careful.

Chapter Fourteen

Ah, the Flower.

She was quick. He had not seen her accept the letter from his agent, though he did not doubt she had done so. Watching her from a window across the street, he should have been able to see the exchange and where she hid the letter.

The Flower was too well trained.

She would be an asset, no matter which side she played on. He'd known it, but until he watched her take the document and hide it without him being any the wiser, he had not quite believed it.

Marchand twisted the heavy gold ring on his right hand. A woman with clever fingers was an asset to a man, and the Flower could be useful in many ways.

"See that you are at the hotel when she arrives," Marchand murmured, gaze still on her form as she continued to wander on the street.

The man beside him slipped quietly away. The agent would be in the appointed room to receive the letter — Marchand himself could not go, of course, as he did not want her to recognize him.

But the little girl, Anne, had never seen him before. Ah, the girl. Delightful, really. So much like the Flower—without the French accent, of course.

Also the perfect incentive.

Chapter Fifteen

"Hold the letter over the flame. *Mon Dieu*, not so close or it will catch fire." Vivienne set her hand over Monsieur Westwood's to guide Marchand's note away from the flame. His hand was warm beneath the glove, and she quickly let go again. "There, just so."

Vivienne glanced down at Monsieur Westwood as he sat at the squat wooden table. He was not looking at the letter or the flame, but up at her with a strange light in his eyes she could not identify.

"What is your perfume?" he asked, brows angling down in irritation.

"I do not wear perfume. Keep your eyes on the letter so we do not burn it."

His gaze snapped back to the paper. Leaning closer, his frown deepened at the corners of his mouth. "The wax is softening already."

"Good." Vermilion wax had become translucent ruby. She would soon be able to pry up the seal, and with care, replace it.

"Does this method usually work?" He gestured with his free hand toward the scrap of paper he held over the flame.

"If the person melting the wax performs correctly."

The paper paused in its path over the flame. "Perhaps you should perform this part of the operation."

"I cannot. I must heat my knife in the other flame." The monsieur's eyes widened when she slipped the weapon from her muff. "If the knife, too, is warm, it will help the seal come away from the paper."

The second candle sat beside the first in the dirty back room of the Goose and Gander Inn. It was not the most pleasant space to be in, but the proprietor never asked questions. He simply rented his secret room to whoever paid him the most.

Vivienne set the knife in the flame, counting the time carefully in her head. The metal could not be red-hot lest it mark the page, yet must easily melt the wax. Pulling it from the flame, she set her finger to the tip of her knife.

"Ouch," she murmured, satisfied with the sharp, lingering sting.

"Are you hurt?" Westwood turned toward her, concern edging his words.

"Let me see the letter."

He grumbled but gave it over to her. "You might answer and tell me if you are hurt."

"I am not hurt." She ignored the sting on her finger. It would cease eventually.

"Be careful." He leaned over to watch her movements, and their shoulders touched, his coat brushing against her pelisse.

"Go away." The seal was warm; she could see the edges were slightly darker. Softer. "You are looming."

"I am not looming."

She could not concentrate with his nearness. He smelled

of sandalwood, of wood smoke. Of man. Concentrating on the heat where their shoulders touched, she let her skin sense it. Feel it. Listening to his breath, she matched her own to it, in and out.

She did not have to feel his body to know how he filled the space beside her. Where his wide shoulders were in relation to hers. How his large, strong hands were splayed on the tabletop. That the handsome jaw could tick as the muscle there clenched.

She sensed him looking at her. Skin prickling, she turned her head to find his eyes were very focused on hers, his breathing uneven though it matched her own. She did not want to think about kissing Monsieur Westwood.

It seemed her thoughts were wayward.

"Mademoiselle." His voice sounded deeper than usual, becoming a rasping whisper that shivered along her skin. "You should proceed."

It was a moment before the words made sense.

The letter. Marchand. Anne.

"Yes." She focused on the paper, the wax, but pretending Monsieur Westwood was not beside her was like pretending not to think.

Vivienne set her warmed knife to the edge of the red seal. So carefully she did not breathe. Beside her, the monsieur held his breath as well. The blade slid beneath the wax, slowly, moving only the breadth of a hair each moment.

The seal released. Candle flames danced as their combined breath shuddered out.

Quickly, she unfolded the letter.

"Is it coded?" she asked, tilting the document toward him. It would take her too long to decipher it.

"No, but it's in French." Angling his head, he studied it with narrowed eyes. He'd forgotten his spectacles. "Very poor penmanship."

"The penmanship I do not care about. What does it say?"

"Very innocuous, actually. Something about a dinner party. They ate roast duck and some sort of pudding with a lemon sauce. The author is going to bring the recipe for the lemon sauce back to France. That is all."

"There is nothing more?" She peered down at the letter. Pudding with a lemon sauce? That was what Marchand wanted her to deliver? It did not make sense. "Who wrote the letter?"

"Georges St. Yves."

"I do not know him." Not at first hearing of his name, but she did not have time to search her memory. "I must complete the assignment. Soon. Can you quickly copy the letter? I must warm my knife again."

Using the paper, ink, and quill she'd instructed him to bring, he quickly copied the letter. She watched his great hands move across the page, dip the quill delicately into the ink, then move again in his bold, flowing scrawl.

He was still too close. Too large and male. Vivienne could not focus on the words spreading across the paper.

"There. It's done." He shoved the letter aside to dry—they had not thought to pack blotting paper—and gave her the original.

She set her teeth, steadied her fingers, and touched the warm knife edge to the wax. Just enough to soften it. Then, quickly, because if she spared a thought to being careful it would cool, she pressed the softened seal to the paper.

"It is done." Was it perfect? Was it set exactly right, so that Marchand would not know? Yes, it was good. "I must go. If I linger too long, they will suspect."

But it was not Marchand that worried her—it was Monsieur Westwood. He was picking up her ribboned reticule, handing her the furred muff, as though she were any lady of the *ton*. It was most disconcerting.

"We must decide the intent behind the letter," he said. "It cannot be simply about a recipe for pudding."

"No. It is not." Pudding was not worthy of cultivating a double agent.

"I don't think we should deliver it until we know." His voice was that of a man preparing to be difficult. She hoped he would not be unpleasant, though she was feeling the need to be unpleasant to counter this thought of kissing him.

"I must deliver it. If I do not, Anne will be at risk. We can discuss it later. I must go."

Vivienne could feel his eyes on her as she walked out of the room, but she did not look back. Nor did she take the copy of the letter. If she were searched by whomever she was meeting, she could have nothing beyond the expected.

She must trust Monsieur Westwood would not turn the letter in to the government.

She was trusting him with Anne's life.

Chapter Sixteen

The door to Room 12 of the Nelson Hotel seemed solid. It was made of light-colored wood, nearly gold in hue. Vivienne might have thought it pretty if she were not concerned with the letter tucked inside her muff. It was a very small letter, folded as it was. Yet in that moment, it seemed enormous.

She knocked, a quick rap on the pretty gold door, then waited. Twenty seconds. Thirty. There was no answer. So. She would knock again. When she had, Vivienne tucked her other hand into the muff and gripped her knife.

She did not like delivery instructions that did not include people to receive the delivery.

Was it a trap? The hair on the nape of her neck rose. Perhaps she was not alone in the hall. She sent a glance to the right. The left. Nothing but empty corridor punctuated by golden wood doors. Curtained windows guarded either end. There was ample room to hide in those heavy, elaborate curtains.

The faintest scratch met her ears. She whipped her gaze back to the door of Room 12. It opened wide, the yawning entrance to the unknown.

"I have a gift of jewelry for your mother," she said to the man in the doorway. Marchand had not conveyed any password, so this must do. Very poor planning on Marchand's part.

The man did not look French—but as with the butcher's boy and the man on Bond Street, he would not look French. If he was in England, he would appear English.

Nor was he the butcher's boy who had delivered the last note. The hair, perhaps, could match, but this man was decades older than Vivienne, with a nose not remotely beaky. He was tall, thin, and wearing the dark coat, light trousers, and high starched cravat of any fashionable man.

The movement of his body told her what he truly was. A man could not hide entitlement. This was no thief from the docks or the rookeries. A spy, most likely, but he was also very much an aristocrat.

"*Merci.*" His voice was low, with a hint of gravel to correspond with his age. He held out his hand for the letter.

She did not give it to him. Could not. Nerves dampened her palms, though she wore gloves so the letter was dry and would not reveal her fear.

"The girl." It was a risk to ask. "She is well?" Holding her breath, she waited for the answer.

"Alive." The man's cool eyes watched her, cataloging every feature even as she cataloged his brow, his cheekbones, the shape of the nose, even the amount of stubble and the pattern in which it grew.

"Good."

The letter was plucked from her fingers the moment she held it out, then the door closed with a sharp snap.

What now? Pressing an ear against the door, she listened for movements on the opposite side. Silence. Not a whisper or the patter of footsteps. He was quiet, this man of Marchand's.

Still, he would have to leave. For food, if not to deliver the letter or relay its contents.

Or act on them.

It occurred to her that he might be standing on the other side of the door, waiting to hear her walk away before leaving himself.

She made enough noise that he would hear, but not so much she did not sound like a spy. A rustle of clothing, but not footsteps. A loud intake of breath, but no words. She began to walk.

Her gaze focused on the curtains at the end of the hall. They were deep crimson and heavy. Brocade, perhaps? It did not matter. They were wide, heavy, and draped in large folds.

She was a very small person.

It was but a moment to ensure she was alone. Sliding behind the curtain, she shook it to cover her feet. It was hot behind the thick fabric. She could not see, nor barely breathe, but she stayed there. Listening.

A door opened. She twitched the curtain aside—a half second only, to see the hallway. A man and woman walked comfortably arm in arm, as if they had done so a hundred times before. They had not passed Room 12 yet and could not have come from there. Eventually they passed the room and moved into the stairwell, leaving her alone again in the hall.

It was stifling standing behind this woven fabric, but she was not ready to leave yet. Marchand's man—or enemy, it could be either—was still here. The heat rose minute by minute until sweat gathered between her breasts, at her temples. The pelisse and muff became unbearable weights.

Perhaps this was not her best idea.

Another door opened. Another twitch of the curtain.

Room 12. The man was leaving Room 12.

She let the curtain fall closed. Her heartbeat accelerated, in that way it did when she was on the hunt. Only now it was not a mission, but a driving force. This man might lead her to Anne.

She gathered herself, her energy, before peeking out again. The man was walking away in long, confident strides. He did not look back as he turned into the doorway to the stairwell.

Darting from behind the curtain, Vivienne followed him. Swift feet, blood pounding in her ears. Frustration blossomed when she realized she was not as silent as usual in her slippers and gown. Pantaloons and boots would be better—she rustled with every step.

It was not difficult to slip down the stairs to the ground floor. The hotel lobby spread before her, not busy, but not empty. She kept her gaze on the toes of her walking half boots, like so, and crossed the room. If she stopped she would lose much ground between the spy and herself.

The man exited the hotel. The door started to swing closed, but she saw him turn left. Picking up her pace, she moved quickly through the lobby. The door was just there—

"Mademoiselle La Fleur?" It was a strange man's voice, a young man's voice. A guest at the hotel, perhaps one who recognized her from the stage.

She did not stop for the man. She did not even look. Instead, she slipped through the door and onto the street, pretending she had not heard. Bright sunlight blinded her. Blinking, she looked frantically to the left. The street and walkway were not crowded, but so many men wore the same blue coat and light trousers of a fashionable gentleman. It was not easy to pick out one from the others. Yet he must be here, somewhere.

She walked carefully, searching for him and refusing to panic. Letting panic take hold might cost her in clear thinking. Carriages moved along the street, as did men and women and street hawkers and boys sweeping the cobblestones and—

There. Getting into a hackney was a man with the right height, the right clothing, the right hair.

She dashed forward, uncaring now what picture she might make, so she could hear his direction.

"To Manchester Square, please," he told the driver.

Then Marchand's man was inside the carriage. Whinnies filled the air as the driver encouraged the horses. Hooves began their rhythmic sound.

Raising her muff, she attempted to call a hack. She must follow, as quickly as possible.

A hand on her arm stayed any potential conveyance.

"Mademoiselle La Fleur!" The man from inside the hotel was young, handsome, and every bit a dandy. "I thought that was you in the lobby. I saw you on stage…"

Vivienne did not hear the dandy's next words. Did not care what they were or who he was.

She was trapped on the street, unable to follow her quarry.

Chapter Seventeen

Maximilian was ready for her.

He squinted into the darkening evening beyond the window. The Flower wouldn't be able to sneak into his study and surprise him this night. He *knew* she was coming to discuss the letter, so whatever mysterious method she entered by would not go unnoticed.

"I shall be on the alert, sir." Daggett straightened a stack of papers on Maximilian's desk with efficient precision, positioning them parallel to the edge. "She will not be able to evade us both."

"I should be working." Maximilian looked down at the paper clutched in his hand, lines of his own handwriting scrawling across the page. Frowning, he set the copied letter regarding pudding and lemon sauce in the cleared center of his desk. "This spy business doesn't pay the clothier's bills."

"Sir, you have been working all afternoon and evening, and have not spent any time on pleasurable pursuits in weeks. I do not recall the last time you attended Gentleman Jackson's for a bout to clear your head." Daggett pulled a wing-back chair near the fire and brushed a hand over the upholstery. "You should rest."

"Rest?" Maximilian eyed the offered chair and wondered when he had last sat in it. He usually sat at the single chair before his desk.

"Yes, sir. Before the Flower arrives. You shall be working well into the night, I daresay."

Daggett did have a point. She would be here soon, with her dark hair hidden beneath a cap and the scent that wasn't perfume. Once she was, he would be distracted for the rest of the night.

"Yes, I shall rest," he said.

"Very good, sir." Daggett beamed. "I shall keep watch for the Flower. Enjoy yourself." He marched from the room and closed the door with a soft but firm *snap*.

Maximilian stood for a moment, looking blankly about the study. What did a man do for leisure? Sitting in a chair by the fire didn't seem to be enough. His eyes lit on the brandy decanter, the liquor glowing through the crystal. Aha. That seemed just the thing. He poured two fingers, then added another splash for good measure. He was trying to rest, after all. He replaced the decanter and began to wander, unsure what else to do.

He looked at his desk. The copied French letter lay there. He could read it again. Perhaps he'd missed something earlier—but no, he had read it a dozen times already. Well, then, what to do? He spun in a circle. Perhaps he *should* sit in front of the fire. Daggett had gone to the trouble of moving the chair. Decision made, he strode to the chair and settled in, the soft chair wings enfolding him. Quite comfortable, despite the strange large flowers carved into the wooden legs. He set his feet on the accompanying ottoman. That was quite comfortable, too.

He stared at the snapping fire, sipping brandy and

listening for the Flower.

She had looked stunning that afternoon, her loveliness a sharp contrast to the filth of the Goose and Gander. In fact, she'd looked like any debutante recently shopping on Bond Street. Hands tucked into an elaborate fur muff, her pelisse a shade of blue that matched the autumn sky. Young and frivolous. Yet her eyes were wise when she'd looked at him in the inn. Her lips had been very red, and the stunning face that had captured the imagination and lust of a city of dandies had been close to his.

By all that was holy, he'd wanted to kiss her. What would she taste like? Fresh and sweet? Or would she taste of temptation? Both. She would taste of both. She would feel the same, if he were ever to touch her. Her skin would be smooth, and perhaps flushed and rosy and warm.

"Monsieur Westwood, have you—"

"Damnation!" He nearly jumped out of his skin. As it was, the brandy sloshed over the rim of the glass. He leaped up and turned to face her, brushing at the stains on his waistcoat.

Her eyes were bright with laughter, and rosy lips parted in a light grin.

"Mademoiselle." How had she entered without him hearing her *again*?

"Monsieur." She gestured toward the chair, then the glass. "Please excuse me. I have interrupted your brandy."

"No." She hadn't interrupted his brandy, she'd interrupted him coming perilously close to imagining her naked. "I was—" Dash it, his mind went blank. He gulped what was left of the liquor for lack of anything else to do and gasped as it caught at the back of this throat.

"The letter, monsieur?" A slim black brow rose even as her mouth curved fully upward.

"It's over there." Using the brandy snifter, he gestured toward the desk. She turned around to look, presenting him with her back—and a round bottom in breeches. He swallowed hard. "I couldn't determine that any part of the letter was coded."

She strode to the desk with her smooth dancer's gait. Black fabric moved over her buttocks with each step, then— God's eyebrows, *she bent over the desk.*

He needed more brandy. To numb his anatomy. He couldn't think what else to do. He moved across the room and quickly poured more of the caramel-colored liquid into his glass, then tossed it back. It didn't seem to help. He stared through the thick base of the snifter to the rug below, its design distorted by the crystal. He was little better than his brother, it seemed, lusting after the Flower.

"I do not understand." She sounded perturbed, and when she turned her head to look at him, there was a line between her brows. "There is no code?"

"I don't believe so. The letter appears to be exactly what it is." He could be wrong, he supposed, but he rarely was when it came to codes. "I have been working on it since I returned from the inn."

"But not just now when you were resting, correct?" Her voice was dry and a little mocking, dousing any remaining ardor he might have felt.

"It was a short rest." He walked to her side, scowling down at delicate features framed by the widow's peak. He tapped his finger against the document on the desktop. "If the letter included a code, I would have seen it by now. I might not have deciphered it, but I would have at least recognized it was there."

"If there is no code, then it may have a hidden meaning." She looked back to the document. "And so we must decipher it."

"Then we had better get to work." He seated himself at the desk again and looped his spectacles over his ears. The simple gesture steadied him.

"The clues will be in the words he uses," the Flower said, her eyes focused on the paper. She stepped close to the desk. Closer to him. "They will have other meanings."

"*If* there is a hidden meaning. You said yourself this is a test. It might mean nothing."

"Yes, a test of my abilities and willingness to follow his orders. That does not mean the message does not have some meaning. If I had chosen not to deliver it, he would know and simply have someone else deliver it."

Confound it. She was right. *Again.*

He set his fingers on the paper and ran them down the lines of text. He played the words in this head, backward and forward. What could it mean?

"Monsieur." The Flower's whisper was nearly as quiet as his fingers skimming over the paper. "What, exactly, does it say? Will you read it for me again?"

"Hmm?" He looked up, fingers stilling on the smooth plane of the page.

"I cannot—" She would not look at him. Face averted, her eyes were not on the letter but somewhere else. "I cannot read it."

"But it's in French." His brain felt as though it were a cart with a horse that had slipped its leads and was now stuck in the middle of the road. In mud.

She shook her head, still not looking at him, though a slow-moving flush colored her cheeks. "I cannot read well. Only the small words."

"You cannot read?" Now the cart had been upended and all its contents spilled. He knew of people who could not read, but not ladies. Or at least, not those who acted like ladies and were mistresses of lords. And she was a *spy*. "How are you unable to read?"

"I know some words." She looked at him now, sharply.

Pink lips were pinched, dark eyes narrowed beneath the brim of her cap. "I am not an idiot. I simply do not know the long words."

Maximilian held his hands up in truce, lest she bite them off. "My apologies."

Shame settled in her eyes, and her face softened. "Please. *S'il vous plaît.* Read it." An entreaty for understanding, for closing the subject, lay beneath in her words. She waited, watching him with dark eyes that could skewer a man's soul if he wasn't careful.

He couldn't inquire further. It would make him a clod. Clearing his throat, Maximilian spoke the English words.

Dear Sir:

Today, we went to dinner before the theater. Our host served roast duck, but it was undercooked. However, there was a pudding with lemon sauce that was well received. I have obtained the recipe for the sauce and will return to France with it.

Yours sincerely, etc.

George St. Yves

"This does not have meaning to me." She cocked her head, as though still listening to the words. "*Maintenant, en français, s'il vous plaît.*"

He didn't hesitate. Doing so would make him that clod and a heel as well.

Mon cher Monsieur:

Aujourd'hui, nous sommes allés dîner avant d'assister au

théâtre. Notre hôte a servi du canard rôti, mais il n'était pas assez cuit. Cependant, il y avait un pudding avec une sauce au citron qui a été bien reçue. J'ai obtenu la recette de la sauce et la ramènera en France.

Veuillez agréer l'expression, etc.

Georges St. Yves

"We must think on this." The Flower began to pace the room. It was not an idle pacing, nor purposeful. More lyrical. Which was the most ridiculous thing he'd thought in ages. A person couldn't pace *lyrically*.

His brain must be addled by the brandy. Or mademoiselle's breeches.

Maximilian dropped his spectacles onto the desk's surface and deliberately turned in his chair so that he wouldn't look at her bottom. Instead, he stared up at the nearest shelf of volumes, where leather covers containing poetry and mathematics sat side by side.

"The letter must mean something to someone, or Marchand wouldn't have wanted to deliver it," he said, mulling over the words of the note. "We should try to think like a spy."

"That is simple." She didn't laugh outright, but he could hear the amusement in her voice. "I *am* a spy, monsieur."

Of course she was. Devil take it, he needed to focus. Perching his spectacles on his nose, he slid a fresh sheet of paper in front of him and took up his quill.

There. Now he felt much more at ease.

"I'll write down some possible meanings. We'll reason this out." Holding the quill in the air, he sent his gaze in the Flower's direction, certain to keep his eyes on her face and not her pantaloons. "First, dinner and the theater. What does that bring to mind?"

"Hmm. I would think of the King's Theatre. It probably does not mean the theater itself—only the king. Thinking as a spy, you see." Her gaze slid sideways at him, sparkling with humor as it had when she'd fixed his cravat.

"A reasonable conclusion, mademoiselle." She was clearly laughing at him. He ignored it and continued to scribble on the paper. "So good old Georges St. Yves met with the king—"

"Or the king's representative," she added.

"—but he went somewhere else first—"

"Where something was not well received."

"—and the duck was undercooked." He frowned at her, confused. "What do you mean, something was not well received?"

"Undercooked. Whatever the duck symbolizes, it was not acceptable. Not finished." She stepped to the fire, crouched, holding out her hands to the flame. She turned them over, as though they, too, needed cooking. "It could be anything. A proposal, an agreement, a negotiation that is incomplete. Perhaps even a person who was not well received."

These ideas were speculative, without any basis in fact. This was no substitution code or cipher with a logical sequence. What if they were wrong?

Except she had delivered the letter, and there was no going back. He sank his head into his hands, gripped his hair. This is what came of consorting with dancers and spies. He should have stayed with his books and letters.

"*J'ai obtenu la recette de la sauce.* I have obtained the recipe for the sauce," she said softly. He shifted his head in his hands to look at her. She was kneeling on the thick rug before the fire now, staring into it. He could all but see her mind sorting ideas, discarding, considering. "A document, do you think, monsieur?"

"It's a recipe for pudding with lemon sauce." Maximilian

did not take his head out of his hands. "*Un pudding avec une sauce au citron.* It's a sauce. Not plans for espionage."

She did not answer, so he dropped his hands, dangling them between his knees, and watched the Flower. Her legs were folded beneath her, torso straight and shoulders erect in that dancer's way she had. The firelight gilded her face so that she was more beautiful than usual, all gold and rosy. Slowly, thoughtfully, she lifted one hand and removed her cap. Thick black hair tumbled down over narrow shoulders clad in a man's coat.

All the working parts of his brain simply stopped. When her free hand began to idly run through the curls, he realized he was holding his breath.

"Citron."

He jumped when she spoke, then pulled in a deep inhale. "What?"

"Citron." She rose in one fluid movement, from crouched to standing, like a waterfall moving backward. Her eyes lit with discovery as she twirled to face him, cap forgotten on the patterned hearth rug. Bouncing up onto her toes and buoyed by excitement, curls bouncing with her, she grinned at him. "I understand the message. It is about Jean-Phillippe Citron. A French soldier in the war. Well, a spy, it is suspected, and an English prisoner. I do not know in what prison he was kept, but he was there for a few months. I believe he has not yet been released."

Maximilian straightened and looked down at the words marching across the paper. "How did you reason that out?"

"Citron, of course. It is written in French, not English." As though it were obvious. "There is also the idea that the author will be returning to France with the recipe for the lemon sauce. He will be returning with Citron, or a plan to free Citron. It might be an exchange, even. The duck for the sauce, but the king, he does not want the duck. So they must find another duck."

He was confused. And, clearly, she was unhinged.

"What of the rest of it?"

"Do you not see? *Aujourd'hui, nous sommes allés dîner avant d'assister au théâtre.* Dinner before the King's Theatre. What does one do at dinner? One speaks to one's companions. They tried to 'have dinner' or 'speak' or 'conference' before they met with the king's representative." Bright with knowledge, glowing with excitement, she was as alluring as a candle flame.

"All right," he said slowly, unsure if he should agree with her or not. "What of the rest?"

"The meeting was not good, and the duck was undercooked. The intended subject did not come about. *Mais attendez.*"

"But wait. *Mais attendez.*" Suddenly he was caught up in the quick inhalation of her breath and the flush of her cheeks. His own breath became uneven, his pulse quick. "What are you thinking?"

"Citron is Marchand's man, and the Vulture wants him returned. A deal must have been brokered." She paced the circumference of the room like a trapped mare. Or a dancer constrained to a space smaller than a stage. "If a deal was negotiated by the king, we cannot interfere."

Dark curls settled around her face as she returned to his side. Lips curving in a triumphant smile, she sat on the edge of the desktop so that she faced his chair, legs extending out to cross at the ankles. But her *breeches*. He gripped the carved edge of the desk, unsure what else to do with his hands. Her clothing had never affected him this way before.

"I don't think ladies should wear breeches. They are too tight on your legs." As soon as he said the words, he wished he could pluck them back out of the air. Most inappropriate. A gentleman never remarked on a lady's body. At the very least, he should have said *limbs* instead of *legs*.

"I agree." She was laughing at him again, her smile broadening with good humor. "Though I am not a lady, as you may have noticed, monsieur. I'm an opera dancer with a protector."

"Of course you're a lady. Your gender, I mean. Not you. Ah. That is to say—"

A laugh tumbled from her lips to bound through the room and lodge somewhere in his middle. "I do not pretend to be anything more than I am."

Pausing, listening to the meaning behind her words, he held her gaze. "I know you are a man's mistress, Flower, but never forget you are more than that."

"Are you sure?" Deep words to match her unfathomable eyes.

"You are a lady of many layers, and every one of them is lovely." Maximilian meant every word and more than he said.

"If I were a lady, I would not be a spy, would I?" Her lips were still bowed up as she straightened, but he saw the dark pain in her gaze. "You are sweet, monsieur, to call me a lady."

She leaned down to look at the document, then turned her head to face him. Her mouth was there. Just there. Lips parted as though she planned to ask a question, though she didn't. She only looked at him, eyes slowly becoming serious and powerful. They were a beautiful shade, dark brown deepening to black in the center. Her lashes swept down to cover those eyes as her gaze fell to his mouth for a moment before flicking back up.

Suddenly he could not think beyond her lips. Beyond her face and the fresh scent enveloping him.

He leaned forward, desperate for a taste, afraid she would bolt, afraid she would not.

And kissed her.

Chapter Eighteen

His lips were warm and firm, pressing gently against hers. A small, yearning place inside her unlocked and opened. She could not stop that place from growing inside her, filling cracks she had not understood existed. Her eyes fluttered closed, lips parting with the slightest movement to accept him.

Fingers slid along her jaw, a thumb feathered across her cheekbone. A part of her, the one fueled by fear, shouted at her to run. The yearning part told her to stay one more moment. If she reached for him tomorrow, he would not be there. Could not be. This moment would be the only one she could have.

Touching his shoulder, lightly, tentatively, her mind learned the feel of his lips against hers, the scent of him, so that she could remember how he felt beneath her fingertips. He angled his mouth over hers, causing her belly to flutter and her body to revel in his touch. She had been right. A man with lips such as his could be a great lover. He could taste her and take her, and yet give of himself so that she did not feel conquered.

Herself. It was all he asked of her. His kiss told her this.

It could not be.

The hitch of her breath rasped loudly in her own ears. She pulled away, heart thudding in her chest. Please, do not let him hear her galloping heart.

He stared at her, the gold bursts in his eyes bright among the green and brown flecks. His breath, too, was harsh, louder even than the crackle of flames in the fireplace. She pressed her fingers to her lips, against the need to kiss him again, and shook her head. She should not have allowed it. Such kisses were not possible in her life.

"My apologies. That was inexcusable." Clearing his throat, he stood up, long limbs decisive and efficient in their movements. "I should not have mauled you."

"I have been mauled before. This was not a mauling." Such things had happened, but this was so much more. She could not hold this sweet feeling inside herself. "I must go, monsieur."

Vivienne started to back away. He reached for her, hands nearly brushing her coat, but she did not stop moving away from him. Could not.

"The letter. Citron." Scooping up her cap meant she could look away from the squared jaw and the lips that could cause such feeling in her. Gathering her hair, she shoved it under her cap with movements that matched the frantic rush of her blood. "I will discover what is happening."

"Lemon sauce. Yes. Good."

"*Au revoir.*" She was at the door now, groping for the handle. It was difficult to grasp with fingers numb with shock.

"Good-bye."

The door opened, and she stepped through. She let herself have a final look at the monsieur, standing tall and straight in a room filled with books and learning. A final memory for tomorrow.

She closed the door quietly and quickly, so that she would not step into that room again.

Heart still thudding uncomfortably in her chest, Vivienne jogged away from Monsieur Westwood's town house and hoped the dark would swallow her. She could not seem to think. Her brain had become like porridge.

He had *kissed* her. Truly kissed her.

Not in the fast, covert way some men did in quiet ballroom corners as they tried to hide it from Henri, or the bruising ways of others when they wanted her to leave him. Those she did not like. Such men saw not her, but another man's mistress who might be persuaded to be purchased from him.

Monsieur Westwood saw her.

Her body had yielded, and something had blossomed in her belly when he'd kissed her. The shock of that remained, just as the feel of his lips on hers lingered.

Running her fingers over her lips, she waited for the feel of her own touch to overpower the memory of Monsieur Westwood's mouth. When they focused the sensation instead, she pushed the thought of him away. There was no time for a code breaker and the breathless moment when he had kissed her.

Tomorrow, there could be nothing between them.

Tonight, she had somewhere to be before her performance at the theater began.

No one bothered her on the way to the town house she had trained in. She used the night to her advantage, merging with shadows as she walked. The dark could be a friend, hiding all manner of details. All manner of emotions.

The door was locked, and she did not feel like knocking. This had been her refuge for too many years. Drawing out her picklocks, she worked quickly and quietly. The spy Angel would not mind. She had free rein in his house as she had years ago. Once, these rooms had been Angel's bachelor quarters and were used to train spies during the war. To train her, when Henri had decreed she needed sparring partners.

The tumbler clicked. A press on the latch, and the door opened. Slipping through the crack between door and jamb, she shut it as quietly as her body allowed and turned around to face the hall.

And found herself confronting a pistol.

The hammer cocking was a death knell in the dark. She froze, shoulder blades pressed against the solid door, and waited for the blast to tear through her.

Nothing came.

"Vivienne. Welcome. Please knock next time so I don't shoot you." Quiet and steady words belonging to Jones, the broad-shouldered, solemn man she had trained with as a girl, rather than his commander, Angel.

She let out her breath, eyeing the small, narrow hole of the pistol. "Is Angel here?" she asked slowly, taking care not to move.

"He and his wife are at their regular home." After a long pause, Jones's arm fell, taking the pistol with it. He was in his shirtsleeves, and the simple cotton fluttered with the movement. Gaze contemplative, he watched her steadily. "You may come in."

A sigh slipped from her lips, and she relaxed the shoulder blades pressed against the door. Jones stepped away to give her access to the hall.

This place was not home, but it was the closest she could think of. Home was certainly not the town house Henri kept for her, where she pretended to be his mistress. Nor the theater, where she pretended to be a dancer. Sometimes it seemed this town house was the only place she could breathe.

Here, at least, were those she could call friend.

Jones led her through the hallways, footsteps as silent as her own. Shadows were deep, as no wall sconces were lit, nor any fires blazing in the rooms they passed. Only Jones, and occasionally Angel, lived here now.

The training room was also empty, but it was brightly lit and warm, fires burning in the grates at both ends of the long room.

"I was preparing for an assignment." Jones stepped aside to let her into the room, inscrutable eyes watching every movement as she entered the space and looked around. Fencing jackets were stacked in the corner. Mounted on the nearest wall were pistols, foils, and knives, though three mounts were unoccupied. Corresponding knives of various lengths and thicknesses were laid out on a table, blades ruddy in the candlelight.

She had not learned to kill a man in this room—Henri had taught her that in the room he used for such things—but she had perfected it in this room alongside Jones. Tears, sweat, even blood had spilled on these floors.

"Is your assignment spying on the spies today?" she asked. It was often his mission to ensure British agents did not go astray and investigating them when they did.

"Not today." Jones slid the pistol into the waist of his breeches. He stepped toward the table where the knives lay blade to hilt in a row. "Why are you here, Vivienne?"

"I have need of information."

Jones did not raise a brow or even flick an eyelash as he inspected the weapons. "I cannot reveal the details of internal investigations, Vivienne. Do not ask."

She shook her head, knowing he would never do so. "It is not one of your investigations."

He relaxed, the planes of his face smoothing out so he resembled the boy she remembered. "Is this a trade, then? Or a favor?"

"A favor that may become a trade if I learn anything useful."

"Ah." He touched a knife blade, as if to determine its solidity.

Leaving him to the inspection of the weapons, she moved toward the pile of fencing jackets and ran a finger over the stitching on the topmost jacket. There was a time she'd lived in such a jacket, day in and day out. "Citron. Jean-Phillippe Citron. Do you know of him?"

"Yes." A very long pause filled the air as he looked away from the knives to meet her gaze. "What information do you need?" Jones cocked his head but did not otherwise move.

She hesitated, wanting to ask of Citron, but also of Manchester Square and any interesting persons who might reside there. Yet she could not risk Jones inquiring into her conduct, nor Henri discovering Anne.

So she would remain silent about Manchester Square.

"Is Citron part of a strategy?"

Another very long pause. There was no inkling as to what Jones thought of Citron or strategies or anything else. His shoulders shifted beneath his coat. "Yes."

Ah. He would not provide details, and she should not disturb the strategy.

"Why do you ask, Vivienne?"

She must tread carefully now. There was much history between her and Jones, much friendship—yet he was not only a spy, but the check and balance of British agents. "Only a name I heard and wondered if it should be pursued. It seems not."

He nodded, sending his gaze once more to the weapons displayed before him. "Is that all?"

"Yes." Though her primary question had been answered, she discovered she was not ready to leave yet. There was more she wanted to know, and no one else to ask but another who had lived this life nearly from childhood.

"Do you ever want out, Jones? Do you ever think of a little cottage with children and a wife?" He would think her weak for asking. Fingers gripped the fencing jacket, knuckles whitening. Deliberately, she straightened them and set the jacket down before turning to face Jones fully.

The planes of his face were even and inexpressive, brown eyes pensive. He picked up a knife, tested the weight. She sensed he was biding his time choosing an answer and a weapon, waiting until she had finished her questions.

"No," he finally said, and took a very long breath. "I would be nothing without espionage, Vivienne. Nothing."

She understood—it was life in the rookeries. They could have lived and died there, and been nothing. "If you had the choice now of something more, would you take it?"

He spoke slowly, as if weighing very heavy words, and watched her with curious eyes. "There is no room for that in my life. In *our* lives. We are spies, both of us, with disguises that run deep. We owe our existence to our commanders and the training provided to us. Turning away from this duty to our country—no. Love and a family cannot be."

"No, they cannot." She should not mourn the loss. Her path was set, and it was a good path. Wishing for everything, or even for something, was useless. "I will stay away from Citron."

"Good." Jones nodded once, picked up his chosen weapon and offered her a light smile. "Now, get out of here. I have a mission to complete before midnight."

Chapter Nineteen

"You are distracted, my dear." Henri bowed over her hand, kissed it, the few gray strands at his temples glinting sliver. When he stood again, his mouth was tight, lips pressed thin. "Your timing in the last song was off."

She had known he would remark upon it, but she could not keep her mind from her visit to Manchester Square. Her clothing for the night's work was bundled and hidden beneath the carriage seat, waiting only for the opera to be complete.

In keeping with her role, Vivienne set her goal aside and smiled at Henri as she adjusted her costume. A soft lover's smile. Many eyes and ears were backstage at the theater. "I was thinking only of you, Henri, as I saw you in your box."

Henri returned her smile, and to others it might seem as lover-like as her own. Still, she saw the tight smile, the narrowing of his eyes. He was angry, as he always was when she did not perform correctly. Fear flared in her belly.

"A compliment, to be sure, Vivienne, but you must be perfection itself if you are to keep your position." His gaze held hers a moment, sharp and blue. "Now, I have brought you a gift."

Hand gripping her elbow, he drew her out of the bustle of costumers and singers swarming around. Intermission was busy as scenes changed and bucks came backstage to ogle dancers and find a potential mistress, the colors and stripes of their clothing as bright as any peacock. Somewhere nearby a soprano practiced a trill, while a boy shouted about costumes for the next act.

When Henri had guided her toward the side of the room, he pulled a velvet bag from the pocket of his evening coat.

"Oh, what is it?" Clasping her hands together beneath her chin, she flashed a wide, anticipatory smile and felt like a foolish child.

"A special treat. Look." A long chain of gold slipped from the inverted bag, loop after loop, to coil in the palm of his hand. The diamonds set into the chain sparkled and caught the candlelight.

"Oh, Henri. It is lovely!" she cried. It was her own, an item she had used many times, for many missions. "You are too good me."

They were in public, or nearly so, and certain proprieties must be maintained. Yet they were still in the world of men and their mistresses. The *demi-monde*. So she set her hands on his shoulders and pressed a light kiss to his mouth. His taste made her want to wrinkle her nose. Tobacco and port. Not sour or disgusting, in the way some men tasted, but not pleasant, either.

She felt his arousal at even that light touch.

"Here, take the bag and I'll put the necklace on you."

Ah, the bag. *That* was the assignment.

"The diamonds will look stunning on stage with your costume." His hand slipped over her shoulder, sliding against her skin just as a snake would slip over rock and stone.

Repressing the shudder crawling inside her, she tucked

the velvet into her palm while he stepped behind her and laid the string of gold and diamonds against her throat. It was long and would hang nearly to her navel, she knew, so he looped it around a second time. Now it hung perfectly in the V of her bodice. When he had clasped it, he pressed a kiss to the place where her neck met her shoulder, lingering there even as his fingers skimmed down the length of chain and across the swell of her breasts. His hot breath hitched against her skin. It would look like a lover's caress, but the fingers of his other hand were hard on her upper arm. She felt the tension in his body as he controlled her position by holding her in place.

From across the room, she heard her name. A moment later, "Lord Wycomb is a lucky bastard to have her warming his bed." The words floated to her ears over the click of many feet and the strains of musicians beginning to warm up for the second half. She saw a young lordling eye her through a quizzing glass, a grin on his lips. "Don't you think, Highchester?"

His tall, blond companion nodded. Highchester, the lordling had called him. Monsieur Westwood's brother was Baron Highchester. She could see a resemblance about the mouth and jawline, as well as the shoulders.

Highchester smiled at her, but it was filled with cunning avarice. "Aye, a lucky bastard," he said brashly, watching Vivienne with a steady gaze as dancers passed between them. "Any man would want his cock in that flower."

The baron was not as good-natured as his companion. Nor as gentlemanly as Westwood.

"Pay them no mind," Henri whispered into her ear. "The mission must be conducted tonight."

Giggling, she pretended he'd imparted a lover's secret. "Tonight, then, Henri, I will do exactly as you wish." She said it loud enough the other men would hear.

The man with the quizzing glass groaned enviously, a

sound that nearly made her laugh. He was silly, that lordling. The other, Highchester, met her gaze again. His brow rose, a charming gesture, before he nodded his head as though she had spoken to him.

The hair on the back of her neck prickled, and it was not from Henri's quick caress before he left her to return to his opera box. As befit her role, she smiled at the baron, then turned away, conscious of the velvet bag clutched in her fist.

Vivienne could not read all of the note Henri had stuffed into the bag. Enough to understand what she must do, but there were a few words that were too difficult.

The theater was emptying out now, patrons whirling through the front doors while dancers and singers poured from the rear exit. The boxes and the pit had long since emptied of most of the aristocracy. She was alone in the room the dancers used to change their costumes, surrounded by empty stools and mirrors, waiting to end the night's work.

Frustration was a sick ball in her stomach. She fought the urge to crumple this note from Henri in her fist. Time was dragging out. Anne had been with Marchand for days now, and there was only Vivienne to find her. Manchester Square was not far from the theater. Yet there was Henri and his assignment that night. She must do as he asked so he did not wonder what else she was about. After, then. When her mission for Henri was complete, she would search Manchester Square until the morning sun brightened the sky.

Vivienne wiped damp palms on the skirts of her gown. The costumer would no doubt rage at the marks she left in the silk, but when she read Henri's instructions again, her hands were steady and dry. There was a long word she could not read. It started with a *P*. "Swiss" she could read. "Italian."

"Papers." "Late supper." These she knew. The long word beginning with *P* she did not.

A throat cleared behind her. She whirled, her hand moving to her bodice and the knife tucked there. But it was only Maximilian Westwood, standing in the doorway of the small room. He clutched a top hat in his fist, his eyes very grave and a clean-shaven jaw firmed.

She looked at his lips. *Mon Dieu*, they were good lips. Pretty, but masculine. She could feel them on her own even now.

This was not good. She needed him for things other than kissing. Still, her body yearned for another kiss. For more of a kiss than the quick, sweet need she'd felt inside.

Very deliberately, she set the yearning aside. She would not allow distraction.

She did allow gratitude for his presence and shame that he knew her secret—though she discovered a strange relief as well. No one but Anne and Mrs. Asher was aware she could not read, and now he shared it with her, too.

"Monsieur Westwood." She stepped toward him so quickly her costume shushed around her ankles like so much rushing water. "I have a note. Can you—"

"Mademoiselle." Interrupting her without any form of civility, there was no hint in his eyes or face that he wanted to kiss her again. It stung—and deflated her yearning. "My brother desires an introduction."

"I beg your pardon?"

In the dim hallway beyond the broad, broad shoulders of Monsieur Westwood, she heard impatient footsteps.

"My brother desires an introduction," he repeated, shoving his hat onto his head and covering neatly styled mahogany hair. His voice was loud—to carry into the hall, she supposed, where his brother waited. Then, more quietly, he murmured, "My apologies. He would have come alone if I had not agreed to introduce you."

She did not have time for this. A bubble of panic rose in her chest. She could not make Henri angry or fail her mission. Anne waited somewhere in the dark. Yet there was no choice but to endure the introduction and postpone both her mission and her search.

The delay did not mean inactivity. She needed Monsieur Westwood to read the letter. Now. Quickly.

She stepped close to him, set the hand holding the note on his shoulder. Cocking her head, she said coyly, "Another Monsieur Westwood? But, of course." Loudly again, so the brother could hear. As she spoke, Vivienne slid her hand down Maximilian Westwood's tensed arm and tucked the note in his hand. There was no skin now to rasp against hers, but only a soft leather glove.

His fingers folded around the paper, hiding it from view. Candlelight shone on the round top of his hat as he angled his head to look at his fist, then into her face.

She rose to her toes to whisper close to his ear. "I cannot read all of the note." Gripping his arm tightly, she held him close to her, so close the ruffles on the bodice of her gown brushed his arm. "Please tell me what it says." Then, stepping around him, she moved into the hall to face the baron.

Yes, she saw the avarice in this brother's gaze, though his smile was charming and face attractive. More handsome even than his brother, Maximilian, and though his bow was as elegant as she'd ever seen, she found she preferred the honest code breaker to the practiced movements of this rake.

"Bonjour to the second Monsieur Westwood." She said the words prettily, with her own well-practiced charm, knowing that he was a baron.

"Not the second," he said, smile widening. "I'm the eldest. Baron Highchester."

"Ah, Lord Highchester." She raised her brows, as if

impressed by his title. "An honor, my lord."

Someone brushed by them in the hallway. A boy who delivered messages and costumes and sets, and usually one of the last people backstage.

She must leave. Soon.

"Mademoiselle La Fleur, your dancing this evening was exquisite," Highchester said.

She laughed and held out a hand to him. "My lord, you have an exceptional ability to recognize talent."

"The others on stage paled in comparison." He pressed her hand to his lips, lingering.

Behind her, Monsieur Westwood snorted. She ignored him, silently imploring him to read the note and tell her what it said instead of paying attention to her conversation.

"Where is your friend this evening?" the baron asked, still holding her hand in his as he spoke of Henri. "I have not seen him since intermission."

"My lord was unable to stay tonight, but he sent his carriage. In fact, I must leave soon." She would not be returning home, however. She would be going wherever Henri was sending her, in the pantaloons she kept in the carriage. If only she could find out what the long word starting with a *P* meant.

She felt Monsieur Westwood move closer so that he stood right behind her. Perhaps the sudden heat at the base of her spine was from his body. Perhaps it was connected to that strange yearning to be kissed.

She looked behind her at the code breaker who knew too many of her secrets. Unsurprisingly, he was scowling, the array of green and gold of his eyes appearing fierce and clever.

"Please, mademoiselle, let us escort you to your carriage so we may ensure your safety." He tried to sound charming, her Monsieur Westwood. Perhaps he attempted to emulate his brother's flirtatious tone. He did not succeed, as he sounded stilted and a thousand times more sincere than his brother.

To Lord Highchester, she said, "Any lady would be pleased to have such escorts."

She looked at Monsieur Westwood over her shoulder again and raised her eyebrows in question. She could not ask what the letter said with his brother there, but the monsieur understood. His nod was clear, and a hundred unspoken words passed between them.

To Highchester the exchange meant nothing.

To her it meant everything.

Relief spread through her. Gathering it, she beamed at Monsieur Westwood. He blinked, as if he were a man sitting in the dark too long and being shown the sun. It made her smile more broadly, until she thought about kissing him. Then it was she who felt dazed.

Breathing deep, she turned back to the elder Westwood. The one charming as a goat.

"A moment, please," she said, smiling at him. "I shall get my cloak."

She went to the small table she used to apply rouge and work with her hair during a performance. A thick mantle was thrown over her stool, black wool spilling over wood.

"Let me assist you, mademoiselle."

Monsieur Westwood's big hands took the garment from her. She imagined his brother was gnashing his teeth for not being faster. Swirling the garment around her, the code breaker set it on her shoulders. He leaned in. Leaned close.

The yearning returned. Breath caught in her throat, and her skin tightened over her body. Forcing both from her mind, she blocked out the scent of him, man and sandalwood. Distraction was weakness for a spy. Hadn't Henri told her this time and again?

Then the monsieur gave her the answer she needed, in a rough whisper.

"The Italian ambassador carries documents that are to be

delivered to a member of the Swiss embassy before morning. You are to see they do not get there. The ambassador is at a late supper at Lord Pemberly's."

"Thank you." *Pemberly.* It was the long word she had not known.

His hand moved on her shoulder as he settled the cloak there. He smoothed the fabric, pressing out wrinkles that did not exist. She reached up, set her gloved hand upon his.

"Thank you," she said again, letting her hand rest over his.

All awareness, all sensation focused there. His hand on her shoulder, heavy, large. Strong. Over that, her own hand. Smaller, but just as strong, she thought proudly, if in a different way. Meeting his gaze, she could not understand whatever swirled in its depths, though she felt it in her toes.

He offered his arm as escort, and on her other side, Lord Highchester arrived and did the same. She smiled and flirted, looked between them, then accepted both arms.

"It is not often a lady has such fine escorts."

Chapter Twenty

Lord Pemberly's town house wasn't an average town house. It was a mansion squatting on the better part of a street, lined by shrubbery and trees beginning to winter over. Surrounding three sides of the property was a tall brick wall. No doubt great lawns led down to the river in the rear of the house.

Maximilian sniffed the air. The *clean* part of the river.

Why he was standing across the street from Lord Pemberly's mansion was a mystery. He should be home, alone and working. He could think of nothing that would drag him out of his home in the early hours of the morning. Except the Flower. Somewhere nearby she was sneaking around, trying to find a way in to steal something from the Italian ambassador.

Quick and deadly — as befit her occupation — the Flower did not need his protection. Still, he stood in the street like a fool. Ten times a fool, as his only thought was she might need him for something beyond protection. Reading another note, or perhaps the pistol shoved in the waist of his trousers. No doubt she had carried out missions alone before — but damn it all, he couldn't leave.

He saw her then. Or someone that might be her. Moving down the walkway across the street was a thin, short, young man. Very short. He was whistling, hands tucked easily into his pockets. A servant coming home after his night off. But Maximilian recognized Mademoiselle La Fleur's walk, even the turn of her foot. When had he noticed the Flower's feet? He could not say, but he knew her rhythm as well as his own. Better, perhaps, as she was trying to disguise herself, and still he knew it was her. Her body moved in a way others' did not—a grace that came from dancing, he was sure. He ignored the low beat igniting in his belly at the sight of her. There was a time and place for such things.

His brain knew it, even if his body didn't.

She ambled down the street, coming closer to Pemberly's. Carriages waited in front, horses stamping impatiently. Drivers called to one another. And then—

Damnation. She'd disappeared.

Concern washed through him, and he took a step forward. She might have turned an ankle and fallen. If so, she would be lying on the walkway, revealed by the oil lamps running along the street.

The path was empty.

Ah, the alley, he realized. A slim space between the Pemberly's mansion and the house beside it, barely six feet wide and dark as a tomb. She would be hiding there, biding her time.

Sneaky wench.

He decided to join her. Not from the front—he was not an unobtrusive shadow—but from the rear. Sticking to the shadows as much as possible, he jogged down the street. Maximilian picked his way through another alley and a rear garden, avoiding any patches of light from the windows.

This spy bit wasn't as difficult as he'd thought. Until he

found the wall. A monstrosity that stood between the alley and the neighbor's rear yard. He was on the wrong side, with mortar and stone between him and the Flower.

"I'm unprepared to climb a wall." He hadn't intended to say it aloud, but there it was. An immutable fact.

"It is not so difficult." A pointed chin appeared above him, displayed by the line of pale stone mortared atop the barrier. "If you are going to join me, monsieur, you must hurry. I do not have time to waste. If the ambassador leaves while I am arguing with you, we will both be dead by my commander's hand."

Her cap was meant to hide her identity, yet with her head angled to the side the moonlight shone white on her face and illuminated her features. Aggravation rather than pleasure at his arrival flitted over her features. Well, the wall irritated him. So did she, even if the silvery moonlight made her look like a starlit goddess.

Bloody hell, she was making him daft. Starlit goddess, indeed.

"Isn't there another way around?" he asked.

"Find a foothold," was her only answer. "A handhold. There are many in the ivy."

The ivy. Yes, that would hold his weight—if he were her size. "That won't work."

She huffed out frustration. "I cannot wait for you." Her hands moved on the top of the wall, and she was gone.

He stared at the empty space where her face had been. Nothing but darkness appeared above curling vines and a rough wall that seemed a foot taller than a moment ago.

"Confound that woman." He would *have* to climb the wall if he was going to help her. Hopefully he did not fall and make an ass of himself.

Ivy for his left hand, rough stone for his right. Digging his boots into the uneven surface, Maximilian hoisted himself up, feet scrabbling to find purchase. He braced himself, shifted his weight, and continued. Fingers reaching the edge of smooth, evenly chiseled stone at the top, he used his feet and arms to hoist himself up.

There he was, sitting at the apex.

"You are much faster than I thought." Her words floated to him from the darkness.

"Huh." It wasn't hard to climb. Rather easy, in fact. He likely wasn't as quiet as the Flower, but—

"Quick!" She sounded spitting mad.

He grinned, feeling much more at ease with this Flower.

She was at the head of the alley, peering around toward the front corner of the house. Pantaloons and boots were just visible in the night. Even in the shadows, her legs had a lovely shape. He jumped to the ground and gritted his teeth against the jolt. When it faded, he crept along the side of the wall, hunched over and trying to make as little noise as possible.

"It is too late to be small and quiet." She did not look at him but continued to peer around the building. "Like a great elephant, you make so much noise. If anyone were to hear you, they would have already done so."

The assumption was likely accurate, which was why he preferred codes over covert assignments.

He set a hand on the wall above her head and leaned over her to see the house. She was the perfect size for leaning over, fitting below his arm and shoulder. Looking down, he saw the top of her cap, the feminine shoulders covered in a man's coat. He imagined setting his hand on her shoulder, just to see if her muscles were tensed, but she seemed confident and quite in control of herself.

She looked up at him, eyes large beneath the brim of her cap. Lips parted on an exhale. He felt it then—her awareness of him. Just as he was aware of every part of her body. The tilt of her head, the measure of her breath, each eyelash in the faint light cast by the oil lamps.

It was her mouth he focused on now. He could kiss her, here in the dark. They were only a breath away, the heat radiating from her body drawing him in. His need for her was suddenly blinding. Did she feel it, too? This primitive pull?

There was still right and wrong, however, and she was with another man.

"What are you planning to do?" He whispered it in the most matter-of-fact of tone he could summon, but it didn't sound like him at all.

Tipping her head back to look at him, her gaze steady beneath the cap. A moment passed, so full of her thoughts he could pluck one from the air.

Deciphering it would be impossible. Irksome, that.

Finally, she said, "I was *not* planning for you to arrive." That tone he knew. The cross Flower when he did not provide the result she expected. She peered around the corner again, her whisper floating up to him on the night air. "Why are you here?"

"I thought you might need my assistance." It sounded foolish, so he added, "To read something."

"I do not require your assistance. I manage on my own."

Her body bumped against his as she turned back to him, which sent lust spiraling through him. The contact seemed to catch her off balance, and she staggered, boots rasping on gravel. He gripped her waist before he could think, curved his fingers around her hips. Her body was delicate and feminine beneath his hands, branding his fingertips despite the chilled air.

Everything in him burned at the contact.

He should back away. Leave her be.

Her arms came up to settle on his shoulders.

They stood there, not moving. The night swirled around them, layered by darkness and the sound of carriages and occasional voices. They did not move, as if a spell held them still and silent. It pulsed between them. Her lips parted, breath slipping out as both sigh and gasp.

He had to have her.

Pressing her mouth to his, he reveled in the heady power of *her*. Soft lips were chilled from the night air. They opened beneath his, revealing the taste of woman and night. He slid a hand up to cup her cheek, tangling his fingers in the hair beneath her cap.

She gripped his shoulders as if she needed an anchor to steady her. Rising on her toes, she met him and angled the kiss herself. Longing was sweet on her lips and dangerous in his heart.

He shifted closer, wanting to feel more of her. To taste more. Her body, with its dancer's strength, pressed against him. Hot in the cool night air. Feathering his fingers over her cheeks, he tangled his tongue with hers, then slid his hands down to grip her waist again.

He could stay this way for a bit, he thought. Just a bit longer. Maybe a lot longer.

It did not last. She stopped, whirling away from him, breath harsh on the late-autumn air.

"Do not kiss me here, like this." Shrinking from him, she crossed her arms over her breasts. "Not now. I cannot think when you—" She broke off, shaking her head.

She was afraid—not of him, but of what the kiss would mean. The thought flashed through his mind in a moment of utter clarity. Well, it sure as bloody hell scared him, too. He jammed his hands in his coat pockets and cursed fate.

Why was it that the first woman he'd wanted with such intensity in years had to be a spy with a body promised to another man?

She shook her head again, eyes wide with emotions too numerous to name. "I have an assignment, monsieur. You are not—shh." Stiffening, she set her fingers to her lips as the front door opened.

A couple descended the front steps, preceded by a footman. The Flower watched, still and inanimate as her namesake, body wound tight and ready to spring. Then she relaxed, her shoulders loosening and breath sliding out in a long exhale.

"Not the ambassador," she said. "Guests are beginning to depart, so it will not be long before he appears."

"What are you planning to do?" he asked again, looking down at the top of her head. The cap seemed colorless in the dark, but he guessed it to be a light brown. Lighter than the rich black of her hair, certainly.

"Now that you are here, I do not know." She pushed away from the wall and swung to face him. "I do not require your assistance. You will only get in the way."

"You didn't think that way when I read the note for you," he said, unsure if he aimed for her pain because he was angry or hurt that she didn't want him.

"*Salaud!*" Hissing it, her fist came up quick as a striking snake, but she held back. At the last moment, her hand dropped away. "I do not expect you to understand."

"That you are practically illiterate?" Damn it all, she'd called him a bastard—in flawless French. Breathing deep, he wrestled with the fact that she could kiss him, but she did not trust him. Shoving that aside, he said softly, "My apologies. That was inexcusable. I don't think less of you, Flower. It's simply fact."

Shock and temper warred on her face as she started to speak, then she spun away as the door to the town house opened again. Two men this time, one walking a little behind the first.

"It is he." Her whisper shot through the dark.

He reached for her, not sure what he was trying to do. His

hands landed on her shoulders, slid down to her upper arms. The lean muscle shifting beneath his fingers was feminine, yet not. Her body bowed up, and the strength in her amazed him. Shrugging off his hand, she faced him with eyes darker than he'd ever seen them. Reaching for his top hat, she tipped it askew.

"Pretend to be drunk." Her fingers mussed his cravat, tugged his greatcoat so it hung crooked. Her eyes widened as they heard a good-night call. "Please, be a drunk peer. I am your servant. Please." Desperation glazed her voice, and he could not fight it.

"Very well," he bit out. He didn't plan to leave her alone, at any rate.

She slipped out onto the walkway, and he followed, though he could not explain how his feet moved. He staggered, pretending to be drunk, with the Flower a respectful step behind him.

"Ho, there!" he shouted to the street at large, not having the slightest idea what her plan was.

The ambassador and his companion paused and turned to look at them, as if determining what danger was heading their way. Light from the carriage lamps shone on the companion's solemn, craggy face.

"Bloody hell."

"What?" The Flower was instantly stiff, shoulders and head snapping to attention.

"It's the Bishop Carlisle."

"He will not recognize me, but you must avert your face," she whispered. Impatience nearly rolled off her shoulders. "We must continue."

It was easier to issue the instruction than for Maximilian to comply. A man couldn't talk to another man without showing his face.

He jerked when the Flower's arm slipped around his

waist as if she were steadying him. Thinking quickly, he put his arm around her shoulders and listed a little to the side. She must be playing at being a sturdy little servant helping her master home—though she was supposed to be a he, given the pantaloons she was wearing. He must remember that.

Damned difficult given the slim, curved, *female* body pressed against his side.

"Come along, sir," she said, as though he were a child she was leading along the walkway. "Not too much farther now."

She guided him down the street toward the watchful ambassador, the bishop, and the carriage. Inquisitive gazes were aimed in their direction. Uncomfortable, all those eyes.

"Do something!" she hissed at him. "Be drunk."

Be drunk, she commanded. *Be drunk*. What did a drunkard do? Be loud. Stumble. Chase women and issue improper advances, if his brother was any evidence.

"Oh ho! A nish night!" he shouted, raising an arm to wave at the ambassador. Had he slurred properly? He could not tell. He leaned harder on the Flower, pretending to stumble over the—unfortunately quite even—walkway.

The ambassador looked down a long nose at them. "It is a cold night. Sir."

"But ishnot raining," Maximilian responded cheerfully. They were nearly to the ambassador and the bishop—then they *were* there, so close Maximilian could smell the faint scent of sweat beneath bay rum.

Bishop Carlisle was peering at him, mouth turned down in disapproval, deepening the lines around his face. Oh, yes, the bishop recognized him. He shifted stiffly in his coat, and Maximilian could almost hear the man chastising him for being drunk in the same manner he had chastised him for reorganizing the family library by author rather than by topic.

What did the Flower want him to do now?

Fall, apparently, as she stuck her foot out and tripped him.

Then she let go.

The walkway rose up to meet him. It was flat and rigid, as his nose quickly informed him. Blinding pain shot through his head as something in his nose crunched. Stars whirled behind his eyes. "Bloody hell," he groaned.

"Signor!" The ambassador's shocked voice rang in his ears, bouncing around in time to the throbbing in his nose.

"Sir!" The Flower was all apologies, her voice rising above the men's, though it didn't sound quite right to Maximilian's ears. "I'm ever so sorry, sir!"

Multiple pairs of hands drew him up to sitting. Small ones there on his right, larger on his left and another set on his shoulders. One of the hands flashed a ring he knew to be the bishop's, but he couldn't tell exactly where everyone was. Lights still hazed his vision.

The blood began. It trickled down his upper lip. He swiped at it, soiling his gloves beyond redemption, and mentally cursed the Flower in every language he knew.

"Are you well, Maximilian?" Bishop Carlisle's stern countenance frowned down at him. "This isn't like you."

No, it was Highchester's usual form of entertainment. Maximilian made a point of doing the opposite. Sitting on the walkway, with the metallic taste of blood in his mouth and the disapproving words of the clergyman hovering in the air, he could only hope the Flower was able to steal the documents.

"Come, you shall ride in our carriage, signor." The ambassador crouched beside him, the concern in his voice as audible as the hairs on his beard were visible. "I shall see you home."

Maximilian waved away the assistance with one hand while attempting to stop the blood with the other. "No, shir. I'm almosht home." This time he didn't have to pretend to slur the words. Tipping his head back, he tried to ignore the taste of blood.

She would pay for this.

"Boy!" he shouted. "*Boy*, help me up."

The Flower was already in front of him. Her eyes glittered as she set her hands on his shoulders. Satisfaction, he could see. She'd accomplished her goal. Damned if he could determine how. Must have been when he was facedown on the walkway.

"Beggin' yer pardon, sir. It's my fault," she said.

"So it is." He was going to wring her delicate neck when he had her in private. He'd made an ass of himself in front of the man who was as close to a father as he'd had since the age of eight.

The Flower's hands latched onto his arm and began to pull him up. Maximilian lurched to his feet, balanced, then tipped his head back again, pinching his aching nose.

"That will sober a man up," he said to the street in general.

"'Ere, put yer arm around me, sir." She slid that strong little arm around his waist again. "There y'are. Steady, sir."

He realized she spoke with an English accent. Not the modulated tones of an aristocrat, but English from the streets. Consonants dropped. Butchered Hs. By Christ, she spoke it like the language of her birth. Gone was the fluid Gallic accent he was accustomed to.

"Enshoy your evening, gentlemen," he said through the fingers pinching his nose. He sounded like a goose and felt like one, too.

He and the Flower staggered off, the stagger not being entirely contrived this time.

Springs creaked as the ambassador climbed into his carriage. They creaked a second time as the bishop stepped in. Maximilian wondered what the bishop would tell his mother the next time she invited them both for tea. Nothing flattering, for certain. The driver clucked at the horses, and they were off in the other direction.

It was done. The mission was over.

"Did you steal the documents?" Anger and embarrassment churned in his belly, an unsettling mixture.

"*Oui.* While they were helping you to stand."

Oh ho, she was back to the French accent. He looked down into that exquisite face. It might be her profession to blend truth and lies and identities, but it left him wondering who was under the characters she played. When a woman became someone else in the blink of an eye, a man could never puzzle out the intricacies of her soul.

Irritation blossomed, though he wasn't certain if it was because of her or himself. "Did you have to break my nose?"

"It is not broken, Monsieur Westwood."

"It bloody well hurts." He jerked away from her and leaned on the nearest area fence. "Am I covered in blood?"

She did not answer at first. He flicked a glance at her. She was very serious and sober. The wide, sensual mouth was neutral. Not angry. Not sad.

"You did not flinch." She said it flatly. "You did what I asked."

"What else was I to do? I didn't follow you to abandon you at the end of the assignment, for heaven's sake." He was in desperate need of something cold for his nose. A slab of meat. Something. He couldn't smell anything—let alone the Flower.

He missed that clean soap. She was right there, and he could not smell her soap.

"I'm going home."

Chapter Twenty-One

Vivienne watched Monsieur Westwood stride up the steps of his town house. He'd walked home alone, though she had not been far behind.

Guilt had settled in her chest at the way she had used him. Yet he had not complained. Oh, he was angry about the nose. It was not broken—probably—but he had not railed at her as she'd expected. Or lashed out, which was a distinct possibility. Men did those things. She knew that of old.

Monsieur Westwood simply cursed at the world. When she assisted him, he did not put his full weight on her. It was as though he were caring for her. Protective, even. She did not understand it. The men she knew—Henri, spies, other men who wanted only her body—they were not gentle. Not hard, of course, but they did not treat her as if she needed delicacy.

Monsieur Westwood's gentleness burrowed into her heart and carved a space there.

The heart was a dangerous organ for a spy.

The door closed behind Monsieur Westwood. Daggett would tend to him, and she did not know how to tend well at any rate. She did not need to stay—and she had somewhere to be. But she lingered, watching the town house for one more minute.

He'd trusted her, without question.

She did not care for that any more than his need to see her safe. Too many people trusted her, to their detriment. Anne abducted. Mrs. Asher locked in a closet, injured. Monsieur Westwood with a nose that was almost broken.

He had kissed her. Again. She had kissed him in return. It was more than pleasant, more than simple want. Or desire. This need for him—she should not have it. That little place inside her had unlocked again.

She had almost forgotten her assignment.

If she were not careful, she would do so again.

After a last glance at the windows of Monsieur Westwood's town house, a final wish for a good night, she spun on her heel and set her direction for Manchester Square. It was not far, as she was in the fashionable area of the West End.

Exhaustion weighed on her limbs, from dancing and the assignment—but the night was not over, and Anne was still lost in the dark. Pushing everything out of her mind but her objective, Vivienne studied the square and tugged her cap lower. It did not cover her chilled ears, however, and chafing her hands together did not stop the frigid air biting at her fingers. It was much easier to keep watch in the pleasant spring and summer than near the end of October.

She waited, as the last carriages of the night came and went, as ladies and gentleman laughed and conversed and whispered while scheduling assignations or returning from parties. Boys held horses' reins, butlers opened doors. It was not the height of the Season, but there were always some aristocrats residing in Town, even in the late fall. They all required entertainment. Those distractions were ending now, and the *ton* was returning to their beds.

Still, it was not the houses bursting with light and families and servants that she watched. It was the town houses with dark windows masquerading as empty. Marchand would not secrete Anne in a busy house, but one full of quiet spies.

Assuming Anne was here, in this square. Marchand himself might be here instead, or the man she had seen in the hotel. But there was no other avenue for Vivienne to explore. She would continue until she found Anne, even if she had to break into each house, one by one, until she located the girl.

Hunching her shoulders against the cold and the dark, she continued her watch.

The arriving carriages slowed, and windows went dark. Silence filled the night more than sound. Still, she saw nothing. Despair tugged at her when she realized dawn was not far and it was nearly time to surrender the watch for the night.

Then the man she watched for, the man from the hotel, stepped out of a carriage down the street. Casually, as though it were his home. She did not need more than a moment to recognize him, even in the faint light from the windows. The height and build, the jaw, the cheekbones. All of these she had memorized at the door of Room 12 at the Nelson Hotel.

He bounded up the steps of a town house as the door opened, revealing the outline of another man, likely a butler. The first man hailed the butler with a raised hand as he reached the top step. Vivienne narrowed her eyes, reevaluating the scene. The other man was not a butler, as he wore no livery. They stepped inside together without a word, each moving fluidly and quietly.

She had her answer, then. If Anne was not here, someone else useful was. Vivienne had somewhere to start searching, at least. If Anne *was* here, she would likely be a prisoner on a higher level. It was too easy to escape from the kitchens by way of the area, and too easy to sneak out a window on the ground floor or the first floor. The second or third floors—it was possible but more difficult to escape, especially for one untrained in such things.

Vivienne carefully studied each window. Each brick and curtain flutter in the rooms above. Some were dark; others glowed with muted candlelight. Someone crossed in front of one curtain, their shadow a specter behind the fabric. Too big and broad to be Anne.

It was another ten minutes before she noticed the movement in the topmost window. The curtain was pushed aside. She could not see a face, only the shift as white fabric revealed darkness beyond, then fell back into place. A minute later the curtain moved again.

Someone was checking the street.

They must have felt safe, as the curtain closed and a light flared. It was dim, as if shielded or only the stub of a candle. A figure flitted across the curtain, this one with small, narrow shoulders.

Vivienne's heartbeat galloped across her rib cage. Hope pummeled at her.

It was Anne. She knew Anne's shape. Every move of her body and angular line that hinted at womanhood. She had watched Anne since the moment of her sister's birth.

Wait. It could be another girl. A servant girl. Anyone. She must not make an assumption. It would be too devastating, too damaging to her heart if she were wrong.

Her mind tried to battle back the hope, but it refused to obey her. She came out of the shadows without any plan. She should wait and observe, determine if it was Anne, then devise the best method for rescue.

She could not wait.

Vivienne loosened her body, hunched her shoulders. She was only a servant returning from a night off and not of importance. This she told herself to prepare her body. No one would notice the young man warding off the cold with a low cap and hands tucked into his coat pockets. They would not pay attention as the young man slipped across the street and into the dark on the other side.

Standing with her back pressed against the wall, she splayed her hands on rough brick. It was frigid and chafed the skin there, but she gripped the surface with numb fingers. She must anchor herself, still her rampant heartbeat, and quiet the screaming in her mind.

Training told her to wait.

Her body moved as though it had no connection to her mind.

Slinking along the front of the building, she passed the front door and around to the area. Skimming her hand along the fence ringing the area and stairs down to the kitchen, she crossed in front of the vertical iron bars and slipped to the other side, between it and the next town house.

Setting her hand on the top of the fence, she fisted the iron spikes. They were always a hazard, but it was the easiest method of boosting herself up to the next floor. Bracing herself, muscles tensed to begin, she set her foot on the railing and used it to lift herself to reach the decorative stones that would allow her to climb the facade.

The front door opened.

Heart hammering against her ribs, fear clawing at her throat, Vivienne dropped to the ground. She tried to blend into the walkway, the fence, the dark. *Anything.* She imagined herself invisible.

It was too late. The man pretending to be a butler was saying good-bye to the man from Room 12, but his gaze slid her way, and his shoulders tensed. The angle of his head—its curious tilt. She did not like it.

Sliding her hand toward her boot, she slipped her fingers around the hilt of her knife. She would be ready. There was no move toward her. When one man had left in a carriage and the other went back inside, Vivienne finally breathed again. Air did not stop the horror and fear building inside her.

Pressed against the walkway, waiting a few more minutes for safety, she knew she could not enter the house this night. The butler had seen her, or at least guessed at her presence, and would be on guard against intruders. It was too dangerous to bring Anne out tonight—but what would they do to Anne between now and tomorrow?

Nothing. Not until they could prove Vivienne had found her and the incentive, Anne, was no longer useful.

She could not decide what was worse—trying now and knowing she would fail them both, or trying tomorrow when there was some hope of rescue but a world of danger in between. Both might result in death, but if she waited the opportunity was better.

While her brain told her this, her heart screamed at her to storm the town house and take Anne now. She pressed her face into the wet fabric of her sleeve. Clutching the bottom of the cold iron fence, her fingers squeezed, released— accompanied by a stuttering breath.

Tomorrow she would return and rescue Anne. The butler would be less on guard than he would be now.

Tomorrow.

Chapter Twenty-Two

"Move the girl."

How had the Flower found her? He'd thought it was clever to hide the girl in the heart of the aristocracy. They rarely looked beyond the end of their noses. After all, they had never suspected him, and he was right in front of them.

The Vulture slung his outerwear over the back of his desk chair, but it was wet and might stain the beautiful wood. He snapped his fingers and pointed at the garment.

"Yes, my lord." The agent removed the dripping fabric from the chair and draped it over his arm. "My apologies for sending for you at this time of night."

The agent had no idea what he'd interrupted. Espionage, politics, money, and women. All of Marchand's very favorite things. But the Flower was important, as was the girl. He had plans hinging on the Flower.

"Where shall we move the girl?" the agent asked.

Anywhere but Mayfair. The Flower was too close now. She would scour the West End looking for the girl. She was proving to be a worthy adversary. Quite clever, in fact — a pity he would not be able to keep her.

"I know of a location." Oh, yes. He had many ideas, but one in particular. "No one will ask questions."

Chapter Twenty-Three

"Maximilian, you must stop Highchester." The words were perilously close to a wail, being rather high-pitched and drawn out. They were also accompanied by the wringing of arthritic hands.

"Mother, he won't listen to me any more than he listens to you." His brother never had, unless Maximilian had pounded the words into him with fists, and Maximilian didn't believe fisticuffs solved anything. "Moreover, I haven't the slightest inkling what you are talking about."

Nor did he *want* to know. The document in his hand needed translating, and he wanted his bed. It was late, and he'd lost sleep the night before while dealing with the Flower, her mission, and a nose that was bruised but thankfully not broken. Also thankfully, it bore little residual damage beyond a vague ache and slight bruising under one eye.

"I would suggest an intervention of some type is necessary, Maximilian." The brisk words issued from the downturned mouth of Bishop Carlisle. The very moral, very distinguished friend of the family who had witnessed

Maximilian pretending to be intoxicated. "Assuming you are capable of such responsibility, of course."

Maximilian almost ducked his head as he would have done as a boy. As a man, however, he simply held the bishop's gaze steadily. The bishop's countenance was grave, the dignified planes of his face sober and full of import, which was why, instead of working, Maximilian was standing in his drawing room facing his almost hysterical mother and a stoic bishop at some time in the evening. Not that his mother was ever anything but almost hysterical.

On the other hand, she rarely visited his bachelor quarters. Nor did Bishop Carlisle, come to think of it. Something truly was amiss, then.

The Dowager Lady Highchester continued to wring her hands together, twisting them in the strings of her reticule. Little frilly things bobbed at the hem of her ball gown, and feathers poked out of her hair. They were drooping, as though exhausted after an evening of standing up straight between white curls.

How late *was* it? He was certain he'd eaten luncheon not long ago. Reaching into his waistcoat for his pocket watch, he flipped open the plain gold lid to study the hands. Not yet midnight, but well past dinner. Well, that explained the gnawing hunger in his stomach.

"I don't know what to do!" His mother's shoulders slumped, mirroring the drooping feathers. "Highchester will surely ruin the girl if he is not stopped."

Maximilian's head snapped up, and he studied his mother's harried face. "A girl?"

"You should have seen him this evening." She shook her head, nearly dislodging one of the feathers. "Strutting about the ballroom with that young chit on his arm. I don't know what her parents are thinking."

Not that kind of girl, then. If she was in a ballroom,

Highchester would be a bit more circumspect. Less chance of bastards and rumors, he though distastefully. Still, Maximilian did begin to pay attention now that he knew the subject matter.

"Calm yourself, Agatha. We will sort this out." Bishop Carlisle set his hand over the strings of the reticule, restricting her fingers' harried movements. "His lordship can be brought to heel."

Maximilian wasn't so sure, but the bishop's low, steady voice seemed to help his mother. Her brows smoothed out and she smiled tremulously. "Yes, of course. You are right."

"Sit down, Mother, and tell me what has happened." He gestured toward a delicate chair that had come from her attic. She perched restlessly on the edge, and the bishop came to stand behind her, leaning on the back of her chair. His chest puffed out as it did right before he delivered a thundering sermon.

Maximilian sighed and sat down on the lumpy settee facing his guests in preparation for the sermon. Only it was his mother who delivered the sermon instead of the bishop.

"The girl was considered the debutante of the Season this spring. *Six* proposals, Maximilian! Though her father is holding out for a better offer next Season. But your brother is *married*," his mother continued in a voice a few registers below a wail. "She should not be seen in his company so often. It's just not done."

"Who?" Maximilian knew few people in polite society, so this seemed a silly question. He wouldn't recognize her name.

"The Lawrence chit."

Well. Perhaps he would. "The Duke of Lawrence?"

The wrinkles in his mother's soft face deepened as she nodded. "The girl is an heiress and utterly lovely—which is why she's caught Highchester's eye. He's making a cake of himself pursuing her, and she's flattered enough to enjoy it, but he'll ruin her marriage chances if he continues."

"Let the duke manage the girl," Maximilian suggested. "I'm sure he'll bring *her* to heel and then Highchester will follow suit." *Probably.*

"The duke has tried, but he's in his dotage." The bishop frowned, his mustache turning down as fiercely as his lips.

"The duke married a girl less than half his age for an heir and ended up with naught but a daughter," his dowager said, amid more wringing of hands. "He coddles her, and his wife is too busy with her own peccadilloes to notice. Maximilian, it is up to us. We must warn Highchester away from her."

Maximilian was certain that by *us*, his mother meant *you*. God's teeth. He wanted to go to bed, not worry about some chit without enough sense to stay away from his brother.

"It won't do any good, Mother." Maximilian sighed, scrubbing a hand over his face. It was rough with stubble he'd forgotten to shave that morning. "He'll go his own way."

"Maximilian." The bishop stepped forward, expression as severe as the cut of the jacket and tight cravat he wore. "Highchester never obeyed your mother and barely obeyed your father. I have little authority, despite our long association and my position with the church."

"Highchester doesn't attend church, my lord." Maximilian couldn't help the vaguely dry tone of his voice. Highchester hadn't attended church since he was old enough to visit a willing barmaid instead.

"Please." The dowager's eyes welled with tears, and Maximilian barely refrained from cursing aloud. "Please. He must not be allowed to ruin the family, or the girl. Society would cast us all out."

Maximilian didn't care a whit about the *ton*, but his mother did, and she was crying. It was the one weapon he couldn't defend against. He supposed no gentleman could.

"I shall speak with him tomorrow." After he finished his

latest translations and was able to sleep. Perhaps he'd even shave.

"Tonight, please. I know it is late, but she was discussing Gunter's and that she wanted to go tomorrow afternoon, and he offered to—" She pressed her lips together, breathed through her nose, then started again. "I told him it was improper. He's married, she's a young debutante. But he doesn't care. It must be tonight, before any additional damage is done."

"Very well." Maximilian pushed up from the settee and strode to the door. "I'll go now."

"Good man," the bishop said, as though Maximilian had redeemed himself from the previous evening's mishap.

"Mmm." Redemption only meant Maximilian had to leave his house when he'd rather stay home.

"Maximilian." The bishop's soft tone made him stop and turn. "Thank you. You're the only one he ever listens to."

"Even then, it rarely happens, Bishop."

"Highchester is at his town house," his mother said, waving her hand in the air as if to remind Maximilian what direction his brother lived in. "I heard him make plans with a couple of other lords."

Oh, hell. If Highchester was with his friends, there was no telling what debauched scene Maximilian was about to witness.

It wasn't as bad as he'd thought it would be.

It was worse.

The gentlemen had brought their mistresses—or at least their women of choice for the night. He could hear feminine laughter echoing down the hall as Highchester's butler led him to the salon.

When Maximilian opened the salon door, he realized half of the crowd was undressed—or mostly so. He was practically struck blind by a man prancing past, wearing nothing but his coat. A laughing woman trailed behind, breasts exposed over the man's trousers. Beyond them was a sea of petticoats, unbound hair, and bared chests.

"A word with you, Highchester," Maximilian said to the room in general, raising his voice to be heard over the laughter. He had no idea where Highchester was among the bodies sprawled on the floor, surrounded by brandy glasses and recently shed clothing.

"Why, little brother! What brings you to my party?"

Maximilian wheeled in the direction of the voice. Highchester lounged in a chair, cravat dangling around his neck. The woman on his lap wore nothing but a corset and a ruffled skirt rucked up to her knees. His brother's hand sneaked beneath her skirt, and she giggled.

"A word, Highchester. In the hallway, please."

"I think I'll stay here." A masculine chuckle followed the words, then another feminine giggle. "I'm quite comfortable."

"Do you want our business aired in front of your... companions?" The amount of perfume in this room made his nose itch. Did they all wear a different scent? It was a battle of sweet versus sweeter.

"I don't think any of *your* business would shock my companions," Highchester drawled.

The room erupted in laughter—not the friendly sort. Maximilian let it wash over him as he met Highchester's amused and maliciously satisfied eyes. "The Duke of Lawrence's daughter," Maximilian said brusquely. "Leave her be."

"She's a sweet little morsel." No apology from his brother. No pretending he didn't understand. "And spoiled enough to want some adventure. I thought to provide it for her."

The girl on his lap pursed her lips into a pout. "My lord, aren't I enough to play with?" She circled her arms about his neck and leaned in for a kiss.

"Indeed." Highchester's hand slid down her thigh, squeezed. "But one does like variety."

"Let the Lawrence girl be." Maximilian knew his words were hard and sharp, but he was finished with this display of debauchery.

Finished with his brother.

If Highchester wanted to betray his marriage vows and tup every willing woman he met, so be it. Young ladies of good family were out of the question.

"Leave her be."

Highchester's lashes flickered as his gaze roved over Maximilian's face. What was he thinking? With his brother it could be anything. It was his actions one had to wait for.

Highchester's eyes met Maximilian's, held, then he broke the connection and glanced away.

Maximilian had his answer. Highchester would obey.

He hadn't anticipated the next words from Highchester's mouth.

"Have you noticed your new acquaintance over there in the corner? Mademoiselle La Fleur?"

Maximilian could not quite hear over the sudden roaring in his ears. Shock coursed through him, twining with bitter cynicism that she should be here. He turned in the direction Highchester gestured and saw her.

The Flower. She lay on a chaise longue, draped over it, her body as fluid as silk. A riot of dark curls fell about her face. Her gown slipped from her shoulders as though unlaced or unbuttoned, its skirt a mound of froth and silk and ruffles. He could not tell, exactly, where dress ended and petticoat began. But he could tell where that stunning face began. Strength showed in her pointed chin, red mouth curved in greeting, the widow's peak raised over cheekbones and jaw and eyes.

Her eyes.

For a moment, all he saw were her eyes. The rest of her smiled, flirted. Her mouth was a complicated mixture of delight and amusement and humor, but her eyes were pleading. Those lovely, dark eyes held him. One moment. Two. Begging him not to reveal more than the public knew.

She was bound by the role she played, there in that room full of debauchery. As was he.

"Mademoiselle, it is good to see you again." He bowed to the proper depth, as if they were meeting in the ballroom.

One corner of her lips tipped up. She inclined her head, just as properly. "*Enchanté*, Monsieur Westwood." She shifted, and his gaze was drawn toward the ridiculously impractical lace stockings covering her dancer's legs.

His mouth went dry.

The entire world became that sweep of leg. The curve of her calf, the way the muscle moved as she flexed her foot. Did all dancers have the slight indentation of lean muscle running the length of the thigh when candlelight played over their skin? Or did that only belong to a spy turned dancer?

His gaze traced the shape, then the froth of her gown, the tapered torso, her breasts and back to her face. Dark eyes no longer begged him. He could not quite read the emotion, but there was no pleading now. A slow, banked fired burned in their depths. Pupils dilated, the whites bright against the deep brown of her irises.

Were his own pupils as dilated? Was that slow, burning heat reflected in his own eyes? Because it was not slow in his body. It was a roaring fire starting deep in his belly and threatening to engulf him.

Maximilian did not notice her companion until the man stepped in front of her, blocking the Flower from Maximilian's view.

Her protector.

Cold fury doused the desire blazing in him. The Flower had an arrangement with this man, and Maximilian was no better than his brother lusting after her.

"Mr. Westwood." Lord Wycomb's voice was smooth and cultured, and a little irritated. "We have not met."

No *enchanté* from this man. He was as tall as Maximilian, with cold, cold eyes. His cravat was untied, his jacket and vest removed. He was otherwise dressed. And older, judging by the silver at his temples. Perhaps old enough to be the Flower's father—though he was handsome and fit, Maximilian thought sourly.

What did a gentleman say to the protector of the woman he lusted after?

Chapter Twenty-Four

She had not expected Monsieur Westwood to arrive at his brother's, nor had she expected *that* look in his eyes.

He had kissed her, but she had not seen that look in his eyes before. A fierce wanting that was more than a desire to kiss. More, she had not expected the same fierce tug inside her. A strange, warm pull that spread through her and made her come alive. She could not put a name to it and had not experienced it before. It felt different. More than the flutter, it was a bright, hot need running along her skin in a most delicious way.

Now Monsieur Westwood, the man who had kissed her, stood before Henri. This she most definitely did not like. Even a word breathed about Anne, of her association with Monsieur Westwood, and all might be lost.

"Sir." Monsieur Westwood bowed to Henri, as he had to her. Most properly. "I must commend Mademoiselle La Fleur. She is an exceptional dancer."

The noise around them lessened. She could feel the eyes of others in the room watching. Gauging. Henri was known to be possessive, which kept her safe from others' advances. He protected her and her missions with this ruse.

Monsieur Westwood was once a code breaker for spies. Henri would know this. The monsieur did not know what Henri was. That left the monsieur at a disadvantage. She could not show this sudden dread that roiled inside her. She could only lie on the chaise, half of her body exposed and men measuring her reaction. She did nothing but continue to smile, to run her fingers idly along the edge of the chaise.

She had not a care in the world. Whatever exchange was to come, it did not concern her.

This was what she told herself so that the room would see these thoughts. She did not want them to see the pings of fire ricocheting through her body from Monsieur Westwood's gaze, or the fear that pinged around with it. She did not want the guests to know she thought about the taste of Monsieur Westwood's mouth, or that she wondered what was beneath his clothing.

"I agree. Vivienne is an exceptional dancer," Henri said in his perfect English tones. "A fact I have known for many years."

Henri stood between them, though he did not fully block her view of Monsieur Westwood's face. She could see the monsieur's frown, his brows drawing together in concentration. Was he searching for an insult? A hidden meaning?

Monsieur Westwood opened his mouth. Closed it. His eyes flicked toward hers, quick as a butterfly's wing. She couldn't read what was in his gaze, but she knew she did not have to worry.

"I was just leaving," he said. "My business is done."

"Surely you would like to stay, brother?" Baron Highchester drawled. His voice, it did not sound nice just now, though he had been nauseatingly kind to her when they'd arrived. "After your private meeting with Mademoiselle La

Fleur at Carleton House, I thought you would enjoy her company."

Henri did not move. Neither did Monsieur Westwood. The room became very quiet, the tension thick and heavy as a slice of the rough bread she'd baked as a girl. But Henri, he would want no difficulty. It was all show. Monsieur Westwood, however, could not be predicted.

She stood, then. It was not acceptable to sit by with nothing to say. Stepping to Henri, she ran a hand over his shoulder. She did not often touch him by choice, and it sent an uncomfortable shudder through her body. It was worse, so much worse, to do so under the watchful gaze of Maximilian Westwood.

"Henri, Monsieur Westwood is a favorite of the prince." She smiled at the monsieur, flirtatious as befit her position, but not inviting. That would not be suitable. "You are not often at Carleton House, are you, monsieur?"

"No." Monsieur Westwood's jaw was tight, the muscles rigid.

"A shame, no, Henri?" Speaking lightly, she hoped the others in the room would think she was mitigating a difficult situation. She could not decide what Henri and the monsieur would think. "Prinny has much respect for Monsieur Westwood."

There, that should do. He would know enough to leave Monsieur Westwood be.

"Indeed?" Henri did not raise an eyebrow. He did not need to.

"Perhaps we shall see you again soon, Monsieur Westwood." She smiled, then turned her back on her monsieur. It sent a pang through her. He was the only man in the room who knew who she was aside from Henri. The only one who did not want to use her in some way.

Her commander, too, turned away. Grabbing her waist as

he had done a thousand times before, he pressed a kiss to her neck. It was a sign. He wanted to leave. Well, so did she. Henri's quarry that night had not even arrived at the party, so time had been wasted.

"Good evening." Monsieur Westwood's farewell was hard and very cool.

She did not turn to look at him, as she did not want to show too much interest, but her heart felt his footsteps as though they were in her chest. Heard them as if they rang inside her.

But that could not be.

They could not be.

"Carleton House?" Henri did raise his brows now, many minutes later.

She stood before him in her breeches and boots in her own boudoir. It had been only a little while after Monsieur Westwood left that Henri said good-bye to their host.

Now he was curious, as he did not like her to act in any way outside his control.

"Prinny introduced us. Everyone saw that we walked the corridor." She cocked her head, shrugged a shoulder. Near truth was more difficult to detect than an outright lie. "You know we had met during the war—I thought Westwood would reveal my identity tonight."

Buttoning a black jacket over her shirt, she began to feel calmer. It was armor, this jacket and shirt—not that frivolous concoction she'd worn to the soiree at Baron Highchester's.

"I am aware he knows who you are, though he does not know who I am." Henri relaxed into the armchair she kept near the fire. Her armchair. The one she had asked to be set there. "Westwood is also considered above reproach by many in the government."

"Yes, he is above reproach, as you say." She pulled on black kidskin gloves. They were tight and thin, to allow as much feeling as possible. "Dawn will be closing in soon, Henri. What would you have me do yet this night? The little lordling with his father's secrets did not arrive at Baron Highchester's town house as we had hoped."

"He did not." Henri took a cheroot from his jacket pocket. With only a quick touch of flame from a nearby candle, it let out a cloud of smoke into her boudoir. *Her* boudoir, attached to her bedchamber. The space she considered her own—except that it was not hers, was it? It was his. When he was in her home, everything was his.

Except the little hollow beneath the floorboard. That space was hers.

"What do you direct, Henri?" she asked again.

"Nothing, at the moment." Smoke curled from the cheroot to form a writhing gray snake that danced above his head. "If the young man does not look for me tomorrow, I'll send you to find out why he was detained."

Vivienne inclined her head in acknowledgment but did not unbutton the top button of the coat. She still had somewhere to be tonight, he just didn't know of it.

Brows furrowing, his fingers tapped impatiently on the armchair.

"What is it, Henri?" she asked. "You appear troubled."

"Marchand."

Her heart stopped. Simply stopped. There was no air in her lungs, no blood pumping through her veins. She could not answer.

Henri did not seem to notice her lack of either air or answer. He continued, as though any words she might have spoken would not have been important. "There are whispers Marchand is active again. He's been quiet the past year or so, and some thought he was dead."

She should take off her coat. Henri would expect this now that she had no orders, but it was difficult to think while her body was numb. *How much does Henri know?* Still, she slipped the first button from its hole, then the second.

"Whispers?" It was the only word she could force past her thick tongue.

"A few. Nothing concrete." He drew in a breath so the cheroot glowed red at the end. "Someone said he visited Lessard's recently, though there was no visual confirmation."

Her mind dredged up characteristics and evaluated possibilities in an amalgam of broken thoughts. Michel Lessard. A brothel owner. Nearly as big as a gorilla and as unattractive. Scarred face, brown hair and eyes. Preferred weapon was a pistol.

Lessard had long been linked to Marchand. It would be another location to look for Anne. Her stomach clutched at the idea of Anne in a brothel, but the idea could not be dismissed.

Manchester Square. Lessard's. There would be other links from those locations, if she could find them.

"You have no need of me this night then?"

"No, my dear. You have no assignments this evening." He looked to the end of his cheroot as if the glowing tip would reveal Marchand's secrets. Then, slowly and quietly, "We have been searching for Marchand for many years."

He did not seem to want an answer, so she did not speak. With a flick of his finger, ashes rained from the cheroot onto the rug beneath his chair. Fortunately, the carpet did not belong to her, or she might have coshed him on the head for such disrespect of her things.

Finally, he stood, but he did not look at her or say goodbye when he left. He simply walked out of her boudoir and into the hallway. A few minutes later, she heard him leave the town house.

Her fingers shook on her coat buttons as she hurriedly redid them. Henri must not know of Marchand and Anne. Not yet. Keeping silent might be a mark on her career, but it would be only until she found Anne. Once she did, she would give Marchand to her commander. She would bring the Vulture to the British.

Stepping to the window, she pushed back the pretty lace curtain. On the street below, Henri stepped into the carriage, and the driver folded up the steps, then hoisted himself to the box. A moment later the carriage moved down the street and around the corner.

She waited ten minutes, fifteen, lest he return, but he did not.

To Manchester Square then.

It could be simple to remove Anne, or it could be difficult. She was uncertain which it would be. Until she bumped into Monsieur Westwood on her front step.

So. It would be difficult.

"*Oof!*" Sound and breath wheezed from her. The muscles beneath his jacket were hard and nearly as solid as any stone wall she had climbed. He steadied her, arms about her elbows. A more proper hold than her waist, no? It made her smile in a way that felt very soft and sweet in her center.

He dipped his head down to see her face, perhaps to ensure the young man he'd bumped into was truly a young man and not an opera dancer.

When his mouth came so close to hers, it was not only something soft and sweet between them. It was more. A deluge of want, of breathlessness and longing.

"Pardon me, Mademoiselle La Fleur." He set her carefully

away from him, even after seeing her mostly undressed and looking at her as though she were as delicious as French brandy.

Breathing deep, Vivienne set aside every sensation reverberating in her body. He would only complicate her errand.

"You must go." She looked up into the face shadowed by night. "Now."

To make her point, she jogged down the steps, hoping he would go away and also hoping he would follow.

He followed.

Her heart bumped a little in her chest. Quickly, she walked down the street to lead him away from her town house, where either Marchand's or Henri's eyes might be watching them.

"Why did you come?" she asked.

"To apologize. For my brother and myself." He kept pace with her, his long legs easily matching her stride. "I thought perhaps we caused difficulties with your...*protector*." The word sounded sour on his tongue.

"No apology is required, as no harm has occurred." *Yet.* She looked to the end of the street. Soon they would turn the corner, and she would not need to be quite so concerned if someone saw them.

"Wait, mademoiselle." He set a hand on her arm, gently, and though she did not stop walking, she did slow. "My brother has a tendency to incite trouble, and it was ill-mannered of me to look at you as I did. I should have averted my gaze."

Affection crept into her heart, mingling with surprise. "No one else did."

"Precisely." As if that settled it. His head swiveled back and forth to study the street, as though suddenly realizing she was not receiving him in her front salon. "Why are we in the street?"

She hesitated. Perhaps it was too long keeping her

own counsel, but she could not tell him her intentions in Manchester Square. He would want to accompany her, and she would want him to, which was why she also could not give in to her need for him. To be kissed by him, or more.

The Flower was meant to be alone.

"I am on a mission, monsieur." Cold night air brushed her face as she turned the street corner. "Thank you for the unnecessary apology. Good night."

Manchester Square was not far, but far enough she must hurry if she was to act before dawn. Quickening her pace to a trot, she expected him to stay behind, but he continued to match her pace.

"Doesn't he wonder where you are every night?"

"Who?"

"Your protector."

She could tell him Henri was her commander, as it was a truth buried deep within espionage. Habit and training prevailed, breaking a piece from her heart even as her mind sorted through a multitude of truths and lies to tell him.

"My protector has imbibed much brandy this evening. If he wakes, I will simply tell him I was in the house but he did not look in the proper location. It has worked before. If he learns I was with another man—that cannot happen. Do you see?" Webs of lies were spinning in the night air. "You must go home. I am busy."

"I did not leave you at Pemberly's when you needed to steal the documents, and I do not intend to leave now. What kind of man do you think I am that I would abandon a lady alone on the street?" Insult rang in his tone, slapping at her the way her boots slapped the walkway.

Hilarity built inside her so that she could not move, and her feet slowed. "Monsieur!" She tried to hold back her peal of laughter, but it would not be stifled. "Have you forgotten who I am?"

"No." He scowled, bending forward slightly to draw a breath.

"You are foolish." It was amusing and charming that he would worry so about her safety. "I am armed, monsieur. All is well, and I must hurry. *Bonne nuit.*" A light fog swirled around her as she trotted once more down the street, its gray bands curling through the darkness between her and the town houses. Mist and fog were useful when one needed to be unseen, but this fog was not as dense and useful as she wished.

Footsteps sounded beside her, again in perfect rhythm with her own.

"Damnation," he said. "Pretend I am not here."

"You are ridiculous," she bit out as her temper rose, but she had very little time to argue. The sun would show its face soon. "The place I am going, you cannot come in. You may stand watch. That is all."

He did not speak again, nor did he lose his breath as he jogged beside her. He was not a soft aristocrat, which surprised her, but she did not have time to think on it. There was no pale light in the sky yet, but she and the night understood each other. The darkness was slipping away.

Suddenly Number 6 on Manchester Square was in her vision. She stopped across the street to study the facade, as she had not studied it the night before. Yes, she could climb it. It would be difficult, but there were handholds in the stone ledges and the brick outcropping. There, above the first window, then the tiny iron railing around the second window. She could move, with a strong leap, to the next railing. If she were quiet and surefooted, it could be done.

Beside her Monsieur Westwood shifted. She felt him rather than saw him, heard the scrape of his shoes.

"Hush," she whispered. "Do not move."

Monsieur Westwood stilled, his body going taut and tense. Vivienne heard his irritated exhale but ignored it to focus on the window where she had seen Anne's shadow. It was high. Perhaps it would be better to pick the lock and go in through the front door, then she would see what she could see on the inside instead of guessing on the outside.

"Do not be in my way." She did not turn toward the monsieur. Looking, now, would distract her. "Wait somewhere."

"Where are you—"

"Just go somewhere. Go."

Chapter Twenty-Five

The confounded woman left him without a bloody backward glance.

Maximilian did his best to slink into the shadows. How did the Flower seem to become the darkness? Feeling like a fool, he hunched between two front doors and tried to pretend he was a brick, just minding his own brick-like affairs. She, however, with her dancer's grace, dashed across the street without even the slightest whisper of boot on cobblestone.

He was coming to admire that stealth now that he knew how difficult it was to achieve.

Her figure paused at the front door. He could not see what she did, but it seemed to him she bent over. He had a sudden image of what her buttocks might look like in such a moment, then cast it out of his brain with a mental oath. What her buttocks looked like was of no concern. Mostly. But the vision was burned into his brain now.

When he looked for her again by the door, she was missing.

Hell, where did she go? The front step was empty. At

what point had she disappeared into the town house? He pressed the heel of his hand to his forehead, rubbed. That should teach a man a lesson. Best to keep your eyes on the spy, not her derriere.

Now he was stuck in the street, unable to go anywhere. Logically, if she were to come looking for him, she would return to the place she'd told him to wait. So he couldn't move, but had to go on being brick-like in the shadows he couldn't hide in, watching the sky lighten above him.

He was ten times a fool.

He should have turned around when he saw her leave her town house. Better yet, he should have stayed at home with his work, but the apology had been burning on his tongue. Highchester and his acquaintances might dishonor women, but Maximilian had made a point of not doing so. Except this little foray of chivalry was costing him. He could be translating something for a paying client. Instead, he was—

A window opened high above the street. Silent, but quickly. Against the white casement, he saw a dark leg thrown over sill, then a small, quick body emerged from the window. The Flower. She was in a hurry, judging by her fast, fluid exit from the building.

Three sets of windows above the street. There were no railings under that window to assist her. Nothing but brick and stone. His damn fool feet were already running across the road. Did they think he was going to climb up there and save her?

The Flower didn't need his assistance. By some miracle of espionage training, she was pulling the window closed at the same time she was nimbly slipping down the side of the building. Watching the black-clad figure dance across the face of the building was a study of strength and proportion, of confident feet and clever fingers that found purchase in nothing but brick and stone.

When she leaped from one windowsill to another, his heart slammed into his chest. The daft woman was twenty feet in the air and leaping over the razor-sharp points of the iron area fence. If she fell— He shuddered and stepped beneath her. Then he realized what she'd done. Moved from the window over the area fence to the window above the front door. There was nothing to stop her drop to the front step.

Except him.

He looked up, saw her body falling through the air, and raised his arms to catch her.

Damn, she was heavy for such a little thing.

The impact knocked the breath from him, but he flexed his muscles to prevent her from falling through his arms. They fell with a tumble of limbs and a bone-jarring thud. He twisted to keep her from landing on the stone, jarred his shoulder, then rolled so that he lay on the ground and she lay above him.

She was not soft in his arms, as some women could be. She was spare. And strong—damn, she was strong. Pushing hard at him, she sprang to her feet. By all that was holy, the Flower was gorgeous, standing above him and blazing like all of hell's fury.

"*Stupide!* I knew where I was landing. Then you were *there*. Just there, where I did not want you." She reached down, her small, gloved hands fisting into his coat. "*Idiote!*"

"Oi! Who's there!" The shout was masculine and above them. A head poked out of a window.

Instinct seized him. He rolled to his feet and shoved her against the front door of the town house. The door was set into the wall so there was some protection from the view above, but not enough, confound it. Not enough.

"I woke him." The Flower's voice was muffled against his chest, but he still heard the fear lurking beneath the velvet tones. "I was not as quiet as I should be."

"Did you get what you needed?" He breathed the words

into her ear. Her body warmed his skin as he pressed against her. Each curve seemed to fit perfectly against his angles.

"No. The room was empty." Not only fear in her voice now. Despair lurked there as well so that her words quavered.

Above them, the window slid closed.

"We should leave," he whispered.

She seemed frozen. Shock, fear, *something* held her in place, tightening her muscles so she was motionless in his arms. When she didn't exhibit any intent to move, he took her hand and pulled her away from the building. Setting their pace at a quick jog, he was pleased when she matched him without question. He wasn't accustomed to the Flower being so biddable.

"What were you looking for?" He waited to ask the question until they turned the corner onto another street.

She only shook her head as an answer, lips pressed together.

"Very well. I won't inquire further." He grabbed her arm, swung her around to face him. "Whatever it is, you can trust me to help you."

Her eyes were huge in the pale light of the coming dawn and seemed dark against her skin. Her chin trembled, then firmed. She wasn't going to cry—he knew that much of her— but she was troubled. The unusual vulnerability tugged at some guarded place in his heart. He gathered her in, trying as best he could to protect her. It would not fix whatever was wrong, but that did not stop his need to try.

"What I wanted was there but is gone now." Her words were like the sun that would soon break over the horizon. Quiet, but significant. "The room was empty." Her hands clutched at his arms, fingers working against the muscle.

Did she know how much information those quick, clever fingers could impart?

"What will happen now?" He didn't even know what he was asking, or what was supposed to be in the room, but despair echoed in her ragged breath and the tightening of her dancer's body.

"I don't know. I had planned—" She stopped. "I must go home and rethink."

Breaking away, the Flower began sprinting down the street. Her footsteps were light on the walkway, despite the exhausting pace she set herself. Even infused with such utter terror that each muscle and sinew was tight and tense, she still moved with fluid grace.

Some primitive, animalistic part of him craved to follow her.

He should not. The gentleman inside refused to let his feet move. He didn't understand the Flower, couldn't untangle the secrets of her heart and mind, and whatever made her so afraid was not something she was ready to share.

Turning away, he hunched his shoulders against the fact that she didn't want to let him in. Very well. He could respect her need to be private. She was a spy, after all, and he a gentleman.

Except he couldn't help her if she wouldn't let him.

Dash it all.

He spun around and studied the black coat and narrow shoulders beneath it as she fled. Her feet flew over the walkway, arms pumping with a desperation that left him sick in his gut.

To hell with being a gentleman.

Chapter Twenty-Six

"Mademoiselle!"

It was no easy task to catch up to the Flower. She was quick, but his legs were longer.

Gripping her arm to stop her and bring her around to face him, he caught a glimpse of a white face and large eyes before her fist connected with his jaw. Stars exploded behind his eyes as pain lanced through his chin and face.

"By all the saints!" He doubled over, as much to avoid her fist a second time as to recover.

"Do not touch me."

He straightened, quick as a whip snapping, to stare at her. "You sound afraid." He hated it. Anger he could understand, but the fear layering over her voice stabbed through him. Seeing it blocked the pain in his jaw, the throbbing of his lip.

"I am *not* afraid." She stepped back. She seemed very small, as though she'd closed in on herself. "Do not touch me," she repeated, more quietly now.

"I would never hurt you." He wanted to touch her again to prove it. His hand reached out, fingers spread to find some part of her.

"I know." She didn't flinch, didn't even tense, but some inner part of her withdrew more than her body did.

He let his hand fall away. If he touched her now, she might run again and never return to him. The thought clawed at his chest, so he took a step back himself and gave her the physical space she so clearly needed.

"What were you looking for in Manchester Square?" he asked.

She shook her head, the delicate features of her face grim.

"Tell me." Whatever it was, he wanted to remove the residual fright in her gaze. It was important, somehow, to discover if he could ease her pain.

"The servants in this area, they will soon be awake," she said, avoiding his question entirely. "It is nearly morning."

So it was. The eastern horizon was beginning to lighten from blue to yellow, so he could more easily see her lashes as they swept down to cover her gaze. He stepped toward the nearest building, into the shadowed doorway where he was masked by pillars and a small portico, and gestured for her to join him. She hesitated, then edged into the space.

"There's time before the sun rises." Now they were partly hidden from the world, he wanted to draw her in against him.

Her inhale was slow and bracing. Impossibly long lashes swept up, and though her eyes were dry when they met his, her chin quivered just the slightest bit.

"The girl," she whispered. "I found her."

He sucked in his own breath and stepped toward her. Gripped her upper arms. "That was Marchand's house?"

She shook her head, and a thick, curling lock of hair fell from beneath the confines of the cap she wore. "It is simply a place one of his agents uses. I have seen the agent come and go, and the room I searched held a prisoner recently, but they were both gone."

Beneath his fingers her arms were taut. He relaxed his hands and slid them down to cup her elbows. "The man that shouted out the window? Who was he?"

"Just a man, I think. A servant hired to keep watch on the empty house." She tilted her face toward his, almost in the same position a lady would request a kiss. "He was bumbling and loud, and he did not pursue us, so he is not a spy. I woke him, as I was careless in my search when I realized the house was empty of any spies—or the girl." Her voice broke, but still she did not weep.

"Who is she to you?" he asked quietly.

A long, weighty silence ensued. He gave her time to think, as it was clear that's what she was doing. If her brain had been made of gears and pulleys, he would have seen them moving.

"She is no one. An innocent girl."

Her face had lost all expression, and he could not tell from it whether she lied—but he did hear the hitch in her voice. Slowly rubbing her arms, Maximilian trying to calm her with long, slow strokes. He continued the movement, whispering, "We'll find her," even though he hadn't the slightest idea how.

"I know you cannot make such a promise, but I wish you could." Her sigh was as quiet as the breeze ruffling the curl spilling from beneath her cap. "I wish I had some assurance that all our efforts weren't in vain."

Beneath his hands, her muscles had gone lax. She raised her face again, and the brightening light beaming through the pillars gilded each delicately drawn feature. He felt her fear and uncertainty as though they were his own, as though they flowed from one to the other of them.

Standing on a street with clouds of gold and pink lighting the sky, Maximilian did something he'd never done before.

Kissed a lady to comfort her.

. . .

In but a moment, she could force him flat onto his back. He would fall hard, this large and gentle man. But she did not want him to stop. His lips were warm and firm, and they filled the cold place left by Anne's absence. She wanted to sigh with relief, cry and burrow into him, all in a single heartbeat. His lips pressed against hers, held, shifted to press again.

She could not say why she found it acceptable for this man to kiss her.

It simply was. *He* simply was.

She should step away. Run away. Plans must be made, and there were people she needed to speak with. Instead, she slid her arms around his waist and gripped the side seams of his coat. She wanted to hold onto something. To someone.

Knowing a spy had no right to this moment, she still chose to remain in his embrace. Heart aching for Anne, body aching for this man, she would stay just a moment longer. She needed him. *Maximilian.* He was not just the monsieur. They had moved beyond that. He was Maximilian to her now.

So when his mouth became a little persistent, when his tongue nudged at the seam of her lips, she parted them. Opened for him. He tasted of man, of mist. Of some mysterious thing that could only be Maximilian.

She sighed and let his body and mouth soothe all the sadness and need swirling in her.

Now, she was not so alone.

His tongue danced along hers. In turn, lightning bolts danced in her body. Her hands no longer gripped his jacket but slid up to his shoulders—the broad, broad shoulders that bore responsibility with such ease. She rose on her booted toes, pressing against him, wanting to be closer.

"Vivienne." The word was a whisper against her mouth.

It stopped her, checking her movements.

Vivienne was not her name.

She wanted him to say her name. Her *real* name.

The idea was terrifying. Utterly, completely, and deeply terrifying.

She stumbled backward, only to realize that the sun was over the horizon now. It was brilliant, kissing London's rooftops as Maximilian had kissed her.

But he did not know her, did he? The fault of that lay on her.

"Vivienne?" Hazel eyes were concerned, but also hot with desire, the gold bright among the green and brown. Awareness trilled down her spine, leaping across each vertebra.

"It is dawn," she said carefully.

He studied her face, gaze flicking over each feature one by one. His translator's mind would be deciphering her expression. She blanked her face. She did not want him to read everything. Some things a spy could not share.

"I must go," she said. "We should not be seen."

"I suppose not." His words were very careful. Measured.

"Good-bye, Maximilian." She had not said his name aloud before. It hung between them in the air. Meaningful, as the easing of her heartache had been meaningful, as the building of liquid warmth in her low belly had been meaningful.

"Good-bye, Vivienne."

Chapter Twenty-Seven

The training room was a comfort. The knives laid out on the table beside her were infinitely soothing. Each one appeared exactly like the next.

Except they were not the same. No two knives were perfectly identical, even if touted as being a matched pair. Each knife had its own personality. The center, the weight, the grip. And once you understood the knife, it did not change. The throw, if one was careful, would almost always be the same.

Maximilian, with his bright mind, would enjoy testing this theory.

She flattened her hand on the table, fanned her fingers apart. These fingers had gripped Maximilian's coat, held onto his shoulders.

Yet the hand belonged to a thief and a spy. She could not recall how many things she had stolen. Hundreds? Thousands? And what of the impact of those thefts? A few pounds as a girl, jewelry, a watch. Anything that could be sold for food. Now it was secrets and politics and strategies that could affect countries, all under the guise of mistress.

Maximilian knew this, and still he wanted her.

Or he knew most of it.

Picking up one of the knives, she tested the weight and found the center. Pinching the blade between thumb and index finger, she eyed the target at the long end of the room. It was the painted shape of a man on the wall and littered with splintered marks. Marchand. If she squinted, this painted target could look like Marchand—if she knew what he looked like.

Measuring the breath that had become uneven and calming the mind that had filled first with Maximilian and then with Marchand, she let the room, the target, the very air settle inside her. Then she threw. Straight and perfect and into the figure's heart, just as she demanded of herself.

"I envy your knife skills."

The words made her jump. "Jones?"

"You *are* in my home. Uninvited, so to speak." He stood just inside the room, leaning against the wall. Pushing away, he stepped forward. "I don't know why I ask every time you turn up, but why are you here, Vivienne?"

She shrugged, not entirely certain how to phrase it. She was uncertain and lost and alone, and yet she'd been none of those things with Maximilian a few hours ago as dawn broke over London. It had scraped her raw, that moment of intimacy.

"I wanted to be home."

He did not speak, but only watched her, handsome and very serious in his shirtsleeves. His brown hair was cropped close to his head, and she could see a bit of early-morning stubble on his chin.

"Do you remember?" She ran a finger over the hilt of a knife. Good craftsmanship, that hilt. "We made love once. It was my first time." Her only time. She turned to face him.

"I remember, Vivienne." His tone was dry, as if to say, *I*

would not forget such a thing. She'd thought perhaps he had, as it been many years ago.

"It was espionage, languages, training, politics. Day in. Day out. We were two lonely trainees." She walked toward him, thinking of those long, exhausting days and quiet nights.

"I remember," he said again. This time he smiled, just a little. Lines fanned out from brown eyes, reminding her they had once laughed together often.

She had kissed Jones, many ages ago, in this very room. They had made love in his bedchamber on the floor above. She was here now, with a strange heat in her body she did not understand and her heart needing something she could not name. It reminded her of that time. They had been two unschooled apprentices in the art of lovemaking. Though she had always thought she'd felt just short of whatever she was supposed to feel, she remembered that fleeting feeling of belonging, if only for a moment.

She wanted to feel that again. There had been no one since, and she did not want to be alone. Except she did not want Jones.

She wanted Maximilian.

Her head knew he was not available—her body and her heart, though, were confused.

She must remember she was a spy, and only another spy could understand this life of lies and secrets. Perhaps it was only here, with Jones, she could belong.

So she walked toward Jones, conscious of the tension in his shoulders, the odd light in his eyes. He was not turning her away, but he was not encouraging her. Somehow, she thought he knew what she needed. She set a hand on his arm and drew herself up on tiptoe. His mouth was cool and firm when she kissed him. It brought memories to the surface that she had not thought of in years.

But there was nothing there for her.

"I am sorry," she whispered, pulling back to look at him. "I thought perhaps—but no."

"You're not here to make love to me, Vivienne." Affection and understanding softened his face, making the line of his jaw not quite so hard. "I'm not stupid."

She sighed and laid her head on his shoulder. It was solid and strong, as was the arm that came about her, but there was no heat. Perhaps that was why, all those years ago, she'd chosen Jones to relieve her of her virginity. There was nothing between them but affection.

If they'd been normal in those younger days, not in the world of spies, they would have chosen others. But when one eats, breathes, and sleeps espionage, one misses the other parts of life.

"Who is he?" Jones asked, laying his cheek against her hair. "You would not be here, looking for me, if there was not someone else you wanted."

"Are you my conscience, Jones?" She could not stay there, wallowing in his support.

"I know you, that is all."

"He is no one."

Jones did not speak. The arm around her waist tightened so that he hugged her. A true, close hug. With his face buried in her neck.

"Love is not for us, Vivienne. Not in the normal sense."

"Then what do we do?" she whispered, and was horrified she wanted to cry.

"Seize the amorphous love that lasts for weeks or months. Because that is all we will ever know." He pressed a kiss to her forehead. "If you want him, Vivienne, take him. Do not look for a substitute."

"If I have no right to him? If the circumstances are such that I should not be with him at all?" Her sister was missing. Abducted. Anne was not dead, but until Vivienne found her, she was in danger, and after—there could never be love.

"Life is for the living, Vivienne. Sometimes, in the midst of battle, when we should think of nothing but survival, we find love. The time may be short and may last only a little while, but we have a right to take love where we can, or we will lose our humanity."

Yes, she understood that.

"It cannot last, though," Jones added. "Prepare to leave him."

Chapter Twenty-Eight

Prepare to leave him.

Sensible. Maximilian was not of her world, nor did he want to be. He had deliberately left her lying, cheating, secretive world of espionage.

Which was where she was just now.

She didn't know where to find Marchand, but she knew where to start. Someone must know something. A man did not work in the underbelly of London without being known. There were always rumors. Always hints. If one listened carefully in shadowed alleys, one could learn much.

She'd always known how to listen, so when a whisper joined a whisper and Mrs. Asher brought those whispers to her, Vivienne asked her questions and listened to the answers.

They brought her to the past.

Vivienne slid onto a stool in the Queen's Bathtub, a pub that looked and smelled as it had two decades ago. Behind her, patrons laughed and drank, barmaids threaded through tables carrying tankards and stews. The air was filled with noise and merriment and memories.

"Well, I never thought I'd see you again. Look just like yer ma." The barkeep clenched a homemade pipe between his teeth and grinned at her. "Ye look well enough, little girl."

In the old days, she might have set her elbows on the bar top and grinned up at the scraggly beard and black eyes above the pipe. But it was not the old days.

"Thought you'd gone and made your fortune on the stage—or on your back. One's the same as t'other." He shrugged, then swished a dirty rag around the inside of a tankard and set it down in front of her. "Can't say yer ma would like that."

"How I make my living is none of your concern, sir." She did not bother with the French accent.

"*Sir*, eh?" He chewed on the pipe a moment, as if yellowed teeth clicking on wood assisted in reaching a decision. "Well, a body does what a body must. The good Lord knows I've done my fair share o' things me ma wouldn't like."

"Aye." She watched him carefully, the rumors she had heard among fog and filth swirling in her mind. "Such as consort with French spies."

"Well, now. Seems you know a bit more about my business than most." Cocking his head, he studied her cautiously over the scarred expanse of bar top. He ignored a young girl who passed behind him, tray full of bread and tankards. "Want a drink?"

"Ale, if you would, please."

"'If you would' and 'sir' and 'consort.'" He muttered the words as he poured pale-gold liquid into the tankard. "Seems you've found some education."

"A bit."

As she waited for him to set the drink before her, she decided she did not feel eight years old again. Nor did she feel French or English, but a strange amalgam of all of them. She belonged nowhere. Not in the drawing room, not on the stage, not in the rookeries.

The ale was bitter in that lovely way good ale had. Better than the French brandy Henri insisted she sip.

"Why are you here, little girl?" the barkeep asked. He'd yet to say her name. She'd yet to say his. Sometimes, in places such as this with patrons such as these, it was best.

"I am looking for the Vulture." She sipped again and watched the barkeep's eyes become secretive.

"Well now. That's not a man to tangle with." He lowered his voice and leaned against the bar. "I can't say that I know how to find 'im, but I know how you can put it about you want to be found."

That was the last thing she wanted. "No, thank you. I only want to know where he is."

"That I can't help with." The barkeep rubbed at the disheveled gray hairs scattered across his chin, then scratched a moment while he eyed her speculatively. "What do you want with him?"

"Business, that is all."

"You wouldn't be interrupting *my* business, would you?"

"No." In truth, she was not certain what business the barkeep was involved in. It could be anything: smuggling, gambling, prostitution, opium. Worse. But she had prodded too much, perhaps, and decided to step back. "A body does what a body must."

"So a body does." He grinned, seeming to exemplify the bustle and humor of this humorless life.

"I should leave soon." But nostalgia was a powerful emotion. She leaned back a little, angled her head up at the barkeep, and smiled the smile that had felled many a peer. "How goes it all, then?"

"Fair to middling, little girl." He picked up his rag again and rocked back on his heels. "Me wife is expecting our fifth little 'un, an' she's hopin' for a boy, but my girls will all make good wives someday. How goes it all wit' you, then?"

"Fair to middling." She said, falling into the patter of her youth. Then, with a gulp of ale to fortify her, she let her heart open to the memories she sought to forget. Memories brought pain, but they could bring happiness. "I miss me ma."

"Aye. And yer sister?"

Her smile dimmed, she knew. "Not as good."

"Eh? That's a shame." The rag moved in aimless circles on the bar top as the man polished dirt with more dirt. "She was a right sweet thing as a girl."

"The Vulture has taken her. I'm trying to persuade him to return her." It was a calculated risk to tell even this much of the truth, but still a risk. Yet the barkeep understood the value of little girls.

The barkeep's hand stilled. "I see." He looked her square in the eyes. "The girl doesn't want that life?"

"No."

He nodded once, decisive. "Check back in a few days. I might hear something."

"Thank you." Gratitude could be all encompassing. "She's all I have."

"No man to watch out for you, then?"

Was there? Henri? No, though there were others. Jones. Maximilian.

Maximilian.

"There is someone." Was that her speaking? Had she said that aloud? Maximilian was not hers. He did not watch out for her.

Yet, he did. He climbed up walls, tripped over ambassadors, broke her fall. All of these things he did to keep her safe, even though she did not need safekeeping. That, by itself, seemed like a small miracle.

"Good." He nodded again, then picked up his rag to start the polishing process again. "Does he treat you well? Your mother would want me to ask."

The barkeep did not look at her now, but he did not need to. The question was there, between them, because they both knew the past.

"Yes." Something went soft inside her as she thought of Maximilian. Men were sometimes easily understood, and sometimes they were difficult. Maximilian was a little of each, but each part of him attracted her. Each part of him was good.

"Keep him, then," the barkeep said.

...

"Are you certain, Miss Vivienne?" Mrs. Asher's thick arms were folded over her equally thick belly.

"Yes. I am." Vivienne laid a hand over one of Mrs. Asher's. "I will be fine alone."

Except she would not be alone. She had made up her mind on that subject somewhere between the rookeries and the West End.

"I don't like it. Thomas is off visiting his ma in Somerset. I'm going to see me sister—"

"I am quite capable of caring for myself. Henri is coming midmorning tomorrow"—which gave her at least sixteen hours—"and I'm well trained."

"Still. I don't like it." Mrs. Asher's frown was ferocious, but Vivienne knew the battle was won as Mrs. Asher reached for her valise. "There are neighbors on either side if you're in trouble. Jones and Angel as well—"

"I know, and I promise to lock the doors and windows." She rose to her toes to kiss Mrs. Asher's cheek and deliver the coup de grâce. "Your sister and her brood—enjoy them. Kiss the little ones for me."

Mrs. Asher's eyes lit up, as Vivienne had known they would. "The girls are four and five years old now, and the little boy nearly two. It'll be a joy."

And so Mrs. Asher bustled out of the house with her feet light and her mind on babies.

This suited Vivienne. She had a note to deliver. It would be crude writing because she could do little more, but Maximilian would receive it.

She hoped he would come.

...

Maximilian looked down at the small scrap of paper in his hand.

COME TO ME. MIDNIGHT.
V

The letters were printed in a square, simple shape. The lines were neatly parallel and perfectly straight. The curves were measured out cautiously, so they were the correct height and width. Great care had been taken in each letter, though they lacked the tutored precision of one schooled by numerous governesses.

The Flower must have written it herself.

He couldn't say why the idea made him grin happily, but there it was.

Tucking the note into his pocket, his fingers brushed against his watch. He pulled it out and tilted it toward the nearest lighted window on her street to better read the time. Two minutes to midnight. Too early.

Waiting on the front step, Maximilian studied the knocker on the Flower's front door. It was plain and similar to his own. He'd never thought on it before, but it seemed an opera dancer should have a prettier, more ornate knocker.

He checked the time again. Midnight. Perfect.

The utilitarian knocker was cool in his fingers and created

a satisfyingly sharp rap on the wood. Frowning when the door remained firmly closed, Maximilian checked the time again. She expected him at midnight, and he was now a minute late. He waited, then knocked again. Still no one came.

Maximilian stepped back and looked up at the windows of the town house. Muted light flickered on the second floor. A single candle, he judged.

Well, *someone* was home.

Fingers curled around the handle, Maximilian set his thumb on the latch and pressed. Unlocked. That was fortuitous. The hall was dark aside from a single wall sconce. The rooms on either side were dark as well. Not a sound was audible in the darkness. Nerves skittered along the back of his neck as the door slid closed behind him. Where were the housekeeper and the footman? The Flower?

Dash it all, after deliberately practicing his marksmanship, he had failed to bring his pistol. Clearly, he had learned nothing after weeks of renewed associations with spies. At the very least, he could have brought a knife.

A thud sounded above stairs. It seemed ominously like a limp body hitting the floor. He braced himself for attack, scanning the entryway. He didn't much care for thuds in dark houses. Which meant he had to *do* something about it. The Flower could be injured. Or worse.

Boxing at Gentleman Jackson's might prove a boon, as he was weaponless beyond his fists.

Hmm. Perhaps not entirely without defenses. An umbrella handle poked out of the stand near the door. Polished wood met his palm as he pulled it from the stand. Dim light masked the color, but he could see three rows of lacy ruffles marching across the expanse of fabric.

Brilliant.

He was confronting an unknown evil with a frilly parasol. Did one hold it like a sword or a cricket bat? A bat seemed the most threatening.

Well, there was nothing for it. He was going up.

He took the steps two at a time, up one flight to the next level, parasol at the ready. It was dark and silent as the floor below, except for a thin line of light beneath a single door. He heard footsteps in that room. Not loud, not running. Just footsteps.

His uneasiness faded a bit. There was no screaming. No weeping. Maybe no one was in trouble after all. Still, he should check—and the Flower *had* asked for him to come.

Very carefully, very quietly, he pushed open the door and peered into the room. He realized he was holding his breath and expecting a French spy to jump out at him. No one did. Instead, there was only the Flower.

In all her naked glory.

His mouth went dry. Good Lord, she was enough to make a man weep with gratitude that woman was created. Dimly, he noticed the hip bath beside her, the pile of black clothing heaped on the floor. A single candle flickered on a nearby table. Beyond that his brain noted rose and gold decor, a bed of massive proportions, tables and chairs and other furniture.

He could only focus on her body as she reached for the thin linen towel draped over a chair back. Candlelight gilded the skin of her buttocks, the shift of her shoulder blades as she moved. He had never noticed shoulder blades before, but the play of skin over bone could fascinate a man.

Fabric billowed as she snapped open the linen and began to dry herself. She was a study of efficiency. Neck, breasts, waist, legs, all were dried with competent movements—and then the linen fell to the floor as she spun around to face him.

His knees buckled, and he dropped the parasol in favor of gripping the doorframe. She was gorgeous. Exquisite. A fantasy of skin and candlelight and contours. He supposed he was accustomed to women with softness about them.

Womanly softness.

Not the Flower. There was a dancer's strength there, in every fiber. In every sinew.

He should look away. A gentleman would back out of the room and give her privacy. His feet didn't move. He could only look and dream of touching. She was so slim. Her thighs and calves were defined in the most elegant of curves. She was narrow hipped, with a dip above to show her waist. Then her breasts. On that small frame they were magnificent, though not large by other standards. Pink tipped, with nipples pebbled and begging to be kissed.

Dear God, he wanted her. The need to touch that glorious body crashed through him, a thousand waves beating against the shore.

"Monsieur." She had borne his perusal without a word, but her skin flushed and her eyes were bright. She licked her lips, and his breath hitched. "Maximilian. We are alone. No one will be in the house but you until the morning."

He didn't understand what she was saying. His ears heard her words, but his brain had disengaged.

Then he *did* understand.

"Are you certain?" Was that rasp the sound of his voice?

She nodded, her gaze never leaving his.

"Thank all the gods."

Her laugh bounced around the room as she held out her hand to him. Suddenly, he didn't care a whit about her protector.

It seemed to him the Flower belonged to no one but herself.

Crossing the floor, accepting her outstretched fingers. He brought them to his mouth, pressed his lips against her knuckle. Then another. He turned her hand over and spread her fingers wide to reveal her palm. It was smooth and soft and warm from her bath. He pressed a kiss to the center, then on her wrist. He felt her pulse jump against his lips, and his own pulse beat out a quick rhythm in return.

He looked into her face and saw her smile had dimmed. Perhaps she'd expected something else from him, given she was naked, but kissing those lovely hands was the only thing he could think to do. Pink lips parted on the lightest intake of air. The breasts so wonderfully displayed for his view rose slightly. Her eyes searched his face, and he saw a question there.

He had not expected hesitancy from this siren.

"Is this how it starts, then?" she asked. She sounded wary now. "I only thought it would be—faster?"

"I don't understand." He looked down at her hand again as her fingers curled into a loose fist.

"I have only done this once before." Her voice was low. Hesitant. "It has been some years. I don't know the movements—the positions."

Shock rippled through him. "What of your protector? Wycomb?"

"It is a ruse." Dismissing both the man and the lie, she shook her head. "I will not say more."

She was not a virgin, but she was as close as possible. Disquiet settled in his stomach, twisting it into tight knots. What if he hurt her? The hands that itched to touch the flesh bared to him became damp with nerves.

"The first time—" He broke off, unsure of what he'd even intended to say.

"Just a boy I knew." She spoke quickly, not looking at him now. "Others have wanted to be with me, but they do not pursue with any seriousness. Because of Henri."

The nerves beneath her skin practically hummed, but she didn't cover her body. That spoke of a confidence he admired. Her voice held the lightest touch of breathlessness—and he had put it there, he thought satisfactorily.

"A ruse." He repeated her words with whatever air he could summon from his own breathless lungs. He was missing a vital piece of information of her relationship with the man. He knew it. Some bit of the code had not fallen into place. Whatever it was, he would ask later. Just now, a naked woman stood before him—but not any woman. The Flower. A spy, it was true, but for now, he could only see the woman before him.

Vivienne.

"There has been no man." She shrugged, delicate shoulders moving up, then down, so that her breasts moved as well. He fought the urge to touch them. To touch all of her. Her lashes rose, and dark, dark eyes met his. His brain told him it was her pupils, dilated in the dim light—his body knew it was desire reflected in her gaze.

"No other man," she whispered. "Until you."

Chapter Twenty-Nine

There was no one else she had ever wanted. Not like this. Something had built in her as he'd looked at her, still damp from her bath. His eyes and their bursts of gold had followed all the lines of her, touching her and warming her as his hands would do if he'd been closer.

And now, after so much *looking*, parts of her ached that she had not known could ache.

"Your clothes," she said. Perhaps he had forgotten he wore his clothing.

His cravat would go first. And so it did, as she untied it and dropped the linen to the floor a moment later. The buttons of his jacket were next. Spreading his coat wide, she set her hands against the waistcoat beneath. His heartbeat fluttered against her palm. Aside from that fast rhythm, he seemed very still beneath her hands.

"Let me." His voice was soft, with a rasp that shivered through her. "You will undo me otherwise."

She smiled and stepped back. His eyes did not leave hers as he began to disrobe, as if he wanted to see each of her thoughts as he bared himself for her.

He was very broad in the shoulders. This was not by the design of his tailor. She saw now that his coat and waistcoat and shirt were removed. Hair was sprinkled here and there across his chest. She wanted to touch him, to feel the light hair beneath her fingertips, to listen to his heartbeat.

He was also narrow in the waist and muscular in the thigh. She saw this as his boots were removed, as his trousers joined the mountain of garments on the floor. And there, his manhood was ready. Very ready. As was she. This, he would read on her face. He would hear it, if she spoke, but she found her throat dry, her voice absent.

Her gaze dropped to his mouth, to the lips that kissed her with need. She wanted it on her, wanted to taste him without fear of discovery. She reached up and set a thumb over his lips. They were full and sculpted and pressed a small, openmouthed kiss to her thumb.

She had no breath. No air at all. Her stomach muscles fluttered and sent liquid waves to the very center of her.

"Maximilian." She had located her voice but could still scarcely speak. "Kiss me. Please."

His eyes went very dark and very focused. He cupped her face, thumbs feathering light touches across her cheekbones. He bent his head, capturing her mouth with a dedicated concentration that could rob a woman of strength.

It robbed *her* of strength so that her body quivered. Again, as he shifted the angle of the kiss. And again, as he delved deep, tongue seeking tongue. His lips were firm and they were strong and gave her the taste of him she craved. He pressed a kiss to the underside of her jaw, then trailed his lips down her neck to press another kiss on her collarbone. Then another. More, here, there, on the curve of her shoulder, again just below her ear.

He made love with his mouth as she'd hoped he would,

so that she was hollowed out and refilled with nothing but urgent heat.

She lifted her chin so that he could access her throat and felt the brush of her own hair against her buttocks. Her hands fluttered over his shoulders, skimmed up his neck to tangle in the hair there. She tugged, not painfully, but enough that he would understand her need for him.

"Do not go slow, Maximilian. Later there will be time for leisure." She pressed her lips against his, and the low hum in her blood quickened. "Not now."

She leaned her body into his. His manhood pressed against her belly, hot and hard. Her breasts brushed the hair on his chest she had wanted to feel, sensitizing her nipples so they rose up.

He groaned quietly, and his hands grazed her collarbone, skimmed over her shoulders, arms, and to her hips—then around so he cupped the round globes of her buttocks, pulling her closer to him. Harder.

"Maximilian." She breathed the word into the space between them and wrapped her legs around his waist, her mouth moving desperately over his. She could feel him pressed against the center of her. She was wet there, and it seemed he would slip right inside her.

He did not, instead carrying her to the bed where the silk coverlet was cool against her heated skin. He laid her down gently, despite the tensed muscles in his arms, and then stood back, *looking* at her again. His eyes moved first to her toes, skimming along her body. They rested on her thighs, then her hips. Darkened as he considered her breasts. Finally, he focused on her face with such intensity she felt his passion burn beneath her skin.

"Come, Maximilian." She reached for him—the man she had chosen.

He moved over her, propping himself up so that he did

not crush her. Always thoughtful, was Maximilian.

His body was long and hard, with muscles not of a trained spy, but of a man who was too disciplined to become soft. She ran her hands over the muscles of his arms as he raised himself up. Over the evidence of discipline he carried with him.

"Are you certain?" He murmured the words into her ear. Desire lowered his voice to a husky, nearly inaudible level.

The sound of his voice, the meaning there, sent her back arching so her breasts pressed against his chest. Her legs came around him, pulling him closer. He was there, at the entrance of her body. At that most intimate place. She closed her eyes, breathed in the scent of Maximilian. Reveled in his strength, his gentleness.

"Yes," she breathed.

He kissed the soft spot beneath her ear and made her sigh. She opened for him, and he slid inside her.

They both stilled. Perhaps time had slowed. Perhaps the earth was motionless on its axis. Vivienne could only revel in the feel of his arms around her, of his strength, of the heat that filled her.

"Vivienne," he whispered against her neck, holding himself motionless. "It seems I have been waiting a long time for you. I didn't realize how long until now."

Why this made her want to cry, she did not know. Blinking back tears, she tightened her arms around him.

He moved within her, shifting, thrusting, but still gently. Always with care and deliberation, using as much science and study as he used for life. He did not thrust wildly, but waited for her reactions, each contraction of muscle and sigh on the air. He saw every movement of her body, every shift in her expression.

He set his lips against hers, inhaled, drawing in a breath that seemed to bring with it her very essence.

Then he drove her to the edge and over.

Chapter Thirty

"Do you know, Vivienne, your face has the most stunning shape. The cheekbones, the widow's peak." It was all there for him to see now, as they lay side by side in her bed. "Your face drove me to madness when it would appear in my study without warning."

"I did not intend for such a thing." Her lips curved up. They were plump and red from his kisses—*his* kisses. Quite satisfactory, when he thought about it.

"You did, nonetheless." He propped himself up so he could look down at her. "Did I drive you to madness?"

She lay on her side, hands tucked beneath her cheek. One shoulder curved inward, and her folded arm lay pressed against her breasts. He supposed it might have been modest of another woman, but the Flower's breasts seemed to be playing hide-and-seek with him.

"Not in the same way, I think." Her eyes seemed to laugh at him. "You provoked me with your scowls and frowns and precise folding of paper."

"My what?"

"Precise folding of paper," she repeated, sitting up. The sheet fell away, exposing her to his view, though she didn't seem to notice.

He nearly swallowed his tongue. She was utterly exquisite, with her hair tumbling around her face and body and—well. His eyes crossed. But his ears functioned properly enough, as he heard her say, "Each corner, perfectly aligned to the other. Every crease, so flat the fold disappeared. This drove me mad. I do not have time for such precision, but I am glad you have it."

"Why?"

"Because." Her eyes were serious, though she still smiled at him. "This precision. You make love this way. No detail of my person is missed."

He had no idea why, but her words sounded much more important than making love. He shied away from that thought and put their conversation back in the realm of the physical.

"The details of your person require proper examination." Amazingly, though he should have been sated, he wanted to have her again. His body stirred to life, hardening. The need for her began to build, stronger this time. "Perhaps I missed some bit of code. We should try again, just to be sure."

"Perhaps we should." She tilted her head, smiled at him. "Only you do not break codes any longer. It is always someone else I must take my codes to."

"Yes." He fingered a soft curl curving around her shoulder and grinned. "I'm busy with all sorts of translations—none of which I can think of at the moment."

"Why do you not work for the government any longer?" She leaned forward, taking his hand and twining her fingers lightly with his. The touch was so much less than their contact only a short while before, but it touched more of him than fingers. She was making him soft inside, like pudding. Or custard. He didn't want to think of code breaking for the government. All of that wild, glorious hair spilled over her body.

She was there—with him.

Waiting for his answer, she shifted so that she lay across his chest, face pillowed on her hands and looked up at him. Her black eyes held the entire world just then, with all the joy and sorrow that could be in it.

"After Waterloo I knew I would retire as soon as was practical. I had only wanted to live my own life in the first place, not be pressed into a world of half-truths after university." He could not help but touch her cheek, running a finger across the smooth skin. "I believe in duty to my country and possessed a useful skill, so they pressed harder until I agreed."

"This I understand," she murmured. "Very much. Though if you had not agreed, we would not have met and would not be here now, like this."

"How did you become a spy, Vivienne? Were you pressed into it?" Maximilian wanted to know more of her, everything before she delivered her first code to him. "What of your family?"

"A fever took them when I was a girl. I was recruited and trained not long after." A shadow passed over her face, quickly enough he might have imagined it. "Eventually, I became a spy. Why was it so long before we became lovers, do you suppose?"

"I don't know." His brain wasn't entirely functioning. "The work, I suppose. You were off doing the secret things you do, and I was—"

"Hunched over your desk, like so." She laughed, pushing up to a sitting position and bending forward, her hair slipping and sliding over her shoulders and breasts. "Then you scowled, like so."

Dear God, please tell him he didn't look like that.

The ferocious frown seemed ridiculous on her, particularly

when she broke into a laugh as bright as the candlelight glowing over her skin.

His hand moved of its own accord, reaching for her. He skimmed a finger down her arm, not quite sure what he had done in his past to deserve such a beautiful woman in his bed. Or, rather, to be in her bed, if he were to be accurate.

"I feel as though I didn't see you for all those years." Perhaps they had not been *meant* to see each other before, he thought. Which was a fatalistic idea utterly without basis in logic.

"It does not matter if we did not see each other then." Her dark eyes had sobered. They were pretty with that seriousness in them. "We are here now."

She rose up beside him, kneeling on the bed. Her leg bumped against his, her skin soft and silky. He could see all of her this way. Every shadow and valley and curve—

She set a hand on his chest, fingers warm and soft. His blood pumped fast, and he realized her hand was over his heart. She would feel every feverish beat.

Her lips curved up in a knowing smile. "Ah, Maximilian. *Oui.*" She leaned over and set her mouth to his, brushed her lips against his. She tasted of sin and secrets, and it was heady.

She was simply too much for him.

It wasn't just her mouth. It was her curling hair, sliding across his shoulders and face. Her breasts, pressing against his chest. The sweetness of her skin. The slow, genuine smile that crossed her face. The quick and clever fingers tangling with his.

"Maximilian." The word sighed out of her.

He drew her down beside him so she was tucked against his side. He turned to face her, traced a finger over her lips. He only wanted to kiss her. To bring her taste and scent and soul into him. A ridiculous notion, but it was what went through his head.

"May I stay?" he murmured. "May I stay with you?"

She looked up at him, her brows drawing together, then at the small clock on the mantel. She was thinking quickly. He could all but see her mind moving behind her secretive eyes.

"Yes. Until dawn."

...

Vivienne stretched, luxuriating in the feel of limber muscles. She had not performed her exercises last night, yet she felt quite flexible this morning.

Making love was as good as exercise, then. Or, at least, making love with Maximilian.

She was tucked against him, back to chest, as he had pulled her in after asking to stay. The hair on his chest tickled her back. It was nice and strange, all at once. His hand was resting on her hip, warm and heavy. And though it mattered that she'd felt his heart bump against her palm like a wild thing trying to get free, and that hers had ached as she'd felt the rhythm, it would not matter forever.

She could not let those things matter.

There was Anne. Always Anne. Vivienne had taken her fleeting, momentary happiness with Maximilian, as Jones had said. It was over now, and though Anne had not left Vivienne's mind, Maximilian must be put from it.

She must say good-bye to Maximilian, then take today for what it was. Dawn could not be far away, and Henri would arrive not long after.

She opened her eyes—and saw the bright light of the midmorning sun.

"*Merde!*" Leaping from the bed, she scurried to the basin. Cupping her hands, she splashed the water over her face. It was icy, but useful. "*Merde!* It is morning, Maximilian!" Her teeth would chatter in a moment.

"Hmm?" He sounded lazy and sleepy. Very un-Maximilian.

"Henri will be here soon. He always arrives at ten o'clock." Henri could not find Maximilian in her bed. If he did—well, she did not know, but one of them would pay. She in blood, Maximilian in some other commodity. Money, reputation.

Perhaps blood. It was possible.

What had she been thinking? It was foolish to take a lover. However much she wanted Maximilian, it was foolish and there might be consequences.

Vivienne turned to look at him, thinking to hurry him along. He nearly made her smile. He was sitting up, his hair mussed, eyes bleary. It was very endearing.

She did not have time for endearing.

"You must go."

His clothes were piled on the floor where he had shed them. She gathered them up and was conscious of Maximilian watching her every movement. He was quite focused on her body. His mouth might not be speaking, but his eyes told her clearly enough what he thought. Had he not had enough of her?

"Hurry!" She straightened, his clothes clutched to her chest.

He only stared at her. Perhaps not all of his very large brain worked this early in the morning.

"Your clothes." She dumped them on his lap—and the part of him that clearly *did* work this early in the morning—in a heap of wrinkled fabric. "You must leave. Before Henri arrives."

"If he's not your protector, then who—" His voice sounded like carriage wheels on gravel.

"It is a ruse, yes." She spun away, searching for a dressing gown. She could not meet Henri wearing nothing. He expected her to be well-groomed. "Still, I cannot have a man in my bed."

"I don't understand." He swung his legs over the edge of the bed to slide them into his trousers.

"It is quite complicated."

"I agree." His tone was very dry. "I feel as though I'm going to be robbed of an answer, which is worse than being tossed out on my ear."

"You are not tossed out on your ear. You can—"

"Vivienne!" The call came from below them. It wasn't angry, it was simply loud. "There is no one to answer the door."

She froze. A strange sort of horror gripped her. Henri.

"Go." Panic could clutch at one's lungs so that there was no air to breathe, but it did not freeze the body. She stumbled to the dressing table and its glass to twist her hair up and pin it.

In the glass, Maximilian's reflection put on its boots. The reflection did not bother with a shirt, but grabbed it, the coat, and cravat and tucked all of them under its arm. She turned, hands full of pins, to look at the real Maximilian. This was not how she wanted the night to end. The need to weep tugged at her heart, but her mind knew it was weak—perhaps not weak, only foolish.

Jabbing a pin into the pile of hair atop her head, she said, "Stay here. Once Henri is in my boudoir, you may leave through the other door." Two more pins. Perhaps one. It would not be perfect, but perhaps would appear artfully *en déshabillé*. "Do not come into the adjoining room. Please."

"How do I get out?" He bit off the words, the short and angry sounds arrowing into the air between them.

There were footsteps in the hall. For one breathless moment, Vivienne thought Henri might enter her bedroom, but he had never done so before, and he did not today.

"Do not be angry, Maximilian. I cannot change what is." Stepping forward, she set her lips against his. "Not just now."

"I know." Mouth strong and hot, he seemed hungry for her. The hand that snaked around her waist held her firmly, yet gently.

One more kiss, she thought.

"Go." Then she turned away from this man who had touched her so deeply. This man who saw her so clearly. His arm fell away. She could not look into his eyes. If she did, she would forget herself.

She pushed open the door to the sitting room—the boudoir, as Henri called it—and deliberately angled the door so Maximilian could not be seen behind her.

"Bonjour, Henri." She stepped through and closed the door. Carefully. Very, very carefully.

"Where are the staff?" he asked.

"Both are on their day off, the others have not yet arrived. I do not mind." She shrugged, making sure the movement was French. Where was Maximilian now? In the hall? "It is nice to have an evening alone."

Henri did not speak. He took a seat in the armchair closest to the fire. It was his usual place, but with no one to light the fire, the room was chilled. His eyes were on her. Just as chilled.

What did he see?

She pulled her wrap higher. It was one she usually wore for him, but she always had stays and chemise beneath. Just now, she was nude. There was nothing between her and discovery but thin silk.

"What is the assignment today?" She walked to the chaise, pleased her legs were steady and her voice calm. Lowering herself to the cushioned seat, she sent her best smile—the one she practiced for the dandies of the *ton* who visited backstage.

Henri watched her steadily. Would he notice she did not have clothing beneath the wrapper? Yes. He would notice everything. She would use this, then. If he was distracted by her body, he would not notice her discomfort. Diversion was the simplest of tactics if one knew one's opponent's weak point.

She slid her legs out along the chaise. Slowly. They were covered, but the thin silk clung to her shape. "Am I not to be active this night?" It was difficult not to grit her teeth. Her legs were still warm where they had tangled with Maximilian's.

Henri did not look at her face when he spoke, but at her legs. She saw the hunger there, the lust. "I have an assignment for you."

"Yes?" It was not difficult to position her body to its best advantage. A shift of her hips, the arch of her back. Her stomach roiled and her mind screamed in protest of such machinations, but she smiled at him as though he were all that was important. She must not let him suspect she had been with Maximilian. But Maximilian's scent was still on her skin, creating a tear in her heart as she posed for Henri. This tear became a chasm, dark and very deep, that nearly swallowed her whole.

"There's a dinner party tonight. A particular gentleman attending is leaving for Brussels. He's been secretive about his reasons." Henri's gaze flicked toward hers, then back again to linger on her breasts. "If you can't find out what he's planning at the party, then I expect you to search his house."

"Of course." She had performed such assignments before. Different circumstances, different diplomats, different parties. But she had done this before. Her apprehension abated.

"Michel Lessard is your second assignment."

Her heart skipped, a hard jolt followed by frantic beating. She could not speak beyond it, but only watched him, waiting.

"The Vulture is making plans. The underground is full of reports. We need to know what is happening." Henri looked pointedly at the empty fireplace, waving his hand toward it. "Do not offer both your servants a day off at the same time,

Vivienne. It is not acceptable."

"My apologies, Henri." It did seem cold in the boudoir. Her bones, even, were chilled. "What of Lessard? Of Marchand?"

He looked to her face again, his gaze arrested. Her skin prickled with unease. Perhaps one's face changed after making love. Perhaps her hair was too untidy, her cheeks flushed. He might read these signs and *know*.

"You are looking lovely this morning, Vivienne." Softly, he spoke, yet with no hint of admiration. Only a chilling lust.

"*Merci.*"

"I am the envy of many a man in London, though I have not earned such envy."

Acknowledgment required only a nod. She could not manage more. Did he suppose he *could* earn such envy? He could not. She *would* not.

"There are many who want the dancer and woman I have cultivated," he continued. "Others who would want the spy I have trained."

"Yes." So many undercurrents. So many things unsaid.

"Lessard would be one such man. He has an affection for beautiful women."

"You believe he would have such an affection for me."

"Perhaps." He crossed his legs. It was not comfort or ease that changed his position. It was command. "Approach Lessard. How you do so is up to you, but he must be turned. He'll be difficult. He's been with Marchand for a long time, but he is known for being first a businessman and second, his own master."

"What shall I offer in return?" she asked.

"Whatever he asks for, Vivienne. Except information."

Fear ran the length of her spine. Lessard would know the Vulture held Anne. If she went to Lessard to turn him as Henri demanded, it would not be what the Vulture expected of her—they would suspect a trap. A ruse. They would expect her to arrive, ready to accept the Vulture's commands. If she asked for something else, it would be Anne who paid the price.

For Henri, she must turn Lessard against Marchand.

For herself, she must befriend Lessard.

The path she walked was thin as one of her own knives, and as sharp.

It was good she was skilled with a knife.

Chapter Thirty-One

Maximilian couldn't work. The words were only random letters on paper.

She'd done this to him.

For years, he'd had the comfort of letters and numbers and the statistical combination of codes, even when he'd worked for the government. Letters on paper were like musical notes to a composer. Except now Maximilian couldn't hear the music. He hadn't been able to hear it all day and into the evening.

"Sir." Daggett crept into the room, careful as a mouse waiting to be pounced upon. Apparently his assistant had developed an instinctive sense for his employer's black mood.

"What?" Maximilian tossed his quill across the desktop. He wasn't going to complete a single task at this rate. The words were crisp on the page but blurred in his mind.

The ever-present ledger hung loosely in Daggett's hand. "The Russian Embassy has sent a messenger asking for the—"

"I haven't finished it yet." He'd barely started the

translation. A headache was brewing behind his eyes. He should be feeling good after his night with Vivienne. She'd been amazing and gorgeous and—well. He didn't want Daggett to notice what Vivienne did to him. But now he was left worrying about her. Did her "protector," Wycomb, suspect Maximilian had been there?

He wished he understood that relationship. Father? Uncle? Friend? God's toes, he was probably a spy—and if so, it grated that she hadn't trusted him with that information.

Whoever he was, Maximilian hated him. Whatever the ruse, Wycomb could see the Flower whenever he chose. He could enjoy her rare humor. Listen to that sultry voice. More, he did not have to hide, to pretend. Whatever else he was to her, the Flower belonged to him in some way.

Breathing deep, Maximilian tried to turn those thoughts into a hard ball he could lob into oblivion. Part of him understood base jealousy, another part understood idiocy. The Flower could never be his.

He stood, not certain what he would do but certain he could not sit.

"Sir. Sir!" Daggett's face popped up in front of him, looking harried and rather concerned. "The Russians."

"Hang the Russian Embassy. I'm going out." He pushed his chair back from the desk and ignored Daggett's sputtering. "What is the time? Is Gentleman Jackson's open?"

"No, sir. It closed hours ago."

"Unfortunate. I shall have to be civilized and refrain from hitting someone."

Maximilian had no idea where he was going when he tossed his greatcoat around his shoulders and slipped a pistol into the deep pockets, or when he stepped out in the damp, cold night. But he should have been able to predict his excursion would end at the Flower's front step.

Light blazed from the windows, illuminating curtains

and the rooms behind. No dark windows for the Flower's residence tonight. The interior looked warm in comparison to the chill of the night air.

He debated knocking on the door, but he was uncertain as to his welcome. She might be happy to see him and invite him in. Or she might toss him out again if her protector were visiting. Or she might be tired of him after a single night.

He was acting idiotic. Like a lovesick swain chasing after his chosen lady, seeking her favor. Lancelot to Guinevere — except King Arthur was King Arthur in name only.

He turned away and began to stride down the street. He should be at home, sitting by his warm fire and working for the Russians, not fancying himself playing Lancelot.

The door to her house opened. He swung around, his heart bumping hard in his chest. The footman limped out first, waving to a carriage coming down the street. Then *she* came out. Something deep inside him leaped at the sight of Vivienne. She was beautiful dressed in full evening wear. A feather adorned her hair — no, two — and her gown seemed to sparkle as the interior lights moved over it. She was smiling at someone in the hall behind her.

A man stepped out.

The protector.

Jealousy bubbled up inside Maximilian. Jealousy and anger and all manner of messy emotions he'd never felt until he'd become involved with the Flower. He supposed it was misplaced jealousy. Wycomb was not Vivienne's lover. He'd never felt her body move around and over him, or watched her eyes flutter closed as she sighed.

Still, Wycomb stood in the open with her. Maximilian was relegated to the shadows.

The carriage clattered to a stop in the street. Maximilian fisted his hands and watched as Vivienne and Wycomb moved toward it. She looked graceful and poised, her hand resting on the man's arm as he escorted her, her head high and the pointed chin proud.

They paused at the carriage door while the footman lowered the steps. Wycomb set his hand on Vivienne's lower back to guide her forward. He glanced up to the coachman, calling out some instruction.

Vivienne gathered her skirts and set one foot on the carriage step. Then she stilled, turned her head slightly. He couldn't see her eyes clearly in the dark. They were too far away. But the gold light of the carriage lamp outlined her features.

It was enough to see her lips curve up.

She knew he was there.

Satisfying, that. Very, very satisfying.

...

Utensils clinked against dinner plates, competing with slightly drunken laughter. Across the table from Vivienne, Henri was chatting with the pretty mistress of the chancellor of the exchequer. Candlelight spilled over the table, the merry guests, the sparkling jewels and diamonds these lusty men showered on their mistresses.

It was a strange little tableau. All of these men, these powerful politicians and lords, had wives sitting quietly at home or perhaps attending a *ton* ball, while their husbands laughed and flirted with kept women.

It was her world, where she mined the secrets and documents she gave to Henri. Tonight, it did not sit easily on her. She was out of place inside her own skin. Still, she must play her role. If she was quick in obtaining the information Henri asked for, then she might have time to search for Anne.

For now, her assignment was the diplomat on her left. Vivienne set her chin on her hand and leaned closer to him.

His eyes glazed over. But then, her breasts would be nearly falling out of her gown and quite within his view. She smiled at him, slow and seductive. He didn't notice. He was still looking at her breasts.

"But what shall London do when you leave for Brussels, my lord?" She set a hand on his arm, squeezed lightly. "The dinner parties shall be boring without you."

"Come, my dear." He set his hand over hers, caressed it. "There are many other men here to entertain you. Shall you really miss me?"

"But yes. You tell the most amusing stories." She cocked her head and pouted. "Why Brussels? It is so far away."

"Duty, my dear." He raised his wineglass, as though to toast with her. So she picked up her own glass. The diplomat had drunk at least four glasses already at dinner, and more before. The cheeks beneath his graying whiskers were ruddy.

She had barely sipped from her glass. Wine made a thief's hands unsteady. Henri, though, was on his second glass. He would likely not have more. Neither of them could risk overindulgence.

"Duty is not pleasurable, monsieur." She set her glass to her lips and smiled at him over the rim. "I much prefer pleasure."

"I am certain you do, Mademoiselle La Fleur." His gaze fell to her mouth and he licked his lips, resembling nothing so much as an aging lion preparing for a tasty meal.

Down the table, their host—a lord who was not her assignment and thus not of consequence that evening—was nibbling on the neck of a pretty blonde she knew was not his mistress. So. That was how the party would end. Some of these men would take home their own mistresses, some would trade for the night. She had been to such parties before. She had always left with Henri and had not been required to be with a man.

She glanced at Henri, who was fawning over a dancer from the *corps de ballet*. She was a brunette Vivienne knew well enough. She was nice, an English girl who would be in need of a new protector soon, as hers was beginning to tire of her. Henri seemed uncommonly interested. She wondered if tonight would be the night he would leave her to her own devices at such a party. Perhaps so, if she did not gain the information he required of her. She had best hurry. She had no desire to be left with any man.

The host ceased nibbling on his guest long enough to signal that the meal was over. "The ladies may retire to the drawing room. We shall join you shortly, my dears," he called out.

The diplomat beside Vivienne stood. It was most fortunate she was quick, as he pulled her chair away from the table without warning. Very impatient, was this diplomat.

"Do escort me to the drawing room, won't you, monsieur?" she asked, sliding her arm through his. Her stomach clenched in disgust, but she stood on tiptoe to whisper in his ear. "Your port, it can wait a few moments, no?" It was an invitation, though she was loath to issue it.

Hidden between their bodies, his fingers rubbed against her stomach. Likely he thought this caress would entice her. It did not. Revulsion rippled beneath her skin.

The women, a few accompanied by escorts, began to retire to the drawing room, where they would forgo tea in favor of something stronger. Some of the men stayed behind to start their port. Henri was one, though he did slide a look at her and the diplomat as if to say, *only a morsel, no more*. It was a warning he had issued before to other men who had sought her favors.

When the men rejoined the women later, there would be more groping of hands and kisses on the sly, until everyone found their partner for night. She had managed it before, and so she did now, when the diplomat pulled her through a dark doorway on their way to the drawing room.

He pressed up her up against the wall, his hips grinding against hers. Hands squeezed her breasts, and his breath came in short gasps in her ear. Bile rose in her throat, shocking her. She had never enjoyed such groping in dark halls, but never had it made her belly revolt in such a way. It was her work, and often unpleasant. But she was trained for it.

She forced the nausea away, forced herself to do her job.

Ignoring the erection pressed against her belly, she tried to giggle. "Sir!"

He kissed her, tongue thrusting. His sour breath made her want to cough. *Enough*, she thought, desperate to flee. "Must you go to Brussels? Can you not tell whoever is ordering you that you must stay here?"

"I cannot." Harsh breathing, rasping voice. The man was ready to take her here, against the wall, with her protector a few rooms away. "I cannot," he said again. "It is too important."

"Important?" She wrapped her arms around his neck and pressed against him. A cold part of her mind said she should kiss him. He wanted her mouth on him in other places, so a kiss might send him into the boughs, but she could not bring herself to do it. Loathing skittered across the surface of her skin, raising the hair. Her stomach roiled and clutched.

She did not want to kiss him. And he would not be able to talk, at any rate.

"I knew you were doing something important. An intelligent man like you," she crooned.

His hands cupped her bottom, squeezed painfully hard.

"What could be more important than this?" she murmured against his ear, in the most seductive tone she could manage while trying not to retch.

"Christ, it's politics, mademoiselle. Just politics."

No more. She could not bear more of this. It was time

to end it, whether she gained more information or not. She gripped his shoulders and said, "Politics are not interesting enough for someone like you. It must be more than just politics that would keep you away from all of this." She shook back curls and raised her shoulders, and knew her nipples were exposed, just a little.

"Dear God," he groaned. "If I wasn't negotiating a munitions trade with Russia, I'd stay here and pay twice what Wycomb pays you."

And now she had what Henri wanted.

Relief spread through her. It did not calm the horrible ache in her chest or the battle of nausea in her stomach. But she was done. She could leave him.

"I would think you are twice the man, as well." What an *idiote*, if he believed women said such things and meant them. "But you are right, he does pay me. I cannot lie with you without his permission, as you know. But perhaps tonight he will allow it."

She prayed it never happened.

"Everyone knows Wycomb keeps you on a short leash."

The diplomat's hands were still kneading her breasts, so she moved away, unable to tolerate any more. But she gave him a fast, bright smile in compensation.

"I shall see you again, shall I not? When you return from Brussels."

He visibly reined himself in, stepping back, though he still reached out to caress her shoulder and run a finger across the top of her bodice. She straightened her gown, gave him another forced giggle, and tried not to flee from this disgusting man and his disgusting hands.

Minutes later, he was bowing to her at the door of the drawing room. Some of the ladies were there; others were noticeably absent, no doubt waylaid in much the same way she had been.

Vivienne poured herself a glass of wine and yearned for a tub. Her skin crawled like so many spiders played on her.

She would do her best not to itch while she waited for Henri to return.

She wanted to ask for a hip bath. More, she wanted to be submerged in water for a week. But she could not. Mrs. Asher would hear her heating the water and come out to help in her nightgown. She would wake the footman to carry it. Vivienne did not want to wake them.

Instead, she used the basin and pitcher in her room. The water was frigid, but she needed to be clean. The homespun soap refused to lather, but she scrubbed herself with it regardless. Breasts, neck, arms, legs. Between her legs. Anywhere that could be cleaned and washed, she scrubbed until it was pink. Then the strip of linen to dry her body, the cotton shift to cover herself.

Her knives were already laid out on the table. One was under her pillow. The pistol was loaded and on the opposite bedside table. This was all routine. Each night. Every night. Whether she stole secrets that day or made love with Maximilian, danced at the opera or revealed her nipples to a diplomat. Just another day. Routine.

Now she would practice her forms. Her body needed to be stretched. Trained.

Plié, deep enough so her bottom met her heels. Count two, three, four. Stand again and step into first position, then fifth position.

Routine.

The tears gathered behind her eyes, bringing with them a dull, throbbing ache. She did not let them fall. It was a point of pride that she was able to ignore the choking ache in her chest, in her throat.

Spin, another *plié*, two, three, four. *Arabesque.*

Routine. Again, then again, until she was hollowed out.

When she was finished, she sat on the edge of the bed to regain her breath. The tear that fell onto her hand came as a shock. It was very round, that teardrop. A second fell. Vivienne swallowed hard.

She did not cry. Not since the day her mother died. She took what came, bore it, and did what was required of her.

She did *not* cry.

The tears did not stop. She pressed her face into the pillow and thought of Anne. Of fear. Baring her body to a stranger.

Being alone.

She did not want to be alone, but the only place she could go was Maximilian's.

Such things were not permanent.

Chapter Thirty-Two

"Ah, you've arrived!" Prinny gestured wildly for Maximilian to come closer.

Unfortunately, if he stepped any nearer he was likely to be splashed by whatever beverage had inebriated Prinny. The bloody glass was waving in the air, gold liquid splashing all over the opera box.

It was a miracle the men around him—politicians and dandies, if Maximilian had any guess—were still dry. In thinking on it, the dancers were likely to get sprayed as well. Prinny's box was perilously close to the stage.

"Your Highness." Maximilian bowed but avoided stepping forward and into the spray of liquor. He only had one coat Daggett considered appropriate for such an occasion, since he'd gotten blood on the last one. His assistant would never forgive him if he ruined this one as well—and good assistants with exceptional filing systems were difficult to find. "I appreciate your invitation this evening."

"Nonsense. It wasn't me who issued the invitation. It was your brother." The Prince Regent grinned and waved the glass toward the corner of the opera box.

Anger settled in Maximilian's belly. Odd that anger could feel icy. Turning toward the corner Prinny had gestured to, Maximilian found the figure he'd missed upon entering the box.

"Highchester." Maximilian ground the word out in the most polite tone he could manage.

"Max." His brother would be characterized as elegant in his evening wear, Maximilian was sure. He rarely looked anything else, so the ladies said. Dark jacket, a crisp white cravat, a striped waistcoat Maximilian would never have worn. Too bad Highchester's nasty grin ruined the effect. It was the grin he used when he believed he had the upper hand.

"An opera dancer, Max?" Prinny waggled his brows in that ridiculous way a roué did when he thought he was being amusing. "Your brother was vexingly silent on her identity, but I'm most curious. Sit down and tell me, which lady do you have your eye on?"

Maximilian accepted the last empty seat, closest to the stage. "None, Your Highness."

Prinny guffawed, belly shaking. His glass was dangerously near to upending itself on the dandy next to him.

The dandy righted the glass quickly enough, saying, "Discreet, are you, Mr. Westwood?"

"Always, my lord." Maximilian nodded his head to acknowledge the man.

Prinny saluted the dandy and took a drink. "Don't be discreet, Maximilian. I want to know." He leaned forward, winked. "Who is she? The little Italian dancer? I've heard she's got a— Well." Prinny slid his gaze toward the stage, where the dancers performed and the soprano wailed. "Who is she?"

Another man leaned forward, from Prinny's other side. "You're not known for dalliances, Mr. Westwood. She must be particular."

"Quite particular, isn't she, Max?" Highchester drawled from his seat. His delight at Maximilian's discomfort was obvious in the relaxed posture, the slight twist of lips, the mocking light in his eye.

Maximilian did not bother to answer his brother. Highchester would do his utmost to make Maximilian uncomfortable. What was most important now was ensuring Vivienne was not discovered for a myriad of reasons, not the least of which was her position as spy.

"We shall guess, Max," Prinny said gleefully. "In the meantime, do think up another code for my own lady, won't you?"

He turned away, and Maximilian was blessedly forgotten for the moment. It wouldn't last long, but a momentary reprieve was better than none at all.

He turned his attention to the stage, his gaze focusing on Vivienne. He'd been vaguely aware of the stage and the dancers since he stepped into the box, he realized. Sort of an instinctive knowledge of where she was in relation to him.

She seemed to him the most graceful dancer on the stage. Though there were other beautiful women there, including the soprano, there was something about Vivienne that caused a visceral beat in his blood.

Maximilian wondered if predators in the wild felt this strange craving when stalking prey. It was a hard and fast churning in his belly—and farther south. A physical pull that kept his eyes tracking her across the stage. Vivienne La Fleur might belong in another man's house, but that man did not hold her mind or her soul.

Or her heart, but that was neither here nor there.

Absently he listened to Prinny and his cronies rattle on about a horse race one man challenged another to, but he watched her. The distance to the stage was not far, and it seemed as if he could feel the air move as the dancers crossed the wooden surface. Vivienne danced at the rear of the stage, providing a moving backdrop for the singing soprano. Yet she was the center of the performance for him.

Her feet moved in time with the music, and with each swirl and beat he could see the delicate bones of her ankles, the flash of the lean calves above. Those quick, talented feet fascinated him.

Until he saw her eyes.

Perhaps he thought she would be blind to anything but the music. Perhaps he'd thought dancing was her passion—in a way, he supposed it was or she wouldn't continue. But it was not all she thought of when she was on stage.

She looked everywhere. No part of the theater was untouched by her gaze—including him. Her gaze flickered over him, registered his presence, and then moved on to this box or that. A twirl, a pointed toe, then her gaze landed on him again.

This time, her lips tipped up in one corner.

He caught his breath. Was it flirtation? Greeting? Laughter? He could not read her half smile. The sight created a yearning inside him. Not for her body, but for the understanding of what she was thinking.

A crafty voice slithered into Maximilian's ear. "You seem to be absorbed in the performance."

Maximilian clenched his jaw and breathed deep before turning to his brother. "I like the music," he answered. Deliberately he looked back at the stage and the Flower.

She made another spin then a series of small, controlled leaps across the stage. She slid another look in his direction. He swallowed hard as her lips tipped up again.

The soprano's voice soared over the music. He heard it, but it seemed like only a hum compared with the rushing of blood in his veins. He was certain there was a story behind the words of the song, but he couldn't translate it just now.

As the crowd began to buzz around him, he realized others watched Vivienne as well.

She's going to steal the show... The soprano won't like that...but look at her. She's never danced better...

The Flower spun on the stage. She was dancing with a fan now. She fluttered it then set it against her face to hide her lips. Her eyes were downcast, demure, just like those of the other dancers as they sank into some sort of low curtsy. The song trailed off in a final series of notes. Things were beginning to draw to a close. He began to turn away, to say something to the prince—

And her lashes swept up. Her gaze latched on his, and he could not breathe. The fan lowered, and her smile bloomed. Sly and sensual. *For him.*

His fingers clutched the arms of his chair as his body began to thrum and pulse and rage. Some primitive male part of him wanted to possess her. To take her from this room and hide her away for his very own.

The crowd was clapping, some enthusiastically like the prince. Others politely, as if they had not watched the performance. All of it was a dim pounding that could not match the beat of his heart.

"She danced exceptionally well this evening, didn't she?" Beside him, Highchester tsked quietly. "You should be more discreet."

He was correct. Maximilian should be more discreet. Yet their gazes were still locked. He could not look away from her.

Tonight, Vivienne. Will you steal into my bedroom?

His mind asked the question. His body screamed it. Could she read it in his gaze?

Her smile curved up a little bit more. Her eyes swept down, the fan fluttering near her breasts. She didn't say the words, but he knew her answer.

· · ·

It was late. The performance had ended, there had been many people—men—backstage to fawn and to flirt and to compliment her dancing. She had left the theater much later than intended.

They did not know it was Maximilian she had danced for, sitting in the prince's box, eyes focused only on her.

Now, here she was. Slipping past the pitiful locks of his window and into his room. She could not see him at first, so she closed the window, set the latch.

"You came." Very soft words. They slid around her senses to play at the base of her spine.

She turned and found him sprawled in his bed, one arm behind his head to prop it up. Watching her. Waiting for her. He was not naked—he would likely think that presumptuous. Still, he wore nothing but trousers. The single candle on the bedside table gilded him. Muscle, bone. Breadth in the shoulders, trim in the waist. His jaw with its late-night shadow.

And the question in his eyes.

"I came for many reasons." She began to unbutton her jacket. He did not look away from her. He saw each movement. Each flick of her fingers on the buttons.

This was one of those reasons.

But there were more reasons, not all that she could share. Maximilian would stop her if he knew what she planned later—with good reason. She was edging the line between treason and espionage. A misstep one way or the other and her plan would fall apart, yet she could not do what must be done that night alone.

"I have a need for you tonight, Maximilian." She pulled off her boots.

He kept those hazel eyes on her. What did he see? Spy? Dancer? Thief? She did not know, but his lids were half closed in that thinking way he had.

It was most arousing.

Perhaps it should not be, but in this quiet moment, when his brain was busy but his body was still, she could do nothing but want him. Pine for him.

What a foolish notion, she thought. One couldn't pine for someone who was right there in front of one.

"I have a need for you, too." He sat up, swung his legs over the edge of the bed. But he did not stand. He only looked at her with hot eyes, his elbows balanced on his knees.

"I have a need that is not only here in your bedroom. In this way." She began to work on her shirt buttons, but her fingers moved irritatingly slowly. "I have need of you much later. After."

"That will be full morning, if I have my way." A smile lurked around his eyes as he stood and began unfastening his fall-front trousers.

"You will have to be quick, for we have somewhere to be." He was handsome with those smiling eyes. She grinned at him and pulled the shirt from her head in one easy motion.

His sharp inhale made her muscles quiver. "Whatever you ask, Vivienne, if it means I can have you."

"Very good. It is important, this night."

He stepped forward and reached for the waistband of her pants. A moment later, they had fallen away. He ran his thumb from the tip of her breast down the curve of her waist and hip.

"Tell me what you need," he said as he took her hand. His was warm, strong. And purposeful. She liked this purpose in him. It was different from before. She wondered if it would be different every time they made love, but she would not know this answer. They would not be together always. Jones had said it. She was not meant for permanency. Love and family did not accompany her line of work.

This did not stop her from wanting Maximilian.

He sat down on the bed, and she knelt beside him. His fingers skimmed over her shoulder, her waist. Gently. There were no groping hands. No men with greedy smiles here. No men with secrets she must steal.

Only Maximilian.

A strange, uncomfortable feeling spread through her. Part pain. Part joy. And part uneasiness. This line between spy and lover, she would not be able to walk it forever. But she *did* need to walk it this night. And so she would not tell Maximilian of Henri's assignment or of Lessard's associates.

...

Vivienne was in his bed. That, in itself, seemed a wonder. This gorgeous woman was his. He couldn't understand the why and how of it, but for this fleeting moment in time, she belonged to no one but him.

"I must speak with someone," she said, setting her palms on her thighs. "A courier. Perhaps not courier—that implies he travels. He does not. He sits in the brothel he owns, sells his wares"—the Flower shrugged a shoulder, as though accepting this selling of flesh—"and he lords over the little kingdom he has built selling secrets."

He was having trouble concentrating on the words. She was too naked. Vivienne slid down to lie on her stomach, pillowing her head on her arms so she could see him. Now all he could see was the curving line of her body, uncovered, unconcealed.

"I cannot steal into the establishment, as it is too well guarded. But I also cannot walk through the front door alone." She watched him carefully, face resting on the crook of her arm. "But I need to speak with the courier."

"Hmm." Walking into a brothel owned by a man who sold secrets to the French seemed like a dangerous proposition. "What do you expect me to do?"

"I need your protection, Maximilian, so that no patrons will consider me available. It would make me vulnerable."

That sent a spear of possession through him. The other men couldn't have her. She was his. For now, at any rate, she was his.

"And when we are inside?" He ran his finger along the curve of her cheek. The candlelight danced along her skin there, and he could not keep from touching her. "What then?"

"If I ask you to leave me alone with the courier, I need you to do so. Alone, Maximilian. Alone."

He reared back, staring down at her delicate, gilded features. "No." He wouldn't be able to. "I'm not leaving you alone with—"

"Please, Maximilian. I must speak with him alone. About Anne. If you are there, it may be more dangerous for all of us." She reached for him, lightly touching his arm. "I will be safe enough. I am well trained."

He gripped the edge of the bed, the coverlet bunching beneath his hands. He supposed he could tell her no, but she would likely go at any rate—alone, confound it.

"Very well." He would have to trust her training and skills.

"Do you give me your word?" Her eyes were serious. Even vulnerable, as though she didn't expect he would make and stand by a promise. "You will do as I say? You will leave if I ask?"

He breathed deep, then let the coverlet slip from his fingers. "My word."

"Thank you, Maximilian." She sounded vulnerable. The tone, the set of her face, crept into his chest and lodged itself there. She smiled lightly, sweetly, and everything inside him twisted and tightened, then loosened as some part of her became part of him.

It was damn near painful to feel so much inside.

She moved, reaching for him to draw him down beside her.

"Wait. Vivienne, wait." He could not let the moment pass. "Stay there."

She stilled with her face pillowed on her arms and her torso pressed against the bed. Waiting. Watching.

Her body was a magnificent thing. She was a dancer, with all the wonders of a dancer's body. The delicate spine, the lean strength. There was the dip at her low back just before the rounded curves of her bottom. And then her legs—dear God, her legs. Dancer's legs. Each contour, each hollow and valley and shift was like watching the entire ballet corps move across her skin.

"No more espionage for now." He didn't care about the courier, or the brothel, or her plans. Just now, there was only her body displayed before him. No shame. No embarrassment. This was the Flower. Vivienne. The woman he wanted in his bed and in his study, with the frown between her brows that meant she was concentrating. The woman he wanted to surprise him, to interrupt him.

"I will always want you, Vivienne. Always."

She pushed herself up so she was propped on her elbows, and his mouth went dry as he took in the line of her back. Graceful as a swan's neck, the curve, the arch, the indentations just above her buttocks. Her breasts swung full and free.

"Do not wait any longer, Maximilian." Her eyes raked over his body, held him in place.

He leaned down and their mouths met, hers as forceful, as demanding, as his. When he moved his lips to her cheekbones, her jaw, she angled her head so he could access the soft skin there. He shifted closer, his hand running along her spine, feeling each vertebra and the smooth skin. As his mouth moved to her shoulder, his hand slid over her buttocks. They flexed beneath his touch and his body reacted, growing harder, hotter, and needing to be inside her.

"Stay on your belly," he whispered into her ear as he rose over her.

Candlelight played over her shoulder blades as she did as he commanded. He kissed her shoulders, her long neck, the most wonderful dimples just above her buttocks. She turned her face to the side and his gaze traced the contour of her forehead, nose, lips against the white pillow. So graceful. The line of brow, furrowed now in concentration, the bow of lips, curved up delight. Each bit of her, each movement, seemed the most extraordinary discovery.

He slid between her legs, moved them farther apart to accommodate his body. Then he moved his hands beneath her torso. She didn't speak, but he felt her belly contract against the palms of his hands. As badly as he wanted to plunge into her, he set one hand to the curls hiding the most secret center of her. With only the tiniest touch, he set her body quivering, and she opened wider for him.

He could no longer wait. He slid inside her. Her soft sigh of pleasure nearly undid him. But he waited, held, then moved in and out. Her hand fisted in the pillow as she angled her body to better accommodate him.

He was lost in her pleasure, in her response. In the way the light played over her back, in the feel of her bottom against him. He leaned over her, pressed his lips to the space between her shoulder blades as he thrust. Buried his face in her hair as he thrust again. Then again.

A small sound escaped her throat, something excited and anticipatory. He couldn't move hard enough or fast enough to meet that sound. He wanted to hear it again. More.

"Maximilian." His name was barely a sound on her lips, but he heard it.

Somehow, it moved him. He slid his hand up to cover hers where she gripped the bed linen. Their fingers tangled as he continued to take her. Her hair, that curling, clean-scented hair, seemed to be his whole world just now. He buried his face in it, kissed whatever skin of her he could reach. Neck, shoulder, that sweet, sweet curve between.

When he felt her inner muscles clench around him, he thrust one final time. This was what he had waited for. This moment, when she came undone and cried out in release.

This was all that mattered.

Chapter Thirty-Three

The brothel smelled like a perfumery. It was also loud. Female giggling, male laughter. Off-key violin music. Voices ebbing and flowing, punctuated by a stray shout or two.

Made his damnable head hurt.

He pretended to enjoy the scenery. He didn't have much choice. Everywhere he looked a half-bared woman was romping around while men leered and fondled. The women didn't seem to mind, either, he decided as he glimpsed a voluptuous blonde giggling as a man did something or other under her skirt. Well, this was their occupation, so he supposed they were used to it.

Still, he was getting dizzy from averting his eyes and trying to find some innocuous place to look. He wasn't having much luck. Even the artwork on the walls was titillating.

Thank all the fates it was the Flower on his lap and not some other woman. Vivienne's hair was loose and curling. She shook it back, laughing at some words uttered by a passing rake, and the dark mass tumbled and flirted with her shoulders. She wore a little black mask decorated with feathers and paste jewels, as did a few other women—likely well-bred ladies of the *ton* out playing for the night. The mask was a silly little disguise, he would know the shape of Vivienne's face, her mouth, even the color of the eyes peeking from behind the mask.

He couldn't understand how these other men didn't recognize her.

Perhaps it was her newly revealed aristocratic tones and vocabulary. Gone was the lilting French accent of her birth he so enjoyed. With the mask covering her face, it was like watching another woman instead of the Flower.

"Oh, my lord, don't be so silly!" She laughed at a passing lord's lewd suggestion then leaned back against Maximilian's chest. He gritted his teeth. Her false laugh grated on him.

Her buttocks shifted on his lap so she was practically lying on him. One of her legs swung easily between his. Her thigh kept sliding against his body. Her gown was some confection of silk and lace and sheer fabric meant for the bedroom, though there seemed to be a considerable amount of it. He tried to keep himself in check, but he felt his body growing hard with each movement.

Damn perfidious body.

"How long do we have to stay in this hellhole?"

"Until I locate the owner, sir." She pressed a kiss against the underside of his jaw. Didn't help his body at all.

"Well, let's get started." He didn't want these men looking at the Flower with such avarice a moment longer. "It's unfortunate you couldn't sneak in through a window."

"Yes, but this is not such a place. Also, I would not get a feel for what type of man he is. I need to see. To evaluate. But you are not playing your role, sir. I believe we talked about that earlier this evening." She whispered the words in his ear, then nibbled on his earlobe.

"God's elbows—" He gasped. Heat bolted through his

body in a single lightning strike.

Now her laughter was real. Full throated and like the Vivienne he knew instead of some disguised English tart. Her eyes sparkled behind the mask, so amused, so delighted. Every one of his muscles tightened, and he fought the urge to just take her mouth with his and bring that laughter into him.

Then he did have to kiss her. He couldn't help it.

Uncaring about who was watching, or where they were, he set a finger beneath her chin and angled her face toward his. Ravenous for her, he covered her mouth. She was warm and responsive, and the fingers clutching his lapel tightened, tugging him closer. He angled the kiss, deepened it.

She pulled away, her breathing ragged. "*Mon Dieu*," she whispered, once again in her native tongue.

He struggled to regain his focus but was drugged by her kisses, by the fresh scent of her soap that created an oasis in the sickeningly sweet confines of the brothel. He was fighting a losing battle.

Until her eyes narrowed, fixating on something beyond his shoulder.

"There he is."

"Who?" His brain was moving at half speed.

"The courier, Lessard. The owner of the brothel. *Don't look*," she whispered as he started to turn in the chair. "He's coming this way."

"How can you tell he is Lessard?"

"The king is always recognizable," she said softly.

He did not turn to look, but every muscle in his body tensed as he waited for the man to appear. The pistol tucked beneath his coat pressed against his ribs, and he fought the urge to retrieve it. He wanted to pull her away from this, to protect her from this brothel owner.

But he wasn't there to stop her, he was there to assist her. He'd given his word.

...

Her brain was fuddled. She could not remember who she was: herself, the pretend English aristocrat in a brothel, a spy, or Maximilian's lover.

She had better decide, because in a few minutes she would step temporarily over the line. But she could not see another way to find Anne. She only wished she were not in the vulnerable position of negotiation. At least she had three knives on her person.

Watching Lessard cross the room toward her, she wished she had three more.

She did not show it. She toyed with Maximilian's cravat. The elaborate waterfall she'd crafted for him after they made love was crushed and crooked from her hands.

"I cannot tell if he knows who I am," she whispered to Maximilian. She did not have time to study the scarred face of Lessard to be sure. "Remember that I must speak to him alone."

"Vivienne, I cannot leave you with him." The words were short and sharp. "I cannot."

"I will not be able to save Anne if I do not talk to Lessard in private. Please, be only my lover and let me go. Nothing more."

She leaned forward and kissed Maximilian. Desperation fueled her passion, and his participation seemed to be driven by protection. He was alert, his muscles poised for action. She hoped he held himself in check.

"You kiss him as though you mean it, mademoiselle. I was nearly deceived." Lessard's voice was low, carrying easily beneath the raucous tones of the crowd.

Digging her fingers into Maximilian's arms as a warning, she broke away from his mouth and peered up. Lessard was tall. Very tall. And wide as a mountain base. This did not concern her. Men the size of mountains could be felled as easily as any other if one knew how to do it properly.

"I *do* mean it, Monsieur Lessard." She cocked her head and set the feathers on her mask fluttering. "This is my escort for the evening." She smiled at her opponent, slow and feline.

Maximilian's arm was tight around her waist, fingers pressed hard into her ribs. There was anger there, and fear as well. Both were layered over with some fierce emotion she could not name while staring into the unattractive face of Lessard.

"I have been studying you this past hour." Lessard's voice carried a hint of steel.

She did not speak but angled her gaze up at the Frenchman. Lessard idly tapped his ringed fingers against the glass in his hand. Gold liquid swirled in the crystal, distorting his fingers. They looked like grotesque pink snakes slithering on the glass.

"Usually when a couple ventures into my establishment, they are looking for a third partner. Or two new partners. This I am accustomed to. But you"—Lessard's fingers tapped against the glass again—"you have eyes for no one but each other."

"Perhaps we prefer to watch. There are those that do." She had heard the other dancers, the actresses speak of such couples.

"I think you are not one of them." He paused, smiled thinly. "My lady La Fleur."

Ah. The knowing tone, the thin smile. He knew she was the Flower. Unwise to think it would be she to reveal her identity at the moment that best suited her.

She must decide how to play the game. In a moment of time, one could generate a dozen plans and discard all of them. Denial of identity. Distraction. Incite a small riot in the room and escape unnoticed. Fight.

She flicked her eyes around the room. She had noticed the footmen in the corners, ready to assist guests. But now each of the large, broad men blocked an entrance—no doubt on Lessard's command.

None of her options seemed wise.

She looked at Maximilian, at brown and green and gold eyes studying her every thought. Beneath her, Maximilian's thighs were hard as stone. He knew of the blocked exits. Despite the women and liquor and laughter around them, he understood there was no escape—and what she meant to do next.

Holding his gaze with her own, she said softly, "I think our plans this evening have been spoiled. Perhaps you should go."

Maximilian did not speak. Only searched her face with those multicolored eyes. He saw everything in her. Despite the mask she wore, he saw everything except the deepest secrets she kept hidden. And she saw in his gaze that he would keep his promise.

Why this should create a tear in her heart, she could not say.

"I think your friend shall not leave, mademoiselle." Lessard flicked his finger, and two of the men stationed at the door began to move toward them. "The three of us, we shall have a private meeting, *n'est-ce pas?*"

Lessard's voice was still low and quiet, his manner mild despite his bulk. He did not want to be overheard.

His weakness. Her advantage.

So she stood. Raised her voice.

"What do you mean, I shall not recoup my money?" A very slim chance this would work. But still she tried, raising her fist, just a little. Shaking it just a little. "I paid for this service!"

Nervous voices, nervous glances. They were all about her, from guests pausing their games and laughter and groping.

Good. It would pressure Lessard.

"Mademoiselle." Not just steel, but anger in his voice now. He leaned over her, towering with his height. In a whisper meant only for her ears, he said, "In seconds, my guards will be able to kill you in a number of unpleasant ways."

Behind her, Maximilian unfolded his length until he stood at her shoulder. She felt him stiffen as though they were in contact, skin to skin. She did not need to see him to know he was angry.

She stepped closer to Lessard. Bared her teeth. "In seconds, the knife tucked in my stays will be lodged between your ribs and into your heart. Your men will be too late." Lessard sucked in a breath. Ah. She had his attention. "Release the monsieur. He is not part of this. A prop only, a man I consider useful when I need a companion for establishments such as these." She could not look at Maximilian as she spoke the words. "I do not want innocent deaths on my hands."

Lessard's eyes flickered, his gaze moving back and forth between her eyes. Judging her veracity. She did not hide the lie in her face. She felt it, lived it, breathed it. It was a truth that she lied. And so the enemy, he would see truth in her eyes.

"I believe he is not important to you. But—" A snap of fingers to summon a large footman. A glance at Maximilian. "He will be my insurance for your goodwill."

Chapter Thirty-Four

She was becoming a liability.

The Vulture watched the Flower as Lessard spoke with her. A very interesting dress she wore. It left little to the imagination. He might have mistaken her for a society whore if he had not made such a study of her. The tilt of her head, her movements, her laugh. The mask she wore did not hide these things. He knew her instantly, once he looked closely.

He might not have done, if Westwood had not accompanied her. The man had given him pause. Westwood did not attend establishments such as Lessard's, so he—and his companion—had warranted a second look.

And so he had seen the Flower beneath the mask.

He had not expected such tenacity in her. Or such loyalty. The Flower had walked into the lion's den—Lessard's brothel—without even the slightest appearance of concern. Still, she had done so, which meant she had not given up her search for the girl.

He had not accounted for this perseverance.

From his shadowed alcove, he watched her confrontation

with Lessard. Neither had the upper hand, particularly. Westwood, too, the Vulture watched. The man bristled like a cur defending his territory, but he did not attack. There was too much control in Westwood.

The Vulture was not finished with the Flower yet. She might not be the double agent he'd hoped for, but he had a very specific assignment for her. Then he would kill the Flower and the girl. The Flower had too much integrity for betrayal, it seemed. But he would have to send a message to keep her in line a little longer.

A very clear message.

...

Around them, music played, women giggled. Men ran card games and drank liquor and glanced nervously at their exchange. Still, Vivienne did not have the advantage.

"As you wish, then, Monsieur Lessard," she murmured. She would need to tread carefully if they were both to live.

"We shall retire to my private quarters," Lessard said just as quietly. "Your guest cannot join us."

"Monsieur—" She turned to look at Maximilian. He was there, ready, alert. She saw it in the fisted hand, the bracing of his thighs, the angle of his head and shoulders. "I have no more need of you, other than an escort home. Do find yourself another playmate for the night."

She turned her back on Maximilian, but not before she saw the fear in his eyes. He had sworn to do what she asked, but there was pain in his promise.

From behind her, in the coldest voice she'd ever heard from Maximilian, "As you wish, miss."

A glance over her shoulder revealed Maximilian executing a short bow. Rigid shoulders were squared, his clenched jaw twitching with the strain of not acting. His gaze was hard and sharp.

"If you'll excuse me." He turned on his heel and strode through the reveling crowd, narrowly avoiding a naked woman pulling a half-dressed gentlemen to the stairs leading to upper bedchambers.

She had never asked for so much from a man—and had never been given so much.

With a heavy heart, she flicked her fingers in Maximilian's direction, dismissing him. "I was becoming bored of him this night."

"Then let us discuss something more interesting." Lessard offered his arm, just as he would on a *ton* dance floor, but the eyes watching her were not the nice eyes of a dance partner. They were canny and perceptive. Daring her.

Taking his arm would mean very close proximity. One could be easily killed in this way. But not here; it would be in private. She had a few minutes before death, at least.

She tucked her arm beneath Lessard's. It was a short walk through the crowd of patrons and to the stairs. This was a different set than those leading to the girls' rooms. The base was guarded by one of those broad-shouldered, brawny footmen scattered about the room.

"Your private quarters, *monsieur*?" She peered up the staircase, surprised to find it well lit by wall sconces. She had supposed friends of French spies would want to hide in shadows. Lessard was not afraid of scrutiny, it seemed.

"I maintain lodgings here."

They walked side by side, in unison. It was perplexing to be in unison with one's enemy. His booted feet sounded heavy on each step; her slippered feet clicked. The train of her revealing gown slid over each step as she ascended. Their movements were an odd sort of measured dance.

"Do you often bring British agents to your lodging?" she asked coyly.

"A question I would prefer not to answer." He slid a glance in her direction. "You did not expect one."

"I did not, but there is always hope, yes?" They were at the top of the stairs now. Fourteen steps in total. There had seemed to be a hundred. She did not dwell on them, looking over the rooms instead. "Very lavish lodgings, Monsieur Lessard. Either Marchand must pay you exceptionally well, or the brothel is quite lucrative."

"Indeed." His arm fell away, and he bowed, ushering her into the space, not pretending he did not understand her.

His quarters were filled with every manner of comfort. Pillows, lush carpet, gleaming furniture. Wine and brandy bottles lay on their sides in a rack covering one wall. She could smell cheroots and male eau de cologne. Various weapons covered another wall, ranging from axes to pistols to sabers.

And the paintings. They were no better than those on the first floor. Naked women in various stages of undress, their bodies on display. Some were beautifully and carefully painted, others were crude and suggestive. All part of men's fantasies, as she knew well enough.

"And so, mademoiselle, you are here."

"So I am," she said. She turned away from the paintings to watch Lessard as he strode to the desk. He lifted the lid of a carved wooden box and extracted a cheroot. He stuck it between his teeth but did not light it. Perhaps there was some refinement in this mountain of a man who ran a brothel.

"I had not expected you as of yet." He came around the desk, stepping closer to her.

As of yet. Which meant he had expected her at some point. She wondered why but did not respond. She waited, quiet, watchful, and was rewarded.

"I must wonder, my Flower, are you here on Marchand's orders, or your own?"

His hand extended toward her, took hold of her chin. She

did not stop him when he forced her head up. Did not stop him when he turned it side to side to study her face, no matter that his hands smelled of onion and his breath of tobacco. Scent could wash off. It would not stay in her nostrils or on her skin forever.

"Mmm." She waited again, let him read her face for a long moment. Let him think, in this short time, that he was in control. That it was he who drove this conversation.

Then she jerked her head out of his hand.

"I am here on both, monsieur." She stepped away from him, shrugged her shoulders. "I thought, *Monsieur Lessard, he is an important man. Marchand puts much responsibility on him.*"

"Flattery, *ma chère.*" He was not falling prey to it—not entirely, at any rate. Only enough for his chest to puff out the smallest of degrees. He chewed on the cheroot with large, unclean teeth before answering, as though the cheroot would impart some wisdom. "I am close to Marchand, yes, but I am my own man. What business is that of yours?"

Now they were coming to the cat-and-mouse game. Reveal information, hold information. Lie, truth. Give, take. It was now that she would walk the line of treason to find Anne.

She began to move through the room, to appear as if she were learning each piece of furniture, each nude painting. "I am one of Marchand's now. If I am to be one of Marchand's, I must learn who among his men is the best. Who is the strongest?" Sliding a glance behind her, she smiled slyly at Lessard. "Whom should I ally myself with?"

"You are one of Marchand's only because of the girl." He spoke harshly, crossing his arms as he leaned on his desk. Lessard's eyes were very unreadable.

"I am." Her heart bumped hard inside her chest. Yes. He knew of Anne. If he knew of her, he might know where she was. "There is no turning back, is there? I cannot ever be on only one side again."

She faced him, let him see that truth on her face. The threat would always be there.

"You are approaching me because you want the girl. *Je ne suis pas stupide.*" The cheroot moved from one side of his mouth to the other so that it was now being chewed by different teeth. They were still large teeth. And yellow. The poor cheroot.

"Yes, I want the girl." That was truth, too. She would not deny it, as he would not believe her if she tried. "But if I am going to be with Marchand, I must know what and whom I will have dealings with."

He was quiet, contemplating her with sharp eyes and a busy mind. She would give him a moment to think. Sauntering away, she eyed the shelves leaning against a wall. Ledgers and books were squeezed side by side, multicolored stripes of leather marching all in a row. She trailed her fingers along their spines, letting the ridges rasp against her fingers.

"What do you expect me to do for you?" Lessard finally asked. Looking over her shoulder, she saw he was both intrigued and confused. "And why should I?"

"You are a businessman, through and through, are you not? Always looking for the profit, no?" There, her tone had sounded admiring. "I want to know about Marchand's organization. In return, I will be of service to you."

He raised a brow. "As though I do not have enough women to service me?" He swept his hand out to encompass not only the nude pictures, but the whole of his brothel.

"Not in that way." She employed an amused smile to stop her shudder. "Using my particular talents. I have a usefulness that is desired by Marchand. I can offer the same service to you."

"An interesting proposal." Removing the cheroot, he examined the masticated end of it. "I have heard that you are quite good, but I have no proof."

"Marchand's interest in my talent should be proof enough." Nerves jumped in her belly. He was not accepting her offer. All of this might be for naught. The risk of discovery, not following Henri's orders, lying to Maximilian.

"Indeed, but you are as useful to him because of your position with Wycomb as you are for your skills. I have no use of your position."

"There are still my skills." This she had gambled on—that he would want them. She turned her hands palm up, uncurling her fingers and spreading them wide.

"There are hundreds of pickpockets in London, *ma chère*." He sounded both mocking and dismissive. As though he did not believe her. This she had gambled on as well.

"*Moi*, I am the best." With a bright, brilliant smile, she pulled the proof from the small thief's pocket she'd sewn into her frilled skirt—and watched Lessard's eyes widen in surprise. "Your watch, monsieur."

"*Mon Dieu.*" He looked down at his waistcoat, now devoid of the timepiece that had hung there earlier. His eyes shot to her face. "When?"

She continue to smile but did not answer his question. Instead, from the thin slit running beneath the ribbon under her breasts, she removed two folded five-pound notes.

"I believe these are also yours, monsieur?"

His fingers flew to the pocket of his waistcoat, dug around, and came out empty.

"You are exactly as Marchand described, mademoiselle. Small and quick." With his eyes on her face, he straightened and walked toward her. Her feet wanted to step back of their own accord, so she locked her knees. He was very tall, very large, and his face was very scarred and ugly.

His gaze did not leave hers when he held out his large, cupped palm. He did not look entirely angry or entirely pleased. She could not read that look, what with the scar running from eyebrow to lip, but she dropped the watch in his hand, laid the pound notes over it.

The notes disappeared into his pocket. The watch remained in his hand. He bounced it. A man testing the weight of something.

Or weighing his words.

Chapter Thirty-Five

"You may not ascend the stairs, sir."

The giant footman seemed quite adamant, and much wider than Maximilian, now that he looked properly.

From his seat in the middle of the brothel, Maximilian stared at the stairs to the second level, to Lessard's chambers. Vivienne had been up there too long. Much too long. He shouldn't have left her. He couldn't think why he had, except he'd given her his word. It had seemed exceedingly important he stand by it, even if every part of him screamed out that he should just punch Lessard in the nose and be done with it.

Dash it all, did he have to choose *now* to make a promise to her?

Well, promise or no, he was going up there. Fear for her crawled beneath his skin, building and building as he watched people go up and down the stairs, none of them Vivienne. She could be hurt in a dozen ways up there, without anyone knowing. She could be waiting for him to save her, and he wouldn't know. She could—

He was making himself crazy.

Maximilian stepped toward the footman and tried to look as large as he could in his greatcoat. "See here. The woman I came with, it's my gentlemanly duty to see she returns home safely."

He apparently didn't look large enough, because the footman was unconcerned. "You're not invited upstairs, sir, by order of the owner."

It would have to be brute strength to get him up there. Well, he'd had rudimentary training with the spies. He knew a few things about fighting. Stepping back a bit, he raised his fists and assumed a proper pugilist position. He heard a prostitute or two gasp, heard a man shout, "Oi! A fight!"

He felt like doing just that. The Flower and her ilk were beginning to rub off on him.

"Step aside," he said to the footman. "Or be prepared to defend yourself."

The bloody man didn't step aside. He shot out a fist Maximilian barely had time to dodge. Maximilian countered and made contact with the man's belly. Then he took a blow to the cheekbone that sent stars hazing his vision.

Now there were squealing prostitutes. He didn't particularly care, what with the throbbing pain and the need to get to Vivienne. He couldn't see well enough to aim precisely, but his fist connected with something that felt like a jaw.

When the man's head snapped back, Maximilian barreled forward, shoulder first, and hit the man square in the chest. They went down in a heap, tumbling onto the first step to the upper floors and sending patrons scrambling for safety. Dimly, Maximilian was grateful the footman was so large. The man was an excellent cushion against the floor.

"Stop!" The shout was feminine. Angry. Blessedly healthy.

A masculine bellow followed. "Enough!"

Relief could be as painful in his gut as a fist to the face. He rolled over and sat up, squinting at his Flower, who looked much taller than usual in her rage. Beside her stood Lessard, who clicked his fingers at the footman and jerked his thumb toward the stairs. In seconds, the footman was standing, then jogging up the steps to the second level without even a hitch in his stride.

The footman must be younger than himself. Maximilian's shoulder was throbbing and his eye was already swelling, but he pushed to his feet and felt his body ache in a hundred small places.

"Mademoiselle." Lessard's irritated voice floated on the air. "Control your escort and get out before I change my mind regarding our association."

They were shepherded out the front door in less time than it took Maximilian to begin to limp and were standing on the street staring at a building blazing with lights and spilling music out of the windows. The rowdy laughter had already resumed.

Apparently they were not missed.

"Idiot. You promised." Her small hands were forceful as she ran them over his arms, his torso, checking for injuries. It warmed him and maddened him that she felt the need to take care of him.

That was the gentleman's task. Not the lady's.

"I kept my promise, for a bit," he said, shrugging off her hands and feeling as though he'd failed because he'd kept that promise. He could think of ten thousand reasons why he should have gone with her, and only one why he left her alone: she'd asked. "You're well? You're unharmed?" Now it was his turn to touch her—arms, face, lips.

"Of course. You are not hurt? Not badly?" She was wrapping her cloak around her body to hide the ridiculously revealing gown she wore. Bloody thing was thinner than paper. She must be freezing.

"No." He pulled her closer, thinking to warm her and

wishing he could just scoop her up and carry her home. His home.

Her hands settled softly on his chest. She looked up at him, the light from the windows painting her face a lovely shade of gold. "Your eye will be quite bruised."

"Probably. Vivienne—"

He broke off when the front door opened. Another exceedingly large footman stepped out to stand on the front step. Maximilian decided that was a message. "We should leave."

He took her arm and started to pull her down the sidewalk. She hissed and tried to bat his hand away, but he tightened his grip. She was trotting along beside him, keeping up with his long strides well enough.

"Let go."

He ignored her. He wasn't about to lose her on the street, now that the worst of the danger lay behind them. "We should have brought my carriage."

"A hack will do, just as it did when we arrived. Now, *let go*."

He couldn't. A footpad might attack them. Or Lessard's men might come after them. The dangers were still infinite. The fear that had gripped him when he couldn't get to her was still running through him. She could have been killed while he wandered through the lower levels of a brothel. But he released her, because again, she asked. It seemed he could not ignore her wishes, however much he should.

"A hack. Over there." She hailed it, waving her arm in a way no delicate lady would do. She appeared unconcerned, this entanglement with the brothel owner of little meaning, their escape inconsequential—his fear for her unimportant.

It was bloody well important to him.

"What happened up there, Vivienne, between you and Lessard?" He jammed his hands into his coat pockets, wishing he could shove his promise and his fear there as well.

"It is complicated." She didn't turn to look at him, but he could see now she wasn't unconcerned. Whatever she felt, she'd lost her dancer's grace. Her shoulders were stiff beneath the heavy cloak, and the faint light from nearby windows shone on the grim set of her mouth.

"I trusted you and your training, Vivienne. I did as you asked and let you go off with Lessard." The moment had probably stolen years of his life. "I deserve to know what happened."

She didn't answer him, as the hack rolled to a stop and let her escape his question. She climbed in among swirling wool and loose curls but did not speak.

He wasn't about to let her avoid the question. Still, he was quiet in the hack, as was she. An unseen wall sat in the vehicle with them, crafted by her life and its many pockets of truth and lies. She did not object when he joined her at the front door of her darkened town house. Wycomb must be out, the servants asleep, or she likely would have turned him away.

Neither of them expected the gift on the step.

...

Anne's hair had always been thick, Vivienne thought. Thick and shining. It was still braided.

But no longer attached to her head.

Or at least some of it wasn't.

Vivienne stumbled into the town house, clutching the silky strands. Fear etched itself on her heart, though experience told her Anne was still well and whole. She swallowed hard and closed her eyes against the sight of the thick hank of hair.

"Bloody hell." Maximilian's oath was very loud in the quiet hall. He gently closed the front door. The night was blocked from her view, but not the darkness. There were shadows in this hall. More in her heart.

"It is the girl's." Vivienne licked dry lips with a tongue that had no moisture itself. "It is Anne's."

Vivienne set it carefully on the hall table and stared at it. It was the same black shade as her own hair. Dark and thick, with the bit of curl that made it unruly. She flexed her fingers, then fisted them to keep from touching it again.

"Do you think she's—" Maximilian did not say the words. She was grateful for it.

"It is only a warning." Blood had not been shed. It could be worse. Much, much worse. Hair would grow back. "Next time it will be a finger or an ear."

"There's a note." Maximilian bent and scooped up a small paper blown into the house to lean haphazardly against the wall.

She had missed it. Stupid. Emotion was always distraction for a spy.

The note was folded and sealed, though not as precisely as Maximilian folded his notes. The corners did not match just so. She was beginning to find this sloppy instead of ordinary.

"What does it say?" She crowded him, hand on his arm and rising on tiptoe to see the paper as he unfolded it. There was little to be decoded here, and nothing she could not read herself.

DO NOT SEARCH FOR THE GIRL.

Beneath was Marchand's mark: the vulture.

"How can I *not* look for her," she snarled. Vivienne plucked the note from Maximilian's hand, but it did not need reading again. She crumpled it. The action, the paper rasping against her fingers—both felt good in her hand. "I must find her."

"Why?" Maximilian's word was not a question, but a demand for an answer. He turned to look down at her, his scowl deep and considering. Not angry, but thoughtful.

"I must. There is no other option." He did not need to know more. No one save Mrs. Asher knew the truth. No one. It had been so for more than a decade. "*I must.*" The balled note in her hand felt hot. A brand against her skin and her heart.

"Vivienne." He set a hand on her shoulder, both heavy and comforting. Damn him. "Who is she to you? I'm not so foolish as to believe she's only a servant."

"No one!" She shouted it, hurling the crumpled note as far down the hall as she could. "She is no one."

They hurt, these words she had told herself for so long. The pain struck her belly, her head. She had told herself these words time and again. Practice meant if she were caught by the enemy or Henri, they would be easy to say and would not reveal the truth.

"Go. Leave me here." She could not look at Maximilian. If she did and saw pity, she would shatter into a thousand fragments she could never piece together again.

She did not say good-bye as she strode down the hall and up the stairs. In that moment, Maximilian's gentleness and attentiveness would not help her. If she ignored him long enough, he would leave her. She could retreat to the confection of ridiculously feminine and flowery decor Henri had provided her.

There her sorrow would not be seen by another. Fear would have no witness, and she could be as she always was.

Alone.

Her room was dark when she pushed open the door. It was late. Mrs. Asher and Thomas had long since retired. Dawn was nearly here. She lit a candle—just a single one.

She would use the pitcher and basin to bathe. Yes. This was good. This was clean. It would not help Anne, but it would bring Vivienne back to where she needed to be.

It was but a moment to unfasten her cloak. The garment fell to the floor, and she did not pick it up. Later, when she knew what to do next, she would pick it up. When she knew how to rescue Anne. How to proceed. What to tell Henri. What to tell her Maximilian.

Her Maximilian.

The sob caught in her throat, stayed there. Perhaps it would choke her.

She refused to let it. There was work to be done. Routine to follow. Routine was important. But she could not unbutton the confounded buttons on the back of this ridiculous gown—and now she sounded like Maximilian. The gown was made for the bedroom, for a lover to remove. The buttons were tiny and behind her back and—

She ripped it. Ripped the buttons, the fabric. She tore silk and lace and the suggestive gown Maximilian had buttoned her into only hours before.

What was she doing? Rescuing Anne, or indulging in her own needs with Maximilian?

"Anne. I am for Anne," she whispered as the gown finally fell to the floor, tattered fabric heaping at her feet. "I have forgotten this. There should be no one but Anne."

A bar of plain soap lay beside the basin. The rough shape was solid in her hand when she scooped it up. It was the soap of her youth she'd insisted Mrs. Asher make for her. She did not want the scented and perfumed soap of the aristocracy. She did not want something soft and gentle upon her skin.

She was of the streets. Anne was of the streets. This soap reminded her of this. She could clean off the spy she had become and simply be herself—only the most important part of her was missing.

Anne was not in the house.

It was her fault Anne was missing and in danger. If she had not done those things so many years ago, if she had not been caught, if she had not joined Henri. If she had not traded her life for her freedom, then Anne would not be tied to Henri or Marchand. But she *had* done those things. All of those things. She had even enjoyed becoming a spy. Now she was forgetting Anne and losing herself in Maximilian.

Worse, she had crossed a line with Lessard she would never return from. She had allied herself with the enemy, however temporarily.

Vivienne stood naked before the basin, shivering in the chilled bedchamber. The soap was round and solid in her hand, but she could not move. She could not complete the routine she so rigidly adhered to.

"Let me help you." The words were so thoughtful, so comforting, her knees buckled.

How long had Maximilian been there? He was behind her, somewhere in the cavernous bedroom she had earned by being a pretty dancer who could steal small items on behalf of His Majesty.

"You cannot help, Maximilian." She turned to looked at him, at this gentle and handsome man whose scowl had become so dear to her, and held out the soap so he could see the round, pale, common shape of it. "You cannot help. The soap will not make me clean enough."

Chapter Thirty-Six

He didn't have the slightest idea what she was talking about, but he took the soap from her shaking hand nonetheless and recognized the scent of it as though he had kissed her skin.

Her nakedness was not erotic, though she looked as gorgeous as ever, even shuddering as she was. Instead, he felt as though he were handling a wounded animal, one who would bolt at even the slightest of rough handling.

"Do you need to be clean?" he asked carefully.

"I always wash at the end of the day." Her pupils were dilated slightly. Panic tinged her tone. This was unlike the Flower he knew. She was upset, beside herself. Beyond herself.

There was no one to help her, save him.

"Tell me. Who is the girl? Who is she to you?" It was the question he most wanted the answer to, and he knew it was this question that would reveal the secrets of Vivienne.

He took her hand, pulled up her arm. Dipping the soap into the washbasin to wet it, he began to rub the soap across her arm. Up, down, slowly. Across her forearm, her elbow. The lightly contoured upper arm. He followed it with a small, damp scrap of linen to wipe away the soap.

"My sister. Anne is my sister." The words burst from her, as though released from long, tight bonds.

He paused, the soap feeling strangely heavy in his hand. "I thought your family died of a fever. You told me that after the first time we made love."

"A lie, Maximilian."

That bloody well stung.

Still, he continued washing Vivienne, moving the soap over her shoulder, following it with the damp linen. Her skin was rough with gooseflesh. "How old is she?"

"Just thirteen, but she is strong. Brave. Anne will know not to anger Marchand. He will not do anything to her, unless it is because of me." Her breath hitched in, then out, her breasts moving with it. "Because of me."

"Why didn't you tell me?" he asked.

"Because I did not know you."

"You started to know me." He kept his voice steady, pushing away the sharp pain in his chest, and focused on the second arm he was washing. Though he wanted to, Maximilian did not look up into her dark, terrified eyes. "You trusted me with your body, why not with the truth?"

"I am not used to— No one knows. Not even Henri. I have kept it a secret from Henri for ten years. If not for Mrs. Asher, I could not have done so and still had Anne near to me." She pressed her lips together, as though she realized she'd said too much, but it seemed her secrets could no longer be stopped. "I have never told anyone. Maximilian, if it were found out, she could be used against me."

"That's already happened."

A shiver rippled over her body, every muscle convulsing. He looked at her face now, the sharp widow's peak and serious mouth. Eyes full of secrets and pain.

"I want the truth about Anne." The churning beast in his

chest demanded it.

"There is nothing to say." There was no heat in her words. Instead, she sounded sad. "No. There is much to tell, but, Maximilian—" Her breath heaved in and out again. "You must not reveal Anne to anyone. You cannot."

He didn't see that it mattered since Marchand knew of Anne already, but he agreed if only to learn the facts. "I will not say anything."

Her arms were clean enough, he thought. Time to focus on her legs. Glorious legs that had wrapped around his waist, he thought bitterly. He dunked the soap in water again, then knelt in front of her and began washing her right foot. Her hands rested lightly on his back, tensed in the fabric of his jacket.

"Anne was one when our mother died."

"What took her?" He ran the soap over her right calf, all the long, lean beauty of it. Inside him, lust warred with fury, but he recognized that if he stopped moving, she would stop speaking. Dropping the soap into the basin, he used the linen strip to dry her skin.

"An ague of some sort. The method is not important. What is important is she took care of us. She worked hard as a seamstress—she was wonderful with a needle—and worked even harder as a washerwoman, a hawker, whatever she could to make sure we could eat."

"Your father?"

"A drunkard." Her fingers dug into his back. Did she even realize it? "He hurt her. Hurt us, sometimes. Not Anne, very often, because I could hide her." Her voice dropped into a vicious whisper. "I remember the back of his hand on my face. Bruises, too, on my ribs. His boots were sturdy."

His heart clutched, but he kept his hand steady as he soaped her thigh. Softly, he touched her skin, cleaning off whatever dirt and memories she needed to shed.

"After Mama died, there was no money. No food. Nothing. Sometimes there was no fire even in the very bitter depths of winter. I remember when we couldn't afford candles. Or soap. I remember being filthy for weeks on end." She shuddered again, hard, then relaxed her hands against his back as he began to soap her left foot and leg. "Do you know true cold, Maximilian? Or true hunger?"

"No." Sorrow that she had known both crept through his anger. "What did you do, after your mother died?"

"I became a thief. A pickpocket. I stole food, water, money, watches, jewelry. Anything I could sell. Anything I could take that would keep us alive. Bread from the baker. Meat from the butcher. Anything." Her words seemed propelled by some unseen force, pushing out of her and into the room. "Because *he* gave us nothing. He only ate and drank and used the back of his hand."

Ah. This was the crux of it. Of Vivienne. "How old were you?"

"Eleven."

He could see it well enough. A young girl with no mother and a drunkard father, doing whatever she must to survive. To care for her infant sister.

"Too young," he said softly, "to support a family."

Her body stilled, like a deer who scented danger but had not yet decided to flee. So he, too, paused in the act of washing to look at her face. Her pupils had regained their normal size and the panic had faded.

"Old enough, Maximilian. There are many younger than I in the rookeries supporting their families." She said the words almost angrily, as if to goad him into a response. "I was a thief. A good one. Not as great as I am now, but good."

He wasn't sure what his response was yet. Except: "You've been a thief since I met you. I've always known you stole for the government. Logically, stealing information isn't any different than stealing food. Why couldn't you tell me of your past?"

"It is not the same. Then, I stole food from people who needed it, or money from others with their own children to feed." She jerked away from him, sprinkling drops of water over the floor. He was vaguely relieved, as the temper in her eyes he could manage better than the aching vulnerability. He stood and tossed the soap into the basin, watching the water slosh over the edge and onto the stand. He dropped the linen he had dried her with onto the floor beside it, unable to think where else to put it just then.

"We lived in the rookeries, Maximilian. It is dark there, and it stinks."

He wouldn't know. He'd never been—saying so wouldn't be the smartest decision a man could make.

She jerked a length of thin linen from a wall hook and wrapped herself in it, apparently clean enough now. "It is also dangerous in the rookeries. My father died there, in the street, when I was twelve." She fisted the hand that wasn't holding the linen. "A knife to the belly. He was in his cups and could hardly stand, they told me. Still, he fought with another drunkard and they both died."

Secrets. There were so many more. Some piece of her puzzle had yet to fall into place—though he was very much afraid he already knew it.

She transitioned from English to French and back to English again, assuming so many traits and characteristics he could not maintain his balance. Now, when she was vulnerable, she spoke English words with a French patter, as if she could not decide between the two.

Which meant one was a lie.

"Are you French?" He asked the question, knowing the answer and knowing that despite what was between them, she had not told him the truth.

"*Non.*" She said it in French with a flawless accent, nasal vowels those of the south of France. Fresh fury rose in him, and he gritted his teeth. "I was trained to be French. It is my masquerade so that I may have contact with important men and learn their secrets. Or steal their secrets."

Through the haze of betrayal, the mystery of Vivienne's life came clear. The man, Wycomb, who controlled her life but did not make love to her—there could be little doubt as to his role now.

"Wycomb trained you."

"And others. I picked Henri's pocket, thinking only to make a profit, but I was not quick enough. He was a trained spy and caught me. He told me I must work for him or be taken up for theft and hanged."

She had chosen espionage. It seemed so young to make such a choice. He turned away from her tight features to pick up the half-empty water basin.

Hoping he could gather himself.

"I do not even know how to think in English any longer," she whispered. "For two years, I spoke only French. I lived with my tutor and studied the language, the accent, the gestures. I could not use the chamber pot without asking in French. I could not eat or sleep or bathe unless I said the French words first."

Setting the bowl in the washstand, he looked once more at Vivienne. She was livid, shoulders tightly held and eyes blazing. Loose hair curled over her pale shoulders to toy with the linen she'd wrapped herself in. "Eventually, it was dancing. Every day until my toes bled."

She breathed deeply, as if in fortification. He rather needed fortification himself, he thought, gripping the edge of the washstand.

"I was a good dancer," she continued harshly. "It was natural, and I learned quickly. Knives, too, and fencing and pistols, so that I moved from weapons to dance to weapons. This was easy. These things—I could do them well. And it was a place to belong."

"Yes, I can understand that." It explained the strength of her of body, of every sinew and bone and graceful movement. His eyes traced the curve of her shoulder, the outline of her waist and hip beneath the linen. Part of him wished he had never seen her naked so he would have never known what gift had been his.

"I loved all of it." She spoke fiercely. Almost brutally. "I loved the training, the weapons, the dancing. I loved having a purpose for my country. But every moment, I had to pretend Anne did not exist. I was afraid that if I did not comply, Henri would send me away. To prison or worse. It is horrible to live in fear, Maximilian. I have never lived without it, not now, not in the rookeries. Even when I was proud of my life as a spy, I regretted every moment I was afraid."

"You could have told me of Anne. Of yourself." He held up a hand when she would have spoken. Oh, there was temper in him now, too. He could not imagine living the way she had—the rookeries, then the training and secrecy and fear, whether founded or unfounded—but that did not explain the present.

"It is logical you did not tell me in the beginning. I understand that well enough. Still, you could have told me later, when we became friends. Lovers." He'd been inside her, had kissed her and touched her body. Yet he'd never known the truth.

Vivienne wrapped the linen more tightly around herself and turned her back, the indentations of her spine peeking between the hair slipping over her shoulders. "I have said already I have not told anyone before."

"Would you have continued to lie to me if I hadn't followed you upstairs tonight?"

"I do not know." She'd tucked the ends of the linen between her breasts to free her hands and was now laying out her knives. One under the pillow. Another on the bedside table. Both positioned carefully. Her pistol she set on the other table.

He was watching a stranger. He might know her body, how it moved and the noises in her throat when he made love to her, but he didn't know the woman beneath at all. She had hidden all of it from him.

"Let me see if I understand this." His words were sharp and biting. "You're an English pickpocket from the rookeries who tried to steal from a spy. He caught you, recruited you to espionage, and trained you to be a French opera dancer. You're now being recruited by a French spymaster because your sister has been abducted."

"That is an accurate summary. Yes." She finally turned to look at him. Her face was blank. There was nothing there any longer, nothing of the dancer, the flirt, the lover. Just a spy.

Very well, then. "What are you doing with Lessard?"

"It does not matter."

"It does." He was furious with himself. With her. He'd blindly followed her lead, when it was all a lie from the start. He'd known it in his gut and had let himself ignore it, first because he didn't want to know and then because knowing would be difficult.

Damnation. He was a fool.

"Did you laugh at me, Vivienne? When I asked you of your family after we made love, when I finally placed what I thought to be your natural accent?" Stomach roiling with humiliation, he advanced until he stood in front of her. "Was it a game?"

"It was not a game." Her hand slashed through air, a Gallic punctuation mark from an Englishwoman. She squared her naked shoulders, ready for a battle.

"I don't know what country you are working for now, or who you are."

Or whether their lovemaking was a lie, and he was very, very much afraid it was.

"I am the Flower," she said fiercely. Her lips were pink and lovely, but anger had crept into her. It darkened her eyes and coated her voice, as real as her body—everything else was a lie.

"Who is *Vivienne*? What of her passion?" He reached for her, wanting to test them both. To test the truth. She brought her hands up to ward him away, but he needed to know if what lay between them was real. He craved the knowledge. "Who are you, beneath the opera dancer and spy?"

"I am the Flower. That is all." She pushed at his chest and was damn near strong enough to move him—but not quite. Hair curled wildly around her face as she shook her head. "There is no more to me. Not any longer. Nor is there anything between us."

"There might have been more." The visceral pain of her lies hit him hard and low, stealing his breath as if he'd been gutted. Run straight through with a knife and all his insides exposed. "I thought there was more."

Her face blanked, features becoming unreadable. Holding her gaze, he studied the dark iris ringing her pupils. Damnation, but her eyes were empty.

"Good-bye, Flower."

...

She did not remember Maximilian leaving the bedroom. She did not remember dressing in her shift or snuffing out the candle or plaiting her hair.

What she knew was that she was in the bedroom Henri had decorated for her. On the hard wooden floor, where it was easiest to curl into herself, arms around ankles, head resting on knees. Here she could simply breathe.

Yet she couldn't think. She wanted too badly to cry. She had told Maximilian so much of her childhood. It was more than she'd ever said before. The words had been trapped inside her for so long, yet tonight she had given them a voice.

It had not been enough. He wanted more.

She could not *give* him more. Not Vivienne.

Her chest was tight, throat aching. Swallowing the lump there, she pressed her face into her knees. It was not her past that made her want to cry. She could admit it to herself, if she was very, very honest.

She could not tell Maximilian who Vivienne was, because she did not know anymore.

Who was she?

Her mind blanked. It was a question that had no answer. She was left hollowed out, with a horrible ball in the pit of her belly and no essence of herself to capture and hold onto.

For a moment, there in the darkness of her room, she was nothingness. She was drowning in that nothingness. Her lungs could not gasp enough air; her head was squeezed, her heart pounded with the rhythm of fear. Her mind scrabbled around for something. Anything. Her hands did the same, searching the folds of her shift for purchase, then sliding over the planked floor.

Her hand found the wet linen where Maximilian had dropped it. Her fingers dug into the cold, wet fabric. Gripped.

Maximilian.

Her body shuddered, her lungs heaved, but her mind focused.

Maximilian.

The beat of her heart matched his name as it echoed through her brain.

Maximilian had been here. In her room. He had kissed

her. He had washed her. He'd brought her back from the edge. Gratitude flooded her. He had brought her back so that she could concentrate on Anne.

Anne. She must remember Anne.

She needed to think of Lessard and their bargain, not Maximilian. Not the soft rug only feet from her, or the empty hearth that called her to create heat and comfort she did not deserve. Lessard would ensure Anne was well kept and healthy, influencing Marchand with the persuasion skills that made him so important to Marchand. In exchange, Vivienne would do whatever he asked of her.

Whatever he asked.

She shuddered, body scraping against the wooden planks of the floor. She did not know what that meant, but it would not be good. Yet Lessard led to the Vulture, the Vulture to Anne.

For Anne, Vivienne would strike whatever deal with the devil that was necessary.

When Anne was safe, Vivienne would bring down the Vulture.

One more moment she would lie here, then, on the cold floor of the bedroom. Just one moment to hide her face, to squeeze her fists as hard as her heart was squeezed by tears.

Chapter Thirty-Seven

Maximilian couldn't bring himself to enter the opera box. No matter that he'd been commanded by the regent. He would be within feet of the stage.

She would be there.

He could hear the music already. The performance had begun, the tenor was singing something or other in Italian, and Maximilian was loitering in the damn hallway because he didn't want to face *her*.

At least the hallway was nearly deserted so there were no witnesses to his foolishness.

He wasn't sure his organs would survive seeing her again. She'd already sliced him to bits—which was ridiculous in and of itself. He'd always known she lied to him. She was a spy, dash it all. Spies lied.

Somehow he'd expected a truthful answer when he'd asked directly. He'd thought he was beginning to translate all those signs and symbols to find Vivienne. They'd made love, had shared something different than he'd shared with other women. He didn't know what it was, but it was different.

Better.

"Back to the opera again, Max?" Highchester stepped out of Prinny's box, brows raised in feigned surprise.

"Prinny sent for me." Maximilian was none too pleased about it. He wasn't fit for company, let alone a regent who was likely drunk. Or nearly drunk. Come to think of it, he wasn't fit for dealing with his rakehell brother, either.

"I know." Highchester smiled, but his eyes were crafty. "He's intent on learning your light o' love."

Maximilian wasn't fooled in the least. It was Highchester who had persuaded Prinny to issue the invitation. Just as Highchester had before, and just as the interest in Maximilian's "light o' love" wasn't from Prinny.

"There's no one, Highchester. There never was." He did not look away from his brother's face.

"No?" Highchester tucked an engraved timepiece in his pocket. "I find myself disagreeing, dear Max."

His brother strode toward him, purposeful. Even stalking a bit. Oh, yes. Highchester wanted something specific from him. Or a reaction from him.

Maximilian squared his shoulders and braced for the confrontation. "There is no one," he repeated, quietly and slowly so his obtuse brother would understand.

"Then you will have no problem if I pursue the Mademoiselle La Fleur, will you? She's a tasty French morsel." Greed lit Highchester's eyes as he let out a mocking laugh. "I've been waiting an age to see those magnificent breasts—"

Something exploded within him. Exploded and caught fire.

Maximilian rammed his brother into the wall. He set an arm against Highchester's throat, pressed hard.

"You will not touch her." His brain had disengaged, instinct gripping him. Vivienne might lie, she might steal, she might even kill. She might have ripped whatever had been building between them into pieces because she wouldn't tell him the truth, but he wouldn't leave her to Highchester. "She's not one of your whores."

"No." Highchester coughed, his hands grasping Maximilian's arm, but he didn't fight. He never fought, only flapped his lips with foul words. "She's *your* whore."

Maximilian's vision hazed, the edges going black. He jerked Highchester forward, then slammed him against the wall again. The sconces above them tinkled merrily.

"You will not call her whore." He bit out the words, barely able to give them voice. There was truth in Highchester's words, and it sent pain spiraling through him. Maximilian wanted to plow his fist into Highchester's face, but that wasn't his way. Not since they were boys.

But by all the gods, the Flower was more than a whore to him.

His fist smashed into his brother's mocking grin, then again. Highchester's head snapped back, banging into the wall. Paintings shook, and the wall sconces rattled again. His grin turned to a slack mouth as his eyes widened and rolled back.

"You will not call her whore," Maximilian repeated.

Another slam against the wall. Highchester coughed, scrabbled at Maximilian's arms.

"Stop! Maximilian, enough!"

Through the rushing in his ears, Maximilian heard the words. He could barely understand them, but they penetrated the livid haze coating his brain. As did the big hand gripping his shoulder, bringing Maximilian back to the present. To his panting brother, to the aria soaring in the background.

"Enough. Let him go." Bishop Carlisle's words were quieter now. His hands pressed hard on Maximilian's shoulder. A warning. "Do not engage in a public brawl. Your mother is here tonight. The scandal will—"

"No more." Maximilian interrupted, still staring at Highchester's face. It was turning from red to purple. He took primitive satisfaction in that. Then Maximilian swung Highchester around and pushed him down the hall. His brother stumbled, recovered, then hunched over to catch his breath.

Hands on his knees, Highchester looked up at him. "There is no woman, Maximilian?" he rasped. The mocking look was back, despite the blood blossoming at the corner of his mouth.

"You will not talk of Vivienne," Maximilian bit out. "You know nothing about her."

"Don't, boy," the bishop said, putting out a cautioning hand. His mouth turned down at the corners. "Don't become too involved. Mademoiselle La Fleur is only an opera dancer. Nothing can come of it."

No. She was so much more than a dancer. More than any of them realized. No one could know all there was to know of her.

Except maybe him.

"You will leave Mademoiselle La Fleur alone, Highchester." He did not wait for an answer but turned to Bishop Carlisle, who puffed out his chest. A lecture was in the offing.

Maximilian didn't want to hear it.

"What is between me and Mademoiselle La Fleur is of no one's concern but ours."

"It isn't only yours, Maximilian. It is your family's concern as well." The bishop stepped between Highchester and Maximilian. He seemed older than Maximilian remembered, but not smaller. Not weaker. "I know you have enough sense—enough gentlemanly honor—to make the right choice."

The right choice. Maximilian stared into the bishop's grave countenance, into the sharp eyes, and saw only Vivienne's eyes when he'd left.

"Give Mother my regrets that I cannot visit her this evening. As for Prinny"—he slid a glance toward the box—"his message must have gone astray."

...

Plié, step, step, turn. First position, attitude.

The crowd in the pit was barely watching. It was thus, sometimes. The tenor was not particularly talented that evening, the soprano very new—only a second-rate performance—so the guests in pit and boxes did not care. They busily gossiped and exchange political news.

Vivienne watched them, as she always did.

Lord So-and-So, a Whig, visits the box of a known Tory. Henri would want to know. She would try to remember this.

Demi-plié. Arabesque.

But her muscles were aching and sore. She did not know why exactly. Her body seemed not quite her own. It was very heavy. The soprano joined the tenor, their voices soaring. Around her, other dancers moved and played their parts.

She stumbled a little—recovered. Had anyone seen? A quick glance showed that the other dancers had not noticed. No one looked at her differently than they had before. Costumes swirled around her, the fresh flowers in the dancers' hair cloyingly sweet.

Her gaze searched the pit for anything remarkable. Henri would expect a report. This was her duty each night. Nothing of note in the pit, nothing interesting in the boxes.

Then she glanced at Prinny's box.

Maximilian.

Her heart lifted, her limbs lifted. She spun on the stage, her *petit fouetté* becoming *fouetté en tournant*. Bigger, more brilliant turns. Her heart thumped in time with it, momentarily glad. The *fouetté en tournant* was not part of the performance. She would be chastised—but she could not help it.

She would be afraid of Henri's reaction later. Just now, she only wanted to see Maximilian.

Turning in a pirouette, she quickly glanced at Prinny's box again. At Maximilian.

Her heart plummeted, belly clutching. It was not him, but the other one. Baron Highchester. He was as tall, as large. The shape of him was similar, but they did not move the same. Eyes were the same shape, but not color, nor did they have the same mouth. Only the same jaw.

She could have wept. So foolish, she was, to dance a *fouetté en tournant*. It was not Maximilian. And if it *were* he, he had left her. He would not come back.

Her feet tangled together. She tried—oh, how she tried—to untangle them. A step and another, but they would not listen to her brain. They did not obey her commands. She tripped, stumbled, nearly caught herself—but she did not.

She slammed into the stage, skidding across the wooden boards. Splinters pierced her palms and shredded her gown. The rip, it was audible. As audible as the gasp of the dancers, the groan of the crowd. The tenor's voice ceased its drone, the instruments trailed off. All that was left was the soprano and the murmur of the crowd.

The soprano's warble also died, and there was nothing but horror in the theater, along with that unmistakable amusement when someone failed.

Chapter Thirty-Eight

"You could knock on the front door, you know." Jones did not look up from the pistol he was cleaning. He continued to polish, the soft cloth penetrating this nook, that cranny, each movement undertaken with deliberation.

"Knocking on the door is not as enjoyable." Vivienne could not help the half smile, though it seemed to stretch her reserve of energy. "I always wonder if I have truly hidden my entrance from you."

"No."

"I did not think so."

She could not decide how best to ask for assistance, so she prowled the room while he continued his careful cleaning. The town house was beginning to lose the look of Angel. Angel had liked richness tempered with practicality. Now that Angel slept elsewhere, she could see Jones here. Weapons carefully arranged, corresponding tools lined up by length. Books stacked on tables and shelves—many more than Angel would have had lying about. Yet each stack was ordered precisely by size.

"How are you, after your fall at the theater yesterday evening?" Jones asked, the concerned tone as deliberate as his care for the pistol.

"Well enough." She ran a hand over the three sets of field glasses lined up on the mantelpiece. She did not know, precisely, what Jones was asking or what information he was searching for.

But she was not ready to leave, and she could not decide how to start. How did one state one was working with a French spy, but only for a little while? More, how did one ask for assistance from the man tasked with ensuring British spies did *not* work with the French?

The matched pistol to the one Jones cleaned sat on the desk. Picking it up, she sighted down the barrel, checked for ammunition. It was empty but needed cleaning. This she could do while she considered her words.

Sitting beside Jones, she began the methodical task of cleaning the pistol. Cloth, oil. It smelled and felt familiar. Side by side they worked, and there was comfort in that. She did not realize how much she needed to be in this world of espionage, where secrets were expected. Where a person did not need to tell someone everything. Here, it was understood that whatever was in your head could stay there.

Secrecy was not always the right way.

She sighed, very long, very heavy. "Do you ever wish to simply tell the truth? All of it?"

"The truth is often frightening," he countered, flipping his pistol to attack dirt and dust on the other side.

"That is not an answer."

"Why are you here, Flower?" Jones did not look at her. He sighted the barrel of the pistol, checking its accuracy. He aimed at the floor, then at a painting, then the bookshelf. She knew the movements herself. Check the sight at each distance, then recheck.

"It is tiring, never being honest." She had not meant to say it in such words, but there it was.

"Would this be about the code breaker?" He blew dust off the pistol, checked the sight again. "Westwood?"

Something heavy landed at the base of her belly. Jones was watching her, the spy among spies. "Perhaps."

"He's the man you spoke of before, isn't he? The one that sent you running into my arms." His dry tone was constructed in part of laughter, part of embarrassment.

"I should apologize for throwing myself at you, no?" Grinning, she shrugged one shoulder to dismiss it. "*Oui*, it is he. I do not know of anyone else I can ask these questions, Jones. You understand me, and where I am from." Though he had never known the whole of it.

It was only Maximilian she had told.

"Westwood is a good man, Vivienne." Jones said quietly, all laughter gone. He laid the pistol in his lap and looked up to study the painted ceiling, as if the curling designs would help him choose his words. "He's not an agent, however, even though he's on the periphery of this world. He doesn't quite understand it. And from what I know, there is little room for error with Westwood. He does not take kindly to half-truths."

"Dire words." She made small round circles on the barrel with the cloth. If she continued these circles, perhaps she would not have to meet Jones's gaze.

"You're under scrutiny, Flower." It was said casually, but there was little mistaking his warning. "And so is Westwood."

"By whom?" She sent a puff of breath over the pistol so that she would not be tempted to hold it while she waited for an answer.

"Your meetings with Westwood have not gone unnoticed." He had not answered directly, which meant only a few knew yet. "A late visit to your town house, a glimpse of you together near a notorious brothel owned by a man known to work with the Vulture. All is noted."

"Henri?" She breathed deeply and carefully, so that whatever skittered in her belly would not show itself elsewhere in her body.

"Knows nothing of you and Westwood, yet, but it will not be long. Nor does he appear to know you are involved in something beyond his assignments." Jones looked at her, direct, with the full force of his intense gaze. "I cannot know either, Vivienne. Don't tell me."

"It is not wrong, what I am doing." It was not precisely right, either. There was much unknown between working with Lessard to find Anne and bringing down the Vulture.

"Be wary, Flower." Jones set a hand on her shoulder, squeezed once. "Your leash is short, and I can't make it any longer."

She understood. He was caught between loyalty to a friend and loyalty to his commander. At some point, he would have to choose. If she told him, he would have to make the choice.

She was alone. Alone, with Lessard and the Vulture on one side and Henri on the other. Anne was in front of her.

There was no one behind.

Chapter Thirty-Nine

"She is on the edge, my lord." Lessard pushed the billiard balls absently across the green baize. He sat on the side of the table, idly swinging a big leg.

"I'm not surprised." The Vulture leaned on this cue, contemplated the end of it. "The Flower seems determined to find the girl." Which was why he'd sent his message. The Flower would take the hair to heart. He'd observed her long enough now to know that.

And she'd fallen during her performance.

It seemed he'd aimed and found his mark.

"Do you think she can be turned?" Lessard stood, ducking his head to avoid the tiered chandelier above the table.

"No," the Vulture said softly, rubbing a thumb along the length of the billiard cue. "No, she cannot be turned. She has a sense of loyalty I hadn't expected from a petty thief."

"Then she's useless to us." Lessard huffed and pushed the balls across the table again. "We should eliminate the girl, then the Flower, and be done with it."

Large man, small brain, the Vulture thought. It was often

thus with the men he used. Muscle and brawn, but little mind behind it. Lessard was a bit different, true. A businessman through and through, but he lacked farsightedness.

"I'm not finished with the Flower yet. I can't turn her, so she'll never be the double agent I'd hoped, but I can use her now, while she's still off balance." More, he needed her quick fingers and access to those around Prinny.

"I do not understand." Lessard's brows turned down in confusion, the scar on his face shifting.

"The Flower will do as I command in the short term. Until she finds the girl, she won't risk noncompliance." The Vulture laid his cue across the table, then rolled it beneath the flat of his hand as he considered the angles. If, or when, the Flower found the girl, there would no longer be an incentive to ensure her silence. The Flower would tell what she knew—and it was unclear just how much she did know—to the British. "If she finds the girl, they must both be disposed of immediately." Before either had the opportunity to provide any information to the British.

"What of her companion? Westwood?"

"I haven't decided whether to kill him or not. He might be useful, given the correct circumstances."

Still, with the Flower panicked about the girl, now was the time to act. Before she determined where the girl was hidden.

"It is time," the Vulture said softly. "We will put the plan into action."

Chapter Forty

Vivienne studied the bright flame illuminating her bedchamber as she performed her stretches. It focused her, that dancing gold light. She could imagine it as bright hope. A silly thing to pretend. Hope was an emotion a spy should never rely on.

Only she had nothing else to rely on now.

She must practice. She had never fallen in a performance. *Never.*

Henri, the conductor, the manager of the theater. All had been livid, though none as much as Henri. He had railed, and like a viper, she'd expected him to strike. He had not, but she had not forgotten that moment of fear.

She shifted from first position to fourth position, held, moved to fifth position, then lowered into a *demi-plié*, held, breathing in and out. She stayed there, testing herself, her strength, her balance. Thighs trembled, her stomach muscles shivered beneath her skin. Still she held it, pushing herself. Another second, just one more—

The door to the bedroom opened. She shot to her feet,

the knife she'd lain on the floor gripped in her hand before she could think. Spinning, she faced the open door, poised to throw the knife and already aiming for the throat.

The throat belonged to Mrs. Asher.

The woman's gasp was sharp on the air, her eyes on the knife. "Miss Vivienne, you put that down."

"*Mon Dieu.*" Lowering the weapon, she sank to the floor, knees weak. What had she nearly done? Henri, Marchand, Lessard—they were all putting her on edge. "I am sorry, Mrs. Asher."

"Miss Vivienne, you need to sleep. Just rest for a few hours." The housekeeper closed the door quietly, leaned against it. Her gown was stained from the day's work. "You're making yourself sick with worry."

"Perhaps." But she could not sleep. She could not rest. Deliberately, she set the knife on the floor. "You do not come into my room at the end of the day for no reason, Mrs. Asher. What do you need?"

"I have a note." The paper seemed very delicate in Mrs. Asher's competent hands. "It was delivered not five minutes ago to the back door. I nearly missed the knock, as I was preparing for bed."

Vivienne leaped across the room, snatching the note from her fingers. In but a moment, the seal was broken and she was scanning it. She recognized the words "viscount" and "deliver," the usual "to" and "this." It was not from the Vulture, as the telltale bird was missing. In its place was a large, ornate *L*. Lessard, of course.

There was a second note, folded into the first. This, too, was sealed, but she did not dare open it. Not until she knew what was to be delivered.

"I remember the boy who brought it, Miss Vivienne. That won't escape me again." Mrs. Asher's eyes were determined. She crossed large, round arms over her equally large chest.

"He was a child, barely seven or eight, and filthy. I could scarcely make out the color of his hair. Blue eyes, for whatever help that is. An orphan from the street, likely enough, paid to run an errand." Her lips thinned out, flattened in that way Mrs. Asher had of showing sorrow. "I've known my fair share of those."

"Yes," Vivienne said softly. Meeting Mrs. Asher's eyes was difficult, but she did it. "You have been kind to them. What did you give the boy before you sent him away?"

"Bread." Mrs. Asher flushed, rosy circles blooming into her cheeks. "It was left from yesterday, so 'twasn't fresh any longer."

"I don't begrudge the boy bread, spy or not." His allegiance could still change, and a kind word and a loaf of bread from someone other than Lessard might make the difference between a future spy for France or some other life. "The note, Mrs. Asher. What does it say?"

She was not embarrassed with Mrs. Asher. There was no need, given their past.

"Is it in English?" Mrs. Asher leaned over. "Aye. Sure enough. *The girl is being moved. Deliver this letter to Viscount Lynley before midnight, and I shall find out where.*" The housekeeper's head jerked up to stare with wide, round eyes. "That's only a few hours away, Miss Vivienne. It's already after dark."

"It does not say more?" It was not enough information. Where would she find Lynley? What information would she be delivering to him? What if she failed? And Anne. Always was the threat to Anne in her mind. "What of the other note?"

"Miss Vivienne, you should take this to Mr. Westwood."

The rip in her heart was large and very dark. "I cannot." She shook her head and hoped the rip would stitch itself someday.

She studied the folded message Lessard intended her to

deliver. There was little time to melt the seal, but the paper was thinner than the note she'd collected on Bond Street.

"Can you read through it?" she asked Mrs. Asher. "Here, like this." She pulled Mrs. Asher over the candle on the bedside table, held the paper over the flame. It became a burnished gold, emphasizing the ink inside.

"It's backward, but I can see it is about money." Mrs. Asher peered at the paper. "Lynley owes Lessard, for gambling and women, it looks like." She scoffed. "Men. Doesn't matter if he's a peer or poor, they fall victim to both."

Not all men, thought Vivienne. Maximilian did not.

"I am going out, Mrs. Asher." She spun toward the wardrobe, intent on the clothing there. In her mind, she was already dressing in breeches and boots. "I must locate Viscount Lynley somewhere in London."

Lynley was ridiculously easy to find. She knew enough about him to know he would be at the most indecent, debauched soiree of the evening. For today, that was a masquerade. This was good, as it was easy to sidle into the ballroom unknown and unrecognized.

But one must have a costume at a masquerade. Her hair was piled high and powdered to hide its color, a mask was added to her breeches and boots, and she'd removed the linen shirt beneath her coat and waistcoat. With the scandalous deep V of a few open buttons and the tight-fitting breeches, it was only a few moments until the guests standing in front of her were intent on her body, not her face—which was as she wanted it.

"Hello, sir!" She sang it as if she did not know a masked Prinny was holding court on a mound of pillows in a ballroom decorated like a feast in ancient Rome. As if she had not noticed Lord Lynley was to his left, fondling the breast of Minerva—or perhaps Venus. "Your little group seems to be having the most fun at this party." She cocked her head and bowed with a flourish. "I want to play, too."

She used her most aristocratic English. It was more difficult than using the French, as Henri had taught her the sound and lilt of *le français* before the refinements of her native tongue.

The men and women around Prinny turned to look at her. Eyes behind masks blinked, even as lips curved in welcome. Men did so love women's skin, did they not? The women with them were as drunk as the men and did not seem to mind another woman cavorting on the pillows.

It was early, yet, for a party such as this, and the guests were not as much in their cups as she would like.

"Welcome, my dear." A familiar-looking man—not Lynley—held out a hand to pull her down to the pillows. No doubt he was one of Prinny's regular hangers-on. "You did not dress correctly. This is ancient Rome, didn't you know?"

She smiled at the man and picked a plump, ripe grape from the plate of food at her elbow. Setting the grape to her lips, she tapped it there as if thinking. "If we all looked like goddesses, a lady would never stand out." Popping the grape into her mouth, she continued to smile coyly at him. "And a lady always wants to stand out, does she not?"

Down the line of the pillows and goddesses and Caesars, a masked Prinny laughed. "Not a shy one, are you?"

"What would be the point of bashfulness, sir?" She leaned back against the tasseled pillows. The coat buttons strained with the movement, so with one hand she unfastened the top button, then another. The waistcoat would cover her, but the hint of removal would entice.

"Indeed." Prinny's greedy eyes followed her fingers.

Ah. She had his attention now, if she had not before.

She must be careful. Prinny would know Vivienne La Fleur, so she would be certain not to be Vivienne. Instead, she would continue to be this English girl, a young lady out to play where she should not be.

For herself, her attention was to Prinny's left. Lynley had barely noticed her, it seemed. This was good, she decided, flicking open the last coat button to leave only the waistcoat between her and Prinny's gaze. Easier to slip the note into Lynley's pocket if he did not notice her. Although he did not have pockets—he wore a toga. She studied the drape and fold of fabric. More difficult than pockets, but not impossible.

Prinny gestured for her to come forward, flicking his fingers at the pillows in front of him. Others shifted to make room for her near the regent—it was impossible to hide princeliness behind a mask and toga.

Sauntering toward him, she set her feet lightly between the pillows and glasses of wine and trays of food. Her mask seemed heavy on her face, and yet too thin. Her powdered hair, the male costume, the rouge and paint she wore on her face—none of it seemed enough. Yet there was no other way to disguise herself but costume and powder and mask.

Gathering her courage and sending an additional sway to her hips, an additional flutter to her lashes, she approached the prince and his companions. Blood hummed as she focused on the man to Prinny's left. An easy matter to position herself just so. An easier matter to smile at Prinny and sense Lynley's body. She was close. A shift, one way or the other, and she would be able to slip the note between the folds of his toga to sit inside the wide leather belt he wore. He would notice it later, as the toga was removed.

Gaze on the regent, she extended her legs and lazily picked up the nearest glass of wine. Through the slits of her mask, she eyed the rotund Julius Caesar before her, and while she did, she slipped the note from her pocket and tucked it into her palm.

"You're holding court, it seems, Caesar. It is good the Prince Regent is not here, or you would lose your throne." She drank deep from the cup. The wine was warm and robust and glowed red in the glass. She hoped it didn't go to her head too quickly. She didn't want to fumble the note.

"What makes you think I haven't staged a Roman coup and overthrown him?" the prince pretending to be Caesar asked.

"Because the regent is too handsome and too powerful to be overthrown, of course," she said, quite seriously.

The royal laughed, belly shaking beneath the toga as though it were a thick sauce being jiggled in its saucepan.

While she watched Prinny enjoy her flattery, her peripheral vision caught Lynley looking their way. The laugh had drawn his attention. Now, then. While Lynley was looking right at her—because he was looking at her face, not the hand tucked among the pillows, or the note she'd palmed.

The thrill of the hunt rose in her. Her fingers moved—

The regent leaned forward, cupped her chin in his plump hand. Fear tripped along her spine as he studied her masked face, turning it side to side. Her fingers stopped their movements. Too many eyes on her. The goddesses, the Romans, the masked faces surrounding them. All were watching.

"A wise lady, indeed, to think of the prince's power," Prinny murmured, breath pungent with the odor of wine. Greed and avarice brightened his eyes as his other hand played with the thick powdered curls she'd left loose to skim her shoulders and breasts. "But what is your costume?"

"A proper English lady who's escaped the confines of her life and is looking for fun," she responded. Coy words, a coquettish look. "What else would I be?"

"A flower, of course." The sly voice pierced her consciousness, plunging an icy fist into her belly. She did not recognize the tones, the tenor. She only knew that voice belonged to a man—and it was not the prince.

The royal hand cupping her chin fell away. The royal face turned to look at the speaker.

"If I am not mistaken," that sly, chilling voice continued, "this proper English lady is none other than the elusive Mademoiselle La Fleur."

Raw terror scraped at her skin. She was discovered. Someone had seen through her costume. But how deeply? To the opera dancer, or the spy? The opera dancer was of no import, as she could play that role and still accomplish Henri's mission. The other—Lessard's note was becoming damp in her palm.

A pickpocket could not have damp palms. Mistakes were made this way. She angled her head to study her revealer, keeping that coy, coquettish look on her face. He was masked, but she did not need the mask removed to recognize him.

He was not Maximilian. The hair was not the same, nor was the deviousness in his bright-blue eyes, so different from Maximilian's hazel ones. But she knew the shape of his jaw, the breadth of his shoulders.

Not Maximilian, but his brother.

"Lord Highchester," she said, slipping back into her French accent. "Monsieur. Are you still enamored of the opera?" She could barely think beyond the note in her hand.

Beyond discovery.

"Not as much as my brother."

Ah. So, that was how the wind blew. It was not that he knew she was the spy, but only Vivienne La Fleur, the dancer, and the elder son envied the younger son. She could make use of that. She was not certain how, exactly, but knowledge was always a weapon.

"Your brother is not as enamored as it seems, my lord." She sipped her wine, then she slid a gaze at Prinny. "It appears I have been discovered, Monsieur Le Roi."

"That was a very convincing act, my dear." The prince was watching her speculatively, eyes very much alert. It was a surprise. He often consumed casks of wine in much the same way a fish consumed water.

But she knew Prinny.

"How else was I to attend?" Stretching like a cat who'd eaten cream so her body was at its best advantage, she pouted at him. "I was not invited, Monsieur Le Roi."

"A travesty." His eyes glazed over, traveling along the length of her body. "Are you recovered from your illness?"

"A misstep, that is all." She wiggled her fingers, dismissing her fall on stage.

Lynley had looked away again, his attention focused on the blond Roman goddess on his lap. He pressed a kiss to the side of her neck. The woman pretended to be uninterested, but her giggle belied her actions.

"I could not allow my favorite men to play without me." She included Lord Highchester with a glance, tipped her lips up on one side. A lure that was effective on most men.

Then her quarry, Lord Lynley, staggered to his feet, and alarm staggered its way into her chest. Lynley reached for the goddess's hand. They were leaving, probably for a tryst in a shadowy alcove or an empty hallway.

She would fail.

If she did not deliver the note on this, her first mission, Lessard would dismiss her. There would be no more opportunities to gain information from him.

She rose to her feet, the note still folded into her hand. "Lord Lynley, have you tired of our company?"

He paused, an ingrained gentlemen no matter his profligate ways. "Never, mademoiselle."

All eyes turned to Lynley, and then to his companion — who blushed prettily.

Vivienne slipped the note into Lynley's toga.

Chapter Forty-One

Vivienne had driven him to Bedlam.

Maximilian couldn't concentrate on even the simplest translations. His brain—a traitorous organ if there ever was one—kept circling round to Vivienne.

Or whatever her name was, because Vivienne likely wasn't it.

He dipped his quill into the ink, thinking to start on the next line of his translation despite it being well after midnight. But damnation, he couldn't think. His mind was buzzing with gossip, of all things. The great Flower had fallen. Rumors were many and varied—she had finally lost her skill, she had taken a draught of brandy before the performance, she was with child.

That last gave him pause. It was strangely satisfactory, even as it terrified him. If she were with child, it would be *his* child. The concept was interesting and warmed an odd corner of his heart. The reality of it made him uneasy, however. He would be a miserable father. He didn't have the slightest idea where to begin. Perhaps there was a treatise on fathering he could read. Yes, if he could find a treatise, then he would know the proper way to go about it.

A moot point, he thought, since she hadn't trusted him with even her real identity.

"Sir." Daggett's voice pierced through the fog filling Maximilian's brain. "Sir. Lord Wycomb to see you."

Maximilian jerked, sending the quill skittering across the page. He stared at the line of ink now crossing through his translation. The Flower's commander. Her fake protector and the man responsible for the twists and turns of her life.

Maximilian had the overwhelming urge to smash his fist into the man's face.

"Mr. Westwood." Lord Wycomb's voice dripped with ice.

When Maximilian looked up and over at the man, he saw Wycomb's eyes were chilled as well. Maximilian had seen him before, of course, fondling the Flower in his brother Highchester's house. Having the man standing in his very own drawing room in the middle of the night seemed an affront.

A single fist might not be good enough. He thought of the pistol in the top drawer of his desk and its mate tucked into the box on the bookshelves. Unfortunately, he couldn't shoot a man in cold blood.

Pity.

"I am aware of your service to our country, Westwood, and I have need of those services."

"My lord." Slowly, Maximilian stood. He was taller than Wycomb, which was absurdly pleasing. "What can I do for you?"

"I need you to read this note. I believe it to be coded." He tossed the note on the desktop instead of simply handing it over. The paper fluttered lightly as it fell.

Maximilian waited a moment until Wycomb looked at him and held his gaze. "I'm busy."

If possible, Wycomb's gaze became yet more frigid. "This

is potentially a matter of high treason."

"That may be, but I don't take kindly to people entering my house without an appointment and making demands." It wasn't true. He didn't take appointments, and nearly all of the people who entered his house made demands of one kind or another, but he disliked Wycomb on principle.

"You will decipher this," Wycomb said softly. Menacingly. "Now."

"I will work on this—tomorrow." He hadn't known he had mulish tendencies. Apparently, they only presented themselves when confronted with an ass.

"I need it now." Wycomb's eyes narrowed. "By order of the prince."

Maximilian picked up the note, ready to shove it down Wycomb's throat. There were other code breakers. Not as good as himself, perhaps, but good enough. Wycomb could go to any one of those men and see the deed done.

He caught the scent on the paper. *Her* scent. Soap. No perfumes, no flowery additions to make a man cough.

Just clean, homespun soap.

It was finished.

Maximilian was sick. His gut roiled and burned, and something damn near fury was growing in him.

She had lied. *Again.*

Wycomb had been waiting in the drawing room for nearly an hour. How Daggett had kept him there was unclear, and Maximilian didn't want to know. It was enough he'd had silence to work in. Nothing to distract him but the letters and mathematics and the smell of the Flower's soap.

"Did you complete the decoding, sir?" Daggett asked, quill poised above a ledger as Maximilian stepped into his assistant's adjoining office. As ever, Daggett was ready to record Maximilian's findings.

At the moment, the thought made bile rose in his throat. He handed the note and translation to Daggett, unable to even look at either one again.

"The letter is from Lessard and outlines an assassination plot against the Prince Regent. It also states the Flower has agreed to be the assassin's courier."

. . .

The back door of the town house was unlocked. She slipped through and into the dark kitchen. There was no Anne waiting for her, sitting in a rocking chair near a banked fire with some household task. No Mrs. Asher working at the counters. There was little need to cook when the growing Anne was not there to be hungry eight times each day and Vivienne never knew when she would be at home.

The night had been exhausting. Monsieur Le Roi was tireless. He'd expected her to stay until dawn. She had not. Only long enough to please him with disclaimers about her health and a few amusing stories. Then she had slipped into the night—early morning, in fact. The guests had imbibed enough so they had not noticed she'd left before the sun rose.

She had succeeded. The note had been placed in Lynley's toga. He had left with the girl—the pretend goddess—to do what men did with pretend goddesses at masquerades. And Vivienne had been left entertaining Prinny. Still, the note was delivered well before midnight, and Lynley would think nothing more of it than a debtor to a creditor.

The stairs were long. Weariness settled over her muscles, her mind. Her bed would be heaven. The door to her room was closed. The hall was dark and still in the last hours before the sun. She brought that darkness into her for a moment.

Exhaustion weighed heavy, and she fought the urge to slide to the floor right there in the hall.

Tired. She was just so tired.

But there was Anne. Tomorrow—today, if one used the clock—Lessard might tell her where Anne was being moved. Or the next day. He had said he would, if she succeeded. She had done so, and she would hold him to his bargain.

She set a hand on the bedchamber door and pushed it open, then stepped into her room. Darkness, here, too. No Anne. No Maximilian.

Only emptiness.

The backhanded slap sent stars wheeling behind her eyes. Fire singed a line along her cheekbone. The shock, the strength of the blow, spun her around. She caught herself on the cold wall, just missing the painting hanging there.

"What are you doing with Lessard?" Henri's voice was low and harsh in the dark behind her. He did not shout when he was angry. He became quiet, so one strained to hear one's punishment.

His hand fisted in her hair, forcing the pins out, pressing her face into the wall she'd sought steadiness in.

"I am doing nothing with Lessard." Now she sought solace in the cool, flat wall. She could not think quickly enough. Her cheekbone felt cracked in a thousand places.

His hand released her hair, and she let out a shaking breath. A candle flared, and the monster in the darkness became visible. She turned to face him, pressing her shoulder blades flat against the wall. It was the only solid thing she could find.

The handsome face of Henri was not so handsome, now, in the candlelight. It was terrifyingly blank.

"You would not visit Lessard for nothing." He stepped forward. She flinched, unable to stop herself, and nearly reached for her knife. But one did not use a knife on one's trainer. "You would not pass Lessard's coded letter to Lord

Lynley for nothing."

"The letter was not—" She could not complete the words. Another blow smashed into her face. The explosion of pain sent her to her knees. She caught herself, barely, before her face crashed into the floor as well as her knees.

Coded? The wooden boards beneath her were hard. She pressed her palms against them and breathed deep to center her thoughts. Center herself. Vivienne fought against the retching pain in her belly. Had the note been coded? What had she delivered?

Henri crouched beside her.

Her fear crouched with him.

Fear of being hanged, fear of leaving Anne. She had lived with this fear as a girl, lived with it when Henri had discovered her. It was worse now. If she was arrested for treason, Anne would be left alone with Marchand. He might kill her, or train her, or give her to Lessard.

Or sell her to the highest bidder.

So Vivienne did not fight. That would be unpardonable in Henri's eyes, and she would die. She would accept anything, any punishment, to keep Anne safe.

"What game are you playing?" he whispered, bending over her and setting his mouth against her ear. Whiskers brushed against her cheek like so many thorns. His breath was hot, his body smelling of eau de cologne and angry sweat.

"I am not playing any game, Henri." The scent of him sickened her. "I am only trying to protect your interests. Protect England."

"Liar." His mouth touched her cheek. A kiss that was not a kiss. "You lie, Vivienne. Do not think I can't see it." His voice was cold in her heart, harsh on the air. "I don't take betrayal kindly."

"Not betrayal." She remained on her hands and knees, hunched over like a dog who had been kicked. Her eye would swell soon. Even now, she could feel it begin. He would take pleasure in this. She kept her face averted, let her loose hair hang like a curtain to block him out. "I would not betray you," she lied.

"I had not expected you would—but that's my mistake. I saved you once from death. I trained you. Kept you. I demanded and expected loyalty. And yet, you met with Lessard."

He moved so that he crouched in front of her now, strong and sure before her abject pose. A long, long moment passed. A long moment when all she could see was the shine of his boots, her fingers curling into the wood floor, and her hair curtaining her face.

He set his hand on her uninjured cheek and deliberately, slowly, turned her face up to look at him. He gave her time to look away, to fight, but she knew he would use it as a reason to kill her. Death shone in the cold, cold light of his eyes.

She would not survive this night. He would not trouble to send her for trial. He would simply kill her. He only wanted an excuse.

"You met with Lessard," he whispered again, still tipping her face up so he could see it. "You accepted his note, and you delivered it. If it had not fallen out of Lynley's toga after he tupped a whore at the masquerade, I would not have known. The prince himself saw it fall."

Despair choked her. She could not defend herself. She had delivered the note, as he said.

"Nothing to say, Vivienne?" Henri gripped her chin, fingers biting into her flesh. "Do you know, I could break your neck. In one motion—in one second—I could break your pretty, lying neck. Then you would be gone, with nothing to show of this life but petty thievery."

No! Her mind screamed it. Her heart echoed it. *Anne! Maximilian!* Terror immobilized her. Too long, she had lived in fear of Henri. Of imprisonment, of death. This fear was so huge, so ingrained, it consumed her.

So cold it had frozen her courage.

Henri leaned down, a mocking smile curving his lips. "Instead of breaking your neck, my disloyal Flower, I shall turn you over to those who excel in the torture of double agents. They will make the closed bud bloom and reveal her secrets."

She did not think beyond a single word.

Life.

Jabbing an elbow into Henri's ribs was satisfying and terrifying and liberating. His gasp of pain was an aria in her ears. Spinning on her knees, she attempted to smash the heel of her hand into his nose. Such a move should have incapacitated him, but he jerked away at the last moment and her blow glanced off his cheek.

Still, it sent him over backward.

Vivienne scrambled up and leaped away—only to be felled by a foot sweeping along the floor to topple her. Landing on her back pushed the air out of her lungs. Without breath, she forced herself to roll over and pushed to her feet.

And so they faced each other. The trainer and the trainee. The spymaster and his pawn.

His eyes—they glittered in the light of the single candle he had lit. Bright and hard.

"There will be no agents who excel at torture, Vivienne. You will not be afforded life for that long." Breathless words. Furious words. "I shall kill you myself."

"So be it." She accepted his vengeance. Expected it—but she would not bow to it. "Another day, perhaps."

He lunged, and though she moved back, the blow still landed in her belly. With a cry she doubled over but used the pain to fuel her. She rammed her shoulder into his chest, then twisted so her back pushed him toward the ground.

It was only a moment of advantage. So she leaped, breath heaving, to straddle him, and plowed her fist into his face.

Cartilage crunched beneath her knuckles. She hit him again and dimly felt the skin of her knuckles split. She could not separate that pain from the pain of her cheek, her belly.

Nor could she keep Henri down. He was twice her weight and stronger. He bucked her off and backhanded her again. She tasted blood, sickeningly metallic, as her head snapped back.

Henri pounced. Some part of her brain recognized this, but he seemed to move slowly, his body light in the air instead of a dangerous weapon. He was large, larger than she could ever remember him being. He filled her vision. Her consciousness.

She could not imagine her body moving quickly enough, but it did. One booted foot slammed into his ribs, then, quickly, she sent the other foot high. Higher. It connected with Henri's now bloodied face. There, at his temple, as Henri had taught her. A woman's feet, he had said, were her strongest body part.

And Vivienne was a dancer.

His eyes rolled back. His body went limp. The floorboards shook beneath her as he fell. How long would he be unconscious? Ten minutes? Twenty? Forever?

A dead woman. This was what she would be if she stayed in England now. She had done the unforgivable—but she had planned for escape. Had practiced for years. If someone came for them, if they had to leave quickly, she would be ready.

She didn't roll up the rug but kicked it aside. She winced as pain rushed through her belly, throbbed in her face, but the loose floorboard moved silently. She had made it so. Money was hidden there. Small bags of it that could be tucked into boots and pockets and bonnets and bodices. Knives were concealed there. Pistols, a musket—she left that, as it was too difficult to carry—and even small vials of poison. All were packed in a drawstring bag. Clothes were already packed in another bag. One gown for Anne, one for Vivienne.

Henri did not move. She did not check for his breath. It would not matter. If he lived, he would look for her. If he died, someone else would. And she could not take a man's life when he could not defend himself. A mistake, perhaps, and the cost could be her own life, but she could not do it.

She would leave him and let fate take its course.

Stepping over him, she moved quickly to the door and the darkened hall. She must remain calm. There was no other way to survive.

It was only minutes before she limped into Mrs. Asher's room. A silent walk to the bed, a quiet hand on the housekeeper's shoulder. She came awake almost instantly.

"Shh." Vivienne set a finger to her mouth. "You must go. Hide."

"What?" Mrs. Asher sat up, her cap shifting over long gray-blond braids. Vivienne had not known Mrs. Asher braided her hair at night. It made her seem younger. "Your eye, Miss Vivienne! Your face!"

It throbbed, more than she'd expected. "I have run afoul of Henri. He is upstairs, perhaps dead. Perhaps not."

"What's happened?" Mrs. Asher asked, her tone brisk now. She pushed the covers back and swung plump feet over the edge of the bed.

"It is too complicated to be explained." Vivienne pulled out one of the money purses tucked into her waistband and ignored the sharp pain in her side as she moved. "Take this. Run. To Scotland or Wales. Perhaps Ireland. Take Thomas with you and look after each other. It is not safe in London for either of you—not even in England."

"Oh, God." Mrs. Asher took the purse. The whites of her eyes shone in the dark as she pressed her lips together. Vivienne would take that image with her. Always. "When can we come back?"

"I don't know." Vivienne's stomach roiled and pitched, adding to the ache of Henri's punch. "When you find a place to start over, to hide, send a note to Monsieur Westwood of your location and I will get it from him in time." She swallowed hard. "He can be relied upon."

Whatever was not between them any longer, she could rely upon him to keep Mrs. Asher and Thomas safe. Maximilian was everything that was honorable.

The housekeeper was already moving about the room to gather items. Vivienne realized she, too, had a bag already packed to flee.

"Mrs. Asher." She could barely whisper the word beyond her aching and bloodied lip. "I will miss you."

The housekeeper's eyes were very large but very sure. "We will find each other again. Make no mistake of that."

Vivienne did not have this hope, and it was drowning her. "But—"

"We will. The gods or the fates or what have you wouldn't have brought us this far only to cut us loose." Mrs. Asher tossed the clothing bundled in her arms onto the bed and bundled Vivienne into her arms instead. They were sturdy and steady arms, her soft body a comfort. "It's not an easy thing to hold the fate of nations in your hands, which is what you do. It's not an easy thing to hold lives in your hands, which you also do. And it is not an easy thing to protect everyone."

"I don't—" She could not finish. Mrs. Asher was too reassuring. Too motherly.

"You will succeed, child. I've never known you to fail." Mrs. Asher gave her shoulder a little pat, the easy gesture warming Vivienne. "If you find Anne, and if you can bring her to me, I'll care for her. Don't even question that."

"Thank you," Vivienne whispered, so desperately grateful she could barely speak.

"What of you?" Mrs. Asher asked, arms dropping away. "What will you do?"

"I will find Anne."

After that she did not know.

Chapter Forty-Two

One foot in front of the other.

Yes, this would take her somewhere, if she just continued. One step, two steps, three steps. Somehow, her journey would end.

She was not exactly certain where. Or how fast she was moving. The star-studded skies had given way to a rain-soaked dawn that pelted her with tiny, cold daggers of water. Uncomfortable on her back, but relief on her hot and throbbing face.

The feet below her continued to move. One in front of the other, in a rhythmic pattern to match her heartbeat. This beat—it also matched the throbbing of her face, and even the ache in her belly. But she had survived. She had faced Henri and won.

It was a hollow victory. The cost might be her freedom, and Anne, and—

She looked up and into the cold rain. A drop fell into her lashes and clung there. Blinking it away, she stared through the gray morning light at Maximilian's front door.

Not intending to arrive here, she had done so nonetheless. A moment later she was huddled in the small threshold between Maximilian's front door and the steps. She was afraid to step inside, and just as afraid to leave. Yet there was nowhere else she could go—even Jones could not help her now.

She leaned against the door, let the solid weight of it press against her back. The thought of meeting Maximilian's eyes again was terrifying. What would she say? He had turned away from her because she had not given him the truth.

Her chest ached. Tears clogged her lungs, pressed against her heart. She needed to move. To hide or run, but she could not. Her ribs ached. They were not broken, she thought, but they were bruised. She tasted blood on her lip and knew it was swollen. Every part of her was abused and sore.

She slid to the ground on Maximilian's front step, set her forehead on her knees—her last uninjured body parts—and let the sobs take her.

The door to the town house opened. Thank the fates she was sitting now and not leaning against that solid door. She would have fallen onto the front rug. She was humiliated enough without that.

But she still had to look up at Maximilian with her tearstained face.

His scowl was ferocious, and very, very dear.

"God's teeth, you are loud when you cry. It's also past breakfast, I'm hungry, and it's raining." He reached out his hand to help her stand. Strong, dependable fingers, there for the taking. "Come in, Flower. You look like hell."

Just like that. No hesitation.

Her heart filled nearly to bursting, expanding and expanding until, suddenly, there was nothing inside her but love for him. Terrifying, frightening love.

His hand was the most comforting thing she'd ever held

onto—an offer of assistance, given without reserve, though with exasperated affection and scowling eyebrows. This was her Maximilian.

She wanted to cry all over again.

The door closed behind her, shutting out the rain and the day. She started to speak, and she was sure the words were important, but Maximilian's arms were around her, drawing her in. He was so male, so large. So comforting. Burrowing into him, she tried to hold back the horrible sobs rising in her chest.

He rested his cheek against the top of her head. "What has happened?" he murmured. "Your face is damn near ugly this morning."

She almost laughed, but not quite. "Everything has gone wrong. I didn't know where else to go."

"Then this seems like a good place, mademoiselle." From down the hall, Daggett cleared his throat.

She raised her face from Maximilian's shoulder to eye the inimitable Daggett. Dressed with careful precision, he carried a single candle to ward away the rain.

"You will not chase me out?" she asked.

"No, mademoiselle." He stopped, cleared his throat again. "You did come in through the front door, after all."

"You've given Daggett fits coming in the windows, Vivienne." Maximilian's lips pressed against her hair, softly. The sweetness of his gesture made her soul shiver. "As you've used the door—and there's that ugly face, of course—I know something's wrong. Daggett, bring liniment and something cold for her eye. That thing is going to swell shut soon. Vivienne, into the study."

And so she was in the study with a piece of raw beef pressed against her eye, her shirt and coat removed, and Maximilian spreading liniment over the bruises blooming along her ribs. His fingers did not linger over her torso or breasts, though they were bared for him. Still, he looked with that dark intensity that so excited her.

She was so tired, so bone-weary and exhausted, that she let him look and felt only the stirrings of desire.

"Why did you let me in, Maximilian? After I angered you?"

"I can be angry at you and still care, Vivienne." With efficient movements he spread the liniment over the first and second ribs as she reclined on the chaise. "Just like I can desire you when you are promised to another man and respect you despite you being a spy. *You* are different than your actions. Now, what has happened?" he asked again.

"Henri believes I am a double agent."

"Are you?" No emotion in those words or change in his expression. Just slow circles rubbing liniment into her flesh.

"Close enough. I delivered a letter for Lessard to Viscount Lynley earlier tonight, right under Prinny's nose at a masquerade. I could not read it, but Mrs. Asher could. It was about women and gambling and money owed."

He was silent and his gentle touch did not change, causing almost no additional pain on the already painful bruises. Cool air raised gooseflesh and puckered her nipples. Maximilian's eyes flickered up to her breasts, then back down to the bruises. Still, he did not speak.

"It was coded," she continued, watching him carefully. The muscle in his jaw jumped. "It seemed innocuous, but it was coded. Prinny found the note, and I must have been suspected, as I was recognized at the masquerade. The letter was decoded—"

"I decoded it." The words were harsh, almost guttural, but his fingers were still tender in their ministrations. "Wycomb brought it to me. It wasn't about money or gambling, but an offer of money to assassinate Prinny. It also indicated you would be the assassin's courier. Lynley, by the way, has already been arrested."

"*Mon Dieu.*" It was true, then, Henri's charge of treason. Emotion churned in her as she stared at Maximilian. Anger, though not at Maximilian, and a thin trail of horror at her own actions. "I did not know."

"No?"

"I did not. I only had until midnight to deliver the note for Lessard, and it was already dusk. If I succeeded, then Lessard would tell me where Anne was being held." Vivienne pressed her fingers to her eyes. "I was afraid to come here to have it decoded first."

"I would've done it, Vivienne, even if I were angry with you." He did not look at her face, but took her hand and examined her knuckles. They were split and sore, and he began to rub the liniment there as well.

"Yes." She should have known this, but hurt and fear had colored that knowledge. Now the damage could not be undone. "If Prinny knows I delivered an order for his assassination, it is too late for me."

"Without doubt." Most matter-of-fact, her Maximilian, even when death hovered over her.

Her Maximilian. He still knelt before her, the mouth she so enjoyed turned down in a frown as he studied her torso. She almost expected him to put on his spectacles, he was so focused on assessing her injuries.

Love burned fiercely in her, hot and bright.

He feathered his fingers over the darkest of her bruises. "How did these injuries happen, Vivienne?"

She looked down at his thumb. Ink stained the tip of it. The dark blot made her heart ache. All he wanted was to be left alone with his books and ledgers and words, but she had drawn him in, again and again.

"Henri confronted me—"

"Your commander did this?" Oh, yes, now there was

temper in his words, but not in the rough pads of his fingers. They had ceased their circles and began to caress her, a trail of fingers over her belly.

"In his eyes, I committed treason. Worse, I betrayed him." In all other eyes it would appear the same. "I fought him. Perhaps, even, I have killed him."

"Good." The corners of Maximilian's mouth turned up in a grin that was both satisfied and bloodthirsty.

"I did not stop to check, or to finish the work. It would be murder."

"You could've checked to see if he was *breathing*, at least." He raised a brow. "Seems simple enough."

"Whether he kills me today or another day is not at issue."

A breeze fluttered over her cheek. A soft one.

Suddenly they were not alone in the room. Jones loomed over them, one pistol pointed carefully at Vivienne, another at Maximilian. His eyes held nothing. She could not read them, even a little.

"It might be at issue," he said.

Maximilian pushed up from the floor, spinning to shield her from view so that both pistols were trained on him. "She's not decent," he barked.

"Aye," Jones agreed, stepping to the side so he could see her again. Raindrops glinted on his shoulders. "At least I know she's not hiding any knives under her jacket. I only have to worry about the ones in her boots."

Vivienne knew that moving would likely result in her death. So she continued to lie there, reclining, naked from the waist up. Jones did not once look at her breasts. He only saw her face, held her gaze.

Even when aiming to kill a fellow spy—a suspected traitor—Jones was a gentleman.

Maximilian lunged forward with a fiercely protective growl. Jones snapped his head around to aim a sharp glance at Maximilian, the pistol following suit.

"Don't move, Westwood. I won't hesitate to kill her if you move again."

Maximilian stopped, though his body seemed to quiver with the need to attack. "Let her dress, at least."

Jones was silent, keeping his gaze on Maximilian, though Vivienne knew he was taking in every element of the room. "Give her your shirt."

Gritting his teeth, Maximilian complied. Coat, waistcoat, cravat, watch fob—all dropped to the floor before he shrugged out of his starched linen shirt. He held it out for Vivienne. "I had a pistol in there earlier today," he muttered. "Pity I removed it."

She accepted the shirt with a small smile. "Thank you." It was said to both Jones and Maximilian.

And perhaps fate, as well. If she were to die, it would be clean and quick and at the hand of a friend.

"How did you know I would be here?" She pulled the shirt over her head. It held Maximilian's scent and was soft against her skin. It was also very large.

"I know you, Vivienne." Jones's smile was dry and humorless. "And you officially became my assignment yesterday. I simply hadn't yet determined what you were doing."

She paused, the shirt halfway down her torso. "I was already under investigation." It was not a question, but a statement.

"What trouble have you found yourself in, Flower?" Jones asked softly. "I wouldn't have believed you could commit treason."

Maximilian opened his mouth to speak. She quickly shook her head. His lips snapped shut again, but she could see it cost him as fists clenched and strong, bare shoulders tensed.

"It's complicated, Jones." It was better, now, with the shirt on, but she still felt naked without a weapon in her hand. Most disconcerting to stare down the barrel of a pistol with no method of defense. "I did not know the note was coded."

"You delivered it."

"I will not lie." She met the gaze of the quiet boy she'd once made love with and hoped he'd grown into a just man. "Yes, I did."

"Then I have to take you in, Vivienne." Jones's expression did not change, though his voice lowered. "I am sorry for it."

"Wait. Wait." Maximilian put his hands up, trying once again to step between them. This time, Jones did not stop him. "She didn't do it on purpose. She didn't know it was coded."

"She still had dealings with Lessard that were not an order from her commander." He looked back at Vivienne. She had not noticed the lines on his face before. They seemed very deep just now. "I gave you what warning I could, but I can't let those connections continue."

"No." Could she kill Jones in exchange for her life? He was outnumbered. Her knives were in her boots, her pistol not far in the bags she had brought. Except the very idea hurt her heart—though she would have no choice but injury or death if she wanted to find Anne. "Do not think I will go easily."

"I wouldn't expect it of you, but if you balk, Westwood dies." Jones jerked his head toward Maximilian, knowing, of course, that he would be her weakness.

"I'm not letting you take her." Maximilian, her brave scholar, seemed very fierce now. He stepped forward, a savagery in his voice Vivienne had never heard.

"The same goes for you, Westwood. If you try to stop me, I'll kill her outright."

Silence vibrated in the room, gossamer thin, but still as vast as an ocean.

"Tell me why, Vivienne." Jones was serious, almost sad. "I'm searching for a reason."

"I—" If she told him of Anne, her final secret might be revealed to all of the agents. But perhaps, if she failed and was killed, Jones would need to know that Anne might be turned against England. "Marchand has taken my sister."

A long pause, then, "The servant girl."

"You know?" She straightened, incredulous. That he should know—how was this possible?

He was slow to answer, as though weighing very heavy words. "I suspected the girl had a relationship with you. Your cover was deep; you had become the Flower so long ago, I couldn't be sure, but I guessed. The housekeeper?"

"A neighbor from my childhood." And the closest person to a mother since she was eleven years old.

"So Marchand has taken the girl, and you are working for him to get her back?"

"In a way. My goal is not to work with Marchand. It is only to find him. If I find Marchand, then I find Anne." She looked at Maximilian. She would not implicate him. "I have delivered messages, but I read them to inform our side if need be—it is why I asked about Jean-Phillippe Citron." She paused, breathed carefully. "I would not betray England."

"That is not entirely truthful." Maximilian stepped beside her, set a wide, strong hand on her shoulder. He squeezed it. "*I* was reading the messages. I knew what Vivienne was doing."

"*Maximilian.*" She could save him if he did not say the wrong words. "Do not be an *idiote*."

"Idiot or no, Vivienne." He looked down at her, eyes grimly resolute. "I read the letters for you. I knew."

She almost groaned out her anger. Pressing her fingers against her eyes, she closed them a moment. "Then you, too, will hang for treason, Maximilian."

"That'll hurt, I suppose."

His hand slid down her shoulder to brush her waist. He pulled her in, settled her against him. She should push him away, but just now her body would not obey her brain. And so they faced a considering Jones, locked together.

"Do you know where the girl is?" Jones asked, after a very long moment. He carefully set one pistol down on Maximilian's desk, moving his hand away. It was a sign of trust. A sign that he would not attack. Yet. He retained the other pistol, though he lowered it now.

Hope clogged her lungs, but words tumbled out nonetheless. "I have an idea. A person is inquiring and will give me an answer soon. I am close, Jones. Very close to finding Marchand."

Once again silence vibrated in the air. This moment—it could decide her life or death.

"Find her, then." Jones uncocked the remaining pistol and shoved it into the waist of his trousers. "Quickly. You can't stay at Westwood's. There are others that will look for you here. You have to go underground."

Relief flooded her. She sprang for her coat and shirt and the knives secreted there, all thought of bruises and aches gone.

"I'm going with you." Maximilian spoke the words as if they were a command.

She turned toward him, opened her mouth to tell him no, she would be faster on her own. But he stood there, broad shouldered and without a shirt, appearing as immovable as a mountain.

He had not hesitated to remove his shirt for her, or to step in front of her. He had not hesitated to draw her into his arms that night, even knowing what she had done. And he did not hesitate now.

His green and gold eyes met hers, held.

"Jones," she said, not looking away from that steady, strong gaze. "How long do I have?"

"I can't give you more than a day. Tomorrow morning, I have to bring you in."

Chapter Forty-Three

The rookeries stank.

They were ugly.

Maximilian was accustomed to the wide, mostly clean streets and graceful architecture in the West End. They weren't perfect streets, but they were not...*this*.

"Why are we in St. Giles?" He was as conspicuous as a Sanskrit symbol in the middle of the Greek alphabet, even with the borrowed clothing Vivienne had found for him that afternoon. He could feel eyes on him, though half of the tiny windows above them appeared dark. He felt them on the back of his neck, and it set him on edge. Every shadow they passed made him want to reach for his pistol.

"No one asks questions here, Maximilian, particularly at night," Vivienne said to him. She walked beside him, guiding him through the warren of alleys as though she were as accustomed to these streets as those in Mayfair.

She likely was.

"I don't doubt it. This is worse than the docks." He shuddered. The stench was the same, either way. "Which pub are we going to?"

"To the Queen's Bathtub to visit an old friend. The barkeep serves a good, bitter ale. Just—do not be friendly, please."

"Don't be friendly with a friend?" He raised a brow and slid his gaze toward her.

She responded with a wry half smile. He liked seeing it, under the circumstances. "There are many nuances in the word 'friend.' In this case, the barkeep is not an enemy. So he is a friend, but one you must watch. It is like the dancer who happily dances beside you until she can push you down and become principal."

"You dancers are a friendly lot." He nodded toward a low, squat building just ahead and to the right. "Judging from the naked woman wearing a crown and sitting in a hip bath on the sign, this would be the place." The woman's crown was crooked, and her legs dangled out of the tub as though she were languidly enjoying her bath.

Vivienne paused to study the sign swinging above the door. Rain clung to her lashes like tiny diamonds. "*Oui.*"

Maximilian stopped walking. His feet were as heavy and useless as the cobblestones beneath them. That single word had twisted something inside him. It was vaguely painful, and made him furious.

"Don't do that," he said. Perhaps it was harsher than he'd planned, but he couldn't help it.

"Do what, Maximilian? I do not understand." The light from the pub windows shone over her face so that he could see her clearly. Wide eyes, confused brows.

How could she not understand?

"Don't speak French to me." He reached out, hand gripping her forearm to draw her close. He leaned forward so he spoke only to her. Invisible ears as well as eyes might be lurking in these alleys. "Don't speak French. It's bad enough I have to call you Vivienne when I know it isn't your real name. Don't speak with a French accent, or speak *in* French." His muscles tightened beneath his skin. "It's all a lie."

"Yes. It is a lie." She whispered it back, with no French words, no French accent. Hearing her voice that way soothed the fury clamoring in him. "I'm sorry for it, Maximilian. I wish I could stop, but stopping means I might lose all that I am."

His hands roamed down her body, gathered her in, before he spun her into the alley and pressed her back against the pub wall. There, away from the windows where no light could reach them, he looked down at the various shadows that formed her face. "Now *I* don't understand."

She rose up a little, curving her hand around the back of his neck and lifting her face so her mouth was near his. They'd look like lovers to anyone passing on the street, which was the intent, he supposed — assuming the watcher didn't notice they both wore pantaloons. Maybe a passerby wouldn't in the dark.

"Explain," he said. He couldn't see more than a few contours of her features, but he could smell her. Still a little of that clean soap, though it was mixed with the liniment he'd rubbed into her skin.

"I have been Vivienne for so long, I do not know how to be only Sarah."

Sarah. It was a simple, pretty name. One any number of women could claim.

"Sarah." He needed to say the word aloud, test the sound and weight on his tongue.

"I am not Sarah any longer." Her thumb slid to his jaw, rubbed there against the stubble, the movement soft and unbearably intimate. "Yet I am not Vivienne. The Flower is not only a spy, Maximilian. She is a dancer. A thief. She is not French, she is not English. She is a little of each. And she is a little Sarah, a little Vivienne. I am all of those things, and they are all me."

"That's very…abstract." He couldn't quite get his brain to think in such a way. The facts didn't add up equally. "And philosophical."

Her lips curved up, though her smile was edged with sorrow. "Your scowl, it is most ferocious."

He wanted to kiss her. Even in the dark, in the rookeries of St. Giles, where he might end up with a knife between his ribs, he wanted to kiss her. Since he wanted to—her lips were there, sweet and curved, after all—he did.

Dear God in heaven. Her body pressed against his, and he could feel each curve of her. The hand on his neck threaded through his hair, gripped. Their tongues tangled, and for a moment, he forgot where he was. He could only taste and smell and feel Vivienne. Or Sarah. Or— He drew away.

"Damnation." He loosened the fingers gripping her hips and let them fall to his sides. "I can't understand it. I don't want to be in love with a woman who doesn't use her real name. Or her real language. It's just too illogical."

She froze, every lean muscle in her body going taut. Her eyes widened. Even in the dark he could see that. The whites of her eyes gave it away.

"Love?" The word was barely audible above the wind whistling through the alley. "Maximilian, did you say *love*?"

"Did I?" He thought back. *God's knees.* "I suppose I did."

"You love me?" She sounded terrified. Utterly and completely terrified.

Well, he *felt* terrified. "I don't know. I don't know who I love. Or what I love. Or—is this feeling even love? I can't tell." Not just terrified. Panicked. "It hurts. In my chest."

"It hurts in my chest, too." She sounded like she was breathing shallowly through her teeth. She gripped his shoulders, fingers digging into coat and muscle. "We're in St. Giles. At the Queen's Bathtub."

"Not the best location to discuss love." He pressed his face against the curve of her neck to suppress the laughter bubbling up. He was bordering on hysteria. Unfortunate that the Flower didn't carry smelling salts. "This feeling can't be love. It's not possible. I don't know who you are, or what you're thinking. I don't even know what *language* you think in. You're a mysterious woman with a past I can't fathom, a present consisting primarily of deception, and an occupation I abhor."

She reared back as though he'd struck her. Guilt twined with panic and the huge, aching knot in his chest.

"'Abhor' is a strong word, Maximilian." She slid out from beneath his arms, stepping out of the dark and onto the street. "Come. Into the pub."

"Wait." He put out a hand to stop her, but it was too late. She had already slipped through the front door.

...

Vivienne heard him enter the pub after her, only a few paces behind. She could not decide if she wanted him there or not. He did not want to be in love with a spy. That was what all of his words meant.

He did not want to be in love with *her*.

Yet this did not make a man follow a woman into a sordid pub. Maximilian had done just that. He had stood in front of her to block Jones's pistol, had shouldered her burden of finding Anne, and now, here in this pub, Maximilian was standing beside her facing the unknown.

She would not cry. Just because a man did what was right, what was necessary, even though he did not want to, did not mean she should cry.

The barkeep would find her soft.

Her old friend stood behind the bar, wiping a gray cloth

over a tankard, almost exactly as he had before. Except this time the pub was closed. No patrons were swearing in the corner or playing dice or getting drunk and fondling the barmaids. Just a young boy methodically moving between the tables and sweeping up spilled food.

She stepped to the bar but did not take a stool. This was not a friendly visit.

Maximilian took a place beside her, but a half step behind. There, but not there. With her, but not in front of her.

She would *not* cry.

"Little girl." The barkeep, he did not look up beyond the merest glance. "People are looking for you."

Fear swirled in her so that her heart bumped inside her ribs, but she did not answer. Sometimes silence was one's best weapon to gain information, as people felt compelled to fill it.

The barkeep was no different. After a minute of humming silence, he said, "Not good people."

"Will you tell them where I am?"

Again, that humming silence as the rag wiped around and around the tankard. Around and around. It would not become more clean, that tankard, but the barkeep did not stop his attention to the vessel.

She could sense Maximilian's impatience. He did not move, but she could hear it in the breath that was deeper than the last, the forceful exhale. She imagined his scowl was firmly in place.

Finally, into the silence, the barkeep said, "For a price, perhaps I'd tell them, but it would have to be a good price."

So. She knew where she stood.

"What if my price is higher?" Maximilian interjected.

The rag stopped its circular pattern, paused, then started again. She wanted to hiss at Maximilian to stay silent, but the words were out. They could not be taken back.

The rag moved, around and around, though the tankard

failed to shine. The barkeep pursed his lips, the whiskers on his chin shifting over skin and bone. It was a considering expression, and Vivienne stayed silent as she waited for him to speak.

"If it's high enough, I'll tell you where *she* is, milord," the barkeep said, ceasing his movements with the rag to blow dust from inside the vessel.

"She? The girl?" Vivienne gripped the edge of the bar top. Hope burst to life inside her. "You know where she is?"

"Aye. Close enough." He still did not look up. It was as though he were talking to the tankard. This was the way some transactions were conducted. If you did not look at the person, then it could be said it did not happen. "The gent, here." He jerked his head at Maximilian. "He good for the blunt?"

Maximilian bristled. This she saw with her lover's eyes. Shoulders lifted, the flare of nostrils. Then he tucked his anger away so all that could be seen was the twitch in his jaw. He reached into his pocket, then laid a coin on the bar top. A coin with a lot of value. Then he laid another. Then a third.

Coins she knew were dear to him, as he was not as wealthy as his brother.

She stared at her hands. She thought perhaps her knuckles were turning white. It was most difficult to tell through the sheen of tears, but blinking the moisture away was impossible. This man—this man who did not want to love a spy and could ill afford to part with such a large sum—was purchasing Anne's life.

For Vivienne.

The barkeep used the rag to sweep the coins into the tankard. Each fell with a heavy *tink* into the bottom, gold onto pewter, then the tankard was set beneath the bar.

"She's at St. Luke's Church." The barkeep stared straight at Vivienne now, with old eyes and craggy brows. "They know you're near. She won't be there come morning."

• • •

Vivienne led him through the labyrinth of alleys. Maximilian was completely turned around in the maze of tight places. One cramped space led into another, then another. Occasionally they'd find larger streets, but she would dart between buildings and over mud and stone to cross them and enter another alleyway.

He'd call her a butterfly or some pretty flitting creature, darting between blossoms and blooms, if he wasn't jumping over pools of sewage and listening to rats scratching in the dark—and half waiting for a knife to slide past his pistol and between his ribs.

He kept his eyes on the narrow shoulders and black-clad body dancing in front of him. He had no idea where they were—or where St. Luke's Church was—but she seemed to know. This must have been where she spent her childhood.

His heart ached knowing she'd lived in squalor, with prostitutes in every doorway and thieves and criminals lurking in the corners. This was no place for a child to grow up. That so many children knew nothing better—and so many more died—tugged at him.

So he focused again on the woman in front of him as she set a comforting hand on the shoulder of a beggar, shook her head at a prostitute, and skirted around the light spilling from a pub window along with shouts and the sound of broken glass.

"There," she said to him over her shoulder. She pointed ahead where the spire of a church speared high into the night sky. Maximilian noted in the dim light from the street that the brass weathervane on top pointed toward the east. Above it, clouds roiled, their color shifting from black to gray as distant lightning flashed.

It was not storming yet, but it would be soon enough.

Vivienne darted into the shadow of the iron-and-brick fence surrounding the church and its yard. She crouched low and Maximilian did the same, the muscles of his thighs tightening in protest after their jog through the rookeries. Her lips were pressed together as she studied the street, the church. No doubt her spy's brain was analyzing the best method to infiltrate the building.

"I don't know where in the church they would keep Anne." She whispered it, perhaps to herself, but then she looked up at him. He couldn't see her face clearly until lightning flashed over her firm, resolute chin. "There could be any number of hiding places."

"Then there's nothing to do but search."

She stilled, and he sensed her gaze searching his face. "You can turn back, Maximilian." Her words were nothing more than a whisper on the air, her eyes wide beneath furrowed brows. "You do not have to do this."

"I'm right behind you, Vivienne," he said, setting a hand on her shoulder. She was tense, her shoulder a thin point of anxiety. "I'd go in front of you, but I don't know how the hell to pick a bloody lock."

One second passed. Two.

Her shoulders lowered a touch, as the tension drained from her. She leaned up, nipped his bottom lip, kissed him hard, then spun on the balls of her feet in a graceful move that somehow or other resulted in her standing up.

By all that was holy, the Flower's body was a marvelous bit of bone and muscle and elegance. And something about that kiss made *him* feel marvelous and strong and heroic.

Addled. He was addled.

And damnation. He *was* in love with her. No other way around it.

"Come." She jerked her head toward the church. "As it happens, I can pick a bloody lock."

He followed her through the dark churchyard, picking his way on uneven ground. Headstones rose like specters from the earth, so many ghoulish shadows surrounding them. And of course, it was foggy. It wasn't London without some fog. If he were fanciful—and he wasn't—he'd think there were spirits in the churchyard.

He suppressed a foolish shudder and kept his gaze on the Flower's back. She slunk between the headstones, as much like fog and darkness as what floated in the air around her. He didn't know how she found the rear entrance to the church, but she did. She crouched, running her hand over the lock.

"Keep watch," she whispered.

"Quite." He removed the pistol he'd tucked in his waistband while she retrieved her picklocks from some hidden pocket, and they both set to work. It came naturally, somehow. He scanned the churchyard looking for men or improbable shadows while she worked her magic with the locks.

She was as quiet as the fog, yet her fingers seemed to fly. He heard the lock open, a quiet *snick* that held promise and fear. The world stopped as he turned to look at her. Their eyes met in another flash of lightning as the first raindrop fell.

There was no turning back.

He nodded once, hard, to tell her it was time. He was there with her.

Her fingers fluttered over the handle, uncertain flickers of rounded nails and sensitive touch. With a sharp, indrawn breath, she pushed the door open a crack. Her picklocks returned to their hiding place, then a pistol appeared in one hand and a knife in the other. It was quite terrifying how comfortable she appeared. He should not be impressed by her weaponry.

Except he was.

Yes, addled. No other explanation.

Slowly, the Flower pushed the door open so they could slip through. The door led into darkness, a deeper darkness than what was outside. In the cemetery, at least, there had been a bit of lightning and some candlelight from windows and lamps in the surrounding street. Inside there was nothing but walls. He couldn't see a blasted thing.

He heard the Flower shuffling ahead of him and hoped he wouldn't have to use his pistol. He wouldn't know where to aim.

A light flared, burning against his eyes and nearly blinding him. The bright flame illuminated her face, casting dancing shadows over her cheekbones and revealing her eyes. Those eyes darted around the room, cataloging every stone, every piece of furniture. His own eyes did the same. A table and chair. A stack of plates topped by a dull knife. An umbrella leaned against one wall. Above it were pegs with various garments hanging from them.

"The vestry," she whispered.

"Anne wouldn't be in here." Not a logical place to hide a prisoner, if one considered it properly.

"No. She would be somewhere less regularly occupied." Vivienne shielded the flame from any breeze and studied the room again. "There's no sign of anything out of place here. No sign of Anne, or a prisoner, or—" She broke off, the last word ending in a choked moan. Clearly, despair had a sound.

"Wait, Flower, wait. She might be in another room. She might—"

"She might not be. Anne might already be gone, or the barkeep might have lied. She could be dead." The candle flame wavered as her hands shook. "What if she isn't even here? I only have a little time before Jones must come for me. I would have wasted it."

"Then we'll keep looking until we find her or they bring us in." That seemed like an immutable fact now. He didn't know Anne, but he did know Vivienne, and he wasn't going to leave either of them to the Vulture or the spies of England.

"We— Did you hear that?" Her voice lowered to the lightest whisper.

"No." Listening, Maximilian closed his eyes to better concentrate. He heard nothing but thunder and lightning and rain pattering on the roof. "Wait." A *clang* sounded from somewhere below.

"Something is not right. That noise does not belong." A quick puff of air followed her words, a fast exhale that sounded suspiciously like—

Maximilian opened his eyes to see nothing but pitch black, the candlelight only a whiff of smoke now.

"Come with me." Her small, ungloved hand found his in the dark, gripped hard, and began to pull him forward.

"Are you a nocturnal creature? You must be, because I can't see a bloody thing."

She didn't answer but tugged him along a dark passageway. He started to protest, but she could obviously see better than he in the dark. There was a measure of safety in that.

"Where are we going?" he whispered.

"Below."

Very nondescript, that word. "Below where?"

Suddenly they stood before another door. It had risen from the dark, innocuous and silent—yet there was a small window with metal bars set into it.

And small iron spikes impaled in the planks.

Spiked doors did not represent enjoyable locations.

"The crypt," she said softly. "There are dozens of places to hide in the crypt. Doors and vaults and tombs." Vivienne's voice caught on the last word, her swallow audible. Then he felt rather than saw her body straighten and strengthen, shoulders squaring and chest rising as she found her courage and assumed her dancer's posture.

"Is this the main entry?" he asked. "Is there some sort of rear entrance?"

"Yes, there are a few different entrances." She set a hand against the wooden slats of the door. "We should use one of those. They are not far—"

"Far enough. And they'd expect us to come in the rear door, wouldn't they? Spies would sneak in from the rear. We should go in through the main entrance and surprise them."

"Perhaps." She spoke slowly, digesting his words, then cocked her head. "It is not a poor idea, except they might see us immediately. We wouldn't have time to search for Anne."

"We'll figure out something." Or die. Either way, it was a bit too late to turn back.

"I don't have a plan." She transferred one of her hands to his arm, squeezed hard.

He shrugged. "Then we devise the plan as we go."

"This does not sound like you, Maximilian."

No, it didn't. She'd done this to him. Improvisation and lack of planning were not his strengths. "It *does* sound like you, Vivienne. Between the two of us, we'll come up with something once we get down there."

"You have your weapon, do you not? It is loaded?"

"Of course." He had two, in fact. "A man doesn't go around St. Giles defending his woman without some type of weapon." He leaned down, touched his mouth to hers.

"*Bon.*" Her lips curved up beneath his, and he took this moment—perhaps his last kiss—to memorize every contour of her mouth. The scent, the taste of her. This might be the last for both of them. "*Bon,*" she said again.

He hoped they didn't die tonight. He wanted more time with her. A lifetime, maybe.

And if it wasn't love that gripped him, it was some kind of illness that made one's heart hurt and one's stomach a bundle of nerves. Influenza, perhaps, with a dollop of palpitations. He leaned his forehead against hers and simply stood there, one arm about her waist. He closed his eyes and breathed in. Her simple soap fought with sewage and rotting wood—and won.

It was how he felt about her. She'd come from these hellholes and had won. However it happened, whatever she did now, she'd won. It had forged her into the woman she was now.

"I love you, my Flower." Not Sarah, not Vivienne. Whatever else she was called, she would always be the Flower. *His* Flower. The one who sneaked into his study and mocked his paper folding. "I don't think I might love you. I'm not uncertain. I don't know why I thought I was. Nor does it matter if you are a spy, or a dancer, or choose any other profession. I simply love *you*, whatever name you bear and whatever language you speak."

He opened his eyes to find her staring at him.

"Right before we are likely to die, Maximilian, you choose to tell me this."

"Seems as good a time as any. I muddled it up before."

"You are becoming soft, my Maximilian." She gave him a short, firm kiss, but he heard laughter behind her words, and it warmed him. "I love you as well, whether you are a scowling code breaker or an irritating translator. Now, let us go fight the Vulture and save Anne. Or die. Whichever happens first."

Chapter Forty-Four

Creeping down a dark stairwell was not frightening, Vivienne thought. Unless Maximilian was behind you. Love made it infinitely frightening. What if Marchand killed him?

Maximilian's death would be etched into her heart. But at the end of stairs, if the barkeep had been correct, would be Anne. For Anne, she must continue.

Vivienne trailed her hand along the wall, noting each brick and the mortar circling it. Rough. Square. There was no rail on either side of the stair descending into the crypt, only these brick walls. She could not see in front of her and dared not go back for a candle. She carefully set each foot on the step below, testing it. She could not go tumbling into the dark.

Behind her, Maximilian was doing his best to be quiet. He was quieter than usual and walked very slowly, as she heard from his footsteps. She counted his slow pace and careful feet as an asset. If he fell, she did not want to be squashed beneath him before she had found Anne.

Then they reached the bottom. There were no more steps. Vivienne paused, waiting for Maximilian to join her. She knew exactly where he stood, where his body was in the dark, and reached out a hand for his.

He jumped a foot. His breath wheezed out.

She nearly giggled, and perhaps she would have, if such a giggle did not mean the difference between life and death. But it did, so she slid her hand up his arm, then to his shoulder and pulled herself up on tiptoe to whisper in his ear.

"Stay close, stay quiet."

He did, as they traveled the length of the crypt. They were not hand in hand, or even touching. Her hands were busy with knives, his with the pistol, but they moved along the passage in tandem.

It was so very dark. Water dripped somewhere, a rhythmic *ping* onto rock. That sound melded with the scent of dank and murk and…something else. Like dirt, only not. Decay. Death. There were many dead buried here. A whisper wound through her mind. *Anne might be one of them.*

A soft glow began to lighten the darkness. She moved toward it, afraid of what she might find. They turned a corner, and Vivienne saw the glow of a single candle at the end of the next tunnel. It scalded her eyes, it was so brilliant against the black.

It was enough to see Anne lying on her side on the floor.

Vivienne jumped forward, heart in her throat. Was Anne well? Had they hurt her? Shackles encircled her ankles and rope bound her hands. Dirty fabric had been shoved into her mouth, the ends emerging from dry, cracked lips. Shorn and uneven hair brushed the edge of her jaw. But Anne's eyes were wide with fear.

Alive! Triumph burst through Vivienne. So close, after so long. Anne was so close. Vivienne broke into a run, feet thudding on the stone floor, heart thudding in her chest. She breached the edge of the candlelight—and skid to a halt.

Anne was not alone. Vivienne should have known this.

Before she ran, she should have prepared better for this, but she had not thought beyond Anne.

"Ah, the lovely Flower. I have been waiting for you." The words were pleasant, friendly, even, which made the man's voice more frightening than if he'd shouted. "I had hoped you would be alone."

The man stepped from the shadows, the candlelight falling first on black shoes and gaiters, then black breeches and coat. Finally, his lined face, floating above Geneva bands.

Behind her, Maximilian sucked in a breath. Held it. Then, furiously, he whispered, "Bishop Carlisle."

"Indeed, my boy. It's a shame you followed the Flower tonight. Your mother will be distraught by your death." The bishop raised his hand. Candlelight flickered on the intricate engravings on a pistol barrel. "And I did tell you not to become involved with the Flower, did I not?"

"You are Marchand, the Vulture," Vivienne said, studying her opponent. He was tall and very solid, but he was not old. Or, at least, he was very fit for his age. She had not particularly noticed this before, but she had not *looked* before. One did not evaluate a man of the cloth for his physical abilities.

"*Mais oui.*" The bishop smiled, again, most friendly. "And so I have been for many years. Right under the nose of the British government." His words moved seamlessly from French to English.

Vivienne struggled to think, to formulate a plan. Anne lay on the floor at his feet, so thin, so small, in that little ball she had curled herself into. Chain snaked from the shackles on her ankles to a ring set into the brick wall so that she could not easily be moved. The iron bands had scraped the flesh raw at her ankles. The angry welts would be painful.

"I don't understand." Maximilian's pistol rose into the air to point at the bishop. "You were my father's closest friend. My mother's confidant. You bloody well stood there on the day of the funeral and promised to take care of our family."

"I did. That has nothing to do with the interests of France or England. Nor the Flower."

He made a little gesture. Two more men stepped from the shadows. Vivienne recognized one as the man from Manchester Square. The other was a stranger, so she cataloged his height, his features. Not as tall as Maximilian, but with a scarred face that would be memorable. She and Maximilian were at a disadvantage. Two against three. And Anne. Poor Anne.

Perhaps, if they all died in this crypt, they would be buried with none the wiser. Still, she would not die without a fight.

"Let them go, Marchand, and I will do whatever you ask. I shall spy for you, for France. Whatever you require." She sounded desperate and did not care.

"Whatever I require?" The bishop's brows rose. "A very intriguing offer, Flower."

He began to circle them, his pistol relaxing slightly. It did not matter, as the scarred man held knives and the one from Manchester Square a knife and his own pistol. Whatever Marchand did or did not do, she could not move fast enough to protect Anne from them.

On the floor, Anne shook her head. Above the cloth in her mouth, her eyes turned wild. She squeaked out a word—Vivienne understood *no!* despite the gag.

"I must, regretfully, decline." Marchand was almost directly behind her, and very close. The words were soft in her ear. "You have proven yourself untrustworthy, going to Lessard's and searching Manchester Square. It is too late for your offer. I would have killed you earlier, if I had not needed you to deliver the note to Lynley."

Beside her, Maximilian tensed, but he did not move. She turned her head slightly and saw he was watching the other two men intently, but she did not want to draw attention to this.

"And the girl?" she asked, speaking as softly as Marchand and turning her head to look at him. He was closer than she had thought. Only inches away. She could see each separate gray whisker dotting his chin. He was not so clean shaven after a long night.

"She is useless to me."

"Bastard," Maximilian ground out.

"You are mistaken, I am not." Marchand turned to look at him and began his slow, circling movements again. "I was born quite legitimately to French parents, dear boy, and was sent to live with English relatives when they died. *Mais, je suis français. C'est aussi simple que ça.*"

What to do? Vivienne's mind screamed the question. She could not see a way out. Anne was in shackles, Marchand's men armed. Any fight would risk Anne. A quick glance revealed exits, tombs, stone passageways. And—

Movement. Something in the shadows.

She held her breath. Was it one of Marchand's men? A member of the church? A rat? Any and all of these things were possible. Whatever it was, it moved behind Marchand's men.

"What do you propose, Marchand?" Maximilian asked.

"Death, of course." The Vulture sounded surprised, as though this were a foolish question. He crouched down to look at Anne. The girl skittered back as quickly as her bound hands and feet would allow. Whimpering erupted from her throat.

Vivienne stepped forward, fear tearing at her heart, at her belly.

Marchand lifted a hand. "Another step, and I shall kill her."

Vivienne froze, the fear building in her until it slicked her skin and filled all the places inside. He was so close to Anne.

Too close. The fear tumbled inside her, becoming an aching pressure against her ribs.

"The girl has been remarkably brave, Flower." Marchand smiled at Anne, as if they had become friends. "You should be proud."

So she was. More, even, when temper filled Anne's gaze. But, oh, her pride was bittersweet.

"My sources indicate you delivered the note to Lynley." Marchand turned to look up at her, then pushed to his feet.

"Yes." She swallowed hard.

"Then your prince will be dead by supper." His eyes lit up. He raised his pistol, aimed it at her heart. "And I have no more use for you."

· · ·

Maximilian leaped. He didn't think about it, didn't analyze the trajectory or proper alignment for effectiveness. He simply leaped at Carlisle—Marchand, the Vulture—and slammed into him.

Marchand's pistol discharged, leaving acrid smoke in the air and ringing in his ears. They tumbled to the stone floor of the crypt. Maximilian felt only the pain of his shoulder and hip where he landed. He decided he must not be hit by the pistol. A quick glance showed him Vivienne was not hurt. Thank all of God's body parts.

So he sprang up and braced for more, started to raise his own pistol, but some unknown man pelted out of the shadows and rammed into one of Marchand's men. Maximilian started, leaping in front of Vivienne—and was immediately pushed aside as she went for the third man. It was the scarred one, approaching the girl Anne with knives drawn.

Maximilian recognized the dark head of Jones as the unknown man from the shadows and felt a moment's relief.

Three to three, then.

Well, that left Marchand to him for now. And damnation, Marchand had a knife, too. It glinted wickedly in the candlelight when he pulled it from inside his coat. Did everyone carry knives?

Marchand took aim with the blade, and Maximilian dived away, skidding along the stone floor. His palms stung from scraping across the rough surface, and his knees would be bruised, but the flying knife pinged off the floor. At least Marchand had missed.

Maximilian sprang up and spun around, anticipating the next attack. From one side he heard Jones grunt as fist met flesh. On the other side, he heard a quick intake of breath from Vivienne. A glance showed she'd felled her man and was spinning toward the shackled girl.

Vivienne began to run, dancer's legs pounding on the stone floor, but Marchand, too, was headed for the girl. For Anne.

Marchand would get there first.

Not on my bloody watch.

He raised his pistol, aiming for the thigh. A small target, and in these circumstances, it would be difficult to get the shot right, but if the bullet managed to find any part of Marchand, it would at least slow him down.

Marchand turned at the final second to look at Maximilian. He might have borne the face of an old friend, but his eyes were nothing of the sort. Nor was the second knife he now carried. The pistol fired, jerking in Maximilian's hand and sending up another round of smoke. The sound echoed between the walls of the crypt, blasting off the tombs and stones. Marchand jerked as well, shock rippling over his face. Then he crumpled as his leg slid out from under him.

The girl, Anne, shrieked from behind her gag as Marchand tumbled toward her, knife still outstretched. He was just inches short of Anne's belly. *Inches.*

The Flower gripped his jacket and hauled him back, fingers clutched in fabric. Her strength in that moment was born of love, her face a mask of utter fury. She jerked Marchand away and slammed his wrist into the stone floor.

"*Non!*" she shouted, before spinning again to see to the girl.

Maximilian rushed forward, and together with Jones pulled Marchand back again. But the Vulture wasn't done. Even as they shoved him against the floor, the knife arced out, wide, aiming for the Flower. Maximilian kicked it out of his hand and felt the crunch of bone beneath his boot.

Jones pressed a foot on the Marchand's bloodied leg, holding him in place with sheer pain. The bishop's face went white, and he breathed hard through his teeth. Jones's face was grim, his eyes impassive. He flicked that unreadable gaze up to Maximilian.

"We need to bind them," he said shortly. A groan echoed between the brick walls as one of the French agents rose to his knees. "All of them."

"Yes." But he had to see Vivienne.

She was crouched in front of Anne, her hands moving quickly with the picklocks on the shackles. The gag was out of the girl's mouth, and her eyes—though still large and frightened—were focused only on her sister.

"They fed me well." Anne's voice was thin and shaking, but Maximilian heard a comforting, reassuring tone he knew was for the Flower. "Don't worry, Vivienne. I was never hungry." She held her hands out as Vivienne shoved the shackles away and began sawing at the ropes with her knife. "I wasn't hurt, either. I promise."

The rope fell away, and Vivienne sat back. Her small, competent hands rested lightly on her thighs, as though she didn't quite know what to do with them now.

Anne threw her arms around Vivienne's neck. Clung there.

"I missed you." Vivienne's voice was a croak, barely understandable. But her face. *Her face.* Raw emotion moved over her features as she buried her face in Anne's neck, hands fisting in Anne's clothing as the girl's arms came around her. Deep, deep sobs racked her frame.

That love, the overwhelming joy and terror of it, tore at Maximilian.

Because he loved Vivienne in just that way.

Chapter Forty-Five

"What now?" Rain sluiced down Maximilian's head and face. He scowled at Vivienne, then up at the gray dawn sky, then at the town house Jones had just disappeared into. "It's damn wet out here."

She wanted to smile, but it did not come. There was too much sadness and confusion and uncertainty in her, though all of it was tempered with joy for Anne. She was safe, ensconced in Jones's town house after a hot bath, and was even now being provided nourishing food and a guard to watch her. Vivienne could not ask fate for more.

Except, perhaps, she could ask for Maximilian.

Only she could not have him. If Henri lived and she were not prosecuted for treason, she would never be permitted to be with Maximilian. Her assignment was to be an opera dancer mistress, and she could not be in love with another man.

If Henri did not live, then she would be tried for murder.

So she looked down the street because she did not know what else to do. The rows of houses were dreary and gray in the early-morning rain, their normally bright surfaces dull without the sunshine. It did not matter. She had business she must attend to. It was only hours ago the Vulture had been brought down, hours in which Anne had needed care and reports had been necessary.

"Now, I speak with Henri's spymaster, Sir Charles. *My* spymaster, also." She was exhausted and heartsore and felt as gray as the row of houses. "Then, if I am allowed to continue in my position, I will bathe the catacombs and your liniment and the Queen's Bathtub from my skin. I will go to rehearsals and performances as Vivienne La Fleur. And I will wait for instructions." Rain blurred the street. Or perhaps it was tears.

"And what of me? Of us?" Maximilian gripped her shoulders and spun her to face him. Through her wet jacket she felt the warmth and strength in his hands. His arms would be just as warm and strong. She wanted to step into those arms. To take comfort from him.

"I don't know." Her heart ached because of it.

"I'm not leaving you." Very fierce words from her scholar, accompanied by even fiercer eyes. "I don't care what your spymaster commands."

"I cannot—Maximilian." She shook her head. Her heart beat frantically against her rib cage, a bird fighting to be free. "Gainsaying Sir Charles would be insubordination. More, he could take away my freedom. My life, even."

"Then run. Go away." Desperation layered over his voice. It was a sound she had not heard before.

"I cannot. If I leave without permission, I will be hunted for treason. And—I am a spy." His desperation echoed in her own heart. She shivered inside her wet clothing and tugged her cap lower to shield her face from the cold rain. "I am the Flower, Maximilian."

"Confound it. Can't you stop being a spy?" He leaned down, very close, to look at her with hazel eyes colored by rioting green and gold spears. He was a kiss away from her, and yet a world of obstacles stood between them. "We could go anywhere. I can find work. I can support you well enough."

"Support me?" Joy battered one side of her as she thought of lying beside him each night, living beside him each day. Confusion battered the other side of her. "It is not *support*. It is not money. I am a spy. I cannot be anything else—I do not even know how."

"Damnation. I *know* you can't, but I *want* you to be something else." Frustration growled out of him. Then, with a sigh, the frustration slipped into the rain and was gone. He leaned down, set his forehead against hers. "I want you to be something different so everything will be easy. Then you could be with me always and surprise me by sneaking into every room of my house."

You could be with me always…

A great rush of deep love swamped her. Not just swamped her, engulfed her. Consumed her. His arms were around her—if they had not been, she might have fallen.

"Yet, if you weren't a spy," he continued softly, "you wouldn't be my Flower."

His lips seized hers. Possession and fury and despair, all of these melded together and became Maximilian's mouth. He tasted so male, and his lips were cool from the rain. She met them hungrily. Hot tears that mingled with the cold rain on her cheeks.

This might be their last kiss. She could not see the future and did not know what came next. But she *could* hold onto him and grip the shoulders that had become so dear to her. She could let her heart be overwhelmed by this man who always stood beside her and never in front, who knew all of her secrets.

She could love him for whatever moments they had together.

Someone cleared their throat.

Vivienne sprang back as embarrassment filled her. Sir Charles stood on the front steps, greatcoat catching water droplets and his walking stick dull in the gray light. He was her spymaster — and he was not pleased. The coldness in his brown eyes was a look she knew. It did not mean good things would be happening.

Often, this look meant someone died. Sometimes they died by the sword tucked into the walking stick he carried now.

"Flower. Mr. Westwood. I expect you to come inside so we don't have to stand in the rain during our discussion." Sir Charles spun on his heel and disappeared into the hallway.

She must follow. Even if her feet wanted to run in another direction. So, she followed. Maximilian's hand slipped into hers as they mounted the steps. His hand was solid and strong. An anchor, just when she needed it.

Except he was not invited into Sir Charles's office.

"I would like a private word with the Flower first." Sir Charles shed his greatcoat, then propped his walking stick in a corner of the hall.

"Sir," Maximilian began, running a hand through wet hair, heedless of water sprinkling onto the tiled floor or the spikes of russet and mahogany he created.

"A moment, Westwood, to debrief my agent." Sir Charles's tone rose, as did the command in the words.

"Maximilian." Vivienne spoke softly, hoping that she conveyed confidence and not the nerves pinging inside her. If her spymaster asked for privacy, she was duty bound to obey. "A few minutes, please."

She imagined Maximilian's teeth would suffer some from his frustration, but he nodded in agreement.

"She'll be safe enough." Spinning on his heel, Sir Charles strode down the hall and toward his office, where Jones stood silent in the doorway. "When I call, send in Westwood," he said as he passed Jones and disappeared into the room.

Vivienne followed, because there was no choice. Jones shut the paneled door quietly as her boots found the thick rug in the center of the room.

Alors. She was alone.

"Sir." Vivienne straightened her shoulders as she faced Sir Charles over his desk. She also raised her chin. Just a little. He might strip her of her position. Prison, even, was possible. Death—she hoped that was not in her future. Whatever her punishment, she would meet it on even ground.

"I've had an interesting talk with Lord Henry Wycomb."

Ah. Then Henri was not dead. "*Oui.*" She did not know what else to say.

"I also had a very brief conversation with Jones." His eyes were colder, perhaps, than they had been before. He did not shift in his chair as he spoke, but regarded her with steady eyes.

"*Oui.*" Her belly flip-flopped. A fish on the line and out of water.

"It seems you've been working on your own these last weeks."

"Yes, sir." This was not a good beginning to the conversation. It was very one-sided, this conversation.

"Why did you not approach Wycomb about Marchand?"

A blunt question, and perhaps it deserved a blunt answer. She would have to reveal her past in any event. "The girl Marchand abducted, Anne—"

"Yes." Sir Charles's eyes did not reveal thoughts, yet he must have thought something as his brows rose most high.

Vivienne swallowed hard. Confession was difficult, so she spoke quickly. "She is my sister."

"I know." He said this as if waiting for something more, as if this was not a critical piece of information.

"You know?" Shock sent her reeling so she had to plant her feet on the rug.

"Of course. Lord Wycomb brought you into our organization. You don't think I would allow that without a thorough knowledge of your background, do you? I know of your parents, their deaths, and your youth as a pickpocket." Sir Charles reached for the bell pull near his desk and tugged. "I must still ask, why did you not speak with Wycomb when Marchand approached you?"

She could not answer. The earth had shaken beneath her. "I have been keeping Anne a secret for as long as—but does everyone know?"

"No. All of my agents' histories are kept private."

"I thought no one knew, and I did not want Henri to force her into espionage as he did me." She gripped her hands together. A very un-spy-like gesture, but she needed to hold onto something. Anything. "To protect her, I brought her into the household as a servant."

"Which I was also aware of. More, Wycomb couldn't have made her an agent without my approval." Sir Charles frowned as he steepled his fingertips and regarded her over them. "What do you mean, 'force her into espionage as he did me'?"

"I—" Confusion rattled around insider her. "Being a spy. A dancer. I did not have a choice. It was either prison or death for thievery, or work with Henri. This is what he told me." Sir Charles would understand her choices if he knew of her past.

Or perhaps not. His frown became most angry. "Espionage is a *choice*, Vivienne. One doesn't put their life in jeopardy without being given the choice." There was something low and dangerous in his voice. "You should have had one."

"Prison, death, or espionage, sir. Those were the choices Henri gave me. And I chose espionage." She did not regret it, until now, when she wanted Maximilian instead.

He did not speak for a moment. This silence seemed loud and full of words she could not hear properly.

"So you did," he finally said. "And in recent weeks you lied to the entire operation and played a double agent, thereby delivering coded instructions for the assassination of our future king."

She thought about his words. There was no error there. "Yes. This is so."

"And somehow or another, you and the code breaker found one of the Vulture's strongholds, rescued the girl, and, along with Jones, felled the Vulture and two of his agents."

"Yes. This is also true." She was not certain their actions outweighed the delivery of an assassination note.

Sir Charles continued to regard her over his hands. She wanted to squirm. A worm on a hook now, instead of the flopping fish.

The door behind her opened. She did not turn. It would be poor decorum to turn away when one's spymaster was inspecting one. Sir Charles lifted his gaze to the door and gestured for someone to come forward.

It was Maximilian. She knew from the beat of the footsteps on the floor and his quiet, steady breath. From the awareness that shifted over her skin. He came to stand beside her, though a step behind as he had in the Queen's Bathtub. With her, but not in front of her. She wanted to look at him. Perhaps they would share a glance. A message. One of those moments when two souls met in time and space, just before they were to be separated.

She did not look at him. It would break her.

"I owe you a debt of gratitude, Flower, for bringing in Marchand." Sir Charles did not sound thankful, she decided. He was still irritated, but perhaps gratitude would not end in prison. "While the result was more than acceptable, however, I cannot condone your methods."

"She didn't act alone, sir." Maximilian's voice was hard and sure, as solid as the body standing behind her. "I was aware of what she was doing."

"I do not condone that, either." Sir Charles stood, his sturdy frame as nearly as broad as the chair. "Westwood, you chose to retire. More, you're a code breaker, not an agent in the field."

Maximilian's body tensed, his breath moving in and out in a controlled rhythm. The quickest of glances revealed a muscle twitching in his jaw, but he did not speak.

"However," Sir Charles continued, "the two of you succeeded. I won't say any more about it—except that there will be no more of this. For the foreseeable future, neither of you will act without supervision. Your activities will be watched, and you will not work together again, is that understood? No further contact."

Vivienne's entire body jerked. Her hand reached for Maximilian's, then dropped away before she made contact. "Sir," she began.

"Do not question me, Flower." He held up a hand to stop her. "Count yourself lucky I don't strip you from service. Prinny believes the note was nothing more than the words printed there, so you are still of use. Lynley will disappear quietly. He's already been arrested, and will be dealt with. As for you, Flower, reassignment. Lord Wycomb will no longer be your commander."

Something rolled off her shoulders. A large, heavy, debilitating, fearsome rock simply rolled from her shoulders to plop onto the floor at her feet.

"He will not be my trainer? My commander?"

"No."

A dry throat was not conducive to speaking. Nor was the relief tearing through her. Still, she found enough of her voice to whisper. "The girl? Anne?"

"She may stay with you. She will be guarded for her safety as well as ours—and watched as well. Is that understood?"

Watched, so that Anne did not give away any secrets. Vivienne understood the danger. "Yes, thank you." She wiped very damp palms on the pantaloons she'd not had an opportunity to change. "And prison, sir? The gallows?" The words barely passed her lips. "Henri said I would—" She could not speak more. The fear was too great.

Maximilian took her hand, its wide, strong palm giving her strength she might not have had on her own. Her knees—they were a little unsteady just now.

"Whatever you've done in your past, you will not be prosecuted. I'm not sure the law would allow it at this late date, regardless." Sir Charles's voice softened to a tone she was not used to hearing from him. "A girl ought not to be prosecuted for feeding her family."

She opened her mouth, closed it. Her response could not be put into words. Sometimes emotion did not have a name. Maximilian, Anne, her future. Everything in her life seemed poised on the edge of a knife blade.

"There is more, sir. Maximilian and I—Monsieur Westwood and I, we are—we have been—"

"Very awkward conversation, sir," Maximilian broke in with the sensible pragmatism that made him unfit for drawing rooms but ideal for a spy with little time for games. "We're lovers."

Sir Charles's eyes closed as he sighed. Perhaps he needed a moment to assimilate this truth. "I guessed," he said drily. "But thank you for putting words to your actions."

"I love her, sir." Maximilian's voice was firm and full of the assurance she needed to still the galloping of her heart and rushing of her blood. Her scholar planted his feet in the carpet and became an immovable mountain.

"Yes, I'm beginning to realize that as well." Sir Charles

leaned on the hand still on the desktop and rubbed the center of his forehead with other. Brown eyes flicked open again, and she could not decide if he was amused or still irritated. "I don't know what to do with you, Flower."

She had to make her stand. Her hand was still tucked into Maximilian's. She looked up at his profile. It was handsome and lean, with frowning brows and full lips and the grumbling beginning to make its way to the surface. Oh, how she loved this man, for all of the foolish reasons such as paper folding and scowling at her and standing behind her.

"Sir, you said before that everyone should have a choice." She looked at her spymaster. Breathing deep, she drew on whatever courage the fates had given her. "I want to have that choice. I want to continue as a spy, sir, but only on my terms."

"Demands, Flower?" A soft statement. A dangerous one.

"Yes. Demands. I am a good spy, sir. I am a good thief."

"I don't disagree. You've ferreted out information where others have failed because of those quick fingers of yours." Sir Charles came around the edge of the desk. It was a little terrifying. He was sturdy and wide—and very authoritative.

"Dancing, stealing. These things I will continue to do." Sometimes, simple words could require digging for courage. She squeezed Maximilian's hand. It was most comforting to simply have him beside her. "I will *not* accept a protector. I am not a whore, though Henri nearly made me one, so I will play the dancer and continue as a spy." Her heart rose to her throat. "But I will be with Maximilian."

"If I refuse?" Low words hung in the air, disturbingly weighty. Sir Charles raised an expectant brow. "What then, Flower?"

Maximilian did not move even the slightest inch, as if the fibers and muscles of his body were waiting for hope to release them. Breathing deep, raising her chin, she gathered herself for the storm.

"I will leave the service. Forever."

Maximilian did not wait for an answer from Sir Charles. He swung her around, all of his male body proving how large he was. He gathered her in, arms around her, lips devouring hers. She could not move, or think, or even fight him.

She did not want to.

"Damnation, Westwood, let her be," Sir Charles said, words both demanding and resigned.

It was a moment before Maximilian's lips left hers. Another before she could gather herself to meet Sir Charles's gaze, as she was still wrapped in Maximilian's arms.

"New orders, Flower." Sir Charles thumped his fist on the tabletop, hard. "You will report to me. Directly to me. Is that understood? I want to know everything you do. I obviously can't trust you even a few feet from me."

"I would not—"

"You will have a new cover. You will continue as the opera dancer. I can't let you be without a protector in the eyes of society, or the dandies of London will be standing on your doorstep tomorrow. So for now, you will have a new protector." Sir Charles narrowed his eyes. "Mr. Westwood."

Maximilian's arms jerked, then squeezed her hard. She could not breathe. Maximilian, too, held his breath. She heard this with her body as much as her ears.

"Sir?" Maximilian asked.

"I know you chose to retire." The commander paused, drawing a long breath. "If you are to be with the Flower, you will need to make yourself available to the government on a limited basis, if only to stay abreast of her assignments and whereabouts."

Maximilian did not grumble, but she supposed that to do so risked all they'd just gained. Instead, he simply pulled her against a body coiled with tension and breathed, "If those are the conditions I must accept in order to be with her, then I agree."

Sir Charles nodded once, a short, grave acknowledgment of Maximilian's agreement before he pinned Vivienne with his gaze. "Your duties will be modified as well, to befit your cover, Flower. You won't have access to the same individuals without Wycomb, but I have uses enough for your quick fingers." Sir Charles pointed at her, his finger no less dangerous than an arrow. "By all that's holy, don't lie to me."

"Yes, sir." Could one's heart hold so much joy without bursting?

"Now, I have a foreign secretary to brief, a French spy to question, and rumors to spread of the good Bishop Carlisle's untimely death by footpads. Good day." He nodded to Vivienne, again to Maximilian, and strode out of the room.

She continued to stare at the place he'd left. Maximilian let out a long, low breath. She looked up at him, her mouth opening to speak, but she did not know precisely what to say.

The slightest sound made her look over her shoulder.

"Jones." This man, the brother of her heart, had given her the gift of time and put his own career at risk. "You did not leave us," she said, a grim amusement welling in her. "You followed the entire time, did you not?"

"Of course." The smile moving across that serious face held the same grim amusement. "I would not be completing my assignment if I did not pursue my quarry."

"Thank you, Jones." It was Maximilian who spoke the words, the arms around her loosening now. "If you had not, we likely would not have prevailed."

"*Oui. Merci,*" she echoed, though there was so much more to be said between her and Jones. Words that went back a decade or more, through friendship and lovemaking, training and knife work.

"Be well," he said softly. "Both of you." Then Jones faded into the recesses of the town house, perfectly silent in that way he had.

And they were alone.

"I'm not certain what happened here, but I think you would have given up espionage for me." Maximilian flicked eyes not quite brown, not quite green, toward her.

"That is correct." She grinned at the dazed expression on his lean features. "I love you, my Maximilian."

"I also think I was just ordered to be your new protector." Large hands took her shoulders, gently, as if he were afraid she would disappear.

"More or less, yes, I think so."

"Well. It'll be interesting being the protector of a spy. Messy business, I'm sure." There was no scowl between his eyes, only a smile. He pulled her in, pressed his lips against hers. "Does that mean I can have my way with you whenever I want?"

Her heart lifted. Desire tingled a path from mouth to toes as she pressed her body to his. "More or less, yes, I think so."

"Good. Then espionage has its consolations."

Epilogue

He didn't hear her enter the study, but Vivienne had not expected him to.

Hunched over the desk as he was, his nose nearly touched the paper he worked on. The candle at his elbow was low, its flame dancing as wax pooled around it. Even so close to his beloved words, even with the candle, Maximilian wore his spectacles.

Her heart simply swelled and grew as she watched his quill scratch across the paper, the fingers of his other hand marking his place on the document beside it. So industrious was her Maximilian.

"Damnation, Flower. I know you're there." Fingers still flew, but she saw he grinned over his paper.

"Anne?" she asked, leaning against the doorjamb and thinking her Maximilian was particularly handsome when he concentrated. Lips made for kissing, eyes not quite green, not quite brown—both made that flutter in her belly come to life.

"Daggett sent her to bed hours ago. She's quite good with the simple substitution cipher." Setting his quill aside,

Maximilian looked up at her with eyes blurred behind the spectacles. "I think I will start teaching her something more complicated."

Vivienne laughed, unable to help herself. "I am surrounded by code breakers." She strode forward, not caring if her boots made noise on the thick rug. There was no longer anyone in this house she must hide from. "What are you working on this night, my Maximilian?" Bending over one of the documents, she squinted at the spidery script there.

"Actually, I'm responding to Mrs. Asher."

Her head jerked up as her heart slammed into her throat. "She wrote you?"

"Indeed." His grin broadened, his wonderful mouth curved and his eyes giddy. "It came today. She's well, as is Thomas, and was following your instructions about contacting me. I'm sending money and my direction and telling them to come home. They can live with us here."

"They are alive?" She nearly wept, the relief was so great inside her. Months had passed since Mrs. Asher and Thomas had left London on her command. "They are truly well?"

"They are." His words were softer now, his eyes, too. Gone was the giddiness of his surprise for her. In its place was understanding. Anne would have companionship beyond Daggett and the agent assigned to guard her. Mrs. Asher and Thomas would be home. They would be safe.

When Maximilian reached for her, she took comfort in his arms. When he drew her to the settee so that they could sit together, she burrowed against him. And when his mouth sought hers, she did not hesitate to give him everything in her soul.

"My Flower, with your wide heart," he murmured against her lips. "They will be in England soon."

"Thank you." Inadequate words for his actions.

"I'm trying to bribe you." Grinning, Maximilian pulled

his spectacles off and tossed them on a nearby tabletop. "Will you marry me *now*? I've asked damn near every day."

"It is too much fun scandalizing London by being your mistress." She shook her head and settled herself more comfortably against him. This was an old joke now. "The great Mademoiselle La Fleur, abandoning her wealthy, titled protector for a poor second son. It is much fun, Maximilian. The other dancers, the dandies backstage and at Prinny's soirees—they are all aghast and fascinated. No one thinks, *Oh, the mademoiselle, she is dropping a note into the pocket of a foreign diplomat.*"

"Just think of the scandal if we were to marry. My mother's nerves will never recover, and my brother will be put out that I am more infamous than he. Prinny will find it amusing, and we shall be discussed at every *ton* gathering. London will dine on it for months—and they would certainly never suspect you of being a spy." He nuzzled her neck, the light rasp of his stubble tickling so that she laughed softly. "It's a good disguise."

"Monsieur Westwood, you are thinking like a spy." She angled her head to look at him, threading her arms firmly about his neck. "This is not like you."

"I'm surrounded by spies," he answered, echoing her words.

He pulled her closer, and she let her head rest on his chest. It was their habit to sit thus each night after she danced or spied, looking into the flames in the hearth. A simple ritual, one that had not replaced her evening routine to keep her body strong, but that fed her heart instead.

"*Will* you marry me, Flower? Vivienne? Sarah?" His hand played idly with her hair, though his heart beat furiously beneath her cheek—not like trapped butterflies, but a team of horses thundering inside his rib cage. "I confess, I want us to belong to each other. I want to shock not only London, but all of England by marrying you. I want you and Anne and me to be a family. I want to make a family with you."

She did not speak. She could not.

He had asked, and she had always said no. It was a jest when he asked, and they both knew it. But he was not jesting now. Not this time.

And she did have a choice. Sir Charles had explicitly indicated so.

She set her hand against Maximilian's chest so that she could feel the beat of his heart beneath her fingers, and looked up into his face.

"Yes." What else could she say to this man? "Yes."

"Oh, thank all the gods. Even the Persian gods." His forehead pressed against hers, every muscle of his body relaxing. "I thought you might say no again."

She laughed and took his mouth. Kissing Maximilian was all that was good in her world. He was heat and strength, love and comfort. His lips were mobile and full, and tasted only of the man she loved.

When he started to flick open the buttons of her shirt, she laughed again.

When his hand cupped her breast, she gasped and arched toward him.

And when they made love, when his body worshipped hers and her heart was full of him, she could only sigh in pleasure.

"I love you, Maximilian," she whispered as he kissed the tender area around her collarbone.

"And I you." He looked clearly into her eyes, holding himself still above her. "Whatever name you use, whatever clothes you wear, whatever weapon you hide. Beneath the surface is a woman of many parts, and I love them all."

"Yes," she breathed, arching toward him, opening her arms to hold the man she had been gifted with. The man who knew each part of her, and loved all of her. "Yes."

Acknowledgments

I must thank so many people for helping to see *A Dance With Seduction* become a reality! Alethea Spiridon and the Entangled Publishing team, my agent Nalini Akolekar at Spencerhill Associates (also known as the Goddess Among Agents), and all those involved in copy edits and marketing and cover art. It is truly a pleasure working with all of you!

To Kimberly Kincaid and Jennifer McQuiston, thanks for reading every single word! And to Tracy Brogan, well, I believe you let me cry on the phone to you more than once.

Also, Mummy, Daddy, and my Sisters, thanks for your unending support! I need to give a shout out to Bruce, the best boss ever, for time away from work to write.

To my Josh, thanks for eating pizza and monster faces and PB&J when your Momma is writing. I love you, baby!

Joe, there aren't enough thanks in the world that I could give you. In fact, there's not much I can say except that I know we drive each other crazy, but I'd marry you again tomorrow if you asked. All my love.

Finally, and most importantly, thanks to all of you, Dear Readers! Authors are nothing without readers, and I cannot wait to share Vivienne and Maximilian with you!

About the Author

Despite being a native Michigander, Alyssa Alexander is pretty certain she belongs somewhere sunny. And tropical. Where drinks are served with little paper umbrellas. But until she moves to those white sandy beaches, she survives the cold Michigan winters by penning romance novels that always include a bit of adventure. She lives with her own set of heroes, aka an ever-patient husband who doesn't mind using a laundry basket for a closet and a small boy who wears a knight in a shining armor costume for such tasks as scrubbing potatoes.

Discover more historical romance from Entangled…

MY HELLION, MY HEART
by Amalie Howard & Angie Morgan

Lord Henry Radcliffe, the sexy Earl of Langlevit, is a beast. The only way Henry can exorcise the demons of his war-ravaged past is through physicality, in and out of bed. Intent on scandalizing London, Princess Irina Volkonsky is a hellion and every gentleman's deepest desire…except for one. Irina knows better than to provoke the forbidding earl, but she will stop at nothing short of ruination to win the heart of the only man she's ever loved.

AN EARL FOR AN ARCHERESS
a *Ladies of Scotland* novel by E. Elizabeth Watson

Lady Mariel Crawford enters an archery contest as a boy but despite her skill she loses to the very handsome Earl of Huntington. When Robert of Huntington realizes she is the runaway daughter of the Beast of Ayr and that her father conspires with the Sheriff of Nottingham, he is compelled to protect her. Even though she wants nothing to do with him, he will risk everything for the Scottish wilding who's pierced his heart.

HOW TO PLAY THE GAME OF LOVE
a *Ladies of Passion* novel by Harmony Williams

Johanna Templeton is on a life-and-death quest. Swept into an intrigue that rivals the tales she pens, she joins forces with a Highland rogue to find the treasure that will save her kidnapped niece. He's as seductive as he is bold…but he may also be the enemy. Connor MacMasters, spy for Queen Victoria, is a man on a mission. Trailing the American novelist who holds the key to the treasure should've been simple, but torn between duty and desire, he wants Johanna in his bed. Loving her would be a fool's game. Blasted shame his heart doesn't agree.

Made in the USA
Middletown, DE
24 July 2017